TO BURY THE
CLOUD
LEAH MARGOLIS

MINDSTIR MEDIA

Published by Mindstir Media, LLC
45 Lafayette Rd | Suite 181| North Hampton, NH 03862 | USA
1.800.767.0531 | www.mindstirmedia.com

Printed in the United States of America
ISBN-13: 978-1-7356910-7-7

DISCLAIMER:

The following story is a work of fiction. It is not intended to reference any particular patient, hospital setting, or colleague; nor is it intended to reference any particular event, setting, or person. Should this work resemble any particular individual or place, it is by coincidence, as these events and interactions are fabricated. Despite diagnosis and treatment cases found within this work, this manuscript is not intended as a source for medical advisement, treatment protocol, or diagnostic criteria. The methods contained herein by which the characters solve or interpret an ethical, moral, cultural, or religious dilemma are not to be considered as guidance towards an appropriate response. The opinions and perceptions contained within this work are representations of the characters which are imaginary. In addition, this work is not intended to serve as a guide for any particular professional organizations or institutions, opinions or action; nor should it be used to create a broad representation of any particular organization or institution's practice framework, or code of conduct and ethics.

DEDICATION:

For the members of my family that are the clear sky on a cloudy day, may we make great memories that we can share in the future.

For my readers who struggle on their path to adulthood and for those who struggle to reconnect with their inner child, may you have many worthwhile goals and a happy journey in achieving them.

And for all those in all facets of healthcare who have worked under the darkest clouds bringing honor to and perpetuating and enriching the cycle of medicine.

Chapter 1: Under a Cloud

Clouds are fascinating entities. They have a way of making me need to see them. They are somehow unparalleled by other natural phenomena. They appear dense and impenetrable, yet they are transparent and seem to vaporize when one traverses them in a plane. Even with the acknowledgment of their intrigue and beauty, I have yet to be able to experience the joy and contentment others do when peering at them in the sky. My perception of them is as gray matter lacking hues. They are vaporous and empty inside but can become dense and heavy. To my eyes, they fail to manifest as a house, palace, or exotic creature. This seems limited to others' perceptions. In a strange way, they beckon to me, enticing me to peek at them as they make their presence known in the sky, and despite my efforts to avoid them as I look into the clear skies, I find myself not only glancing at them momentarily but glaring at them as if they can divulge a secret that has been waiting to be told.

I, too, have a good understanding of what it is like to vacillate between feelings of vapor and nothingness to a heaviness that seems all-consuming. I would venture to say that I am a pessimist, and despite my best efforts, I can't seem to ever see anything other than that of the present stark reality. I am cognizant of the fact that I embody the density and heaviness of the world which has provided me with some foreground of my perceptions.

On this day, as on many others, I sit on a park bench gazing at the sky, waiting for the clouds to appear and manifest themselves as something more than gray matter filling pockets of the sky. There is always a time when every notion we have is eventually challenged, morphing our perceptions into something else. Perhaps today would be one of those days.

Ironically, I enjoy nature. Perhaps it is because there is a stillness and calm without the clutter generally experienced in other environmental arenas. I practice deep breathing which never comes naturally despite my daily routine. In the midst of a deep breath, I feel a quick brief shiver emanating from my thigh. The cherub cheeks of a young boy suddenly appear. He seems to be just over two years of age. His clothing is a size too big, basically hanging on him, making him appear even smaller. He peers at me with sunken eyes.

"I sowwy, my dwink on you," he says. His curly black hair accentuates his green piercing eyes nicely, his hair covers the top portion of his eyes, and despite the sad expression on his face, it is difficult not to smile at this angelic creature. I also note that his eyes, though beautiful, are wide open like a child ready for terror to strike. He lifts his head ever so slightly saying, "I sowwy," and he looks like he is waiting for me to mete out some punishment. I had never heard a young child who appeared to be not yet three talk like that, his words filled with heaviness and guilt.

"It's okay," I respond. A woman quickly grabs his arm, pulling him away, then walks briskly with him toward the park gate. A smile remains on my face a few seconds longer as I watch this child, whose name I did not catch, walk away while catching small pieces of scattered leaves on his legs. I return to deep breathing, which does eventually calm my nerves, and before leaving the beautiful scenery that envelops me, I take one last look at the clouds above. The cold shiver on my thigh is reawakened as my eyes meet the cloud. While walking away, I whisper under my breath, "I am a cloud." I am either empty or dense, just waiting to burst. I wrap my jacket around my waist, not so much for warmth, but to weigh me down in order to feel grounded.

After noting the time on my watch, I hurry along, as I do not want to return late to work. It is an eleven-block walk, but the various aromas and visuals in New York City make the walk feel like a significantly shorter distance. I take in deep breaths, as a host of smells tickle my nose. The air carries the intermingling scents of the bakeries, restaurants, coffee shops, and especially the vending carts that one can find throughout the city. The loud and bright colors are a stark contrast to the quiet I felt in the park but serve as a good alerting mechanism to walk briskly. I take note of the massive overshadowing buildings and the endless stream of people that usually walk the sidewalks regardless of the time of day. Walking in the city, you barely sense the distance as your legs tag along while your eyes take in the scenes.

Aside from the well-dressed window shops, there are small vendors on each corner waiting for someone to choose a scarf, a watch, sunglasses, or some other trinket or souvenir. There are the food vendors whose aromas seem to deflect the unpleasant odors emanating from the New York City sewers and construction sites. There are always people carrying signs requesting something, some with the interesting choice of self-advertisement like "need money for weed." The long lines of people waiting to secure a ticket for some show or museum stand there, often with youthful enthusiasm, as if the ticket is being supplied free of charge.

In New York City you expect the unexpected because even though you can't predict what will occur, something is always brewing; however, the persistent flow of dramas is insufficient for those who live with, and have become accustomed to, the ever-changing daily goings-on, causing them to await the next amazing thing to reignite their attention and renew their interest. The guy with fanged teeth, split tongue, tattooed face, and shimmering ears wearing the leopard costume barely garnishes a second glance. The guy giving something away for free is also ignored and will often need to chase you down because he is no competition for your cell phone, earbuds, or earpieces, and you walk, by rote, past him in a hurry toward your destination.

Those who choose to live here, however, are thankful for not being that person sitting peacefully in his or her backyard admiring the birds' vocals or the swaying of the leaves. As a result, they learn to wait in the endless lines, assume they will be stuck in traffic, and willingly rub shoulders with people on the street in order to get by as they walk.

You watch the people protesting something, but don't know what they are protesting as it is commonplace; you only know that they contribute to an already noisy city and are a source for blocking traffic yet further, that is until you realize that their voices are protesting unfair practices or wages directly related to your own care, life, or wallet, and then, they are no longer a nuisance but voicing a right.

Although I am considerably fit, the ache in my back accentuates the fact that I will be turning thirty-four in a few weeks and no longer have the tone and strength of a youngster. My pace, however, is speedy enough to get me to work with a few minutes to spare. For the last ten years, I have been working in a local hospital as an occupational therapist on staff and have assisted patients in becoming independent in the cardiac, neuro, and orthopedic units of the hospital. Yet, most people have no clue as to what occupational therapists do. Perhaps this is why I chose this field, as I am just as undefinable.

After high school, I dabbled in a host of jobs, remaining in each one for a short burst of time because I was either bored or under/over-qualified for a number of fields. I earned a bachelor's degree in marketing, but marketing wasn't my thing because I don't feel I can sell anything to anybody. On the other hand, I knew I liked helping people, wanted to employ variety and imagination, had scientific curiosity, and was into fitness. Meghan, my older sister, had injured her arm following a sports injury and was referred to an occupational therapist specializing in hand therapy. This was my first introduction to the field. I subsequently read up on the possibilities available to me which made me gravitate to it.

On the first day of graduate school, I noted how cheerful everyone was. I had never met a more eager and enthusiastic group of people. It seemed that I was the only one that lacked that optimistic frame of mind. I seemed to be the only one that didn't know how to make everything okay. I did do well in my classes, ultimately leading to a master's of science in occupational therapy.

As I entered the workforce, I tried to let go of my pessimism, but it wouldn't let go of me. In some sense though, it has proven to be a gift, facilitating a successful work habit. I am usually the earliest attendee at the morning meetings. I am particularly organized and submit paperwork in a timely fashion. I tend to speak in a factual manner with detail. I generally conclude that the patients in question are doomed. Nonetheless, it doesn't make me give up. Quite the contrary, it makes me work harder, investigating all avenues and methods available to enable these individuals to return to a semblance of their former selves. I am not the person that tells everyone else, "Don't worry, it will be okay," or "Go pray." In its place, I overcompensate, always providing them with a host of exercises, an extensive list of community resources, and assistive devices, and then reference other disciplines that perhaps can provide the guidance that is beyond my domain. However, my smile is genuine when I greet them, and although they don't often know it, my patients are generally the welcomed novelty in my daily routine. They provide the impetus that creates the change from day to day. My pessimism also lends itself to additional compassion, as when you know that someone is doomed, you feel their pain all the more.

The hospital day's routine is simple: get a client list for the day, make sure all necessary doctors' orders are in, attend to the client, and document progress in a highly advanced computer database while ensuring correct codes and details for accurate billing. Subsequent weekly summary reports and updates follow. Then there are weekly meetings. They are brief, extremely brief. Despite the healthcare world's best intentions and belief that we have become so efficient that a fifteen-minute meeting for fourteen clients will suffice, I beg to differ. Gone are the days of forty-five to sixty-minute meetings, a few times a week, where we actually spoke about clients rather than about the particularity of documentation and paperwork.

Here I am, heading towards one of those meetings now. I think that getting there on time is not only a reflection of my timeliness but that if I am two minutes late, there will be only thirteen minutes left to the conversation, leaving me able to only update medical personnel on twelve and a half patients instead of fourteen.

My stride increases, and I reach the hospital with five minutes to spare, leaving me just enough time to navigate the hallways, wait for the elevator, and ride up to the ninth-floor conference room where the afternoon meeting is to take place. These gatherings are generally in the morning, but given the influx of patients this week, the time was revised. I sit down at the table. Dr. Tromblone, a neurologist, motions to me to fix my wind-blown hair as he sits down opposite my chair. The meeting commences with nurses, doctors, therapists, and social workers.

When it is my turn to present, I discuss Greg Lawton, a twenty-eight-year-old architectural student who sustained a right lower extremity amputation following a car accident. Greg had borrowed a friend's BMW and was racing it down the highway, resulting in a devastating impact. I go through the motions naming the course of therapeutic treatment the patient has undergone and his current progress. The meeting is presented under the guise that we are attempting to improve our overall care, whereas I know, as has happened in the past, we are attempting to cut costs. Given time constraints, my mind tries to decipher the most important facts, but my tongue is throwing out words lagging behind my thoughts. I run through the treatment. "Desensitization of the stump through tapping and touch . . . vibration has been encouraged . . . use of physical agent modalities and biofeedback for phantom limb pain, exercises to improve trunk control and balance. Lower extremity dressing . . . bed mobility . . . safety concerns." I take a deep breath, and more air enters my lungs, allowing me to continue on this linguistic marathon. "Use of pillows under stump to avoid contractures in a flexed position and muscle strengthening for scapular depressors and wrist extensors."

The meetings are often routine in nature. I had become so accustomed to their routine that I failed to note Dr. Montauk, chief of staff at the hospital, trying to catch my attention. "Ms. Westcott, are you alright?" Apparently, I was preoccupied with my thoughts and failed to hear his question, which was whether I had attended the tech support seminar, as we were updating the hospital system. I blush, but answer in the affirmative, and note my need to pay better attention to administrative staff in the future. I wonder why the chief of staff is in attendance. This was supposed to be a general meeting with no particular administrative or special interests concerns requiring the attention of the upper echelons of the hospital. The fact that Dr. Montauk recalled my name further boggled my mind. It was nice hearing my name from someone of his stature; still it provided yet another opportunity to bring shame on myself.

Dr. Montauk now turns to my coworker on my right and then to the one on my left, asking them if they, too, attended the seminar. I lean forward in my chair, this time assuming an active listening posture and smile at my good fortune of having secured a seat between two great colleagues and friends, Dr. Kevin Chase and Dr. Jonathan Slate. Dr. Chase is a third-generation orthopedic surgeon. He is a risk-taker, a pioneer in his field, and outgoing to a fault. He is thirty-seven years old, but he has the stamina and appearance of someone in his early twenties. Dr. Chase is definitely a confident speaker. I have always thought that if he failed at medicine, he could become a marketing or advertising agent, as he knew how to sell any idea. His pearly white teeth sparkle as he speaks and are accompanied by two flirtatious blue eyes. It was even rumored that Dr. Chase had two years of law school under his belt, but no one ever confirmed its truth.

True to his name Dr. Chase was definitely *chased* by all the single female members of the staff. I, however, kept my distance. I once sarcastically remarked that I would like to chase him away. I always thought him way too chipper for someone who functioned on four hours' sleep and way too perfect to be a true human. There was just one area in which an imperfection lay. Kevin was the type of person I would classify as generously flawed, as he was the guy that purchased a clear Lucite coffee table for his visually impaired grandmother's birthday and bought his college girlfriend an expensive ticket to dance on stage at a Broadway show when she suffered from panic attacks.

The meeting went overtime, approaching eighteen minutes, and the attendees and chief were in quite a rush to leave. They glanced at the clock on the wall more than once. Once again, my mind wandered during the meeting, albeit briefly, not because I was daydreaming but rather overthinking a particular rehabilitative strategy mentioned; overthinking was part of my inner being so it was no surprise.

As the meeting ends, Kevin nods toward Stephanie, another surgeon, Jonathan, and myself. We congregate at the door momentarily, and he informs us that a new bar has opened in the vicinity. In light of the fact that it is his birthday he is inviting us out for drinks. Although Kevin and I don't always see eye to eye on matters, we are friendly and have known each other for a long time. He has always been gracious despite my attitude, so I agree to come.

Kevin and I have a strange relationship. On one occasion, I had actually agreed to pretend to be his wife and accompanied him to his high school reunion. To this day, I have no idea why an eligible bachelor with so much going for him needed a wife, but I never inquired further as to why he asked, or more so, begged; begging didn't become him, so as crazy as it seemed, I agreed. When I asked why Kevin hadn't chosen Stephanie or his many potential suitors on the floor, to my surprise, he answered, "I thought the two of us would make a more believable fit," so I went along with it. As expected, Kevin had been a perfect high school student. This led me to believe that even someone like him had secrets or insecurities, and that was the first time that he became a bit more human in my eyes.

In truth, as compared to past dating experiences, that date with Kevin really was quite amazing. In all honesty, my longest relationship had lasted seven months. It was with a psychologist named Peter. Peter was handsome, well dressed, and generally courteous. He was talented at writing poetry, which he regularly presented to me, but it felt like none were ever really written for me. It was more of an expression of his writing talent than personalized to my existence. He frequently complimented my choice of clothing but never anything else. In theory, I thought we should have been a great match, but all I really gained from that relationship was a greater understanding of cognitive behavioral therapy, psychoanalysis,

EMDR, systematic desensitization, and other psychological methodology. One can only imagine the boredom inherent in our dates when my greatest surprise was when he presented me with a pamphlet written by Dr. Ellis, known for developing yet another psychological therapeutic technique, rational emotive therapy, which I admit I still have to this day.

Although pessimistic, I am not a shy girl. I am extroverted, and my dressing style reflects that. Under my white lab coat, I often wear a colorful garment. I also enjoy accessorizing, as besides attesting to my great style, it further serves as a method of self-expression. When I first started working in the hospital, I hated the fact that my lab coat, while making me outwardly appear important, covered my fashionable and chic clothing and accessories. What was even more horrifying to me was when I stopped wearing rings, necklaces, and bracelets to avoid injuring patients. The first time I walked in devoid of these accessories, I felt bare and defeminized. However, after almost hitting my patient in the eye with my dangling necklace during a transfer, or almost scratching another with my ring, I figured forgoing my accessories for safety was a wise choice.

At the entrance of the conference room, Stephanie is attempting to initiate a conversation with Dr. Chase. Stephanie has jet black hair, olive skin, and soft brown eyes with delicate features. She has graded herself a four on the beauty scale. I think her to be way more beautiful than she thinks of herself. She prides herself in being exceptionally funny and is the true optimist of the group. She is everyone's cheerleader, particularly

18

mine. Stephanie is a hugger and had even gained ten additional pounds at one point, sharing jokingly that she was in pursuit of improved hugging capabilities.

Stephanie's mother was a nurse, and her father was a military man. Her father had lost a leg in a war which had prompted her interest in orthopedics. She married in her early twenties and had three kids, but was still the most fun-loving adult ever. She is an optimist but has this way about her where she doesn't shove her optimism down your throat. It is subtle and in good taste. Her husband is a chemist and researcher who travels frequently, leaving Stephanie a seemingly single mother. This is particularly difficult for a woman who is frequently up at odd hours performing life-altering orthopedic surgery. Stephanie often espouses her husband's virtues, proudly declaring that he always gives them quality time when he is home. She imparts that he is a positive force in her life and in her children's lives. She rarely finds flaws with anyone. Even with her hectic schedule, Stephanie makes time for me. She isn't a talker, she is more of a doer, and her actions, though sometimes annoying, are definitely acts of caring. Stephanie is constantly trying to set me up. She has even paired me with her brother, Taylor, at one point, which could be a tale all on its own. Unfortunately, Taylor did not possess the same virtues as his sister.

Stephanie's husband's mother, Qiao, came from China. Qiao believes that once you're ill, the doctor has already failed at his job. This prompts her love for herbs and natural scents, as they are preliminary measures undertaken to avoid illness. She has attempted to instill this love of nature within her son's household. Stephanie always smells of nature, not like some other over-perfumed coworkers. Her mother-in-law often babysits the children in their parents' absence.

I enjoy frequenting Stephanie's house, particularly in her mother-in-law's presence to hear her talk of her native country. As a teenager, I was introduced to the book *The Chinese Cinderella*. I had read it so many times that the page edges were considerably frayed. It was one of those books that left a lasting impression on me, perhaps because the source of the main character's distress were members of her own family. There were no glass slippers popping up magically. I have never enjoyed fairy tales, like my sisters who knew the words from *Cinderella* by heart. Fairy tales, in my opinion, are disappointing. They make you believe that things magically turn out okay when they generally don't. They are stories that encompass hardship followed by a miraculous triumph. Hardship is more in line with good reading material.

Kevin continues to urge me to come and join the group at the bar tonight, and Stephanie notes my hesitation. As is her custom, she wraps her arm around my shoulder and says, "Come on Jules, you will have fun." Despite the internal debate pulling me in the opposite direction, I agree. The next thing I know Stephanie is giving me a ten-second hug for which she was famous.

As I walk through the hallways toward my next client, Nurse Randy advises me that I have an envelope waiting for me at the nurses' station. I think that perhaps I have a long-awaited secret admirer, but when I open the envelope, I find it unmarked. I peek inside to find solutions to a math equation coupled with a picture of a young man named Mark sitting at an upright desk with a smile on his face. The back reads: "Math is predictable. You aren't." and signed MIT admittee.

You know those people whose knowledge far exceeds your own, and you have a hard time trying to speak their language. This was the case with nineteen-year-old Mark, a math genius applying for the prestigious Massachusetts Institute of Technology. He sat in bed, solving math equations, the type of equations that are challenging when you're just attempting to copy them down. The one thing we shared in common was a sarcastic tone and pessimistic life outlook.

Mark had gone to a party with a friend. That friend ended up driving him home drunk. The car rolled into a ditch and Mark sustained a number of injuries. Convincing him to perform muscle reps, or core strengthening, or balance training was difficult. He viewed these suggestions as trivial in the grand scheme of his life. Mark haggled with every member of his healthcare team. It was like he was scheduling these arguments.

The one thing that he struggled with and really cared about was his ability to sit upright and face a laptop, mobile device, or notebook. Solving equations was to Mark what listening to running water, deep breathing, and yoga is to others. It gave him a sense of tranquility and purpose. It put him in a Zen-like state and increased his motivation to get better. Luckily for me, the medical staff wasn't upset when I borrowed their chairs, mobile desks, and any other office material. I scrubbed it all down until my hands ached and brought it into Mark's room. His roommate looked on as he was wheeled toward the hospital gym. Initially, Mark looked at me like I had gone mad, but quickly became intrigued when he caught sight of a math example peeking out at him on the laptop. I sat down, showing him the postures one would need to sit at the desk with correct positioning and demonstrating what compensations he could then make to achieve the same.

Mark finally allowed me to help him and followed my demonstrations. I borrowed a math book from the library and copied down some equations, which I may mention took a really long time with back-checks five times to ensure I had copied accurately. At every session I handed Mark an equation, and at every session he complied. Mark never said good-bye, and it's been seven months since he left, but I guess this is his version of 'thank you,' "Math is predictable. You aren't . . . MIT admittee."

I walk away from the nurses' station in a better mood than I had come. I see Gabriella. She shuffles her feet as she walks. She is a client I had treated many years ago. She takes a seat in the waiting room at the outpatient unit. I say hello, and she barely nods in return. Near her sits a woman named Mini whom I recognize from the physical therapy unit. She is memorable because she is Southern and you don't often hear an accent like that in New York. Mini is a petite-framed woman with a perpetual smile. Aside from her accent, she is very animated as she speaks. She originally moved to New York in support of her husband's new job. He accepted the offer of a promotion that was worthy of the move, and in the interim, she gave birth to twin girls. She has been having some pelvic muscle weakness and is having biweekly therapy sessions.

Gabriella, on the other hand, sits stone-faced. She, too, has been suffering pelvic weakness following childbirth. Gabriella has been on her own since she was sixteen. She had suffered abuse at the hands of her fiancé throughout her eight-month pregnancy, after which she gave birth to an underweight little boy. Gabriella also has significant scars on her arm due to limb reattachment at age twenty-one when her then best friend pushed her into an oncoming car in the midst of traffic during a drunken stupor.

Mini sits smiling and making small talk with the other women in the waiting room. She shows off pictures of her twins, her eyes sparkling with greater and greater intensity as she shares her pictures with each person. Her accent makes her even more interesting and personable. Gabriella sits there tapping her feet in anticipation, her eyes cast toward the ground looking up every so often to see if it is her name they are calling to be seen next. She crosses her arms, stabilizing herself as she sits. She increasingly retracts towards the chair as the minutes tick by.

I think Gabriella is annoyed by Mini's cheerfulness and her squeaky girlish voice. I see Gabriella's wounds, the below-elbow reattachment, the scratches, scrapes, and gashes her fiancé left her with, but her emotional wounds are also somewhat transparent. She has been living in a shelter for abused women, with no end goal in sight. She has no family to return to, no job, and no partner. She has a child that she seems to be numb to. I remember the way Gabriella worked through sessions following her reattachment. I can attest that Gabriella was an excellent patient. She did her exercises with no complaints, but there was no motivation or attention attached to it, no expectation. It was just something she did. There are patients who follow regimens because it is something they do.

Stephanie always makes fun of my perpetual state of analysis. Once, when we traveled on a train, there was a group of acrobatic performances, complements of the youth of NYC. This performance could only happen in New York City on a moving train car. The performers did cartwheels and demonstrated a range of dance moves on the subway car bars. I observed that they never knocked into anyone and came within a quarter of a hair's breadth of the man reading his daily newspaper.

"They have great spatial skills, coordination, and balance," I noted.

Stephanie laughed, "But did you enjoy the show?"

"I guess I did," I replied.

As a child, I loved to watch people's muscles contract and relax; it was almost like a dance being performed. In upper grade school, I learned that the coordinated lengthening and shortening of muscles transpires as a result of a complicated sequence of activity of various structures and bodily components, including the crossbridge sliding action of actin and myosin filaments. I also learned that the face is constructed of over thirty muscles, and the hands, too, have their share of muscles. I discovered the reason why we are required to stretch and perform a warm-up before a sporting activity. My science teacher, in his baritone voice, said, "Warm muscles contract more easily and receive more oxygen. This allows for a greater span of performance." He continued, "When there is repetition of muscle use, there is significant use of oxygen that may not be sufficient to support the activity and this results in the buildup of lactic acid which creates a cramp, denoting a need to rest."

It was lucky I enjoyed science because his voice didn't quite capture the excitement of the actual content he imparted. It was only when I began to work that I truly understood the workings of the body, particularly when my patient had a lactic acid buildup, a side effect from a given medication. As I moved into adulthood, these same principles took on new meaning. Your body works towards a given goal, creating a complex network of feedback and feedforward to make you move, perhaps dance, or perhaps to remain steady. My patients would become living proof that only when something in this complex network goes awry do you begin to recognize its value.

I find out about people's lives, their daily routines, the activities they perform, the people in their lives, the environments they live in, their support system, and then I find out what drives them so that an illness or injury doesn't need to indicate an end; it may be an alternate beginning.

There is another thing, perhaps most important, that I consider; it is the patient's emotional state. It is like the driving force behind everything else. I remember this as I walk into Cara's room. She is twenty-seven years old and suffers from diffuse scleroderma. She and her peers had never heard these words before her diagnosis. Now, she finds herself explaining what her diagnosis is, and all it entails, on a regular basis. Her body also reminds her about her disease each day. She has changes in her skin, and blood vessels, and her organs are already falling victim to this disease as well. She complains of the cold in her hospital room, her fingers changing color, yet I barely recognize any change in temperature. The skin of her hands has hardened and stiffened and she has significant changes in connective tissue, making movement restricted and, of course, there is lots of pain. She has some shortness of breath and says that her pain level is a six out of ten.

What scares her the most is not the significant restriction of activity or fatigue; it is her wondering what will happen next. She particularly worries about constrictors of the face, her beautiful freckled face. Aside from the beauty element, she worries whether she will be able to move and smile properly. Scleroderma manifests differently in different patients and even its cause is debatable. It is not one of the more popular diseases, so its patients are yet in a world that hasn't been fully navigated. The same collagen that is responsible for our youthfulness, the one that's touted as

26

an ingredient in expensive beauty products, is a possible facilitator in this disease. It wreaks havoc when it continues to synthesize without limits.

I look down at my research article entitled "Functional Limitations in Diffuse Scleroderma Patients Five Years Post Diagnosis." I have gathered some data about what activities these patients can't perform or aren't performing easily and even have a measure for pain, but it doesn't tell me how the pain feels. Does it burn? Is it shooting, sharp, or stabbing? Does it feel claw-like, spasming, or extremely tight? It definitely doesn't tell me how fearful these patients are about what tomorrow brings. Cara doesn't want the literature I brought her and throws down the pamphlets on the chair beside her bed. Her father enters the room, and I give him pamphlets of adaptive equipment and stretching exercises that may increase productivity, while Cara covers herself with yet another blanket to keep warm.

The day passes slowly. Despite there still being some sunlight as I make my way home, I could feel the darkness making its way earlier and earlier into the day, as is generally the case in fall. I will need to freshen up and change clothing for Kevin's get-together. On my way, I pass a young girl seemingly in her early twenties panhandling for cash. Her clothing is a bit worn and her demeanor a bit solemn. Her hair and eyes match my own in my early twenties, and I think that could have been me. I open my wallet and give graciously and attempt to ask her about her life, she recoils into a dirty blanket that's wrapped around her. In an attempt to help, I try to advise her about her options, but she seems to be lost to the notion. Still,

I hope to meet her again.

As I reach my house, I walk straight to my closet and decide on my black dress, intending to dangle my beloved metal jewelry over it. I imagine my jewels smile as they are taken from a gilded jewelry box that is only accessed on rare occasions. "Ah," I take a peek at my general physique in the mirror that hung on my closet door and was pleasantly surprised by the image staring back at me, given that I had gained five pounds recently.

I take the subway to the bar, Googling its exact location. As I open my phone, I notice a text from Kevin which reads, "Time moved up by twenty minutes." I move about quickly, as I am already running late and will likely miss half the festivity, but am happy when there are no surprises or delays on the subway that would prolong my trip further.

I enter the bar, and there sits Kevin already in the party mood, holding his glass in a cheers position. Stephanie waves and motions for me to sit next to her, and I notice Jonathan Slate sitting beside Kevin. He has a full smile on. "Glad you came, Jules," he says. I take my seat quickly and let the partygoers know that I saw the text a bit late.

Jonathan Slate is a coworker. He is one of the most respected doctors in his field and is an innovative thinker. We have an unidentifiable relationship. He has a unique quality that makes me want to trust him. We discuss and debate about the nuances of life, but the one category which is never broached is emotions. Like myself, Jonathan lingers in the universe of misery. I would come to find out a few years after our initial meeting that his younger sister had been raped and murdered in her teens. She had borrowed Jonathan's car to meet an ex-boyfriend and never came home. There was insufficient evidence linking her boyfriend to the crime, and as such, Jonathan never had the closure that he needed. At the time, he was in his early college years, pre-med, and instead of taking time to mourn the death of his sister, he put his energies into his studies. He never spoke of his sister's death to anyone around him and became what I would consider a thespian optimist. That is, he would pretend to find the positive in a situation and would always be heard saying, "It will be great," or relaying, "All will be okay," when, in fact, he really believed otherwise. On the surface, he, too, resembled Dr. Kevin Chase, walking around, exuding a happy disposition.

My first introduction to Dr. Slate was when we met at a meeting in the hospital when he was twenty-seven. Jonathan was six feet, two inches tall with bluish-gray eyes and curly black hair, two dimples peeked out from the shadow of his growing beard. It was evident that he was of athletic build. During that initial meeting, his forehead was crinkled as he appeared to listen with the intensity of a man about to find out the secrets of the universe. His demeanor and speaking mannerisms were similar to that of a man many years his senior. His arms were folded the entire time as if shielding him from guttural bullets. When the meeting was adjourned, he stood near the exit door with his arms still folded yet even closer to his chest. He broke into a smile every now and then, as if forced, and greeted everyone as they exited the meeting. I had started working in the hospital six months before Dr. Slate's arrival, and given the fact that I had not yet been introduced to our most recent member of the hospital staff, I thought it would be an opportune time to introduce myself. With a sarcastic tone, I said, "Are you folding your arms to protect yourself from me or from the world in general?" After he further crinkled his forehead and evidenced a look of surprise, he broke out in a genuine smile, and from that moment forward, a mutual friendship and good working relationship evolved. I am not sure why, but I have always referred to Jonathan by his last name, Slate. I easily call all other coworkers by their first name but not him.

Slate is different from other doctors. Medicine is like an art to him rather than a science. He studied the history of medicine and surgery and has all these theories about how the body works. He attended a prestigious medical school but isn't convinced that everything he learned is an exact truth. He is particularly interested in studying the liver, despite being a vascular surgeon. He feels that all ills stem from, and could be healed by, the liver. Slate references ancient Greek mythology, particularly its notions about liver regeneration. He studies articles relating to the role of stem cells in liver regeneration, always thinking of bioartificial methods that may re-vitalize the liver. The medical department hates and loves him for this. He is good at making suggestions to revitalize health care at the hospital but finds it difficult to go along with the preset medical routines that others easily follow. He goes way above and beyond for the care of his patients like an older brother that doesn't want yet another member of his family to die.

Slate had been an art major earning a bachelor's of arts in undergraduate studies. At the time, he minored in the sciences, particularly physics because he enjoys the nuances of shapes and angles. In his spare time, he frequents art studios. He is particularly awed by artists that study the physical environment. On one occasion, I caught him looking at Ned Kahn's artwork, which included the *Cloud Portal, Cloud Arbor, Cloud Rings.* Art is one of the few things that seems to bring him some joy. In its presence, he becomes less factual and less in-tuned with time and its burdens. To everyone else, Slate is perceived as this outgoing, cheerful man who is detail-oriented and conscientious and smiles rather often. Slate does smile rather often. The same forced smile I had seen during our initial meeting is evident when he greets others. In all the time I have known him, I only recall him laughing once, although our coworkers are actually quite funny people. I laugh a bit more frequently, but generally try to suppress it. Even though Slate can easily be a ladies' man with his chiseled features and athletic build, he is gentle and seems to fail to recognize, or perhaps avoid, the frequent flirtation that he encounters.

Slate generally keeps things to himself. The only time I ever witnessed his lack of control and the onset of confrontation was with a superior who was advising a patient. An eighteen-year-old patient was admitted for suspected appendicitis. She appeared more like a fifteen-year-old and came in with a man who stated he was her father. Slate had come into the room to get a bandage wrap for one of his own clients when he noted a suspicious exchange of glances between the man and his daughter. It was as if he was giving her some kind of warning. He also observed a mark on the girl's arm. He left the room to tell a superior that something was wrong, but the onsite physician didn't do anything, claiming that Slate was overly concerned, perhaps due to his own experiences. Slate tried to follow them out to record their license plate number, but they were already gone. He only saw the front make of the car. He never learned what became of the girl. The phone number they left had been disconnected, but the insurance charge came through. Slate took that day off and didn't show up for work the next day; he called in sick. When he came back the following day, he had significant bags under his eyes, but he wouldn't talk about it.

Slate and I are often in each other's company. We attend concerts, frequent museums, eat at restaurants, and partake of many other treats available to us in the city. We discuss world events, analyze movies and documentaries, and even discuss and employ better means of adaptability and coping for our patients. Yet, we never verbalize our own struggles or how we feel about people or family. It is always limited to observing and discerning gestures and facial expressions, but nothing more.

It was a few years after our initial meeting that Slate made reference to his sister's murder, and I only came to find out that he had yet another sibling after a brief run-in with his significantly younger brother, a brother that had been born after his sister's death. A brother that he had never spoken about or even alluded to in all our conversations before that meeting.

In contrast to Jonathan Slate, his brother, Matt, had a youthful silliness about him and seemed like the happy-go-lucky type. When Slate introduced us, he sarcastically stated, "This is my brother Matt. Yeah, he is noticeably much younger than me. My parents apparently like each other too much." Matt erupted in a hearty laugh which was in great contrast to Slate's disposition. Matt barely knew me at the time, yet disclosed that he was on his way to meet his beautiful, gregarious girlfriend, sharing a picture of the two of them from social media.

Even though Slate seems restrained on sharing personal matters, we somehow understand each other. Whenever the need arises, we are always there for each other to lend assistance, guidance, or moral support. There was the time Slate had to give a speech in front of a large audience. He kept mumbling, "I'm going to die!" over and over again. Once he got to the podium, he displayed that "smile" that he typically displays even while sweating through his designer clothing. This was his first public speaking venture since college when he messed up rather royally. The panic was only diminished by the fact that he didn't know these people and would never have to see them again. I traveled close to three hundred miles to attend the event just so he could see me, and to enable him to set his vision firmly on me, rather than the other three hundred nineteen people in the room, knowing that he needed that distraction to concentrate without tension. It further served as a reassurance that someone was there for him. While visiting friends in another state, my car was hit by an oncoming driver who was blinded by the sunlight. My car jumped the fence from the impact, defacing the exterior of a house. Slate traveled over four hundred miles to pick me up and attempted to calm my frazzled nerves with hot cocoa and cookies. He then assisted me in filling out all the necessary paperwork for insurance to lessen my load.

Slate has this sort of uncertainty as to what he wants out of life. He has a hard time defining himself besides being an M.D. with a specialization in vascular surgery. When we engage in "meaningful conversation" with friends, they often say, "I hope someday I have my own practice, or I am trying to get something published, or I want a big house in the country, or I want to travel the world," while Slate and I remain silent. We have goals, but they are concrete day-to-day goals with limited vision for the future.

Future is not a word I like. I want to forget the past. I am barely getting by in the present, so why do I need to constantly consider the future. During my senior year in high school, I was asked by basically every member of the academic staff what I wanted to do in my future but had no clue how to respond. I did all my schoolwork and joined every club and extracurricular activity available to me, but it was mainly to pass time, not intended as a resource for my future. I conversed with everyone in my school without feeling the quest for a particular social standing like many others do. Aside from making small talk, I generally only had deep personal interactions with two good friends. At the urging of my grandmother, I also attended workshops at a community center near my home.

I opted for ballet class, thinking it was movement-based and I would enjoy it, but I turned out to be the worst student in the class. I basically endured two semesters of class, after which I decided, no more. One needed to be poised and elegant in his or her movements to achieve in this area; I was neither of those. Worse yet, my ballet teacher was a particularly critical woman, and the last thing I needed was someone else nitpicking at my flaws. My rosy cheeks accented the tutu and ballet slippers nicely, but that was the only positive of that experience I can recall at the moment. To this day, I veer from donning anything pink to avoid recollection of my experiences in that tutu.

I did enjoy the piano lessons, though. My long slender fingers lent themselves well to creating pleasantries. In addition, piano lessons required less interaction with other students than dance did.

Slate has chosen to mask his misery, but mine is quite evident. When speaking with peers and colleagues, Slate often makes remarks such as, "This or that will work out great," or "We will have a great time," even though it kind of sounds like a rehearsed speech. I am the Debbie Downer in the group and make note of all the risks or negativities involved in an activity or venture. Somehow, when actually engaged in the task or activity, Slate participates unenthusiastically while donning his usual forced smile. I, on the other hand, generally participate with greater enthusiasm, yet usually armed with a sarcastic or satirical remark when something does go wrong.

Slate is a member of the cardiac and vascular department's faculty, whereas most of my time is spent within the rehabilitative and orthopedic departments of the hospital. As the two departments are nearby and we share some patients, we generally pass each other in the hallways or at the various nurses' stations where people are constantly entering or exchanging information. It is here that one can observe Slate's distinct posture as he sits near a computer station.

Slate isn't fidgety. He sits upright displaying a perfect ninety-degree posture. He isn't one to turn towards others making small chitchat, only occasionally lending his two cents to a given conversation. He holds a Cross pen in his hand, gifted to him by his grandfather and although he doesn't need the pen for computer entry, he twists and twirls the pen incessantly as he spends time thinking. It seems to help him focus and be precise. It is only on the occasions when I catch him glaring at this semi-crunched envelope addressed to him, that he keeps hidden in his jacket pocket, that he begins to fidget and appears agitated. However, when he notes someone else around, he quickly returns the envelope to his pocket, and sits back up in an upright position, returning to his usual serious demeanor. Although curious about its content, I recognize that he is entitled to his secrets, as I am entitled to mine.

I look at Slate now in the bar, he is sitting in his usual upright position as he holds his alcoholic beverage in his hand. He stretches out his hand in a cheer towards the group and drinks. Everyone else downs their drinks easily, even Slate enjoys two rounds. I order a rosé spritzer and drink a quarter of it. Stephanie eyes me, to which I reply, "What? I am drinking!" picking up my cocktail for her to observe the missing portion of my drink with her own eyes.

Stephanie comments, "That's not called drinking. If it doesn't look like something or smell like something, it isn't something."

To which I retort, "You know me, I can get drunk on water."

I glare at my watch. It is getting late, and we all have to be up early to get to work the next day. Stephanie had baked Kevin a cake and distributed a slice to each of us to take home. The cake was perfectly shaped and designed. The creativity and dexterity of her surgical skills seem to play out well in the kitchen. "Stephanie, you're a superwoman," I say.

She whispers in my ear, "That was the second version. I only perfected it after I messed up my first." After the others bid us goodnight, I walk with Stephanie toward the door, coddling my piece of cake. Stephanie laughs, "It's not a baby, you know; it is okay if a bit breaks off."

"I never had one of these," I respond while still admiring the beauty of the cake.

"You never tasted birthday cake, Jules?" Stephanie asks in a surprised tone.

"Of course, I have tasted birthday cake! Although I have never had my *own* celebratory birthday cake." Birthdays were not big celebrations in my house. We would, on occasion, receive an extra pancake or something like that for breakfast.

Stephanie knew that my family wasn't wealthy, but they could definitely afford a cake, which prompted her to ask, "Why not?"

"Well, I don't know. It wasn't considered important, I guess." She wasn't aware that not having a birthday cake was the least of my childhood problems. Stephanie puts her arms around my neck, giving me a side hug while still holding her piece of cake, and we enter her vehicle heading homeward. Overall, the conversation flowed well. There had been a lightness in the air, and I wouldn't admit it to anyone, but I had enjoyed the night.

I get home only to discover an alcohol stain on my black dress. The black dress that fits perfectly, yet still allows me to move and breathe. The black dress that is my staple and has accompanied me more loyally than any other to many events. As I hang it up, readying it for dry cleaning, I think of my clients and whisper, "Better alcohol than blood."

I walk to work the next day, waiting to greet the young homeless girl that graced the street the day before. With resources in hand, I pass the area where she sat yesterday, perched against a gate, but she is no longer there. In her place, sits a new young man, less worn from the hardships of living on the street and more willing to talk, so I give him the list of resources I prepared, and he makes his way toward a local café. The landscape has changed as noted not only by the additions of some more greenery but also by the youthfulness of the faces living on the street. They are not only younger, but appear healthier; they speak articulately and don't appear to be under the influence of drugs or alcohol. They are not the veterans of yesteryear or the disabled that I used to meet on these streets years ago, and I am left wondering what has affected this change in the landscape.

I spend my walk looking up at the trees, but at the same time avoiding bumping into the workers delivering boxes. The trees are vivid. They are no longer just green. The light green ones' edges have turned different hues of yellow. In contrast, the dark green leaves are changing to a beautiful orange color. However, as is often the case, my calm is interrupted by two drivers bantering about something. One is talking expressively with his hand while the other is pointing his finger at the car. They are within close proximity to one another, and as I approach, I take note of the dent in one man's car. Soon the police arrive and begin the questioning. A block down, a man returns to his vehicle to find a bright orange ticket lying on his dashboard; he mumbles under his breath, grabs it, and drives off. As I turn the corner to reach the hospital, I observe a beautiful tree that has a reddish tinge bearing a resemblance to the trees I have only seen on my trip to Costa Rica.

As I reach the hospital and approach the revolving door, a little girl pushes the door out and warmly invites me to come in, as if it were her home. She has no hair, and a few tubes are protruding from her arm. Her mother soon catches up with her. "Thank you," I say to the little girl who dons a smile, feeling some excitement at having ample strength to hold the door. Then I motion to the reddish tree at the corner. "Isn't it beautiful?" The girl nods in the affirmative. "I never saw it before," I say. "It must have come to life just for you," and her mother smiles as they exit. She breathes in the fresh air like it was magic.

The elevator at the end of the hallway takes me upstairs where I am greeted by a list delineating my caseload for the day.

CHAPTER 2: ABUSE IS A BOX

Life at the hospital was basically my life. I worked there from seven thirty to five thirty, five days a week, which included time for paperwork, with a few mandatory breaks. On Sundays, I worked in the outpatient clinic for a few months at a time, to cover other therapists. I had initially gone in as a favor to a friend who was on sick leave but ended up committing for a longer time frame.

After graduate school, it took me close to a year to find my specialization in occupational therapy. My classmates had long been employed in one steady job and found the contentment of commitment. I was still in this need-to-make-a-decision mode for quite some time. I volunteered or interned at various departments, including: neuro, acute care, subacute care, mental health, and hand rehab. I had an interest in everything, but no particular specialization drew my attention. Given my indecision, I chose to work in a hospital that had multiple subunits that would provide me with some variability. However, there was one department that I would frequent as a visitor or volunteer only, but would never consider for employment. That was the pediatric wing. I enjoy watching the children on the wing and entertaining them but don't want to see them regularly. For the last ten years, I have been working for the same hospital in NYC, making short visits to the pediatric wing in my free time.

I generally seek out fast-paced work. Other than on breaks, there is little downtime during the day. I have encountered patients from all walks of life, many of whom don't speak fluent English. The persistent change and constant activity don't allow my mind to overanalyze or go to places I try to avoid. I also enjoy the quick thinking and problem solving; it is like a living logic puzzle. Sure, there are always coworkers bordering on annoying, but for the most part, we work with each other, not against each other. We have acquired an understanding of each other's strengths, weaknesses, likes, dislikes, and have even come to appreciate each other's quirks. Perhaps that is why our staff turnover is low. We have the incentive to stay in each other's company. Our common interests include food and movies; other than that, our interests and pastimes are quite diverse.

Sutton, the nurse practitioner, is a sports enthusiast, spending twenty percent of his income on sports. Evette, the physical therapist, is obsessed with geography. She can name the origin of any dish in restaurants. Evette is also the only person I have ever known that holds a bachelor's degree in archeology. Shana, the speech therapist, has taken screenwriting courses. She uses her talents when volunteering and hosting charity events. Delya, another occupational therapist, runs a silk-screen printing business with her husband. She was a national spelling bee champion and is an expert in word etymology, which is why she can comprehend even the strangest most complex medical terms. Her combined passions have contributed to the inspirational messages and interesting slogans that adorn her accessories. Slate is an art enthusiast. Kevin knows how to source every type of material or fabric possible. This likely contributes to his eclectic yet sophisticated wardrobe. He also has an encyclopedic knowledge of all things pertaining to baseball. Stephanie is an avid animal lover and good with mechanics. She has already fixed my car more times than I care to count. Dr. Sarim, the psychologist, is an extraordinary puzzle-solver. We also have an inventor of a multipurpose tool, a salon enthusiast, as well as a software and coding expert. Another staff member is a machinist, a job title I didn't fully comprehend because as society has evolved, it has decreased in popularity. We share our interests with each other, which creates a system of greater trust and communication. Our interests foster different skills, providing us with a wider range of professionals to interact with.

Some are skilled at tool usage, others can advise about pet care and pet assistance, yet others are skilled with color and form. The better we understand each other, the better our collaboration and ability to improve patient outcomes with a greater magnitude of improvement. One staff member helped me figure out what materials to use for a patient project, a software engineer helped me build the model to maximize efficiency, another helped me secure funding, and yet another advised of changes to make the project more aesthetically pleasing.

The doctors on our unit reattach limbs, revitalize blood, restructure bone, change organ placement. They can restore eyesight and hearing, change facial structure, identify the content of body fluid, reinstitute brain structure, and remove tumors. They are preoccupied with the makeup of the body and see the sadness and fear emanating from a projected surgery, or the initiation of a course of treatment. Their interactions with their clients are critical, yet brief. Supporting staff have insight into the patients' daily functioning and the particulars of patients' lives. They see the frustration of a patient not being their old efficient self in daily tasks and activities. The job they need to alter or leave, the house they no longer can navigate or care for, the child's meals they can't prepare, and the financial toll the disability generates. It is within the course of this staff's functioning to identify how successful a given course of treatment truly is, whether the side effects outweigh the treatment, and whether the person remains a functional and complacent human being. Ultimately, we rely on each other's expertise.

Microbiologists, pathologists, and some other vocations examine things in their smallest detail. They see things which human eyes cannot see. Their jobs are of extreme importance. They have been able to prevent and cure ravaging diseases. They have been able to substantiate the effects of good nutrition and lack thereof for mankind. They appeal to the masses by examining detail, intricacies. My job, however, requires analysis of activities and tasks viewing the person as a whole in a larger contextual environment. An image emerges as to their needs and wants, their lifestyles, the people in their lives, their physical surroundings. The overarching reach of a failing in the body's systems. My eyes are trained to view the overall image that is perceived based upon facial expressions, observation, interviews, physical examination, and assessment.

I don't rely upon a microscope to find specs, and while my daily tasks aren't consumed with plagues and diseases that affect the masses, I care for each individual as if they were their own microcosm. What modern medicine still fails to understand is that the world needs the constant cycle of interaction between those that particularly seek out the specks and those that concern themselves with the general image. We are an ever-changing system that requires the exchange of information from each other, particularly in the age of chronic illness, where cures are often nonexistent, necessitating ongoing treatment. We have the potential to become each other's greatest champions or each other's worst enemies. A good institution cultivates a positive relationship, while a bad one puts us in competition wherein there are only short-term winners and losers.

As I walk in the hallway, I pass a surgeon, nurse, physical therapist, speech therapist, tech guy, and the janitor who helps keeps germs at bay. We greet each other and then continue on to do our jobs.

Oliver Edwin Hawthorne is my first patient of the day. He has been diagnosed with Guillain-Barré syndrome which is a polyneuropathy that unfortunately progresses rather rapidly. His thirty-third birthday was just over six weeks ago, and he suffered from an upper respiratory infection in the weeks before his admission which formed the foreground for this viral infection. Oliver's weakness began in his hands and feet and then progressed upwards. Although he has been on a ventilator for respiratory support, at present, with the aid of the respiratory therapist and nurse, he is able to breathe on his own. Despite the fact that he has made some strides, he still has many challenges ahead. Initial measures have been undertaken to prevent muscle atrophy and to prevent contractors, or muscle shortening, with additional measures to prevent further infection and to help him deal with his gnawing fatigue.

Oliver was working as a freelance writer. He has traveled to many parts of the world that others only dream of. His articles and short stories have been predominantly about nature. After reading some of his work, I noted that he had, on a number of occasions, written about disease and disease prevention techniques in respective regions that he had visited. The fact that he is scientifically aware makes me feel even more compassion for him.

Guillain-Barré syndrome can be quite scary. Sometimes ignorance is bliss. Having a greater understanding that something horrific is attacking your body when you are limited in what you can do is beyond frightening. Sometimes it is easier to have limited medical knowledge, thus entrusting your entire care to medical professionals and believing them when they say they are doing everything they can to help you get better.

Oliver's eyes always express some level of horror, particularly when someone in the medical field enters his room. Aside from sadness and fear, it is also evident that Oliver is a pessimist, always assuming that he will be among the small percentage of individuals that will never fully recover from this illness. Once he was able to speak, he often said, "This will probably do me greater harm than good." In the early stages of his disease, the staff was only able to passively range his muscles using the force of their own bodies to create movement and maintain the integrity of his muscles and surrounding tissue. From the onset of paralysis, Oliver's nerves have taken quite some time to show sufficient improvement to perform functional tasks.

It took time, but Oliver has been bumped up the therapeutic ladder, finally showing greater range of movement and able to tolerate light-weight objects. He provided me with a less than enthusiastic, "Yippee," evidently assuming that he would never fully return to his former self. When he had ample breath support and his tubes removed, the first thing he relayed to me was that despite having amassed all the scripting gadgets a writer can amass from all the corners of the world over the years, he still opted for writing in a journal. It is only after he completes a full work that he transfers it onto electronic media. I was, therefore, careful to splint his hands as necessary to prevent deformities and contractors until the small muscles of his hands had sufficient strength to support activity.

Oliver was beginning to tolerate movement for greater intervals, spending more time out of his bed, and evidencing less discomfort with changes in positioning. It was at this point, when he was better able to contract his muscles and was able to produce more fluid movement, that he was provided with some utensils and tools that were modified with built-up handles for assisting him during grooming and eating activities. I could often hear Oliver comment under his breath, "I am strong, I can do this," and then muster up all his energy to do what was asked of him; however, he would become frustrated with himself when unable to achieve what he thought he could.

It was also at this point that Oliver returned for very brief increments to using a writing tool, although modified, to write down some thoughts. There was a glimmer in his eyes that signified the return of life. Although he evidenced some difficulty with facial muscle movement, he conjured up a smile. Oliver never spoke of any relatives, only stating, "I have been on my own for a long time." In the course of his hospital stay, thus far only one friend has come for a visit.

I pity Oliver, and yet, from all my patients, he reminds me most of myself. I don't like Oliver's negativity but believe that had I been in his shoes, I would be voicing his words and having his feelings. I, too, have always believed myself to be strong, thinking, *I can take it*. Yet, when reflecting upon my own challenges, I am awakened to the fact that I might be weaker than I thought, and that notion scares me.

Part of my job is facilitating the process of performing activities of daily living, the stuff you do every day, whether by remediation or compensation. Sexual activity is one of the activities of daily living. Patients who have sustained a pelvic injury, who suffer from urinary or gastric conditions, joint and movement issues or are experiencing side effects from medication, may suffer from sexual dysfunction. Sometimes patients will need information related to repositioning, or they may need to engage in additional exercises for improved strength related to this activity.

Additionally, they may also be suffering from the emotional ramifications from this inability and feel less human. As I am not a sex therapist, I can only have limited exchanges on this topic with patients, but sometimes I am the person whom they choose to confide in. I once befriended a fellow occupational therapist, who was most knowledgeable about sexual dysfunction. She was a shy, timid individual who rarely spoke up, and I only found out her name from a name tag she was wearing at the time of our initial meeting. I think I had my own preconceived notions about what people who talk about this topic are like. This area has been less frequently addressed than others, as most clients won't initiate their concerns. My level of comfort has increased over the years, but at first, I would only supply a pamphlet about the topic, not even allowing one word to pass my lips, avoiding any further discomfort. But on September 12 of this year, a patient asked me a question that would challenge that level of comfort considerably.

Mr. Galston was scheduled for therapy in the gym and as always, I came to get him. He was lying in bed bemoaning the fact that he hadn't seen his girlfriend in days. I hadn't shared the fact that I saw his brother give her more than a friendly kiss on one occasion. My blood boiled at the lack of loyalty one brother had toward another. I wasn't one hundred percent certain that what I saw was accurate, but I would guess about ninety percent. I felt guilt, like I was betraying a trust at not sharing this information and at not being certain as to how to address it. What department in a hospital does one go to for advice on such a dilemma? This continued to weigh heavily on my conscience. Mr. Galston was a particularly nice man. He also seemed sentimental, as he would pile his get well and good wishes cards next to his bed and read them more than once. Then it happened out of the clear blue; he didn't even turn to me; he just asked, "What do you think of a sexual surrogate?"

I was so caught off guard that I dropped my pen and tried to prevent Mr. Galston from noting the small tremble that had just overtaken my hands. I felt my face flush. I wasn't even certain that I knew what a sexual surrogate entailed. The only thing I knew was that other countries had employed the use of surrogates with people whose sexual needs were difficult to be met due to disability. These patients had often only experienced touch related to machinery, devices, and blood draws. They had lacked that intimate touch.

What came to mind was my old coworker and friend, Ashley, who sits for hours on end in the neonatal care unit watching over her premature little boy, Landon, who is barely two pounds. I see her approach him as she moves the various tubes attached to his little body so that she can access his barely visible limbs. She caresses his paper-thin skin, so thin that his ears appear attached to the side of his head. She retreats only momentarily to allow a nurse to draw some blood from his heel, for the third time this week. Yet, Landon's small frame seems to relax as she resumes stroking his little arms because a loving human touch has no competition. It was something he earned just by existing.

I directed my eyes toward Mr. Galston but was unable to make eye contact, and responded that all people crave touch, something that makes the body relax, a way to express their emotions; it's part of the overall human design. It is what makes people human and non-robotic. I looked up at Mr. Galston, this time semi-eyeing him, recalling that this is the man who had undergone a fecal transplant, had catheters, was frequently prodded for blood. I allowed myself to gulp hard before responding. "We all want to be human." Mr. Galston nodded. "To be honest, I am not the most well-versed person on this topic, but I can try to answer any questions you may have or will find someone you can talk to." As I said these words, I found that once again, I failed to make eye contact because I couldn't. I assisted him in transferring to his wheelchair, and then we made our way to the gym, concentrating only on the exercises at hand.

At the last meeting, the decision was made as to the date that Mr. Galston would be discharged, as he had made considerable progress. Today that date has arrived. The day is coming to a close soon, and I make my way toward Mr. Galston's room to say good-bye. His girlfriend never came back, his brother skipped town, and he never asked me any additional questions on the topic. Apparently, he left his cards behind, and the janitor tossed them into the garbage. I observe the cards in the trash bin and see the empty bed. I am too late. I sit down on a chair in the room, feeling defeated. I have failed Mr. Galston. It wasn't skill that failed him; it was my own insecurities about a topic that I don't feel comfortable discussing. In general, forging close bonds is not my strong suit.

The day is thankfully over, and I have checked off all the boxes: see patients, documentation, signatures, put in orders for equipment. I walk steadily on my way home remembering mid-way that I have run out of shampoo and make my way to a convenience store, only to find out that the day is not yet over.

The choices are endless, and I try to decide whether I want my hair to appear unrulier, wave-like, or sport a full curl. After a few minutes reading the descriptions, I end up taking the shampoo with the most refreshing fragrance and then get ready to leave the store. I am distracted by a woman chasing me down and yelling after me in a high-pitched voice. "Jules, is that you?" She is holding her receipt and it's flailing in the air. I recognize her; it's Dana Lampert.

Dana was a sixty-nine-year-old woman who had been happily married for forty-seven years. She had suffered from bouts of chest pains for a while, and ultimately, heart blockages were identified. In her youth, she had undergone an appendectomy which was unsuccessful and required supplemental surgery to repair the additional damage done by the initial attempt. Given her past, she harbored a fear of surgical procedures.

Dana had failed to tell her primary care provider how frequently she experienced chest pains coupled with increased fatigue. It was while I was treating her for lateral epicondylitis, otherwise known as tennis elbow, that she would come to learn of the blockages. It was only after her primary care physician, who initially discovered variances during a routine check-up, strongly encouraged her to make an appointment with a cardiologist that she summoned the courage to schedule an appointment.

Dana enjoyed therapy, as she loved to talk while she "worked." She spoke about her four grown children, her husband, her dog. But she never discussed anything relating to herself. Her passions, habits, interests. I had only known her as a figure navigating through others' lives. The one obvious thing was that she was always a particularly good dresser. One day, as her therapy sessions were ending, she mentioned that she had seen a cardiologist, at her primary care physician's request. She relayed that he discovered blockages and she was advised to have surgery. Looking at her, one could not conclude that she would need such extensive surgery. She was a thin, beautiful woman, well dressed, with seemingly no evidence of swelling, shortness of breath, and no self-reported complaints of fatigue or pain. She was actually a model patient, always compliant and with a happy disposition. She would only say in an amusing tone, "The stairs are not my friend." When she spoke of her impending surgery, her disposition changed and an initial sense of anger and then sadness became evident. "I refuse to go through that surgery," she relayed. "I don't care if it's the end of me without it. I refuse."

The change in her shocked me, but also made me aware of how strongly she felt about not going through with the surgery. It was the first time she had disclosed something about herself and her own emotions which made me realize how much she tended to hold back. I believe she had forgotten about her own care while preoccupying herself in her role of wife and mother. It wasn't my place to give medical advice, but I tried to urge her to reconsider the surgery. She was entitled to a second opinion at another institution that could either refute or confirm that surgery was her only option. I think the fear of her surgery was so overwhelming, given her experience in her youth, that it was blocking her ability to be rational.

Our session ended, and she went home to return a week later, failing to have gone for a second opinion and was consumed with refusing surgery, as that was all she could talk about. There was definitely a psychological component involved. "You know, Dana, riling yourself up won't help your heart heal." But she wasn't listening. I made her take deep breaths for a few seconds throughout her session, and I advised that I would end the session prematurely if she did not try to calm down. At the end of our session, I peeked out from the therapy room in search of any of her family members thinking that they may have escorted her there but no one was around. I was to have my lunch break right after but couldn't let this woman leave in this condition.

"Dana, wait a minute." She turned surprised at my request but stopped short. "Can we have a chat?" My brain was on overtime, trying to think of someone to pose this dilemma to, but nobody that could advise me was available at the time. I started to wonder if what I was about to say would help this woman or hurt her, and I definitely felt that I was over-stepping my bounds; nevertheless, my gut kept prodding me to continue talking. "Dana, I see that you're really upset and scared about your surgery. Perhaps there are other avenues you can explore. Have you ever heard of EECP? I realize how committed you are to others, but please keep in mind that you deserve to take care of yourself." The words weren't really coming out in continuous sentences, but rather broken-up fragments. I repeated, "Have you ever heard of EECP?"

"What?" she said.

"It's a type of a treatment where medical personnel attach a cuff to your lower extremity that inflates and deflates, continuously pumping throughout the session, in order to facilitate improved circulation through-out your body and heart. You get to lie down during the whole process, but you would probably need multiple sessions to achieve some results. I know how you were committed to therapy, so I thought this would be a possible option for you. But please keep in mind that it is not guaranteed to work."

After the words exited my mouth, my mind was volleying so many thoughts: EECP is controversial; it isn't used that often, but then again it may be relaxing for her; she is very conscious about therapy sessions, and she will likely go, whereas she is refusing surgery. Then again, she hasn't even attempted to get a second medical opinion. She doesn't have aortic insufficiency or any other contraindicators, or does she? Yet, I found myself giving her a sticky note with the words "enhanced external counterpulsation."

She grabbed the note enthusiastically. "Great, an exercise," she said.

I called out after her, "Make sure to check it out with your doctor." She walked out with her head held high and waved good-bye to me at the door.

The next week, Dana returned for her final therapy session. She was in a good mood and more invigorated than ever. She thanked me profusely and said she had an appointment at an EECP center.

It was at that moment, I self-criticized. *"What have you done, Jules? This woman can die as a result of your actions. It wasn't your place; you're not a doctor, let alone a cardiologist."* Perhaps my desire to help her clouded my judgment.

I thought I would never see her again, particularly as I had only been at that outpatient unit for six months, but here she is, Mrs. Dana Lampert, chasing me down and laughing at her husband's hat, which was blown off as he chased her. My initial reaction was to be glad she was alive.

"You look well, Dana. I hope you're doing well," I say with a bit of apprehension.

"I am fantastic, Jules! I finished my EECP sessions, and I feel great, better than I have felt in a long time. I loved the sessions; I would just lie down and relax and close my eyes and conjure up images in my mind of swimming in school. I was a competitive diver in high school, did you know that? I barely felt the pressure rise from my legs during the EECP sessions. It was really great. Oh, and the doctors say I have gotten much better."

"That's great," I repeat. Dana shakes my hand good-bye with such great enthusiasm, she almost takes it with her. I walk home wondering what to learn from my actions. Despite the positive results reported to me, *"Was I correct in going against medical advice, or would it be better if I keep my mouth shut next time . . . What's the lesson?"* I look up at the clouds in the sky as I continue to walk home. They are being covered in darkness and are silent. Despite the crisp, brisk air, I walk slowly, taking in the New York City scenes while trying to calm my nerves.

I go home and use my new fragrant shampoo, which creates a nice aroma in my small home. I then cover myself in two blankets, not only for warmth but for feeling cuddled by something, and I finally doze off.

The morning sky appears a bit overcast; today, my weather apps show predictions for rain. I lug my oversized umbrella in one hand, which can't compete with the weight of my handbag. Furthermore, I am carrying my black dress to the dry cleaners, which I ironically shield from the elements even though it is going for a cleaning. Upon arrival, I see a particularly long line, and personnel are tagging another four black dresses that are waiting to return to their former selves. I make a mark on the label of my own, J.W. for Jules Wescott, just in case.

I turn onto the block of the hospital noting that my favorite tree with the red hue has turned even redder, but that the leaves have begun to shed. My hand picks one up, examining it to further gaze at the reddish-pink color. Soon it gets knocked out of my hand by a pushy passerby who unsteadies me on my feet. The wind blows the leaf further toward the traffic and I watch it get crushed under the wheels of a tire. I cringe a bit. "I guess better you than me, little leaf," I say as I spin through the hospital's revolving doors.

Today I would visit the pediatric wing. The wing that fills me with a certain indescribable sensation; it is like fear and anticipation all in one. I have some time as it is early, so I make my way up to the wing before starting my official workday.

The pediatric wing is filled with a host of different age groups ranging in age from birth to eighteen. As I am not an official occupational therapist for the unit, I come in the capacity of a volunteer and often read to the patients or organize short craft projects for patients who can endure an activity for a few moments. Other visitors might bring pets or well-known personalities to help the children pass the time. Today, a music therapist is scheduled to arrive but has been detained due to an automobile accident. It is a rainy morning. Her car had skidded into another vehicle on the highway. Although she has not been injured, she called in to reschedule, as her car needed to be towed. *As usual, something goes wrong*, I think, as I

58

pass by the pediatric nurses' station. I begin to mentally think of alternate methods of entertainment or activities for the young patients on the wing to "keep busy and distracted." In the midst of my search, four nurses enter a patient's room that is within direct visual contact from the station. My curiosity gets the better of me and I peek into the room.

The four nurses and a doctor are standing over a young boy who appears to be between two-and-a-half to three years of age. He looks frightened and recoils toward the hospital bedframe as the medical team attempts to bandage the sores on his legs. One nurse turns toward me, and with a look of despair, offers me entrance into the room. I feel like a giant in comparison to the small creature curled up in bed. I have no previous knowledge of who this child is or what his story is but note the lacerations and strange marks, perhaps from friction or burns. Worse yet, there are odd imprint marks on his torso and legs. These are not injuries associated with an accident. It is easy to deduce that this child has been subject to some kind of physical abuse which was likely preceded and followed by emotional abuse as well.

Despite his appearance, I can see beautiful green eyes that, although downcast, are picking up the light from the corner windows of the room. "His name is James," the nurse advises. As I approach him, I detect the extent of the strange, unidentifiable indentations running up and down his arms and legs, with a few scrapes that look like a metal hanger had scratched him up. He has some red blotches on his thighs, but as the doctor examines this further, he identifies it as oil paint. His arm had been thought to be broken, but the doctor has just received the results from X-ray, confirming it was just a sprain. The nurse turns to me, advising that his wounds had been inflicted by his mother.

My initial inclination is to turn around and leave. I am so bothered observing this child's bruises that it facilitates a strong visceral reaction. In the past, I have encountered children whose bodies had been ravaged by cancer, infection, burns, skin disease, and allergic reactions, but there is something sickening about looking at a child whose bruises have been inflicted not only by another human, but by a human that should possess an unconditional love for her own child, attempting to protect him or her at all costs. I run my hands through my hair over and over again, still contemplating leaving, but in the end, I stay.

At that moment, I recalled my youth and the verbal and physical abuse I endured at my mother's hand. My mother was a well-dressed woman who was always adorned with the latest fashions and wore aromatic perfume whose scents lingered after she left. She was strikingly beautiful; by looking at her, one would never know what type of rage she was capable of. She often grabbed my long curly hair almost like claws and banged my head against any vertical surfaces in the area. She threw readily available household objects at me. My reflexes were significantly sharpened as I tried to duck and maneuver myself around the object. My mother often pulled at my arms, which made my arms pop out of their sockets on more than

60

one occasion. Although I was a good student, kept my room and objects tidy, and rarely complained, my mother found reasons to criticize everything I did. Perhaps her beauty and grace made the abuse that much worse, as there seems to be an incongruence when a beautiful creature commits monstrous acts. It also requires reframing and increased effort on the part of the victim to believe that this creature has actually abused them.

Being hit has a sound. It resonates even when low in frequency and magnitude. Even hair being pulled has its own sound. Abuse is accompanied by a particular visual image that becomes embedded in your memory, that plays itself out more than once in your mind, although the event has only happened once. You not only experience the act itself, but also the wrathful look on the perpetrator's face, coupled with the unsympathetic looks on the faces of others that ignore your presence and what is happening to you.

My mother never looked at me as her child. Her eyes portrayed a look of disgust or anger. My father never looked at me at all, and when he finally did, his eyes reflected the same pain that I imagine my eyes held. These vivid images appear even now when I close my eyes. Abuse has a distinct feel, sometimes the feeling is shock. Sometimes you feel the reverberation of the wall when you are thrown against it. Other times you feel that nudge of your center of gravity being displaced by an unwanted force, or sometimes you just feel frozen and muddy, like mounds of snow exposed to the elements. Sometimes you relive the feel of the bruising occurring, like your veins are collapsing, and sometimes you just feel small, like you're shrinking into the ground.

The question, "What do you want to be when you grow up?" would make my six-year-old-self want to vomit. It wasn't only the thought of future failings that scared me, but the fact that most of my classmates would say, "I want to be a mommy." In contrast to today's society, most of my classmates just wanted to be a mom. In truth, I was afraid to be a mother. I was afraid to have a daughter that looked like my mother and that I would have to stare at and care for her, all the while recalling my mother's face. But what scared me even more was the thought of becoming like my mother and actually hurting my child. The very first time I read an article discussing genetic engineering as it relates to choosing the sex of a child, I remember thinking that I would make sure to have boys. That way, they could never definitively look like my mother. My mother was a bit critical of others and would make her opinions known to my four siblings, but I was the only one of her five children to endure physical abuse at her hands. I had three sisters and one brother. My sisters had inherited my mother's coloring and beauty and there was a stark contrast between my looks and theirs. My sisters, at least the two younger ones, were initially empathetic to my plight and seemed to want to console me, but, with time, they became accustomed to my mistreatment.

My older sister, Meghan, who was perhaps the most beautiful of my sisters, generally ignored my situation. However, she had once gotten really mad at me for waking her up early in the morning, and as she walked past me in the hallway, she slammed me into the wall. For a few seconds after it happened, she looked at me with such surprise at what she had done that she genuinely appeared shocked by her own behavior. Although she never apologized, she refrained from any future violence. Within a few months however, she did revert to verbal denigration. Overall, we never shared a close sisterly bond but were more like related acquaintances.

My father was a kind and considerate man but extremely passive. He never allowed me to be hit in his presence, but he failed to stop my mother's behaviors in his absence. My father was a contractor and was particularly talented in creating molding and other intricate details, giving character to a room. In an alternate universe, he may have been a sculptor. After being hit or hurt, I would run to the room I shared with my sister and stare up at a small skylight between our beds. I would look up at the sky in a semi-numb state and usually see a cloud in the sky. I couldn't see the full body of the cloud but would lament the fact that the clouds blocked my view of the sky, a sky I desperately wanted to make eye contact with.

The one element of luck in my life was when, at age nine, my grandmother moved in with us, and the abuse stopped. She had beautiful piercing green eyes which were accentuated by her olive skin and curly, jet-black hair. She was tall and statuesque with a beautiful operatic voice. She was the strongest willed and most inspiring woman I had ever met. I modeled myself after her, thinking that this must be what people are supposed to be like. I behold this little boy's eyes, this little James. His eyes are green, a beautiful shade of green. They do not evidence the strength and fortitude that came with my grandmother's green eyes, but rather, the sadness and aloneness evidenced by other green eyes I had encountered. I suddenly feel a quiver in my thigh which cues me in to where I have met this young boy before. He was the child in the park, the very one who spilled his drink on me days before. I hear Nurse Abbie say, "Don't worry, James. We won't hurt you. We just want to clean your boo-boos and put some medicine on them."

It isn't within my authority to chase out medical staff, particularly given that I am only a visitor on the pediatric ward, but I feel it necessary, as I feel certain that to James, these do-gooders are probably being perceived as a pack of wolves ready to pounce on him. It isn't that the pediatric staff are not caring individuals. It is just that they are already understaffed and overburdened and that they have watched children suffer for such lengths of time that it has become commonplace, and has somewhat lessened their patience and their empathy.

Perhaps it is because I am hypersensitive to this situation that I could feel his pain, or perhaps, I am feeling my own. I still feel exceedingly uneasy around children who are suffering, particularly children who had sustained injury by abuse. Although I have convinced myself that I am numb to my own experience, I continue to vicariously experience a renewed rawness of trauma when meeting children who have experienced the same.

To my own disbelief, I make the bold move of chasing out the doctors, requesting that only Nurse Abbie remain in the room. Shockingly, instead of being met with resistance, the remaining medical staff quietly exits the room. I am not a trauma expert, and in truth, that is what they needed, but for some reason, they are willing to allow me the opportunity to try. Abbie turns to me and, under her breath, says, "He hasn't spoken a word since he was brought in." I turn to Nurse Abbie and ask if I could briefly turn off some of the monitoring systems in the room. She looks at me wild-eyed, but given that it isn't life-threatening, she agrees.

"There is too much noise in this room," I say. I then go to the window to close the shades slightly, allowing ample light to peek through. I momentarily catch a glimpse of a cloud, but turn quickly away. I take off my lab coat and push my chair over to the young boy's bed, maintaining an arm's length distance. I bend my head slightly, moving away somewhat to avoid being in his face, yet trying to meet his eyes. In a soft voice, I say, "My name is Jules." His eyes peer up at me for only a few seconds only to return downward.

My hands are always cold. My grandmother used to rub her warm hands over mine and say, "Cold hands, warm heart." Children's hands, even in illness, tend to be warm and cozy, and I always retract my hand apologetically when touching theirs, saying, "Sorry for making you cold," but they are generally receptive to the gesture. However, there is no way

I would risk startling James with my touch, especially not with my cold hands. Instead, I start to hum a gentle tune as the sound of raindrops in the background provides a good backdrop, all the while keeping eye contact with him. After four to five minutes, James extends his legs and looks as if he might fall asleep.

Nurse Abbie is growing more impatient by the minute. "I thought you were here to help," she says. "I have two other patients waiting for me, and you're just wasting precious time."

"He needs time," I say. "His body needs to relax to allow you to help him." Nurse Abbie agrees to allow him fifteen minutes of relaxation. Then I extend my arm to Nurse Abbie and say, "I have a boo-boo. Can you make it feel better?" Abbie smiles and plays along, bandaging my arm. Even in a tired state, James looks at me curiously, and then I say, "Can Abbie make your boo-boo better too?" I receive no response, but James extends his legs as if relegating control of his muscles. Abbie hums my tune as she medicates and bandages his wounds, and soon after, James falls asleep.

I return to the acute-rehab ward downstairs with thoughts of James on my mind. I take a brief detour on my way to Mr. Simmons's room. I enter Mr. Simmons's room quietly, almost tiptoeing to reflect the state of quiet in the room. The room is eerily still, reflecting the lack of vitality that a comatose patient brings. Mr. Simmons fails to evidence basic pupillary reflexes and is starting to evidence contractures, shortening, in his hand from lack of movement. His wife said he had been a philosophy professor for close to thirty years. Now the man that had lectured for so many years about the nuances of life was the subject of that very debate. I feel there is still life in him, but know he will be unable to respond. While standing a few feet from Mr. Simmons's bed, my mind is still preoccupied with James's situation. I let my frustrations out and state, "How can someone do that to a child. It is so unfair." It's strange how you want someone to hear you and not hear you at the same time. After my brief venting, I stand there looking at Mr. Simmons, and with sudden guilt, I come close to his ear and say, "I'm sorry for this display; you deserve better."

As I exit his room, making my way toward the hallway, I feel a light touch on my shoulders, and there stands Dr. Civian, orthopedic surgeon, with a stern look on his face.

"Jules. Where were you? Your patient is awaiting your assistance."

"Sorry," I say, walking briskly toward my client.

I make my way through the day, which thankfully goes by without any additional drama, yet I feel this overwhelming heaviness. Some images don't readily leave your mind, and little James continues to occupy my thoughts even as I walk home. I try to recall every last detail of my encounter with him in the park days ago, but no new revelations come to mind. I know he was able to talk and I don't recall any limp or scratches on him, only remembering his oversized clothing. The stress of having seen little James in that state compels me to swing my apartment door open. I allow my jacket to fall to the ground and leave my shoes at the door, something I generally don't do. I sit with my feet up and attempt to indulge in a six-hundred-calorie treat.

In comparison to a typical house in a suburb of Texas, my home is a shoebox. Its dimensions lend itself for entertaining about two people at a time, three on a good day. My apartment has no remnant of the life I lived before arriving in the city, no pictures of home or my family. There are only two beautiful picture scenes that grace the walls, compliments of Jonathan Slate. It's the type of apartment where you can't escape the smell of smoke when you occasionally burn suppers. Nor can you escape to another room to find light when a lightbulb starts its last round of flickering, like small lightning bolts trapped in glass, then finally succumbing. I have all the storage units possible and have tried to maintain some floor space to weaken the shoebox effect.

As in childhood, I am once again stuck with objects as my permanent companions. Given its dimensions, few people frequent the apartment; we mostly meet in outside quarters. I constantly reorganize, throwing things out to make room for new. It's difficult to sort and decide what is important, what is worthy of being salvaged. Books are always keepers. The electronic books just don't do it for me. I love the weight and feel of the book, I enjoy shifting from page to page; in its hard volume, I feel ownership and possession. The luxury items are predominantly composed of my good china and silverware. I always set the table; it's a habit from early childhood. Sweatshirts and vests are usually the first to go. "Sorry," I say as I toss them into a bag destined for charity. These have done their job and have kept me warm and fashionable. I, likewise, toss in the small boxes that housed my accessories for the season, like fashion belts and jewelry. I wrap them as they had been wrapped upon purchase, to allow for that same impression and spark, that element of surprise, for the next owner. Then I find the cosmetics and makeup bags, along with their respective small tools that I just had to have at the time, but of which only twenty-five percent got used. I generally enlist Stephanie's help for sorting through my shoes, not that I buy that many, but it is hard to see the way others see you amble in shoes, it's more something you feel. Stephanie is a shoe person; she graciously provides her opinion and critique within minutes.

As a child, I grew up in upstate New York, where greenery surrounded me. I received a fairly good education. I saw the same people every day. People mostly dressed in similar attire. The streets were rarely congested, but my life was not immune to gossip, expectation, or conformity. Neighborhood parks were good areas to frequent as a child. My brother, Dean, would spend hours riding his bike, particularly following the outline of the circular path in the playground. I would watch kids engage in hopscotch on worn painted boards, and we would throw sidewalk chalk as the indicator of where we had landed.

The air quality was quite good. I didn't know that air quality was a thing back then, but I do now. We would swing for hours and pump our feet really high, in competition, aiming to reach our legs farthest over the fence. We would always find a willing partner for the seesaw ride, which generally ended in one partner vying for his or her stability, like being on a riding bull. Despite having three sisters, my general play interactions were with neighborhood kids or friends from school. The one activity which was solely with a sibling was attempting to scale the playground wall. I would watch Dean go up and down the playground gates. My own hands and legs would try to mimic his, but I was never able to reach the top. I didn't trust that Dean or my siblings would catch me or help me if I fell, so I never gave it my full vigor to try and reach the top.

I admired the trees as their leaves changed in fall and created snowmen and snow castles in the park yards in the winter. To this day, I still live in the outdoors with friends as my apartment lends itself to only a little more than nothing. The streets are congested, the air quality not great, there is diversity in clothing, and despite actually having mastered rock climbing, the only scaling of something I have done recently is attempting to reach items on the higher shelves in my apartment. There are few, if any, swings, hopscotch boards, and seesaws, but I still marvel at the great outdoors, the parks, the playgrounds, the way kids become more alive outside, more curious, and evidencing greater comradery in a shared space. My few positive childhood memories were created in the outdoors. It was only there that I felt a sense of freedom. I can't imagine being chained to video games or TV, which today's youth so often chain themselves to, sitting in one spot, with my body frozen, staring for hours at one target. It is bad enough spending a significant amount of time at work, documenting my progress on various databases and systems. These activities are the most boring part of my day.

My apartment is home to only one other living thing, that is, my plant. Due to the nature of tropism, the plant is leaning toward the window, like a bent-over elderly person, the angle at which it stands looks like it wishes to escape through the large pane of my window. Being cooped up in the shoebox all day, I cannot blame it. Stephanie often watches me water the plant and comments on my use of filtered water.

"Why do you need filtered water for a plant to grow?"

I readily respond, "You know how much construction goes on in this neighborhood and how dirty the water must be."

Stephanie retorts, "Perhaps you should just talk to it. That's free. Filtered water is costly."

Even in its bent position, it provides a vitality to the apartment and is worth the space and filtered water it takes advantage of.

As I open the door to my apartment, I am greeted by a near growl coming from my next-door neighbor, Mr. Dawson. Mr. Dawson is a very angry man. I have yet to see him smile or greet me. He doesn't like noise and will sometimes bang on the wall when music is playing in my apartment. I have never seen people enter his apartment. When I first moved in and tried to make light conversation, he ignored me and literally banged the door closed in my face. He had some fingers missing with partial amputation of other fingers. I realized that he must have some kind of dramatic story, but the story was his to tell, so I respected his privacy. The day has drained me so much that I just ignore the sound, making my way, while dragging my feet toward the kitchen to where I find a cheesecake. I look at it and say, "You will do just fine." I then sit myself down on the sofa, curl up and take excessively huge bites that will fill my mouth and maybe my head.

Overnight I toss in bed so much that I wake up with an aching neck. I could vividly see my mother. I could see her anger and the facial expressions she would make. Sometimes the anger was mixed with pleasure at hurting me. It was like some kind of payback was being meted out, and justice being served. I could feel my body's response to the force, and the sadness from the sound of the negative words she spewed at me. I could see myself covering my wounds so that others' eyes didn't see them too and brushing through my hair that became disheveled in the struggle. I could see myself retreating to my room for safety, but there was no room in that house that was off-limits. My mother often threw objects at me. It not only strengthened my ability to anticipate a flying object and ducking skills, but it also taught me to distance myself from people. You can only see something flying toward you and duck if you're a far enough distance away. After the object cracked and shattered, my mother made me clean it up; she wouldn't have a mess in the house. I would clean the area and throw the shards in the outdoor garbage bin as I smiled at the neighbors like a good girl. On those occasions, I often heard the sound of the neighbors' children laughing and screaming in delight as they played in their own yard. I was also assigned the chores of cleaning the mud or snow off of everyone's shoes and boots. My mother never let me wear gloves during these tasks, and I was never given hand cream or a lip balm like my siblings were.

My mind filled with so many other instances that it began to feel heavy and overflowing. After the mixer broke, my mother blamed me for carelessness. She gathered its accessories and threw each piece, one at a time, at me, specifically at my head, and a mild scratch emerged on the side of my forehead as the mixing apparatus hit me; the pain was considerable. I thought there would be a large gash there, but there wasn't. My mother handed me an ice pack, and I held it to my wound for fourteen seconds. I know this because for those fourteen seconds I thought my mother cared and regretted her actions, but it was only this length of time before she grabbed it from my hands and said, "You don't need it." My mother neatly folded laundry for my siblings, often placing them in their designated area in their dresser drawers. Mine would be thrown on the floor or at the edge of my bed to further gather dust and dirt. When my dad bought us fruit drinks one summer day, I relished mine, sipping slightly throughout the day. My sister did the same, but my mother threw only my unfinished one in the trash. It was placed upright so I could see it. When Grandma taught me to ferment food and make yogurt, I had two glass canisters fermenting in the kitchen every day for close to three weeks. I stared at the concoctions, waiting for them to be ready. As the time approached, I found the two canisters in the garbage can, my hopes dashed.

I don't have those deep scars like people who may have been more severely abused by their parents, bludgeoned, poisoned, or with gun holes, cigarette marks, or more severe burns. Mine were more subtle, yet frequent. They still infringed upon my personhood, and I still questioned, "Why?" in my mind.

My mother would often say, "Good for you," if I tripped or banged into anything, which was rare. That felt bad enough, but when she raised her arm against me to hit me, she seethed with rage. I recall the night I was hit so hard that I went tumbling to the ground, hitting my ankle against a nightstand as I dropped. Nevertheless, I explained to the doctor I was clumsy, and that I fell from my bike as I attempted to get off. Now the abuse was accompanied by a lie and the one thing other than becoming an abuser that scared me was becoming a liar.

My father is the only one of my immediate family who contacts me on occasion. He calls me two to three times a year, generally once on my birthday and once before the holidays. My father is very tall and extremely strong; they used to call him "the ox" during middle school, but he is an emotionally meek figure. He never stood up for himself, and he never asked his boss for a raise. It was only due to his brother's prompting that he became self-employed as a carpenter. My father wasn't to blame for my mother's rants, but he didn't know how to handle the situation. Before my grandmother's arrival, I used to sit in bed and wish that my parents were divorced, and I would go live with my father's side of the family. My cousins Samantha and Tilly were kind and considerate girls. They showed an interest in my life, and seemed loyal like their fathers, my uncles. My dad's brothers, however, had both moved to Canada and married young women they met when they went to school there. My dad was a kind person. I think he felt sorry for me but was not astute as to how to peacefully improve the situation. Dad loved roast beef sandwiches and would always give me half of his. I never told him that roast beef wasn't my favorite, as this was the primary gesture attesting to the fact that he cared.

As I lay in bed tossing, my bad memories were mixed with one really good memory, the sight of my grandmother. I could visualize my grandmother coming in, and her warmth enveloped me, as it still does. It was this memory that allowed me a short period of reprieve, enabling me to catch at least some sleep. She was kind, courageous, fearless, beautiful, a good listener, and had always been tidy. I don't have enough positive adjectives to describe her.

Unfortunately, my grandmother died of Alzheimer's disease when I was sixteen. She was one of the lucky ones, if you can call it that. Her body gave out relatively quickly; she didn't suffer for decades like some others who are afflicted with chronic conditions. I also felt fortunate that she never got angry, at least not with me, which so often happens with patients that suffer from Alzheimer's disease. For the time that her decline was quite evident, I pretended that she was a ghost that was with us to protect me. A small part of me feared her, as well, but in the end, my love and respect for her won out. I took walks with her and tried to make sure she had familiar objects around her. I wasn't sure if it was the right thing to do at the time, but I gave her my stuffed animal to stroke, to calm her. Sometimes I substituted my head for the toy and had her stroke my hair. It was a familiar routine, as she used to massage my head in my younger years, to calm me down.

Ironically, the only good memory I have of my mother was during this time. My grandmother went missing one day, as she wandered from our home. When she returned, she appeared disheveled and was wearing a slip and T-shirt, with socks. It was a far cry from the high-heeled, well-dressed woman with perfectly placed makeup that she was known to be. I remember my mother, almost lovingly, brushing Grandmother's hair and taking out her finest clothing and dressing her. My mother's gaze emitted some warmth toward my grandmother, and to my surprise, there was no trace of disgust at what my grandmother had become.

Alzheimer's generally progresses in stages. Even when my grandmother's face changed, becoming flatter and less expressive, which happens with this illness, nevertheless, I felt some comfort and happiness peering at her face because it was still hers. I am fortunate that I didn't fully comprehend the disease then. I just noticed slight changes as time went on—the lapses in memory, poorer sense of direction, decrease in problem-solving skills. Her clothing became simpler, and she no longer donned makeup. She had more of a persistent nervousness about lots of things. Looking back, I do recall her confusing two of my sisters' names, but never mine. She misplaced her reading glasses often, but there was generally someone in the house who found them rather quickly. She would ask, "When is your play?" three or four times, but I excused it as being something important to her that she didn't want to forget. I never perceived a change in my grandmother's mood. She would enjoin me in picking out her clothes for the day, which I relished, particularly the accessories. I thought it was my superb taste that inspired that decision. She also began being up later at night and waking later in the day when it had generally been her style to wake at five a.m. religiously. She would still tell me stories which she had fabricated, helping me pass the hours. She loved listening to music, which became almost a given in the household. I remember the last days when she sat in a wheelchair, and I placed my favorite pillow behind her back to increase her comfort. I now know about the stages of Alzheimer's, but at the time, the lack of knowledge was a saving grace. I didn't analyze her or check off symptomatology; I just allowed her to be my grandma. I have no negative memories of my grandmother. I still remember her feistiness, her laugh, her melodic voice, her beautiful thick hair, and soft skin. I recall the way she knew the exact amount of sugar or spice to put in a recipe and the way she pointed out the new flowers in every garden. Mostly, I remember her eyes that were protective and caring.

I often wonder if she knew what was happening to her. When her Alzheimer's was advanced, she began needing help with everything. Her swallowing ability was failing, her ability to sit and stand had failed too. She would ultimately succumb to pneumonia, but her progression was rather quick. Knowing what I know now, she was fortunate to not have lived out double digit years with this threat looming over her like a tormenter, waiting to distribute its next torture device until the body finally would say no more when the mind could no longer say it.

The last time I saw Grandma before she went into the hospital, I kissed her cheek and asked her if she loved me, knowing that I would never get a response. I refrained from revealing my love to her because my mouth would not allow such emotional words to come out despite feeling it in my heart. At her funeral, the second I had ever attended, I stood next to her coffin, guarding it, and when a fly flew onto its perimeter, I quickly shoved it away like a good soldier protecting its queen. In truth, the body ultimately goes to the ground where many of the world's insects have their home, and I wasn't able to protect her from that.

Abuse is like a box, open at times, closed at times, even locked and stored away at times, but somehow it still exists in some capacity as long as one lives, even when one is one hundred years old. I realize there have been many that have suffered far more than I have. I have been comparatively lucky, but every now and then, that locked away box rears its ugly head. Abuse shapes a person's life. I am more vulnerable, less trusting, and more cynical because of it. But I have also become more independent, more emotionally mature, and empathetic. I was the first to move out of my house as a teenager and get an apartment, the youngest of my siblings to finish college and get a job. I became the person who always gives some extra change to panhandlers, who notices the old or disabled person crossing the street, the one who sees and greets most of my neighbors with a friendly smile, the one who has held strangers' hands when getting blood drawn just because they needed someone to be there. My imagination has also grown, as I have had to imagine what normal looks like, and since normal really did not exist in my life, my imagination took me to an extreme, the extraordinary. For many years I was able to endure my mother's co-existence because my mind was generally elsewhere.

I had realized from a young age that being hit is not okay. I once had a classmate, Molly, who, at age six, stole my snack, one that I had worked hard to earn. I felt the anger building and I began to lift my hand in retaliation, but I felt my hand begin to weigh heavily and slowly lowered it because even at age six something didn't feel right about hitting someone else.

One of my first writing endeavors was writing a note to this little girl on primary paper with my far-from-perfected handwriting. I remember writing the words "treat" and "hard," but other than that, the exact verbiage fails me. I don't think Molly read the letter. I think she was so enthused by receiving a letter that she started to invite me over for playdates.

I don't know what became of Molly, but I can still see her brown hair and coordinated outfits and her skip-like walk. Molly was a lesson in restraint. It was a lesson that I didn't need to mimic my mother's actions despite the fact that I was biologically her daughter.

In the morning, I wake up stiff, as I find that I must have slept in the fetal position for the duration of time that I actually garnished some sleep. My muscles and bones ache as if the bed held me captive. My eyelids are heavy from the lack of sleep, and my nerves feel raw. I make myself a glass of chamomile tea to calm my nerves and stomach. I continue to stretch to feel less of the torment suffered, compliments of my bed. I know the day will be hectic. I get dressed slowly. I anticipate that the day will be difficult because there have been more admittees, in addition to a scheduled data entry meeting and a host of other small tasks to contend with. Of course, this is what is to be expected when you're agitated and have barely slept. I do some stretching exercises, and I attempt to imagine myself a trapeze artist flying through the air. I remember the day, about a year ago, when the phone rang in the morning as I was trying to catch up on my TV series. A guy identified himself as Max Cabbot. Max told me he had gotten my number from a Dr. Kevin Chase. "*It is nice that Dr. Chase is sharing my number with strangers,*" I thought. Apparently, Max had sustained a minor shoulder injury a year ago and wanted some help getting back into his sport of choice. He relayed that Dr. Chase thought I would be able to help him.

"What sort of sport?" I asked, waiting to hear the proverbial football, baseball, or basketball, maybe competitive swimming, perhaps even horseback-riding, which I had heard on more than one occasion.

"Trapeze," he said. I had yet to meet someone who wanted me to help them with the trapeze and had been so out of the loop with the fads of the day that I thought perhaps trapeze was code for another kind of sport or a game within a sport.

"Like the aerial sport trapeze, is that what you mean?" I asked, almost thinking a definitive, "No" will be the answer.

"Yes," he said. I stood there in my almost nonexistent kitchen mind-boggled, then harbored a bit of resentment toward Kevin Chase for throwing me under the bus. Besides the fact that I know very little about the art of trapeze, Kevin knows I have a fear of letting go, like I can rock climb really well, so long as I have a firm hold on the terrain, but I am extremely fearful of the free-floating that diving and trapeze art requires.

Max took my mind off my thoughts by stating, "Okay, so you will do it then?" and before I knew it, I agreed. Max apparently just wanted an extra opinion about his technique to renew his confidence in returning to his most beloved sport. Two weeks after our initial conversation, I met Max on his way toward the pedestal from which he and his fellow trapeze artists practiced. I watched intently as a professional trapeze artist ascended to the pedestal, bent his knees, and rocked back and forth on the trapeze bar. I watched how he moved to enable the catcher to catch him, and took note of the net on the floor, there to prevent injuries should something go wrong. One could hear and see the passion that trapeze artists have for their art. During my initial interview, Max had disclosed that he was a victim of a mugging that transpired when he was nineteen. The perpetrator threw him to the floor, cut open every facet of his jacket, and he lost two of his front teeth from the impact of hitting the floor, subsequently requiring implants. His face and the area around his ribs had been swollen for weeks. They healed, but he began to fear everything and everyone, constantly looking over his shoulder. His best friend took him to an aerial show which was only a two-time event in that vicinity. Max had watched the aerialist carefully, noting the beauty and enthusiasm they have for their art. As he saw them fly through the air, he harbored a bit of jealousy at their freedom. He disclosed, "While other people try to feel grounded, I wanted the opposite extreme. I wanted to feel ungrounded with this ability to be immortal or to fear everything and nothing all at once." Max said the first time he went on the trapeze, it was like a burden was lifted off his shoulder and his fears started to dissipate. For the last eight years, he had been using the trapeze as a release.

Trapeze art takes a toll on the rotator cuffs, which are small muscles that enable us to move our shoulder but are vulnerable, particularly with repetitive use. They can't take the brunt of repeated trapeze swinging, which requires the arms to be overhead much of the time. Max had also been painting the ceilings in his apartment, and the combined force of overhead movement resulted in a partial tear of his right rotator cuffs. He felt intense pain and required subsequent rehab to return to normal. But it had been a year since his last swinging escapade, and he wanted someone to examine his technique. In truth, I wasn't the best contender, but as a favor to Dr. Chase and Max, who was a really nice guy, I gave it a shot.

I watched over and over the dance between the shoulder muscles, the movement of the abdominal muscles and the back, the vestibular challenge of being upside down, the coordination and timing necessary to get to the catcher, and the constant need to follow directives. Perhaps most importantly, it is necessary to believe that the catcher will catch you, thus reinforcing your sense of security. Max looked fine out there. I think he just needed the confirmation and validation from a so-called professional to confirm what he already knew, that he can do it successfully. I had agreed not to take any money for the exchange.

Max kept prodding me to attempt the trapeze and said, "You will see. It feels great!" I had already ascended to the pedestal to study the art but never contemplated actually holding the bar, let alone ever allowing a catcher to catch me.

As we so often do, I started talking to myself, *You can do this, Jules; you're tall but limber; you have good core strength and upper body strength. Your timing is quite good; you used to be the best at monkey bars in school. At worst, you fall on the net . . . what are you scared of?* I couldn't decide if I feared failure at the task, a brain injury, spinal cord injury, the ability to trust another human being to catch me . . . My mind raced with these thoughts, and Max must have noticed my embarrassing self-talk.

"Listen, just try it."

So up I went to the pedestal. I am generally not afraid of heights. I kept telling myself, *This is the perfect setting for balancing mobility and stability,* thinking where are my college professors now who espoused these terms so freely.

Max's coach, Ella, kept repeating the instructions. I practiced swinging and allowing myself to fall in a designated manner to the net. Surprisingly, my stomach and heart were still intact and in the correct place. I kept convincing myself that my fears were unwarranted and that my trainer and safety bell would surely provide for a successful attempt. At first, Ella would remind me, "Lead with your hips!" Of course, I should lead with my hips. At one point, I had almost convinced myself that I can allow the catcher to catch me, but for a long time, I just let myself fall into the net.

I went home, disgraced and disappointed. Here I was mentoring Max and I couldn't do it myself. It wasn't the physical aspect that was my true concern, it was the trust necessary to allow someone else to catch me. I went back to the studio almost every day for two weeks failing miserably. All the self-talk and self-reassurance and any cheerleading at the sidelines hadn't helped. I decided to give myself three more days of trying and then quit. There was something about quitting a sport or activity that you have just encouraged someone else to do; it is like the ultimate failure. It made me feel like a hypocrite telling someone else to do something when I couldn't.

On my thirteenth attempt, I looked up and realized that the catcher was a different guy. At first, it worried me further, but as I got closer, his face had a familiar look which helped to calm me. I kept thinking of his face until I reached the top of the pedestal and then stood there ready for takeoff. That face, it was like Slate's. A sense of contentment washed over me. This time I allowed myself to move, so that the catcher, who was named Mazin, would catch me. I successfully completed the jump. During my travel home that day, I acknowledged the fact that I trusted Slate. Apparently, I trust him with my life. He is one of the few people I truly believed cared about me; thus, he would not allow me to fall. I truly trust him. When I came home, I found myself feeling like I had just done fifty sit-ups, noticing how out of shape I was. Ella had taped my sessions and allowed me to view my aerial experience for myself. I sat down on my couch, viewing myself flying through the air over and over again. I was pleasantly surprised at how graceful I appeared. I always thought myself athletic, but not graceful. Perhaps those ballet lessons as a child did teach me something.

I tried to recall that exact moment that I went flying through the air, the weightlessness, and silence of floating, where my brain was in sync with my body, and the thoughts make my body ever freer. With these thoughts, I get through my morning routine. The wind howls outside like it's reminding me of the hour and suddenly, I am no longer an aerialist flying in the air. I am an employee attempting to get to work on time. This time I fly through the door, making my way out of my apartment to the outdoors in record time. Before I know it, I am out of my house and on my way down my block.

I generally have a choice of three routes to work. This morning, a construction crew has blocked one of them, leaving two left, so I choose the shortest route. As I walk, I realize that even after many years of passing by this route, the grandness of the city isn't lost on me. Although I love the nature and the landscape of the suburbs, I prefer the drama of the city. Amid all this noise and traffic, I can still hear my own voice clearly, a voice that was stifled in the chaotic atmosphere of my old home.

CHAPTER 3: UNGROUNDED

I reach work in record time. As part of my duties today, I lead a vestibular rehab group that convenes weekly. This group came to exist by way of my extraordinary eavesdropping skills.

The vestibular system is like the talent without the celebrity. Our knowledge of this system of the body is quite old, yet it is usually overlooked. Its existence is commonly unfamiliar to the general population. One familiar medical term associated with this system is vertigo. Yet, most who haven't experienced it don't fully comprehend its magnitude. It is responsible for many successful bodily activities, but is often only associated with seasickness or dizziness. Yet, when this system is malfunctioning, its impact is significant. Those with dysfunction may use maladaptive and abnormal movements. They may be clumsier and less coordinated. They may begin to shift their weight in one direction, perhaps becoming a toe-walker. They may seek out the next available chair or scan their environment for the next beam or structure to make them feel stable again. They may feel more fatigued. Some may experience that annoying ringing sound of the ear known as tinnitus. In addition, this system is related to oculomotor dysfunction making many daily visual tasks laborious.

The chief talent in this system is the inner ear. The otoliths are small structures in the inner ear that contain calcium carbonate crystals that detect linear movement, acceleration, or gravity-related movement.

We need this information to successfully travel by car, or ride on an elevator. Other talents in this show are the semicircular canals presenting themselves in groups of three. The semicircular canals direct a specific set of eye movements so that one can, for instance, look toward the ground or behind or overhead. They help us continue to feel safe and steady even as we move back and forth, bend, sit up, lie down, reach, and roll. The vestibular system helps our eyes move in conjunction with changes in head movement so that we maintain a steady gaze at objects or people in our environment even as our head moves.

The vestibular system's messages don't end in the eyes and ears. They are ultimately transmitted all the way to our feet. Our feet give us more feedback about where we are in space so that we continue to change our posture and positioning accordingly. When this system is efficient, it allows us to move and explore our world freely or allows us to just sit quietly at a desk performing a given task, feeling still and stable without movement. This is the system that allows us to maintain an upright posture, yet feel grounded.

As I walked along the hallways one Wednesday a few months ago, I stopped short when I observed the following scene and overheard the following conversation taking place in the waiting room near the gym.

A group of patients had just exited after a vestibular rehab session. A small group of women were sitting in the waiting area near the gym, sipping coffee or hot water. One woman was waiting for her husband to pick her up and was surrounded by a few other women sufferers of the same malady.

She said, "It is hard to know where your body starts and where it stops. It's like an out-of-the-body experience; everything is removed from me. There are no natural automatic movements. It's no longer just a walk to admire nature. It is another struggle I need to overcome."

Another woman piped up, "I can't go to the department store. It is hard enough navigating the aisles, but when I am walking and scanning shelves for objects or articles of clothing, it's brutal. What is worse is the small dips and dents in the floor. I can feel every one of them, and it just puts me on another planet. Also, can someone please tell me why in the world a bowling alley would have changing flashing lights as you bowl? I went bowling with my kids the other day; it was hard enough watching the ball roll down the alley, but those lights flashing in my eyes created such chaos, it felt as if they were trying to pick a fight with me."

"I hear you," said another woman, nodding her head in agreement. "My favorite pastime used to be watching the boats go by at the lake; now, just watching small, barely visible waves move is a feat unto itself."

"I wouldn't ride on a boat if you paid me a million dollars," another woman says in response. "My worst day was when I stood at the dock which moved ever so slightly as I watched a boat pull into the harbor. I thought I was going to pass out."

"Before rehab, walking down the block felt like running a marathon. Forget about chasing my dog. I won't even attempt that feat; I would sooner kill myself. Other people don't understand; they comment on my perfectly slim legs and manicured toenails with no evidence of outside injury, but it is like my brain and body have some kind of disconnect. It gets even worse when there are changes in temperature when I suffer from dreaded seasonal allergies, and during my period. I just feel so unstable."

A young man couldn't help but overhear their conversation and, despite being the only male in the room, was edging his way toward the group of women. In a mild voice, he added, "Going on an elevator is like having your insides fall out, and going on the bus, that's like having a war with your own body." The women looked up and smiled; the young man smiled in return. They all started to laugh until the first woman's husband picked her up. She leaned against his arm for stability as they traversed the hallway. I saw those few moments of joy as they conversed. Maybe these people are on to something; maybe they need a group, like a support group.

Now came the real feat of trying to persuade the head of rehab that yet another item should be added to his already-long list. I walked into Dr. McConnel's office the very next day like I was on a secret mission. My heart was pounding out of my chest. Dr. McConnel isn't the easiest man to talk to; he is always busy holding some document and very impatient. I planned an entire speech, but it wasn't meant to be, as I was told, "Jules, you have two minutes, no actually ninety seconds."

Feeling the burden of time, I got straight to the point. "We need a vestibular rehab group. It will not only provide the clients with support but will give us better data as to what works and what doesn't." I had to add that last part because everything in a hospital is about data and cost. "It may increase patients' willingness to do home exercises, it may decrease dysfunction associated with—"

I try to plead my case further, but my ninety seconds are apparently up, as McConnel says "There are no funds."

"How much funding do you need to allow people to talk to each other in a room? A room that already exists in the hospital?"

McConnel scratched his head and then gave me that look as if he were angry but thinking. "Fine! Then you coordinate it . . . and you run it . . . and then we will have a group."

I think McConnel was undermining me and was condescending, using a sarcastic tone, but I responded with enthusiasm. I felt almost as optimistic as Stephanie and as chipper as Dr. Chase. "Great!" He looked in my direction, assuming I would fail. This is the same Dr. McConnel that called me Samantha and thought I was a physical therapist when I first started to work. That was until I gave him a cupcake and coffee. The cupcake read, "I am Jules, the occupational therapist." At the end of the day, I felt assured that I would succeed with the vestibular rehab group plan because people need others to understand them whether they are sick or not; it's a basic human need.

No one can advise anyone else unless they have a basic understanding of a problem. What else could I have done to understand the vestibular system other than to subject myself to some torture challenge of my own? I took two shoes, one high-heeled, the other low, and tried to climb a ladder; it was fazing and a bit difficult but doable. That's not enough, I thought. I considered the times in the shower and those few seconds when water hits your ears, which become clogged and suds cover your eyes, which can barely adjust. You feel kind of weird and displaced. Then when your eyes and ears emerge unscathed, you say, "Oh, here I am," and resume your shower routine.

In preparation for the group session I was to lead, I spent time closing my eyes and navigating the areas around me with changes in head and neck motion. I went to a local park, and despite being in the presence of onlookers, I spun myself silly and then tried walking a straight line. Stephanie outlined the path for me. I ensured that I was a distance from the railing or people so that no enabling crutch was available. I felt the anxiety rise within me for a few seconds at the sensations going on in my body. Apparently, I hadn't spun around enough in the last few years. Then I walked, eyes closed, on a tiny balance board only a few inches off the ground, designed for preschoolers. I felt the panic, wanting to open my eyes, but didn't. Stephanie cheered me on. I watched a 3-D movie with, and then without, the specialized glasses. I had arranged for the images projected to be improperly aligned. As a result, I was so busy adjusting my seat and visual focus to get a correct viewing of the image that I only got fragments of the storyline. Watching the little hamster run up and down in one of the scenes made my brain feel disorganized, and I found myself averting my eyes to escape the image.

On another occasion, I entered an amusement park tunnel, watching the changing colorful images as I walked. During my third round, I was desperately attempting to grab hold of the moving wall. Then I watched a spinning and changing wall design on a computer screen, and discovered that my optokinetics aren't what they should be. I walked down the aisle of a toy shop wearing two different shoes of different heights, and an earbud with blasting music in one ear only, all the while trying to turn my head and scan the shelves. The sensation in my ear didn't feel all that bad, just weird. I was glad I didn't get arrested.

I returned to the park, trying to navigate block towers of different sizes. Attempting to descend from the top, the glare of the sun obstructed my view of the next block, and for a moment, I felt a bit strange, standing there in a half-crawling position, not knowing where to place the rest of my body to go on. When I finally realized that I was half hanging off the block tower and might fall, I gave myself a brief period of rebuke for participating in an activity that I would generally classify as, "Don't try this at home."

Imagine living like this. Every step is methodical. I found myself planning movements rather than automatically moving freely. I went to bed at night, inching my way toward the headboard. I held my head straight, then planned the angle at which my head would hit the pillow. I put down two pillows to ease the transition to side-lying them removed them. I drank two cups of water, ensuring a midnight walk to the bathroom, which lucky for me isn't that far from my room in a shoebox apartment. I woke myself every time I turned, opening my eyes, pretending that I needed them open. I then sat myself up in bed methodically placing each limb of my body in a designated manner necessary to ensure that I was fully upright and supported. In the dark, I walked to the bathroom and refrained from turning on the light. All this was only a mild nudging of my vestibular system, not the full onset of havoc which others experience daily.

As I sat there the first day of the group, I was quite anxious. Firstly, I was concerned that no one would attend, and secondly that if they did, they might find no benefit from participating. This wasn't the first time I would lead a group, but this experience would be vastly different from the first leadership position I held.

When I was nineteen years old. I led a youth activity group near my apartment. The kids ranged in age from eleven to sixteen. I wasn't much older than they were, but they had lived lives far worse than my own. Many, too, had experienced abuse, but that was often coupled with poverty and sometimes absentee parents. They were often raised by extended family members, and they had become belligerent and angry. A part of them yearned for a bit of love and caring, but they felt so far removed from it that it had become an impossibility in their minds. The center's approach was to provide them with a variety of activities to improve self-esteem and offer a positive venue to let out their frustrations. I predominantly associated this with a sports center, as many of the activities were athletic in nature, which was right up my alley. On my first day, I found sweet, curious kids not at all resembling the picture others had painted for me. What I did find, however, was a group of kids that had sometimes failed to evidence basic skills. They had difficulty with positive affirmations; "please" and "thank you" were not words in their vocabularies; they had difficulty with turn-taking, with preparing and organizing, and with time management routines. These were primarily the type of things you may learn from a parent, not a necessary part of academics. I compiled a list of activities that I thought they would enjoy, particularly geared toward hardcore juveniles.

Maurice was one of the unofficial leaders; when he did something, the others followed. He was six feet, two inches tall with a grin that showed his large teeth. He was also large-boned and towered over me. I felt like I was contrasted with the Empire State Building. I wasn't certain if I should fear him, but something inside me relaxed as he approached with a serious look on his face, blurting out, "Can we learn to make cupcakes?"

I made certain to repeat the request anticipating that I had misheard. "You want to learn to make cupcakes?"

"Yes, and like try them right out of the oven," he said. As he spoke, his grin widened yet further.

"So, you want to have a baking class?

"Oh, yes, that would be great!" Maurice said, flashing yet more of his teeth. Maurice nodded to two boys and a girl standing there who evidenced that same look of anticipation.

I was a bit concerned about the actual taste of the cupcakes they were so looking forward to. It is not as though I possessed exceptional baking skills. My theory was don't burn anything, don't over-sweeten or over-salt anything, and don't break anyone's teeth. Yet, it worked for me. I had always been more of a cook than a baker. Thus, each treat was very simple, like chocolate chip cookies, brownies, cupcakes, the types of baked goods one may make with a child on a rainy day.

I think the kids enjoyed the process more than the end product. They laughed and cheered each other on. They read instructions and followed them. They experimented with various toppings and ingredients. They made certain to prepare the ingredients before they began. They said, "Please," and "Thank you," and made appropriate requests. They shared the ingredients and basked in being able to create a product using their own skills. They learned to set a timer and to wait patiently for their baked treats to be ready.

As the year came to a close, Maurice approached me and said, "You're gonna leave, aren't you? Everyone always leaves." Maurice knew me as a guide, a person who saw him every Thursday night religiously, but he didn't know I was an escapee, that I tried to escape from my family while he desperately sought one.

"Yes, Maurice, I am going to leave, but that's the way the world works; we always have an ever-changing group of people we interact with. And with every interaction, there is a lesson and a memory, and you get to choose how to use it. I am going to remember a guy named Maurice who helped me perfect my baking skills and taught me how joyful baking can be, and who made me relive a little giddiness of childhood."

Maurice blushed and nodded his head. "Thanks, Jules, really, thank you."

"And thank you, Maurice."

To this day, I enjoy baking and cooking. It is an art form to me. Moreover, I learned that I could lead a group. With this thought in mind, I contemplated my upcoming vestibular group, and I told myself, "It will be fine."

Only two people attended that very first meeting of my vestibular rehab group. I sat there in anticipation as I made my first observation of the first and then second individual that arrived. I had already concluded the specifics of their respective cases based upon their physical presentations but waited for their stories, which gave me insight into who they were and what this condition had taken from them. I watched a twenty-two-year-old girl, who had been on a high-dose intravenous antibiotic whose vestibular organs had all but been destroyed and who had to learn significant compensations for daily activities. She admitted that getting to the center this morning felt like a full day's feat, only made more complicated by the fact that there was a last-minute room change. I then heard from a seventy-six-year-old man who vented his frustration, while the twenty-two-year-old nodded in agreement. I feared that the differences in age and life experiences may make them reluctant to join future sessions, but the next week they returned, and a thirty-five-year-old athlete joined the mix. He related that he couldn't do his job, just turning his head upward makes him feel out of sorts.

As the weeks progressed, a middle-aged mother joined the group. She previously ran PTA meetings, often accompanying classes on field trips. She was no longer able to easily navigate her child's school when attending simple school functions and firmly asserted that she wouldn't attempt school trips in the near future. A young man who was also present relayed that he had sat in the corner during his brother's wedding, not even attempting to dance. When he watched the dancing, it was like being in the throes of a moving circle over and over again. He felt that he had failed his brother and family. Another participant was a young woman who wrapped her arms into her sixty-eight-year-old mom's arms as she exited the meeting, not to assist her mom, but rather out of her own fear of falling. There were those with extreme stories and others who had had relatively minor changes in life, but they all spoke a common language. There was an exchange of ideas, techniques, and frustrations, but there was also an exchange of laughter and smiles.

Now, eight months later, twenty-five people are sitting before me. In addition, there is a waiting list for more, as the room is filled to capacity.

It's eleven thirty in the morning, and the meeting begins. I watch the participants as they walk in. Some sit with a forward posture, with their arms stabilized on chair ends. Some walk on their toes. Others' shoes indicate significant wear and tear on one side, attesting to uneven weight-bearing. Some tilt their heads while others demonstrate extraneous movements of the head.

The first patient suffers from Meniere's disease and has had hearing loss. She can't tolerate the sound of the buzzing coming from a water tank machine in the background that may be in need of repair. I hadn't even detected its sound until she arrived. I attempt to go find personnel to shut it off for the duration of the group's meeting but am unsuccessful. The patient takes a seat, willing to endure the discomfort to attend. The patients discuss the balance training that they undergo to improve equilibrium. They also discuss how they feel when they are performing tasks with changes in head movement over and over again to decrease the effects of a malfunctioning system. Some have twenty-four hours of light in the hallway to avoid falls during nighttime bathroom stops, and some have rearranged their houses or sleeping positions to decrease other obstacles. Some admit to changing their shopping venues, like grocery stores, others have been doing their shopping on off-hours. A few have chosen being driven to work over enduring public transportation. Some have mapped out their days to avoid too many challenging movements in one time period, and others have done the opposite in an attempt to be what they deem to be more "normal." Some with unilateral hearing loss admit to being particularly stressed in the presence of noise. One woman says, "It's scary not knowing where you are in space, like your body is moving without you, perhaps floating on something like a cloud. It is like you're trying to find out where you are without recognizing the starting and endpoints."

Sara's long hair had not been cut in decades. It flowed beautifully and dangled around her neck creating almost an accessory to her outfit. However, today she walks in with her hair tied in a bun. Her hair is bound so tightly that it tugs at her face creating a mask-like appearance. Unlike her usual pleasant and welcoming appearance, her unexpected new look makes her appear less sociable or approachable. She admits that she has restyled her hair because she has found that a slight blow of the wind would dishevel her hair, temporarily covering her face, and for those few seconds she becomes ungrounded; without her vision, she is lost, and the fear creates a panic as her hair covers her eyes.

Nykeisha admits that getting out of bed is a constant struggle. "That first moment of sitting up in bed is like a tornado has hit and I am twirling about in no man's land. The sensation eventually gets better, but I relive it the next day."

Trista says that she has suffered numerous ear infections as a child and was never able to follow the music nor the beat as classmates engaged in marching and rhythmic activities. She observed herself on a childhood video and realized that she had been significantly out of the line when marching alongside peers at her preschool graduation. She still feels a particular pull toward one side as she walks, often attempting to reconnect and reconcile the two sides of her body. She has also noted herself leaning toward one side in family photos. She says that for some reason carrying heavy bags makes her feel more evened out.

Alejandra says that she is not exactly sure why, but seems to always feel the need to grab hold and push a shopping cart in the grocery or department store even when she is just browsing.

Ted says that he feels more lost in open spaces like open parking lots. He uses objects in his environment as visual referencing points. He only came to this realization when he was hiking in an open road with nothing but dirt, and he felt himself seeking the next tree or boulder.

Lini says that turning her head when driving is still a bit difficult, momentarily disorienting her, but she has been doing better lately, making her a more confident driver.

Kane admits that his vestibular issues aren't as bad as those of his peers but continues to have difficulties. His cousin's wedding was on a yacht. They had rented the yacht at quite a cost, and the event was extravagant. He couldn't sleep for three nights before the event, thinking of how he would cope. When he actually attended the wedding, he refused to walk to the restroom because it required walking to the opposite end of the boat, which was just too much for him to endure, so he waited until they docked.

Jim says he never reads street or storefront signs when walking to work. They just look like they are bouncing around, making him feel like he is jumping along with them.

Tally says that she recently needed new tiling for her bathroom. When walking through the store scanning the merchandise, she went over to scrutinize a set of tiles. Suddenly, while looking up and over, she felt somewhat off, and feared she would fall into the salesman. "I held on to the store shelf for dear life," she adds.

Guy had a bowel re-sectioning and just felt a bit off-kilter as his body composition had changed a bit. He mentions that he kept leaning to one side after the surgery, but that with training, he has much improved. He adds with a smile that his digestive tract is healing too.

Yuan says he had a bad vestibular day this week, and shamefully bumped into the wall at a local bank, misjudging its distance. It was only for a second, but the surrounding twenty-two people in line turned to ensure he was okay.

Misti says that whenever she remains in bed past breakfast time, her five-year-old daughter kisses her on her forehead, asking if she has vertigo ouchies.

Favi says she turned abruptly to take note of her toddler's whereabouts and almost went tumbling into her child.

Hazel admits to have come on behalf of her daughter, lamenting the fact that recent cancer treatments have left her daughter's vestibular system with significant impairment. A few tears cross her cheek as she says, "Youth should be filled with many activities, such as, twirling, spinning, swinging, bike rides down winding paths, somersaults, and headstands, visiting haunted houses and choosing amusement rides, that are defeated by holding ones stomach but making it through alive. My poor little girl can't do any of that right now."

Belig had suffered from a fear of heights, otherwise known as gravitational insecurity, as a child but admits he is otherwise fine. He recently experienced a car accident resulting in a broken leg, which compromised his standing balance. He continues to have a mild limp as a result of the damage to his leg, and he feels less balanced. He refuses to go on a ladder, requesting that his eleven-year-old son change the lightbulbs in his house.

Manny says that although his vestibular system is only mildly affected, a recent job change requires much air travel, and he fears the effects of acceleration on his system.

Glenda admits that dietary changes and mineral supplementation have improved her vestibular functioning and adds that although it's been a lifestyle change, it's well worth it. A few have formed social walking groups helping each other, and others have created logs for sharing.

Lucia, the most cheerful of the group, shares that persistent vestibular training has left her with increased strength and tone in her legs and core, which has not only improved her physique and her footing, but seems to have enhanced her breathing.

Ally thanks me before she leaves. She relates that her symptoms are quite extreme, and she suffers from related anxiety. She admits that she has barely left her house in over a year, and has only been engaging in social activity via interfacing on the web. "It's nice to actually sit with people and remember there is a real world outside," she says as she walks away, fixating on all the objects in the room while she makes her way to the hallway.

I have learned many lessons from this group. Not only appreciation of a functioning body and patience but the need for social connection even when there are significant differences in disability, age, and socioeconomics. To further give credence to the group, I document each client's preclass admission of activity participation, followed by what activities they perform after twelve sessions, and I find not only improvements in activity participation but in their self-reported perceptions of ability.

The group session ends. I attend my data meeting and then go to teach one of my patients the proper steps involved in washing laundry. He also has difficulty with positioning himself and using proper body mechanics. My patient is mumbling obscenities at me and then rebukes himself, calling himself stupid as he is aggravated and frustrated at the loss of his ability to perform basic activities. This time I don't attempt to say anything. It hasn't worked before; he needs to prove it to himself. As I walk into the room, there is the speech therapist, Saja, sitting with a patient at the other end of the room. Saja is a guru when it comes to swallowing. He owns every gadget and knows every technique to improve a client's swallow. Yet, today he is using a party favor toy to improve a client's lip closure. He also lets his client know it would be wise to get new dentures. It will likely improve his ability to chew and lessen the burden on his digestive tract, given that he already has a poor swallow. My patient looks on in wonder.

Lana, the other speech therapist who generally isn't in the room, is using fictitious blow out candles with a patient to increase breath support. She doesn't forewarn her patient that it will be tricky to blow out, and her patient comes to the realization that it won't go out easily. He starts to laugh, and despite poor breath support, it turns into a semi-hearty laugh. It makes me laugh too. I try hard to suppress it, but it is coming out in increments and, lo and behold, my patient begins to laugh, his body less guarded and looser. He starts the activity again, this time his reach is farther and longer, his body moves more fluidly and his trunk more gracefully, as he moves his hand toward the dial and pushes. He hears the sound of the machine, that swish, swish, swish, and perceives his own victory. "What are we doing next?" he asks. Everyone's day just got a bit better.

Just as our outer beings need balance, so do our inner beings. I go to visit James again, looking at him through the window. He is sleeping, and I'm trying to figure out how to create a balanced individual, one that can be disciplined and follow rules and limits, yet feel loved and have positive feelings toward those instituting the rules and limits. I then think of Stephanie. She is a great example for her kids; she institutes rules yet is available to them and comforts them when they need it. I guess when one senses the love associated with the reprimand, it is more easily assented to.

I leave James's room, happy that he is resting even though it would have been nice to spend some time with him. I finish my notes for the day and take a shortcut through a local park. I see an empty swing, the only one that is not covered by the falling leaves from a nearby tree. It beckons to me, so I sit down for a few moments to feel that sway that carries me briefly "through the sky," but the lightness doesn't come. It only serves to create a feeling of loneliness.

It reminds me of the one time I allowed someone in on my secret as a child. I remember sitting on a swing at school next to a boy named Kabe. Kabe was a rambunctious seven-year-old at the time. He had curly red hair with blazing blue eyes. Kabe was a bit mischievous but in a good kind of way. He was also a bit of a class clown. Kabe would pronounce words in a funny way when reading in class, spurring class outbursts. He accompanied the words with the addition of a funny face like his famous fish face. He was pretty good at sports, and he seemed to know a lot about everything except for that which pertained to school. I'm not sure why, but I trusted Kabe more than other classmates.

On one occasion, as we sat swinging and pumping our legs high, I bluntly stated, "My mom hurts me a lot. I think she hates me."

106

In turn, he said, "My dad thinks I am dumb. I think he hates me too."

"I like being around you. You're fun," I said as my cheeks rose in a smile; and we sat there swinging away for the rest of recess and never spoke about the topic again.

Kabe finished books by reading the first few and last few pages. I actually thought him to be a genius. He could concoct a great story in a matter of minutes and had a great imagination. However, he was never able to easily put his thoughts down on paper. The teacher was often annoyed with him. He had a very hard time learning to write his name and to form simple shapes. Kabe ended up successfully running his own company. However, his brother Macky, who had suffered from the same learning disability and wasn't as socially regarded, ended up committing suicide when he failed his exams in high school and subsequently lost a sports scholarship. Macky was known as an innovator, but I had heard from the grapevine that his dad left the family when he was a teen; I am sure this further fueled his demise.

In retrospect, I am fairly sure Kabe was dyslexic, but youths only take what is presented to them at face value. I now know why Cindy continuously blinked and why Edmond, who stuttered, was still able to sing well in his choir group. I understand more clearly why Sammy never laughed or initiated conversation. I realize why Donald, a neighbor, constantly washed his hands and would count everything multiple times. I now understand even more clearly why Linda would just stop talking, staring into space. I finally came to the realization that it wasn't that I had been boring her, but rather it was because she had suffered from petit mal seizures for a few months following an illness. I am armed with much more information.

"Oh, Kabe," I say under my breath as I stare at the empty swing next to mine, "I wish I could talk to you. Hope you are okay." A sudden rush of the wind blows the leaves on the ground onto my face, so I sneeze, and a few leaves now make their way onto my swing. I pick one up and blow it back to its source, a large oak tree with massive branches. Its upper branches appear to be almost touching the clouds in the sky. The clouds are whimsical and thin, and I walk back home.

Chapter 4: Frozen

When I return home, I see the gift that I had purchased for an upcoming wedding sitting alone on the counter. I wrap it gingerly, ensuring that each corner is as beautiful as the first. I admire my wrapping skills and place it on top of the shelf for safekeeping. I take out a host of ingredients, mix them together and place them in the oven, all the while recalling Maurice and his friends from the center. I treat myself to a gourmet dinner, and shockingly, as my head hits the pillow, I fall asleep.

I walk to the hospital at a slow and steady pace finding nothing significantly unusual during today's walk. However, just as I am about to locate my cell phone, which is buzzing, a policeman approaches me. *What now?* I think, only to find out that I have dropped a glove that must have been hiding in my jacket since last winter. "Thanks!" and I continue to walk on. I now pull out my phone that shows a missed call from my father, but I don't open it. I shove it back in my bag and continue to walk.

My first patient today is a forty-two-year-old woman. She suffers from adhesive capsulitis, otherwise known as frozen shoulder. It is strange when you're moving someone's arm with great force to try to lessen its tightness. I almost feel strange applying force to anyone's arm, as I recall my own arm wandering out of its socket several times when my mother yanked me so hard that that was its natural course. Yet, on the contrary, this force of application is intended to heal. It's the pain that works through a problem, not its cause. Sandra has a history of thyroid disease, hypothyroidism, and has developed adhesive capsulitis. She is quiet during the session. I can see that she is in pain, as indicated by her facial expressions. The bags under her eyes were probably the result of decreased sleep from pain, but she always classifies her pain as three out of ten. I look over at the robust six-foot four-inch guy with massive muscle architecture on the opposite side of the room, and he is crying like a baby, as structures of his own shoulder capsule are stretched. Sandra's arm is freezing, and synovitis is present. Growth of new blood supply and nerves are supplying the area only increasing the pain; fibrosis and thickening of the area are apparent. I note that the posterior part of her posterior-inferior capsule is affected. I bring in some everyday items, placing them in different positions and on different surfaces in the room to demonstrate which functional movements are being affected. She nods and agrees that household chores and daily activities are more cumbersome, but seems to be going through the motions. Her lack of emotion makes me wonder whether she suffers from depression as well.

With all the pain, Sandra still fails to care for her thyroid, which likely caused the problem in the first place. She knows that therapy will last a few weeks, but caring for her thyroid will be a lifetime, so she opts for the therapy. She admits that she is stressed daily by life and adds, "What do you want me to do? I have three kids to care for, and no one else to help me." She hasn't changed her diet, fails to maintain a regular medication regimen, and hasn't gone for a sonogram of her thyroid, even knowing that her mother had such a severe case of hypothyroidism that it induced mental health challenges, including psychosis.

As I complete my therapeutic course of action, I tell her that for a time afterward, she will feel some discomfort, but it should dissipate. She listens as I talk, nodding her head, but there is no fear or enthusiasm nor any real emotion. Sandra is a patient in the gym; she isn't being seen in the nutritional department or the endocrinology department, so basically it is my job to care about her arm and get it moving, not to provide advice about other matters because patients are "little pieces" at least that is what Sandra has felt from her medical past.

"Sandra, this isn't going to help you in the long run if a year from now you come back with the same problems in the other shoulder or worse."

She turns to me and says, "Let's just stick to the shoulder, okay?" I nod in agreement, even though I want to state otherwise.

I look over at the other guy, who came in with the costly leather jacket accented with metal hardware. He still appears to be in distress but less so. He has sustained less damage than Sandra. His therapist is stretching structures around his scapula. Despite some pain, he looks content now, like he is on a path to something better. Sandra, on the other hand, seems frozen, just as her shoulder; she is frozen in her life situation.

By the time the day ends, I look at my list of things to do. You know when you have only fifteen minutes and are supposed to complete two hours' worth of work in those fifteen minutes, you spend the first three minutes deciding what the priority is and trying not to feel overwhelmed to the point of dysfunction. Then you use the other twelve minutes to complete whatever it was you needed to do. Thenceforth, you have this lingering feeling of incompleteness, so you spend the rest of the day thinking about everything you didn't finish, and the rest of the day takes up more time than the two hours the actual tasks would have taken.

Well, today I couldn't figure out how to juggle my time, neither for work nor for personal matters. My father has left me a message to call him. He calls me three times a year, but never leaves messages. His voice doesn't indicate urgency or the need for an immediate return call. Slate wants to enlist my help with his quest to find a new car, or I can visit with James. Slate wasn't high on my emotional priority list today as my knowledge of cars is limited, and he still has a very functional and well-taken-care-of car. I know it is more for moral support to help him believe he is making the right decision. My dad can be called later. At least that's what I imagine. That leaves over-sensitized James, alone in a hospital with little understanding about what is happening around him and with no voice to make his needs or wants known. Emotional prioritization is way worse than prioritizing chores. In the end, this choice was simplified by the fact that it was only James who was truly alone, the most vulnerable.

James had the same expression on his face; it was like he was there but wasn't. The fact that James hesitated to be touched and harbored a distrust and fear of staff, coupled with a minor injury to his wrist and right hand, inhibited completion of many necessary daily tasks. As a child not yet three, he hadn't had the chance to master many activities, but even assisting him was cumbersome. It was difficult to get him bathed, and he wouldn't even attempt to wash his own hands. He wouldn't allow a toothbrush near his mouth nor allow anyone to brush his teeth. He would generally be dressed in a hospital gown but would squeal when someone tried to tie it for him and made the staff's life really hard during wound and infection management. He needed to become at least somewhat more involved and compliant in allowing others to assist with daily care. He barely moved when Nurse Abbie's earring came undone, tumbling down on him, but later became hysterical and screeching when someone shut off the lights in the hallway.

I sit there rummaging through my belongings and only come across a penlight that I use for visual testing. *This will do.* I open and close it in his presence, trying to encourage him to try it, but he doesn't even make an attempt. Thankfully though, he doesn't overreact when I turn off the lights in his room to create small circles on the wall, which I try to catch with my own fingers. He shows the first signs of interest in something, making small movements to view the circles, and slightly lifting his finger to model my own. As I put the penlight back in my pocket, James scrunches his forehead as though I have just insulted him. I take the penlight back out

113

for one more round, and I create waves on the hospital wall. This time, as I end, the penlight is tucked safely in my pocket, and James is under the sheets and more peaceful.

Before I go to my next client, I return to my unit and grab some hot water. My throat feels parched. I encounter Evette, Slate, and a few nurses in the office. Dr. Sarim, the resident psychologist, walks through the room. He seems a bit distracted, as he attempts to get the coffee grinds in the cabinet. He clenches his teeth and briefly rubs his upper arm, as he seems to attempt to reawaken its power. His teeth-grinding becomes even more apparent, and his opposite hand is now guarding his arm. He then looks at his arm as it leads toward his wrist, in this most peculiar manner. His facial expression transitions from what appears to be pain or confusion to a more relaxed state once he releases the container of coffee grinds and once his neck returns to a more neutral position.

Evette and I eye each other and simultaneously announce, "C5-C6!"

"We are worthy competitors," I say, as I grin. Dr. Sarim looks at us, wondering what we are talking about and why his pain has become some type of competition.

"Dr. Sarim, how long have you had these symptoms?"

"For about a week. My wife had been nagging me to redo our crumbling steps before the onset of winter weather. I admittedly had three months to do it, but life got busy, so last weekend, I just started and kept going until I finished it. I had to carry the bricks out from the garage to the front steps. I didn't feel anything at the time, but I definitely do now!"

Evette asks if she can try something. Dr. Sarim agrees so long as she doesn't make it worse. She moves Dr. Sarim's head so that it's flexed toward the same side as the pain, moving his head slightly back. She applies a bit of pressure, and more pain is evoked.

"Are you trying to kill me?" Dr. Sarim says as he holds his neck and shoulder. He faces his own frailty and fails to employ his own strategies for calm. Evette applies some mechanical traction and force to increase the space around the nerves, thus relieving the pressure briefly, and Dr. Sarim admits that the pain has somewhat subsided. He looks up at Evette, "I have been your perfect patient. Now would someone like to tell me what is going on?"

"You need some imaging, but I am pretty sure it's coming from this part of your neck." Evette references the point of origin of Dr. Sarim's pain. She points gingerly to avoid further discomfort.

I look at Dr. Sarim's briefcase and add, "You have been carrying around that suitcase?"

"It is not a suitcase. It's a briefcase."

"It's a briefcase on steroids," I say. "Why can't you just scan some documents onto your laptop instead of schlepping twenty-five books everywhere." Dr. Sarim is an erudite, intriguing, well-read man. His analytic skills have surely surpassed those of many others. He can solve a puzzle or riddle in minutes, but as we often do when it comes to our own pain, he fails to reasonably think about what is in his *own* best interest.

As Dr. Sarim leaves, I whisper to Evette, who lives in a shoebox like my own, "Aren't you glad we don't have a staircase to repair, or a yard to mow, or the proverbial shoveling of snow on an acre lot, or pulling out weeds that may possibly be poison ivy?"

Evette laughs, "Yes, it is great living in a non-house, and you forgot the best part, Jules. The best part is not having to watch the squirrels dance on my roof wondering how much damage they're going to cause and the associated cost."

I smile, "Yes, we have it made, don't we?"

Dr. McConnel informs me that another occupational therapist has had a family emergency and has left suddenly, and provides me the name of another patient I need to treat in her stead. I look at her records, and it's a burn patient.

I hate to admit it, but I often avoid treating burn victims. Their suffering does something to my core. Perhaps it is because I could see their scars, making my brain conjure up the high level of pain and distress that they feel. My aunt Emily, my father's sister, died as a result of burns. She was his only sister. When Emily was six years old and my father eight, she had been playing at the local playground with her brothers, and after dinner and a bit more play, she was ready for her nightly bath. The hot water scalded her and unbeknownst to the family, her little body was dehydrating. She ultimately died a few days later from dehydration. My dad's mother, Grandma Meg, was a quiet woman, and I always thought this was a trait she shared with my dad and his brothers. Perhaps this quiet nature was not their nature at all; perhaps it was a way of refraining from expressing pain and bottling everything up. My grandma never spoke Emily's name. I only heard her name when my dad lectured us about playing with fire or playing with water faucets. His whole demeanor changed, and he would always say in a raised voice, "You want to die like Emily?"

Grandma Meg was one of those people who always knew what to say; her words seemed like they were scripted. She only spoke briefly and usually kept to herself. She had that same smile as Jonathan, the one where a good set of teeth are shown, but to a trained eye, it is masking something. Grandma Meg was a kind and considerate person. I remember her shooing insects out of the house, then rebuking my brother for trying to kill them. She added, "We don't kill God's creatures." She always gave small gifts to everyone in her life, the postman, the gardener, the hairstylist. She was sure to show her appreciation. Grandma Meg ultimately died as a result of a heart attack when I was ten years old. She probably died from a broken heart. I once asked my dad what Aunt Emily was like, while he was busy with some woodwork in the garage. He briefly glanced at me, then immediately returned to his work. He answered, "Why would you want to know that?" and allowed the sawdust to cover his face and eyes rather than look me in the face and answer the question. Before I exited, he made one brief statement. "Emily was a good girl, funny too . . . it was a shame." And before he allowed himself to continue, I heard him ramp up his tools to drown out the sound of his own voice.

Perhaps in some existential realm, when I see a burn victim, I think of death and feel the vulnerability of mortality, or perhaps I mourn the fact that a burn caused an entire family, people close to me, to not be themselves. I found out Emily's date of death from my uncle Travis and every year on that day, I donate some toys to a children's charity. I also give an annual lecture on the danger of fire, and when I do, I say her name out loud.

I enter the room with some apprehension. Sara's most extensive burns formed as a result of her going to her brother's bedroom, which was quite a distance from the door, as their house burned. It was Sara who saved her little brother and shielded him from substantial injury. She had just turned eighteen. Her parents, who had sustained minor injuries from the fire, were a constant presence. Her hospital room basically looked like a living room with books and trinkets and magazines. She was a heroine and a young girl all in one. She had undergone many skin grafts, therapy to improve her range of motion, strength training, and lessons on maintaining skin integrity. She had received a lot of care for many months in a burn unit. As she was still in need of care, I would be seeing her at her later stages of treatment. She embodied strength and motivation, the likes of which I had never seen. Although her arm didn't have full range to create a complete good-bye wave, she nevertheless made a great attempt and thanked

118

me for my help. Her personality, coupled with the way she allowed me to treat her, made something within me grow, and when I exited her room, I felt a sense of calm that I hadn't felt in a long time.

I walk home in a pleasant mood, with a bit of a spring in my step. The hallway in my building was just waxed, and I tread carefully as I traverse the area. The floor sparkles, and I can almost see my reflection. I am happy as I enter my own apartment, noting that my floors share a similar sheen due to my cleaning skills, and I get an additional sense of pride.

The night passes rather quickly, and I watch the evening news, which, as usual, has a robbery, a shooting, and an attempted rape. I generally spend the full segment feeling sorry for those who lived through it, but tonight I can't keep my mind off James. I take out the penlight that had given him some level of entertainment today. A wide smile extends across my face as I think of his curious expression. I recall that I had purchased a small sailboat with two accompanying plastic figurines for a friend's son, but decide perhaps James might benefit more from these toys. I don't know how many, if any, toys he had received in his past, or if he even knows how to play. I put them in a box, preparing them for tomorrow.

As I enter the rehab unit in the morning, I bump into Delya. Delya is the occupational therapist whom I covered for the day before. She looks okay, and I ask, "What happened?"

"My dad slipped on a banana peel. Can you believe it? Who actually slips on a banana peel? He is, thankfully, okay. It was only a sprained ankle."

I think of my own dad's message, but don't feel ready to return the call.

My rotations for the next few days will be in the traumatic brain injury unit, otherwise known as a TBI unit. The unit hosts stroke patients, patients following neurological surgery, or patients that have had poor surgical re-sectioning outcomes. The TBI unit is the unit that makes me marvel at the wonders and intricacies encompassing the structures of the human mind and body. People on this floor are generally in need of both physical and cognitive rehabilitation. A further challenge is that some patients can't speak or they may have difficulty with comprehension. It is here that I learn to recognize the true complexities involved in the completion of the simple tasks in life.

On this unit, one can often observe an asymmetry of the body, as one side lacks strength and tone. The asymmetry manifests itself based upon where the patient's brain injury occurred. Although there are protocols for care, each patient is different and is treated accordingly.

My first patient of the day is a thirty-four-year-old male. He continuously fails to use his affected side, so his good arm is now constrained in a sling to force him to use his involved extremity. This patient has been moved from another facility to ours after brain tumor removal surgery. The therapy is generally intense, and the patient begins to use his affected extremity for longer time frames, thus increasing his functionality. His

120

wife visits him daily despite working a twelve-hour shift. He is thoroughly annoyed by the sling but really wants to return to work, recalling that he barely managed their monthly mortgage fees before this injury.

A large part of therapy in the TBI unit focuses on the core musculature. Your core helps your limbs complete their task by providing a stable foundation from which they can move. In addition, the trunk provides a base for the head and neck, which helps control the function of the visual system, and helps the mouth and neck move appropriately for good swallowing. The gym will often include individuals having difficulty sitting straight up, accessing things from above, below, and at their sides, as well as standing upright and moving limbs in a coordinated pattern.

I wheel my next patient to the other side of the gym. As I navigate to a safe spot to work with him, I observe another patient that has difficulty flexing forward as she reaches for the cover of a magazine that features a well-known and adored singer. Despite hardship, she doesn't give up, humming a tune that seems to summon up the additional strength she requires to finally move forward and grasp hold of the magazine. As her hands finally make contact, a wide grin covers her face.

I then sit on a rolling stool and observe my own patient, Latti. Latti is a wife, mother, sister, daughter, and shopkeeper. She suffered a stroke in the midst of reading a good book, sitting on her favorite chair. Her son noticed her odd behavior and poor responsiveness and got her to the ER. I look at her rib cage; it's rotated; her head and neck are misaligned, and her pelvis sits in a posterior pelvic tilt, in a slouched position. The pelvis is also one of our unsung heroes, as its movement helps to realign the trunk, changing the spinal curves and moves the shoulder into a particular position. Aside from the need to be in a correct posture for various tasks, left unchanged, the soft tissue that surrounds given areas like the tendons, ligaments, muscles, skin, and lymph system may undergo further changes, thereby creating additional problems. Sitting in an efficient seated posture, which is a central part of our daily existence in and of itself, is contributing to improved soft tissue health.

Latti is relentless, though. She turns to me and says, "Jules, let's get started already." She knows she can't wash her hair and stand in the shower, and she comments that her hair is her pride, and we need to get the show on the road.

I assess another patient who seemingly can't roll onto his side. This is problematic as he is more likely to form ulcers or sores without regular intervals of movement. He only maintains a seated posture for twenty-one seconds, with compensation that is. I document my findings and then greet the man's roommate, a thirty-six-year-old male who is on nerve-blocking medication, evidencing swelling and edema. He has been in such great distress and pain that he is suffering from a pain syndrome and can't shut the pain out anymore.

The hand is yet another area that usually requires addressing on the TBI unit. The hand is beautiful and complicated. The anatomy of the hand is more complex than one would know from its outward appearance. The metacarpophalangeal joints connect the bones of the palm to the fingers. They move in opposition to the interphalangeal joints, the joints of the fingers. When metacarpophalangeal joints are flexed, the interphalangeal joints extend, and the small muscles of the hand shorten. When the metacarpophalangeal joints extend, the interphalangeal joints flex, and the muscles of the hand elongate. It is their ability to work in this seemingly opposite pattern that makes our hands work efficiently.

My next patient, Amy, has suffered from spasticity as a result of a stroke and injury to the brain. It caused a prolonged contraction of the muscles, and the muscles tightened, increasing stiffness and rigidity. I must fabricate a splint for improved tone and function. I take the necessary measurements for her splint, then place her wrist and fingers at the appropriate angle. Once presented with the splint, she examines it and inquires, "So you're telling me this constricting contraption that causes tension in my hand is going to help relieve the tension in my hand?" Her question makes me re-examine the splint, a splint that I have fabricated on many occasions, yet this time my eyes see it differently. Perhaps this is yet another one of life's many ironies.

The hand not only has intricate musculature and bone, but it also has these unique palmar arches, the lines in your hand that allow us to accommodate our hands to objects, further increasing our functionality. Following a neurological insult, some patients may lose their palmar arches making functional tasks cumbersome. The unit is quite cold today, and I grab some hot water to warm me. My hands conform to the cup, allowing me to successfully drink without spillage. I am a bit warmer and return to the unit.

I observe Evie, a fifty-six-year-old stroke patient whose brain insult has been quite substantial, attempting to roll in bed, unsuccessfully. She extends her back, head, neck, attempting to bring her hemiplegic leg across her trunk. I teach her the proper way to roll to her sides, mostly using the power of my own hands with some visual guidance. She has difficulty speaking and comprehending, but she looks up at me like her eyes are saying, "Thank you."

As a member of the human race, your morning routine will likely be chaotic given time constraints. Every movement has an intended goal, no matter how simple. Most people can generally anticipate the steps necessary to accomplish their goals. They then gather the objects necessary and use correct movements in a required sequence to carry out their goals. For some people completing simple parts of a morning routine like dressing and brushing their teeth can take on a life of its own. The chaos comes not from a lack of time but from the inability of the body and mind to perform these tasks efficiently and effectively. Dina has good strength but is brushing her hair with the opposite end of the hairbrush. Clarisse, a young woman, barely twenty, was in an auto accident. She is washing her face but is unable to stop, as her brain continues to perseverate. Mike is on his way to physical therapy. He attempts to give his wife a thumbs up because that is the gesture he always uses for "okay" but he can't seem to find the correct way of positioning his finger to get it right. His wife looks on lovingly, waving and blowing him a kiss. I walk Thomas, Mike's roommate, towards a kitchen display. He has difficulty preparing food, as he can't figure out how to proceed despite knowing he wants to. The more instructions you give him, the more flustered he gets. Less is more, and I cue him ever so slightly, directing him towards the proper sequence.

Patients don't always greet me with enthusiasm; some can't greet me at all. Others use my existence as a verbal punching bag. Genie is a forty-four-year-old woman. She has been a single mother and has one son that is currently in foster care. She has no parents and only one sibling who lives outside the United States. A stroke which occurred during a friend's party left her hemiplegic with decreased ability to swallow. She doesn't allow any friends to visit, as she still carries the shame of what happened to her, the fact that everyone close to her witnessed her during her most vulnerable moment. Today, toileting is on the agenda. One needs to be able to get to the toilet, assume a squatting sitting position, and actually maintain it for the duration of the task.

Although we only engage in a simulated act, the act, in and of itself, is so very intimate, and Genie says, "I am not going in there with you! You got it? What is the point anyway? These meds, they constipate me so bad that I may never go. I'm not human anymore. I can't turn in bed and sleep. I can't eat, and I can't go to the bathroom." I attempt to validate her feelings, but she refuses to hear me out. She also adds, "And with the constant beeping and lights and blood-taking, one can go nuts here."

But she is already in a wheelchair, so I wheel her over to the bathroom. She yells at me, but I move her, and she begins cursing at me. I park her wheelchair, not in the standard position to access the toilet, but rather at the front end. She looks at me curiously, and I demonstrate the motion of where the wheelchair is, how to squat, and the required seated position. All the while she watches me, and I note she is absorbing something. I don't say a word, just demonstrate how my body needs to move. I move her wheelchair over at the exact angle that will give her greater efficiency for accessing the toilet, and she allows me to provide physical cues to assist her in moving her body to an efficient posture. We both say nothing. I fix the positioning of her upper garment so that it sits correctly on her shoulders, and I look her in the eyes, sustaining eye contact throughout. I initially find her facial expression to indicate discomfort, but it fades quickly, and a look of shock emerges as she realizes she has mastered the transfer as well as she did.

When she is back in her wheelchair, sitting near her bed, I allow myself to talk. "You are very much human. You know how I know? Because many people on this unit can't talk, and they definitely can't express emotions like you." Anger and frustration are normal parts of the human repertoire of feelings. I want to add that I am aware that loneliness doesn't

126

help either. I have lived on my own since age eighteen, but I don't allow the words lonely to pass my lips. Instead, I just say, "I like your feisty spirit."

Genie gives me a slight nod and asks, "When are you coming back?"

"Tomorrow," I say, adding in a low voice, "by the way, lying in bed all day doesn't really help the constipation situation."

One of my clients greets me in the hallway and leaves me with some parting words which I don't understand, but imagine to be a Latin American proverb. She is very warm and thankful as she leaves the unit, so I assume it is something nice. Language barriers and cultural differences don't often create havoc on the unit, particularly when you become accustomed to reading patients body language and using your own body with postures and gestures to help them understand. That is not to say that there are never miscommunications.

I once had a patient who was cognitively intact, an older woman who was generally sweet, donning a smile. She had suffered a stroke, and we worked on normalizing developmental sequence patterns. In order to accomplish this feat, I employed a technique known as PNF, specifically the D1 flexion pattern, to elicit more functional and efficient movement. The woman didn't speak English fluently and had many rituals as part of her culture. I did what I most often do; I explained the exercises and gave a demonstration. I lifted my hand to demonstrate bringing my arm and hand inward and across. As I moved to extend it back down, she became panic-stricken and started shrieking, looking horrified and failing to communicate the source of the distress. I thought she was having yet another stroke and enlisted the assistance of a nurse to help me settle her down and take her vitals. Everything seemed stable except for a mild rise in blood pressure.

I left the room and returned the next day, assuming it had been a passing physical episode. She began shrieking again, this time the moment I entered the room. I was obviously the problem. I couldn't figure out what warranted that reaction. She was willing to work with Evette, the physical therapist, but not with me. Her sons later approached me a bit apprehensively and said that their mother had relayed something odd to them. She said that I had displayed the *Sieg Heil*, the salute used to greet a Nazi soldier. I was mind-boggled by the thought. They further relayed that their mother stood in a ditch for nearly three years during the Holocaust to survive, and that occasionally odd occurrences would trigger memories. My movement intervention, though well intended, seemed to have revived her horrific experiences. I nearly lost my breath at the notion of being a perpetrator of such a dreadful emotion. I didn't even know the exact hand motion for that particular gesture.

"Perhaps you can tell us what you were doing when she began to act out?" one of her sons asked. I demonstrated the D1 movement, which seemed to be the trigger. During my break, I accessed the internet, looking at what the *Sieg Heil* salute looked like; biomechanically speaking, the movements did not resemble each other, but for some reason, this conjured

128

up the memory.

This wouldn't be my last miscommunication. A woman from Haiti rebuked me when I demonstrated a forward and backward spinal motion. Trying to add some pizzazz to it, I incorporated a bit of a sway. Apparently, she associated my dance with the voodoo dancing in her country and seemed genuinely afraid, stating that her house was burned as a child because she had something wrong with her soul. Otherwise, she was quite chipper and funny, and appeared perfectly fine to me, always saying please and thank you, and initiating the same pleasantness with other patients. I apologized profusely and clarified my actual objective. Sometimes it is just best to apologize, not because you have intentionally done something offensive, but for giving someone else a few extra moments of discomfort in their already complicated life.

I note Dr. Sarim still schlepping his twenty-five books through the hallway, still rubbing his neck and his shoulder a bit, so I commit to buying him a gift tonight, a portable scanner.

The next morning, I feel a bit groggy. I don't want to go to work and push my way through my apartment in that slow, uncoordinated gait. I generally don't drink coffee, but I need my mind and body to be a bit more alert, and so I walk myself into the kitchen, locate the coffee mug, then go through the motions in preparing the coffee in sequential order. I fill the urn with water and plug it in to boil. I then locate the coffee grains, add sugar, and boiled water. I even detect the small bit of water that dripped on the floor and go to clean it up. I become cognizant of the fact that I have grabbed the decaffeinated coffee instead of one with caffeine. As the former won't suit my purpose, I start the process again.

I sit at my small kitchen table with my posture intact and upright while leaning slightly forward to enjoy small sips and avoid burning my tongue. I answer the phone call that disrupts my morning coffee to find it's Stephanie on the other end asking me if I want to walk to work with her, as she is in the vicinity. I agree. I return to my coffee, noticing it needs more hot water and continue the process. When I am done, I go to the sink and wash my mug. My eyes are more open and more ready to face the day.

I meet Stephanie outside, and we walk, comparing who is dressed more warmly today as the weather is expected to be more like a day in winter than in fall. Still, it will be a good day, in some ways, it already has been. I have started on a good note, independently completing my morning routine without any assistance or major hitches, and for that, I am grateful.

I return to the gym at the TBI unit today. I sit down and reach for a timer on the shelf using my right hand extended up and out, and my left trunk shortens as my right trunk elongates, my left hip follows by hiking itself up a bit, allowing my weight to shift towards the timer and pick it up. The whole process is completed so quickly and efficiently that I don't even take notice of my actions.

I look out at the sea of patients, taking note of the movements and positions that pose hardship. One patient attempts a forward reach.

130

Another patient's right hand attempts to cross his body, reaching his left foot to attempt shoe-tying. Yet another crosses his left hand over his left shoulder and then above his head and behind his head in an attempt to reach the tissue box after a really loud achoo. This motion is only made more difficult by the fact that the box had been misplaced on a shelf and the patient has difficulty gaining a firm grip on it. The tissue box begins to fall, only missing the patient's head due to the swift-moving action of his therapist. Yet the therapist delights in the fact that the patient knew to make use of a tissue altogether.

Each task is made more challenging by changes in surface type, chair height, and size, coupled with the type of objects or tasks they attempt to complete. Their bodies move according to their capabilities given an injury, trying to eat, groom, dress, in an attempt to become an independent and more capable person. I watch Yvette flex forward to gather food from the table and bring it to her mouth, which, thankfully, today she completes successfully. She evidences a smile like she was just awarded a trophy.

I watch a young man, barely twenty-two, attempt to button his shirt. Despite his best attempts, he is unsuccessful, and the buttons don't match up with their respective holes. His shirt is too short on one side and too long on the other, making him appear lopsided. His younger brother, aged twelve, who has come to visit, helps him out, saying, "There you go!" as he completes the last one.

I walk toward the room nicknamed "the house," where we practice many daily activities. It is not quite a house, having bare walls and two cabinets. It is small, allowing for only three or four people at a time. It has some dishes, a stove, a fridge, a table, and a washer and dryer. At the corner of the room, one can find a full-body mirror. It is there that I meet up with my next client. There is no one else in the room today, allowing us privacy and quiet.

Unilateral neglect is a neurological sequela often associated with stroke. To me, it attests to one of the most fascinating workings of the human body because this neglect can create a state of havoc in one's life. The patient fails to acknowledge objects or space related to the opposite side of their lesion. They use compensatory strategies like scanning or guided hand movements to better attend to that side to complete tasks and activities.

Mrs. Pratt, a victim of left-sided neglect, only notices her right profile. She fails to note all left-sided objects on the table, like spoons and forks and the bottle of ketchup that someone left out before, unless directed that way. She also doesn't acknowledge her own left hand that is an inch from the spoon. Thankfully, however, she is motivated to compensate. She is visually able to see and comprehend only part of herself. She is both oblivious to space on her left as well as her left side of her body. This makes all activities difficult. She has learned to walk to acknowledge her left foot and swing her left hand. She has difficulty dressing the left side of her body. Recognizing people or objects on her left is also difficult. Reading is yet another challenge, as the page requires scanning from side to side. Still, with all these challenges, she chooses to feel whole and not allow what she is told is missing to make her feel fragmented or unwhole. Unlike some other stroke patients that suffer from decreased motivation and initiation, Mrs. Pratt is quite motivated to improve. Ironically, I employ the use of mirrors to help her attend to her full self. In addition, greater attention is brought to her left side with verbal reminders and stimulation of the left extremities. All these techniques are employed to bring attention to something that is already there.

A month before my grandmother's move into our home, my mother purchased a dresser with drawers to house some of my grandmother's beautiful clothing. It was vintage, meaning old and worn, but it was within budget and could accommodate a large wardrobe. My mother had asked my sister and me to clean it in preparation for placing Grandma's articles of clothing inside. I remember gathering numerous household products and rags. At first, my sister and I worked as a team, scrubbing off the exterior goop for fifteen minutes. It was very cathartic, the rubbing back and forth; there was some release of energy that was gratifying and enjoyable. I also enjoyed my sister's company, as she was willingly engaging in some childhood banter, which was unusual for the two of us.

Unfortunately, the excitement only lasted those fifteen minutes. Before long, my sister stated she was tired, and went to watch TV, leaving me with the majority of the exterior surface and the entire interior surface to strip and clean on my own. I stood cleaning with such intensity that the marks on my hands and wrist lasted for hours and some for several days. I inhaled so much of the cleansers' aromas that I had a cough that lingered for a week, but on the other hand, the furniture looked spectacular. I caught a glimpse of my right profile in the mirror, only a part of myself, but I noted how interesting my half-smile looked and could feel the full smile that emanated from within. I stood there, proud of myself for having accomplished the feat of restoring something, recreating it instead of throwing it away, and for someone I loved.

My mother never came to check on the work in progress. She only later examined the end product. When she finally arrived, she looked at it from all angles, very pleased, and then went over to my sister, kissing her on the cheek, raving about her good work. My sister said nothing. She acted as if it had been her lungs that breathed in the fumes, her hands and nails that were filled with the dirt, her arms that had an ache from pushing back and forth. She never even bothered to apologize for taking all the credit. Then when I looked at the dresser's large beautiful mirror, I noted my right profile, only a part of me, unable to see my full face. I felt like half a person. The joy I had experienced turned to sadness and would later turn to anger.

For months, I dreamed about how I should have spoken up and taken the credit for myself and how I should have addressed my sister when she said nothing. I think, in the moment, I was just relieved that I hadn't suffered my mother's negativity, only her neglect, which in my book was just fine. In the end of it all, however, it robbed me of something of myself that would continue to haunt me into adulthood.

I look at Mrs. Pratt as she needs to learn to reattend to a part of her body that is still there and ultimately know that I, too, am whole. Despite her upbeat attitude, Mrs. Pratt is somewhat frustrated, having knowledge about a deficit that is both there and not there at the same time. The long, standing mirror in the corner of the room is intended to help her dress, and when she is told she is now fully dressed, she sighs with relief.

I walk into Mr. Landers's room; he is dressing. He places two legs into the same leg hole, as he can't figure out where in space his leg is in relationship to the pant hole. His roommate doesn't know where his left leg is in space, secondary to neglect of his left side, yet a third patient can't scoot over to lift his leg into the hole, and a fourth puts on his socks and shoes before his pants, failing to denote the correct order of dressing. Another man looks at his pants, trying to recall the word "pant" as he moves into it easily.

A woman who is taking her husband home in a wheelchair today asks how to rearrange the furniture for unobstructed movement in her home. "How much clearance do you need?" she asks hospital personnel. She then dials her daughter and asks that she measure all entrance ways in her home. She paces in the hallway indicating her agitation and momentarily releases her lip from successive lip biting, as she grumbles to her daughter, "It's an older home with way too many nooks and crannies. Maybe we should move."

Some will return home near normal; others will require a host of changes in door capacity to fit a wheelchair or walker, improved household lighting, sturdier stairs, or handrails in the shower. Chairs may need to have armrests; shower doors may need to be removed and replaced with curtains only to accommodate a shower bench. Items are made more accessible for easy reach, commodes placed near the bed, and the list goes on.

I see small sparks of happiness as patients master skills: I can eat, I can walk, toilet, brush my hair, turn in bed. When these patients make these little strides, it is like a breath of fresh air, giving me a renewed vigor, as I learn not to take my own bodily competence for granted. I go home to my little shoebox and count my blessings. I enter my apartment, appreciating the confines of my home where one person can reach, amble, and sit. It makes me want to return to work with greater vigor, be more inventive, so that I can restore some fairness to the world, to enable good people who have had bad things happen to them experience an improved life.

CHAPTER 5: SEEING IS PERSPECTIVE

I treat myself to a fruit drink before going in to work today, which is a bad decision. It has some ice in it, and it gives me brain freeze from the cold. I enter work, making my way toward the office to get a warm drink, to bring me back to some state of equilibrium. I ensure that it isn't too hot based on the lack of steam emanating from it. My teeth delight as the warm water washes over them. I notice the time and quickly exit the office.

As I walk through the hallways, Slate's mother appears. She is a long-legged woman with blonde hair and blue eyes, and more than a few freckles lining her nose and forehead, making me question if she had been a natural redhead rather than blonde. Her great smile further complements her already natural beauty.

Mrs. Slate visits the hospital from time to time and brings some lunch or snacks for her son in an attempt to see him. Slate generally avoids interacting with his family members. All conversations and interactions are always brief. I go to find Slate. He is leaving his office and immediately encounters his mother. He rolls his eyes briefly. His parents seem to be nice and caring people. I can't figure out what had transpired to evoke this reluctance, but Slate never told me. Mrs. Slate looks at her son like he is a polished diamond. She reveres even the sight of her son, and she beams as he strides through the corridors toward her. She doesn't even bother to attempt a conversation. As she has on other occasions in months past, she just hands him his lunch to which he responds, "Thank you," and concentrates on an invitation or piece of mail that requires his attention. Mrs. Slate pecks him on the cheek, as Slate tries to extricate himself from a further embrace.

She says, "Good-bye," and goes back on her way. I couldn't understand this strange exchange. Here was a caring woman, nonintrusive, for the most part, making an effort just to see her son. It was hard for me to trust people, and I started thinking at one point that if the person others perceive as my perfectly presentable mother had been guilty of abusing me, then perhaps Slate's mother may harbor some other unapparent identity as well.

Dr. Sarim is in the hallway and I run after him. He is sporting his generally friendly disposition. "Hi Jules," he says, still coddling his neck as he stands. I invite him to the office where a gift awaits him.

"What's this?" Dr. Sarim asks with that inquisitive look he has when he makes a discovery.

"It's a magic wand!"

"What?"

I take out a long wand-like object. "It can scan your books or magazines. Use it. This way, you aren't carrying around half the American Psychological Association's recommended reading choices."

"Thank you, Jules." He examines the wand as he walks through the corridors.

I go to the TBI unit, teaching others to roll in bed, transfer themselves, dress, eat, and complete daily routines. I then complete a few additional interviews and assessments. It is my break, and I still have forty-five minutes to spare, so I go to visit James with my sailboat and figurines in hand. I enter his room in anticipation of what is forthcoming.

He has apparently refused his lunch, and during the instance where he was open to eating food, he refused to pick up the spoon. He is now being fed by Nurse Abbie, who was supposed to switch shifts. Given how little he was eating, the doctors were volleying the notion that he had sustained an injury compromising his swallow. Nurse Abbie knew better and was standing there humming yesterday's tune while placing small bits of food on a colorful spoon with cartoon characters, yet to no avail.

Nurse Abbie gestures for me to come in, and James tilts his head and looks up at me with increased eye contact, as compared to the other day. I take out the box that housed my gifts and say, "Let's see what is inside the box." James's gaze shifts toward the box with a slight look of wonder. I pull out the sailboat and figurines. I place the figurines in the boat and create a short story of who the figures are and where the boat is headed. I place a weighted, cuddly blanket over his thighs, which he thankfully does not refuse. I place the sailboat on his lap and wait in wonder to see if he will attempt to play with it. He stares at it for some time and then leans forward and gently pushes the boat. He looks up at me, and I place the figures in and out of the boat, so he attempts the same. He seems to enjoy mimicking my play, so I place a straw coated with his lunch mixture next to the sailor's lips pretending to feed the sailor. After several rounds, I take another straw placing some lunch mixture on it and move it slowly toward James's mouth. He hesitates momentarily but then opens his mouth for another eight rounds before shutting down again. He never does make it to using the spoon, but he eats a minimum to sustain his small frame. I have six minutes left to get to the TBI unit and leave with a quick wave good-bye.

As I exit his room, I see Sally and Mia, two little girls with different respiratory conditions. Their sweet young voices are slightly less exuberant due to decreased breath support. They both, however, don large smiles that appear to overtake their small faces. Mia's father is standing down the corridor, exchanging words with hospital staff while referencing a piece of paper. Mia eyes her father and frowns as she senses a bit of distress in her father's face, even from the distance. Sally tells Mia that her mother also looks like that because she is poor. Sally is seven and a half while Mia is one year her junior. Sally has heard her mother complain about paying for meds for most of her young life. Sally has been sick since birth, while Mia has only begun her medical journey. Sally says, "It is better to be rich."

When Mia's father returns, she turns to him, "Daddy, are we rich or poor?"

Mia's father looks at his daughter in wonder. "What do you think it means to be rich?"

"I don't know," Mia says, looking for some direction at her new best friend, Sally.

Sally interjects, "To have a lot of money, money or maybe things." She is a bit puzzled.

Mia turns to her father. "Do I have a lot of things, Daddy?"

"You have lots of love," her father responds and confirms her status as rich, as he holds back tears when looking at his daughter. Unbeknownst to her, the paper he is holding has the name of the malignancy they have just found in Mia's little body.

"Yay! I am rich!" Mia responds and tells her new best friend that she will give her things to make her rich too. Sally is confused by the change in the definition of rich but nevertheless smiles along with her friend. I look on in wonder at the simplicity of this discourse. I go upstairs to my office to finish paperwork containing much verbiage conforming to definitions and codes set forth by various health-related institutions for reimbursement purposes. I look at all the words on the page that truly fail to capture the meaning of life. I conform.

I walk home at night feeling the change in weather that comes with autumn air. I fail to feel that extra step in my walk that comes from the heat and energy of the summer. As I walk, I pull my sweater closer to my core to create a warm and cozy feeling. I examine the various shops and businesses that are closing up. Some windows become barren, lights shut down; some shop owners look weary, others walk back and forth frantically. I see people come and go, not knowing if they are on their way to the city nightlife or going home for their night routine.

Although I prefer daylight, I can't ignore the sparkly lights of the city at night. As I walk, childhood nostalgia envelops me. The beams of light make me recall the fireflies that I sought out in the company of my siblings. The warm breeze encapsulated us as we sat outside with my grandmother holding our jars in anticipation. As the first firefly emerged, we ran enthusiastically, and although we each wanted to be the first to jar the firefly, it became a group effort, a source of sibling comradery. As more fireflies emerged, we shared short giggle sessions admiring our lighted captives. My grandmother stood there and cheered us on. Then in unison, we freed our little friends back into the world and stood there transfixed as they created a string of lights that seemed to light up our entire universe. For those brief periods, I understood what it felt like to be in a family.

I arrive home, thankful that the weekend has arrived. I prepare a casual dress and then pull out a dressy outfit deep within the confines of my closet for the wedding. I find matching accessories to accentuate the fabric detail. I intend to make my way to Brooklyn tomorrow to visit a friend that's staying in another friend's apartment that is also a shoebox, just a bit bigger than my own. Her apartment gets bragging rights though, for having a small lawn in front of her apartment building.

I get on the subway bright and early, reading an article about the effects of air pollution in the city. I could attest to its effect, given my daily dosage of smells and sights, which I witness day by day. As I arrive, I notice

142

that the small lawn hasn't been cut, and for a brief moment, I smile. My apartment is apparently winning this competition. We spend the morning together, admiring the changing architecture every few blocks. As we traverse a child's playground, my friend Cary attempts the monkey bars when no one is looking. She isn't that great at climbing anymore and massages her sore arms.

The late afternoon arrives, and we dress for the wedding. Before entering the hall, we take sneak peeks in the mirror, and a pleasant atmosphere welcomes us. The bride looks beautiful in her vintage dress; it's almost as if the hall décor was custom-made especially for her. The groom laughs out loud and makes jokes, and the kids are generally well behaved with only one or two dipping their little fingers into the food. The photographer is a serious man shouting commands to which everyone complies because pictures are the only way one's wedding lives on.

Before long, I am on my way home; it's six fifty p.m., and I take a rideshare. When we pass the FDR Drive, there are a host of emergency vehicles blocking the path. I wonder if there was a shoot-out, or terrorist attack, or a really bad accident. Then as I peer through the car window, I note a woman who looks young from a distance on the bridge, her hands flailing in the air. I hear my driving companion complain about the traffic, and the driver just bangs his hands against the wheel in frustration. Another man calls home to tell his wife he will be late, but I just see an image of this woman in my mind even after other vehicles have blocked my view.

"Why are there so many vehicles for just one person?" the man shouts.

I sit there in horror, looking out my window, waiting to see the image of the woman again, to learn whether she is still alive. It is hard to be so close and so far at once. *"Don't do it. Don't jump!"* I whisper under my breath as if she could hear me. It is like when you cannot move the subway car, and you push on the bars as if that will magically make the subway car move. *"Just don't do it,"* I say to myself again as the car begins to inch away.

I was bullied as a child. The majority of my bullying took place at home, however. Sisters barked at me for what they wanted, and needless to reiterate, my mother was the biggest bully. In school, though, it was generally only about insignificant stuff. Why I like to answer questions in class, or why I didn't answer something. Why I had an old knapsack or why my teeth weren't the straightest. I eventually did get braces once my grandmother moved in.

Tracy, however, got the brunt of the classroom bullying. Nothing she ever did was right; it was like every choice she made would warrant a comment: horrible hair color, wrong dress style, wrong locker number, out-of-date shoe style, not reading loud enough or fast enough, gave her test in last, and the list goes on. Tracy was really sweet and a great artist. She would doodle while the teacher spoke, and her notebooks were filled with characters and other illustrations. She was especially good at shadowing and color combinations. She started using markers to write with in class which didn't sit well with the teachers and brought forth a whole

144

slew of additional problems for her. She sat alone at lunch and at recess, all the while drawing and doodling. Years later, she would draw her first and last masterpiece. It was a red and black inkblot design that she splattered, displaying the silhouette of a person, a painting that she painted just before her suicide attempt. As her attempt failed, she remains in a hospital bed in a vegetative state to this day. To complement her final drawing, she painted streaks of black and red on her own person in various lengths and widths, almost in a checkerboard pattern as if she consisted of the culmination of small jigsaw pieces put together. Tracy was twenty-four at the time. She barely gave herself a chance to live. I remember where I stood in my apartment when I found out about what had happened to her. At that point, I dropped the phone along with the milkshake I had been holding, splattering it across my kitchen floor.

Tracy had a great dad, and she knew it. Her father was a traveling salesman making them move quite often. She had remained at my school longer than in any of her other ones, but it appeared as if life just happened; there was no novelty or excitement in her life during the time she spent with us, and she never really found a place where she fit in. She continued to be just an image projected by the people around her, where nobody seemed to value her worth.

The last straw was shortly after Tracy was laid off from her job at an art store. She could no longer afford to pay for her education, and she left graduate school. It was her dad who found her near-lifeless body.

Consequently, he now works only part-time, spending his days with her in the hospital. It is not the daily trip to the hospital and seeing her in that state that torments him most. It's the fact that he didn't see it coming and didn't stop her. Her mother was affected in her own way, generally staying at home and obsessing about her other daughter's whereabouts. She is also constantly riddled with anxiety, depression, and chronic pain. That's just the thing; suicide makes a statement—the wrong one.

The fact that Tracy still exists, however, continues to provide the mild hope that she will once again regain her life, or better yet, have a more meaningful one. There is an endless flow of people that now come to talk to her and attend to her, some admitting the errors they made in their youth, but now she can't talk back, and she may not even be capable of listening to them or hearing them. Tracy may be gaining some inkling of the repercussions of her actions. If not now, maybe someday. The dead cannot. The dead don't see the sad faces, hear their own eulogies, see their own obituaries. They don't get to witness the remorse on people's faces for having had a hand in killing them, or to hear the words, "Perhaps I should have been nicer." I am not sure that Tracy spared her father the pain of finding a cold, dead body by covering herself in paint; it may have further fueled his pain. The paint now gone has been replaced by tubes and wires so numerous they create their own work of art.

I have limited my visits to Tracy to only two occasions because when I visit, I recall my own contemplated suicide. It was during my early sophomore year, a point in time when I had established some social standing in the previous freshman year, which, as it turned out, had not been as fulfilling as I had hoped, and it made me unhappy. At the same time, studies were becoming difficult, and life's challenges increasingly problematic. This can result when you no longer have those childhood birthday parties with friends or simple exchanges in the playground, or memories of purchasing your fun, new school supplies in the store. It is when your mature body starts to take shape in ways you don't enjoy, and, in my case, it was compounded by my grandmother's recent passing, coupled with my mother's increased verbal abuse. She was my tormenter.

This stage can become a vulnerable time in life when you can be most easily influenced and prompted to do the unthinkable, no more the egocentric child of your youth. Your eyes open up a bit, not only to your own tormenting factors but to the greater world, which at times seems more bleak than pleasurable. It's a time that you generally become moodier and less balanced, with few outlets to reinstate that balance, like how many teenagers perform deep breathing and have morning yoga routines. How many have deep conversations rather than taking selfies and engaging in teenage banter via social websites? Well, my method of choice was simple suffocation. I would lay in my own bed and suffocate myself. I started writing a note delineating all my life's ills, and the writing felt good, somewhat cathartic. I peeked over at the pillow that would provide me with this "salvation", but it didn't hold the fascination that I thought it would.

I had imagined the revenge I would get on every person that harmed me, particularly my mother. I was glad my grandmother was no longer alive to witness my demise as I didn't want to cause her pain. As I held the pillow over my face, not yet with increased force, my hands trembled, and my mind raced. I looked over at my sister's bed which was now empty, Jessica shared a room with me since early childhood. Although we weren't best friends, we would sometimes share stories during the evening hours and have some youthful chatter. I imagined Jessica looking over at me and seeing my cold dead body, and I imagined my father's face like the face he made when I asked him about Emily, and it was those images that made me stop. I could see my grandmother's disapproving eyes at my decision, which ultimately sealed the deal. I refrained from further action. I placed the pillow back on the bed, stroking it to decrease the creases that I had created. The decision hadn't brought me an unexpected delight at having been alive. I yearned for that cathartic state I dreamed of, the raw pain still there, the problems still there, but I lived. It took me a long time to realize the fortune of my decision. There would be no long talks with Stephanie, no museum and art visits with Slate, no joking with Chase, and so many other benefits that came along with my being alive. My regret, however, is failing to form a close enough bond with Tracy; perhaps that extra phone call or visit all those years ago could have changed the course of her life.

On the bridge, I sit silently in the car, thinking. I can still see the outline of this woman; I am quite happy she is still there. The car starts to

148

drive off as traffic finally moves. Everyone else sighs with relief that the vehicle is finally moving, that is, everyone but me. I get home and go to sleep trying to delight my mind with visions of the vintage dress the bride was wearing at the wedding, the dancing, the food, the silly face Cary made as she climbed her way up the monkey bars or the different casing of windows and roofs we had noted on Brooklyn streets, but my mind keeps returning to the woman, who I hope is alive somewhere, getting help for healing.

It's that dreaded Monday morning, the morning where your foot is half in and half out when you get to work. You push yourself through the morning, knowing that there will be at least four more days of the same. Slate is sitting at the nurses' station tapping his Cross pen against the table as he speaks on the phone ". . . vascular clamps . . . angiogram . . . anastomosis microscopic polyangiitis . . . granulomatosis . . . cryoglobulinemia."

Stephanie is on her way to a surgery and passes me by with a hello, then turns and shouts, "Great day, Jules!"

"You, too!" I yell after her as I walk by.

Diane is an eighty-one-year-old former literature professor and author. She had minored in languages, making her résumé quite impressive. While in her home, Diane sustained a right hip fracture as a result of a slip and fall over one of her own authored books which had somehow made its way to the floor. She also had an old shoulder injury, which made overhead reach a bit difficult.

When I first met her, I identified myself as Jules Wescott, to which she crinkled her nose, asking, "What type of a name is Jules?"

"Well, it's actually Julianne," I replied.

"Dear, why would you refer to yourself as Jules when you have a perfectly good name like Julianne, which to be quite honest, is more befitting for a young lady like yourself." *Young being a relative term*, I think.

I was not about to explain to this woman the actual event that turned this perfectly good name of 'Julianne' into 'Jules'. I was sixth months old when my parents made their way into some kind of pub while traveling to the Midwest with my siblings and me. I heard that a burly drunk guy referred to me as Jules and, somehow, that name stuck.

The conversation with Diane was apparently not over when I relayed my job title. "I am an occupational therapist."

"Oh," she said, "You're a physiotherapist, not a physical therapist, is that it?"

I attempted to explain my function within the hospital system but try and clarify the complexities involved in defining occupational therapy with sufficient eloquent detail to a noted author who probably wrote more books than the number of years I had lived. I saw that perplexing look pasted on her face. *Perhaps too many words were thrown into the mix*, I thought. I imagined Oliver Hawthorne, who is also proficient in the written word. He would likely be better able to explain to Diane my exact function in terms she could understand. However, unlike Oliver, Diane is cheerful and conversant. She is also a linguist, often peppering her words with other languages. I tried to speak her language, adding a bit of humor, which isn't my forte, "We are like dangling participles or run-on sentences; we have value and can add to a sentence, but no one knows what to do with us."

Diane shook her head, smiling at me, "That's the first happy thought I have had in a while."

"I am glad to be of service," I answered. Diane was one of the few patients that appreciated verbose responses. She enjoyed the flow of words. For other people, I would often demonstrate movements and activities by minimizing instructions or explanations, relying on visual or physical cues. Diane, on the other hand, was sharp-witted and a conversationalist. When I provided her with an abductor wedge to avoid crossing one leg over the other, which was prohibited during the initial stages of recovery, Diane's face evidenced disdain for the word "abductor wedge." It was as if I insulted her own being.

"Abductor wedge? What type of word is that? It sounds so sterile for such an interesting object."

To her delight, I began to refer to it as "the hip sculpture." Then transferring it to French, "la hanche sculpture," knowing full well that I have about three percent proficiency in this language.

"Well, you could do worse," Diane said, at hearing the name change.

Diane was inquisitive. She liked knowing everything about the people treating her as if she was interviewing them for her next literary piece. Diane had once asked me why I chose my profession. I thought for a few moments, as I had never been asked that by a patient before. Sure, doctors, family members, and friends posed the question to which I would provide a vague response, but Diane was a patient, and she wouldn't let me get away with a darted answer. I told her about my sister's injury as my first introduction to occupational therapy, but Diane was persistent.

"That just generates an interest in a professional field. It doesn't compel one to make the commitment. What brought you to the commitment, Julianne?" There were still another fifteen minutes left to the session, so I knew Diane would continue to harass me until I provided more details.

"Not to diminish the role of physicians, as they selflessly give of their time, sleep, and energy and endure attending to people in the worst of situations. They endure many years of medical school only to endure more years of criticism during residency by often elitist higherups, and only to have brief interactions with their patients, and are, furthermore, obligated to carry hefty medical malpractice insurance. Well, while doctors are indispensable, their day is comprised of taking or referencing vital signs, communicating using accurate medical jargon, writing prescriptions, paperwork, and then more of the same. I found occupational therapy to be empowering; it has that humanity about it. I guess that is what appealed to me. When you teach someone to eat, sit, dress, and bathe, these tasks are core human tasks that are purposeful and relate to the human race. Unlike medicine, that prevents or hinders the furtherance of disease, occupational therapy looks not at how many beats your heart produces per minute but whether that heart can endure a good game of catch with your grandchild, or whether you have the upper body strength to participate in sports, or enough to allow you to sit on a chair at a desk for a long enough time to perform your job or enjoy a pastime like reading."

Diane turned to me as if she was satisfied with my answer. "Now I understand, Julianne. You're better at this than you think," she said. "That's right, Julianne. You're getting better. You're not just that three-word girl anymore."

"Better at what?" I asked.

"Expressing yourself, saying what you think. You are learning not to hold back," she said.

I didn't know how to respond to her answer. She obviously wanted that response to make me open up, I decided. It is not my job to open up to patients, I thought. Or was it? And, am I sufficiently emotionally available to share my feelings, thoughts, or ideas? Perhaps not. My mind was racing, only to be stopped by Evette asking me to order a piece of equipment for a client. By the day's end, Diane would be discharged and gone.

As I walk through the hallway, with the end of my workday approaching, I come across a boy sitting in a chair in the hallway. I take a second look and recognize his face. He is Denny, Dr. McConnel's eight-year-old son. Denny is sitting across from his father's office waiting for him to complete his day's work. Denny has been visiting the hospital more frequently, as his mother has been working additional hours lately, and he has been shuffled over here from school. I wave and smile, and he waves and smiles back with great enthusiasm. Unlike his father, Denny is gracious and personable.

Denny is holding a book. It's a recent publication, as denoted by its fresh face, and the pages appear to be crisp. I watch his eyes as he scans the page while he reads. He shifts in his chair. He turns his head quite a bit, particularly as he approaches the ends of each line. At one point, he touches his neck from all the head movement.

"Looks like you're reading a good book. Can I see it?" He hands me the book with a look of anticipation at what I might say. I observe the word size on the page and where the pictures are relative to the page. I read a page out loud and comment, "Sounds interesting." As I read, Denny sits upright, his eyes slightly widen and a smile emerges as he is attending to my read- aloud. I return the book to him. "Do you like stories, Denny?"

"Yeah. Lots!"

"Do you like to read?"

To which he thinks for a moment, then answers, "I guess."

"Oh, this part looks really interesting. Can you read it to me?"

"Yeah, I guess."

I watch him again. He pauses before the start of each sentence. I see him move his head as he reads. He seems to reread words and reference the accompanying illustrations in an unorganized pattern.

"Enjoy the rest of the book, Denny. Catch you another time." He waves.

I feel that internal struggle come on, like when you should do the right thing but don't want to. I look at Dr. McConnel's office then walk on, but my conscience gets the better of me. I go to the door, pause for a second, and then knock. I hear his voice. "Enter. Jules, can I help you?" The words are at the tip of my tongue but don't flow out freely.

"I just saw your son, Denny. He seems like a really great kid."

McConnel has a perplexed look on his face, morphing into curiosity. "Okay," he says, "is that all?"

"Sir, I just thought I would relay an observation." I reiterate the observations I had made while Denny was reading, and McConnel looks at me with the same look he has on his face when we convene for a meeting about the hospital's failings. I reiterate that it is just an observation and that he may have a visual deficit.

"Denny is a good reader," McConnel states with a firmness in his voice as if you can feel him holding his shield up to protect his son or maybe himself. "I think I know my own son, and I did, after all, go to medical school. He doesn't have a problem. Trust me."

I take a deep gulp and reply, "I think he is very persistent and motivated to do well, all great attributes, but I think he is working really hard to get there, and as time progresses, this may become more apparent. What harm could there be in just checking it out a bit further?"

McConnel is speechless which invokes even more anxiety in me. I continue, "With all due respect Dr. McConnel, it was you who created a mentorship program for medical students in the physical medicine and rehabilitation department, as you astutely noted that one has difficulty spotting their own difficulties." I attempt to quote him verbatim. "I think you really love and care about Denny, and it may be difficult to spot his weaknesses." My teeth are now chattering a bit due to my anxiety about discussing this issue further.

"I will speak to Olivia tonight, and we will look into his possible visual issue a bit further."

I nod, and as I turn toward the door, I hear a faint, "Thank you," coming from McConnel.

"Good night, sir," I say quickly as I make my way out of his office.

I go to get my coat from the office, and when I attempt to exit, the door doesn't open. It's locked! I scratch my head, thinking about what to do next or whom to call. I sit down on the cold floor, thankful that I have my cell phone in my pocket, and get ready to dial. As my fingers touch the number pad, a missed message pops up. It is my father, yet again. I locate Slate's number, ready to ask for help, but my fingers stop me, instead accessing my father's number. It rings for the third time, then a fourth. *Oh good, he isn't available,* I whisper to myself. My hands are cold from the lack of heat in the room. Then I call Slate who seems to unlock the door in record time, still panting from running in the hallways. "Thank you,

Slate," I say.

"Sure, anytime." And he walks me toward the hospital entrance, opens the door, and waves good-bye. As I leave, I note Stephanie on her cell phone, letting her mother-in-law know she is on her way home.

I decide to take the long route home to my apartment, at least for part of the distance. Stephanie graces me with her presence. As always, she brings a lightness to my mood. As we turn a corner, I'm struck by a beautiful woman, and when we make eye contact, I shudder, recognizing the figure before me. It is Ivy Harway. Ivy was that girl that everyone wanted to be, the perfect one, perfect at everything except being kind. I avoided her like the plague in high school. She was never perceived by others as a bully, but her words were often sharp, and she often brought attention to an already shameful, spiteful, or negative moment. Most memorable was when she pointed out the rip in my prom dress, the tear I had spent the last hour trying to hide from my classmates. My gown had gotten caught on the door of the limo. She definitely wasn't a person I want to meet on a day like today.

We greet each other with an awkward smile, and then she asks, "How are you doing?"

I almost believe her to be sincere for a second, but know better. I say what everyone says," Oh, I am great." For a moment, I totally forgot about Stephanie, so Stephanie introduces herself, but Ivy fails to acknowledge her presence, which, in a strange way, makes me feel better. For the first time ever, I think that if Ivy can dismiss a great human being like Stephanie, she must really be egocentric. This idiosyncrasy would likely eventually destroy her relationships, or so a part of me hopes. I rebuke myself for my ill will, then turn my thoughts toward another element of this meeting. If Ivy doesn't care for Stephanie, amazing Stephanie, then her attitude doesn't reflect on me, and it wasn't that something was particularly wrong with me, and it wasn't only me and my existence that Ivy perceived as someone less than her.

Stephanie gives me a big smile, and we continue on our way. "Stephanie, do you ever wonder why people bother asking each other how they are doing when you know they will automatically say, 'Fine. Everything is fine, and those few who do relay their true circumstances are often ignored. Why are we a culture of extremes? You're either perfectly fine, or you take to social media or another public forum, to rant about how terrible life is?"

Stephanie smiles again. "You're just so you, Jules," She turns to me with a partial smile and says, "So, how are you today?"

"Well, I had a horrible day, a linguist/author tried to teach me how to better express myself. I got locked in an office. I almost threw up when I had to approach McConnel about a personal matter, and in general, life kinda sucks. Thanks for asking." It is too bad there aren't more 'Stephanies' in the world. It would be a much better place.

"What exactly is the deal with Ivy?" Stephanie asks as we approach the corner.

158

"Well, she is one of those perfectly imperfect people."

"Jules, Ivy is definitely imperfect. Didn't you see her folding her hands, to hide some document? She looked rather panicked about it."

"What? She probably was just thinking about rubbing my nose in some grand venture she has going on."

"No," Stephanie says, "her hands were shaking. She actually looked like she was avoiding us. Let's continue our walk and stop having Ivy on the brain."

That night I go home and meet Mrs. Watts in my building. I am a bit apprehensive about approaching her as she greeted me with an intense stare yesterday when I met her in the lobby. The elevator was being repaired, and she was carrying a small bag of groceries. She kept looking at my face like she was doing a thorough examination. I thought I had a sauce stain from some baked ziti I had eaten at lunch. I rebuked myself for failing to look in the mirror after lunch, as I so often do. She looks at me again today, almost as if I were a stranger, and fails to return my hello when I enter. Mrs. Watts is a very presentable lady. She actually epitomizes the term "lady." She is like one of those people that you try to imitate when you are trying to show off good manners. The elevator is out yet again today, making life more miserable.

I start to walk up the stairs, heading in the same direction as Mrs. Watts as I eagerly await the comforts of my own home. I recall that I forgot to get my mail on the ground floor, so I walk back down. When I return,

Mrs. Watts, although carrying only a handbag, is treading up the stairs methodically, walking each step like she is trying to locate a diamond in a mine. She holds on to the banister for dear life and seems to be counting the number of steps she has thus far ascended. She pauses briefly but doesn't appear out of breath. Her eyelids slant inward, and she presses her lips firmly together. She tightens her fist then mumbles something. She then takes slow deep breaths to calm some underlying frustration. I can't assist her under the guise of helping her with her groceries as there are none, and I fear hurting her pride by offering her assistance in walking the stairs. Instead, I choose to gently walk at her side at first, slowly watching her steps then almost serving as a guide at her side. She takes note of my ploy.

"Jules, what are you doing?"

"Walking up the steps to my apartment," I say nonchalantly. I am a bad liar and am often so transparent that I feel my avoidance of the truth is printed on my face as I speak. Mrs. Watts admits to having come from the eye doctor, acting as if her eyes had only been dilated.

"Jules dear, you're a pest. I am fine."

I start to recount a particular circumstance warranting help and say, "I wish someone had helped me when—" and she cuts me off as I try to finish my sentence.

"Okay," she retorts, "I will take your arm." I help her climb the stairs to her apartment. She struggles to locate her keys. She struggles to locate the keyhole and is placing her fingers around the hole with more force than warranted, and then, pushes the key into the hole rather ungracefully. I guess Mrs. Watts has difficulty lying too, as she soon admits she has undergone laser treatment to stave off the progression of macular degeneration. I say my goodbyes, pretending to leave as if I am not continuing to observe her failings. In truth, if I know how to help another, I will, even when that someone isn't yet ready to ask for help. Perhaps this is my flaw.

Mrs. Watts turns to me, reiterating her previous contention, "You're a pest, Jules, would you like to come in?" Upon entering, she states in a matter-of-fact tone, "Well yes, it's macular degeneration, and yesterday I didn't recognize your face in the elevator as you entered. It was only later that I realized who you were." She shows me pictures of her grandchildren but can't make out which is which without referencing the pictures carefully and uses the bold coloring and texture of the frames to assist her in making out who is who.

"Mrs. Watts, I can only imagine the frustration you feel at your circumstance."

She nods and says, "I am only seventy-nine, and my husband, Harry, is long gone. I only have myself, so I can't lose myself."

I look at her apartment, noticing some things I can change immediately. Mrs. Watts is quite the put-together woman. Every outfit has a matching pair of shoes and accessories. She is the timeliest in paying her rent and is the first to get mail from the mailbox. I know this because she has, on occasion, made remarks to me about how she never meets me at the mailbox like other tenants. I suppose she loves to read as her dining room is flooded by books, many whose covers attest to their ages. When I first met her years ago, she held not one, but three books in her hands. I soon came to discover that books accompanied her frequently as she was rarely seen without one in hand. The numerous photos that line every room in her house displaying family members indicate the great affection she has for her children and grandchildren. She lets me know that all but one live out of state. I never considered myself a nosy body, perhaps I am, as I find myself rummaging through her home, in search of things that can make life easier.

Mrs. Watts was not the first person I met with macular degeneration. Sadie was. Sadie was a ninety-nine-year-old woman soon to be one hundred. She had a pleasant disposition and was sharp and witty. She was worldly and possessed the ability to be in-tune with those around her, befriending anyone in her midst despite being legally blind. Sadie had been diagnosed with macular degeneration, thus her central vision was compromised. She, too, had undergone laser treatments to stop the progression of the disease, but her eyesight kept failing nonetheless. Sadie would say, "People spend way too much time remembering the dead and not enough time remembering the living." She would know. She had suffered a still-birth shortly after her marriage when she expected to give birth to a daughter. She had lost her husband at age fifty-nine. Her older son passed when she was eighty, and her younger son died the day after her ninety-second birthday. Three of her grandchildren had already passed. One as a result of a motorcycle accident; another two, unfortunately, succumbed to cancer. Sadie had only one living friend who was a mere youngster, age ninety. Her friend lived in another state, and they would generally only chat via phone.

My own problems, unlike Sadie's, arose not from being able to forget the dead but more so from remembering the living. I spent a considerable amount of time avoiding my family, specifically my mother whom I'd have liked to forget. Sadie was correct in one element, I spent too much time mourning the loss of my grandmother; she just continued to exist in everything I did, and not one day went by that I hadn't thought of her.

Sadie was a person to admire. She lived alone and refused any help. She was a self-admitted stubborn woman. She had few pieces of furniture, as she enjoyed the freedom of navigating her environment using her walker. She admitted that, on occasion, she imagined her walker to be a dancing partner and she would twirl it around, holding on tightly. The persistent smell of VapoRub accompanied her, but it wasn't to fend off congestion. She said it relaxed her nasal passages from the lingering smell of gasoline emitted by the gas station, which was located at the end of her block.

Sadie was initially a patient of mine post-right-hip-replacement surgery nine years ago. She subsequently found me, for the second time, in a grocery store and actually recognized my voice, despite her already failing eyesight. She had likened my voice to that of an actress, one whom

I didn't particularly admire, but she said it with such love that I appreciated the comparison. Sadie had this inner peace that was admirable. Her macular degeneration had limited her ability to read, a pastime which she had loved, and made everyday tasks a hardship. She also faced additional safety concerns, preparing food with sharp utensils and with the flames of the burners while she was cooking. She had to be careful when navigating around furniture and to be aware of where there were dents and deviations, tripping hazards, in the flooring of her apartment, noting where they began and ended to avoid falling. She had difficulty locating household items without implementing necessary cues and adaptations. She had to overcome difficulties, such as reading food labels and differentiating between medicine bottles. In addition, she was unable to read the keys on the remote control which controlled her stereo system. This prevented her from finding the accurate controls that enabled listening to her grandchildren's homemade CDs. She wasn't able to find emergency numbers nor the numbers of her friends and relatives that were not yet committed to memory. Additionally, her balance issues were compromising her ability to locate clothing on upper shelves, and she required a raised toilet seat and a grab-bar in the shower.

There were simple modifications like books on tape, enlarged reading materials, voice-activated command technology, applying additional textures to items for touch classification, but what Sadie loved most was the reading group I arranged for her with members of her community. They

164

came and discussed not only current reads but politics. Sadie evidenced a small giggle, almost childlike, as they gathered. This allowed her a forum to share her witty remarks and to gain greater insight about the world around her as she shared her own perceptions. Reinforcing the human bond also made her feel more comfortable taking help from others when she really needed it.

At the conclusion of our last visit, Sadie said, "You're a lifesaver Jules," accompanied by a wink. As she closed the door behind her, she added, "Don't forget to live—truly live."

I turned to her. "I thought that was my line." And Sadie smiled and closed the door. Here was a woman with balance issues who could barely see, who craved interpersonal communication and who engaged in life like a twenty-year-old. Sadie eventually required some homecare for a few hours a day, still she was one of my heroes.

I turn toward the door of Mrs. Watts's apartment, ready to leave, but I can't. I can't because I haven't put in my two cents yet. "Mrs. Watts, I think we can rearrange some of your items to make your life a bit easier." Mrs. Watts looks at me, annoyed, but nevertheless, listens to my suggestions. Before I leave, she makes me some flavored tea with herbs I have never heard of but willingly try. During my lengthy visit, I organize her cabinets with colored bins, quickly retrieved from my apartment, and place food inside by category for easier access. I use a variety of fabrics and materials that she has in her apartment to form little tags glued on to them that will help her feel and differentiate similar objects like keys. She has my teabag in hand and moves less effortlessly when pouring the liquid with the minor strategy I suggested, using the table and counter as a guide.

As I sip my tea, which has an unusual but interesting flavor, Mrs. Watts then asks, "Will you be back tomorrow, Jules?" The phone rings, and she recognizes the name on the phone because her phone is now programmed to announce the caller's name, matching names to numbers and is voice-activated for when she desires to place a call. She lifts the receiver and activates the speakerphone. "Jules, meet Jack, my grandson," she says, and she continues to speak with him with a sparkle in her eyes. As they exchange words, I make my way out of the apartment.

I unlock the door to my apartment, enter, and turn on some classical music, the type that doesn't distract you as you complete your chores. When I raise the volume a bit, I hear the persistent knocking on the wall from my annoying neighbor, Mr. Dawson. In response to the banging, I lower the volume, but shortly after that, raise it ever slightly again. This, once again, elicits Mr. Dawson's loud pounding on the wall. *"Sorry,"* I say, thinking, it is not like it's rock 'n' roll. It's classical music. As I sit down, I note a stain on my coffee table, which I rub vigorously against the backdrop of Beethoven. The flavor of the herbs in Mrs. Watts's tea must be lulling me to sleep, as its barely nine thirty, and I feel the need to hit the sheets. I sleep like a baby at least for the next six hours, waking up refreshed and ready to go.

Today, I leave my humble abode, walk outside and take a short cut by traversing a park. As I pass the outskirts of the park, a stylish woman passes me. She sports a designer handbag and coat, both with very distinguishable logos. Her clothes drape her body well, and they are accented by the sparkle of diamond earrings, which play off of the ray of sunlight. A group of teenagers passes her as well, and as she departs, one young lady, and I use the term loosely, comments in a distinctly audible voice, "Did you see those clothes she was wearing? What a waste. It's a total waste on someone like that."

These kids were degrading the same woman whose beauty I had just admired. Why? because she was in a motorized wheelchair. I could feel my blood starting to rush forward. "I think the clothes suit her just fine, I think she looks refined, elegant, and put together. Perhaps you can take a lesson!" And, as I am speaking, the teenager moves forward and looks down at her boot that has just stepped directly into the dog poop which someone else forgot to clean up. Karma, I thought, just plain karma.

I know it was a teachable moment, and perhaps I should have attempted explanation rather than rebuke, but I find crassness and lack of compassion intolerable. I look back at the teenager who is still wiping her boot clean. Perhaps this incident lends itself to a different interpretation of Aristotle's term, social animal, I thought. We attempt to rise above others in social settings precisely by projecting the wild, ferocious uncouthness of a beast. If this is what human interaction entails, perhaps I choose loneliness. I personally prefer to view humanity as compassionate, disciplined, and restrained. I take one final look at this woman who is already down the block and ruminate, *Besides, that woman carried off her look way better than I could have.*

The surge of energy that accompanied my little rant has made me arrive to work quite early, giving me plenty of time to review my patient roster for the day. I look at the roster and note the title before the names. I see reverend, rabbi, imam, and a few other surprising titles. This conjures up a bit of anxiety. Religion scares me. I attempt to dodge the conversation of religion at all costs. I know it sounds like an old joke, but today I will have the privilege of treating a rabbi, minister, and an imam. "Wow!" I say to Cam, a physical therapist. "What luck I have. Maybe I should play the lottery today."

I walk to the gym, ready for some religious banter to greet me. I imagine a great discourse taking place with theological ideation and life philosophy, sharing commonalities and conflicting viewpoints. I enter the gym, and just as I thought, I see three men shifting in their respective wheelchairs, talking to one another. They look a bit animated, and when I approach, I hear fragments of the conversation. They are discussing their respective dietary restrictions and how they hate the consistency and the taste of hospital food, particularly Jell-O. One observes the perplexed look on my face, asking if I am okay, followed by another one asking, "Why so serious?" and for the duration of their session, they are cordial and willing to work, and not one mentions faith or belief. They are humans, I think, as am I.

Next, I enter the room of a petite, energetic woman who is approaching age ninety. She suffered a transient ischemic attack, like a mini-stroke. Kayla Silver is a feisty woman. Despite her age, she wants to reengage in the world as she had for so many years. She still wants to be able to dance, to prepare gourmet meals for her family members and friends. She wants to continue to quilt and to photograph her great-grandchildren. I examine her arm for strength, muscle tone, and skin integrity. Her balance is somewhat compromised, and she has reduced strength in her right arm. As I move her arm, I come across a group of numbers seared onto her skin like a tattoo, approaching her wrist. I know what those numbers are. I had learned about them in history class, where I had been shown videos but had never seen them etched in real human flesh with my own eyes. Kayla was a Holocaust survivor. I stand there for a few seconds examining the numbers, and Kayla makes eye contact. Apparently, while I examined her arm, she was examining mine. She points to the small tattoo near my wrist and asks, "What does your mark mean?"

I look down at my arm to view my tattoo and find her choice of words interesting, 'mark' versus 'tattoo' or 'symbol'. "It's a symbol of freedom," I say.

After leaving home at eighteen, the first thing I did after finding an apartment was getting a tattoo. The freedom symbol is small, sitting on the internal surface of my wrist, mostly for my own eyes to view. It wasn't an act of rebellion or to show comradery with anyone else. It was a small sign for my own eyes to remind me I am free. Mrs. Silver uses her left hand to assist in lifting her right hand ever so slightly for better viewing of her own numbers. As she does, she explains that these marks were intended to indicate shame and bondage, but, she says, "I am free because I create my own freedom." Mrs. Silver works fervently through the session. As I leave her room, I look down at my own mark. *Are you free, Jules?* I ask myself, but am unable to respond with a resounding yes. My thoughts are interrupted by Stephanie, asking me to join her for lunch in the cafeteria.

During the lunch break, Evette invites Stephanie and me for apple picking during the weekend. But Stephanie declines and says her husband will be back from his travels by then, and they intend on having family time. I, however, readily agree.

The rest of the day passes quickly. I complete my paperwork and am soon ready to go home.

I meet Slate in the hallway. He looks a bit tired but greets me with enthusiasm. He has just come from performing hours-long surgery, restoring and reconstructing critical vascular pathways in a patient. It always surprises me how surgeons walk around human-like after performing long surgeries. It is almost like they have specialized genes for attention, endurance, and patience, aside from the obvious need for sharp eyes and steady hands. He walks toward a computer station as his work is not yet done. He

170

lets me know that it is raining outside. It was not part of the daily forecast, and I hadn't checked the hourly one yet. He, then, asks me to wait for a second as he needs to grab something, and before long, Slate brings me his umbrella.

"Such chivalry," I say, chuckling. I ask him to wait momentarily so I can get my own umbrella from my office and give it to him.

He laughs, "I guess we are both prepared for a storm."

CHAPTER 6: APPLES IN A DAY AND MANY DOCTORS

The rest of the week passes quickly, and I find myself getting ready for apple picking on Saturday morning. I put on a houndstooth skirt with a flared bottom and pair it with a solid black shirt and black boots. I am not sure what one wears to apple picking, but I think it looks good, and I can move freely in it—that is, in case I need to climb some trees.

I meet Evette at a local shop where we enjoy a cup of coffee and croissant before we go. The taste lingers in my mouth as I drive toward the specified location, while Evette confers with some apps to ensure that the weather and traffic are optimal for an anticipated joyous experience. I do enjoy these seasonal outdoor adventures. There is a crispness to the air, and the apples give off a fragrance that reminds me of fresh apple pie. We pick the apples ever so slowly, enjoying each moment, all the while reminiscing about shared life events. There really isn't any tree-climbing, just picking, but my outfit doesn't go to waste. My skirt flows effortlessly as I make my way toward the next apple, and my boots shield my feet from the dirt of a previous day's rainstorm.

Evette takes me aside to inform me of a new job opportunity, and that she will likely be leaving at the end of the year. I meet this news with a sense of loss, but I am also pleased for her. People come and go, I remind myself, and they help us form memories. Evette and I reminisce for the remainder of the trip and bring back a hoard of apples for our fellow co-workers.

I return to work the following Monday with ripe apples and an apple pie, compliments of my grandmother's recipe. I take a few apples upstairs to the pediatric wing. I cut a slice, peeling away the skin, fearing that it could be a choking hazard for young James. James fixates on the apple in my hand, seemingly interested when I present him with the peeled white version instead of the nice, shiny, red version. He is confused, but I show him that it was taken from the interior of the red one, and he takes the slice willingly. He brings it toward his little teeth and begins to crunch away at its edges. "Oh, so you like apples," I say. In his case, though, it won't keep the doctors away, but he continues to crunch while seemingly also enjoying the sound it produces.

I watch for a few moments being overly cautious that he is able to swallow the apple or what is left of it after I scrape away the skin and every questionable dot. Nurse Abbie notices my overly cautious state watching James take bite after bite. Abbie comments, "Don't worry. It is not an apple he is eating; it's a bald, holey fruit . . . You can chill." I smile, not knowing Abbie has a comedic side. I leave some apples for the pediatric staff before making my way downstairs.

Today there would be yet another meeting, this time about hospital financing, not under the guise of patient care. These were the most boring meetings. One would find some colleagues holding back the ever-growing urge to snooze as their eyelids became heavier with each word. Others would spend time crumpling papers, or clicking pens, or twirling writing implements back and forth. Some would gesture at each other.

As I am about to cross the threshold, Dr. McConnel stops me. He is clenching his teeth somewhat as he speaks but asks if I have a moment, and my heart drops. "Jules, would you happen to have the name of a good developmental optometrist? Olivia has been observing Denny a bit more, and the teacher did corroborate your findings. Olivia also finds he has a hard time searching for designated objects in his room."

"Sure," I say, and I observe McConnel's upper lip become less stiff.

He turns back momentarily, adding a "Thank you," as he walks toward the meeting.

The meeting begins, and as usual, I sit and listen, but very few new provisions apply to my area of practice, that is, at least directly. I sit with my full attention, almost playing a game of seek and find, like trying to find the Waldo in their words. They generally won't mention the words "occupational therapy" directly, but I would listen for any related keywords like "therapy," "rehabilitation," "alternative modalities," "equipment," "gym," "functionality," but these are rarely referenced. I count two in total.

I also listen carefully for words like, "benefits," and "insurance," as those words conjure up some fear when I hear them, particularly at meetings discussing costs. I have already heard from the grapevine, via our extensive hospital gossipers, that the hospital intends to change our health insurance policy, and there will likely be higher associated deductibles and co-pays. Thankfully, those words don't come, at least not for now. I make it through the meeting alive and untethered.

One of life's many ironies is that I work for a hospital, which covers my health insurance, and even though I live in one of the most famous cities in the world, it is still difficult to find affordable and accessible health care. I hate to admit it, but I have, on occasion, skipped being treated, either because I wasn't properly insured at the time, like during my youth, or had adequate insurance but felt uneasy taking time off for treatment. When I developed a rash following a short trip to the islands last year, I found that I had to wait three months to see an infectious disease specialist due to few scheduled openings coupled with the need to get a referral from my primary care provider, who initially felt that infectious disease personnel weren't necessary. The hospital allowed me to continue working even given the rash because there was no associated fever, chills, or cough. In truth, it turned out to be just a health scare, nothing more, but the episode left me with some unanswered questions.

I empathize with the hardships the uninsured and under-insured face. I also see the difficulties involved in navigating the insurance world.

Generally, those in inpatient hospital settings are focused on regaining their health and battling their illness with vigor, but once they are discharged, they are often bombarded with a host of administrative and financial stressors that exist, aside from the ongoing continuous care they commonly need. This is a double whammy. The medical profession strongly advises that you not get stressed; it will only exacerbate your symptoms. Yet, there is no direct formulation to ensure that one can go about de-stressing with mounting medical bills, decreased functionality, and limited work opportunities, and all the while having to contend with a stream of caregivers. All this, aside from the continuous medical care they are presently undergoing. For some just getting a ride to the doctor's office, or making contact with an insurance carrier or billing department are feats unto themselves.

I once had a patient who persistently asked during the session if I was certain this therapy was covered by her insurance. It was only after a few sessions that she received an explanation of benefits evidencing proof of payment that she came for therapy in a calm working state.

My next patient is sixty-four and trying to navigate the Medicare system in preparation for her sixty-fifth birthday. She knows she still has time but is quite concerned. She asks me a host of questions, like when she could actually enroll, what the parts of Medicare are, and what coverage, including supplemental insurance, she actually needs. She is particularly concerned, as she suffers from a chronic condition and is asking many questions to explore in what direction her care is going. I advise her of the personnel in the hospital to direct that question to, but to assuage her fears for the moment, I provide her with tidbits of information as we engage in therapeutic activity. She works so effortlessly through her session, almost automatically, as her brain focuses on financial matters. She even provides a two out of ten for pain, which she reported had been six out of ten just a few hours ago. Her session is over, and I wheel her back to the waiting room. As soon as she enters, she gets her purse, taking out a host of crumpled papers, and while saying, "Thank you," begins going through them with great speed, speed I didn't know she was capable of.

The hallway is filled with people apparently waiting to enter a particular patient's room. They take turns, one or two at a time, and I wonder who this person is who commands such attention. I peek in to find it's a little old woman who is a grandmother. She kisses each person as they enter. *Oh, grandmothers,* I think, *the kingdoms they run.* But my next patient isn't a sweet and innocent little grandmother, it's a nineteen-year-old gang member.

Sometimes you know whom you are treating and other times you don't. Early in my career, a man had requested me as his therapist. I felt elated by the request, assuming that he sought me out for my skill. I entered his room with enthusiasm. The man was gracious and allowed me to tape his shoulder for improved stability. He complimented my work and agreed to perform all the exercises I recommended. I felt quite productive, almost leaving the session with a spring in my step. He was a particularly put-together individual, and I noticed the pin that graced his lapel. It was vaguely familiar, but I couldn't place where I had seen it before.

That night I went home researching on the web for an image that bore resemblance to the pin. My weary eyes zeroed in on the small letters inscribed on the pin—it symbolized a supremacist group. *"That can't be right,"* I whispered under my breath. I maximized the screen and zoomed in a bit, wiping my eyes for greater clarity. The visual once again confirmed the truth. The symbol jogged a memory from my youth. There was a guy that fixed my father's equipment in our garage. His white T-shirt had a novel pin. As he approached my father with the news that he needed additional parts to resume working, my father vehemently pushed me back. I wondered why my meek father was so forceful that day. I wondered whether he felt I was not competent to understand or worthy of understanding his machinery.

After a bit of reflection as to the composition of the staff on that day, the day I was assigned to this gentleman, I realized that I was the only one with pale skin. It wasn't my skill; it was my skin color. The man returned for his next session, proudly stating that he had done his homework. My enthusiasm was replaced with terror and confusion, but I continued through the rehabilitation process until he achieved his goals. I was drained. I worked through the sessions like a robot, afraid to think. I forced myself to be cordial, but the hypocrisy was gnawing at my existence. As I improved his being, I felt my own humanity losing bits of itself. This memory brought me back to the present. This time, I am armed with information. I walk toward Kenny's room. He is a gang member, and now I know whom I am dealing with. I stop off briefly to drop some additional apple treats at Dr. McConnel's office. It was reminiscent of the apple placed on the teacher's desk. I know he has had a hard day. I then continue on my way toward Kenny's room. When I finally lay eyes on the nineteen-year-old before me, I wonder if I truly do know whom I am dealing with, because my observations are inconsistent with my preconceived notions.

Kenny was rendered a paraplegic following a gunshot wound ensuing from a heated exchange with other gang members. I admit that my exposure to gang members has been significantly limited, and that all the knowledge I have amassed about them was based upon information disbursed by the media. I had anticipated meeting a muscular, well-trained, tough guy who would dismiss my presence in a harsh voice. As I enter the room, I find a small-framed nineteen-year-old, with a curious smile on his face.

I introduce myself. "My name is Jules."

Taking note of my lab coat, he interrupts me, "The doctor was already here."

"I am not a doctor; I am a member of the rehabilitation team. I'm an occupational therapist, and I am here to do an evaluation."

He looks more confused and asks, "Oh, you're going to help me get a job?" Once again looking up and down peculiarly at my white lab coat.

"No, lots of people think that I am here to help them find a job." I elaborate a bit further, "Basically, at different life stages, people sometimes have a hard time doing something they used to do, and they may need to find a new way of doing it or relearn how to do something the way they had done it before. I help people learn to eat, dress, bathe, transfer themselves. I also help them learn to do activities that they enjoy and find meaningful." I take a deep breath, hoping he has understood me thus far. "Is there a particular activity you like to do?"

Kenny looks at me like an alien invader. Apparently, no one had ever asked him what he liked to do. I would learn that his father had been killed in a shoot-out in his home, and when he backed up to protect his then girlfriend, Kenny's mom, in a weird twist of fate, she fell on to a shelf and suffered a hematoma. They both succumbed to their wounds, and Kenny ended up living with his grandmother. He had witnessed his parents' death, and I detected from his lack of shock at having been injured, that he had anticipated that something like this would ultimately be his fate, as well. I would also learn that his grandmother's health was failing, and he had recently broken up with his girlfriend because she cheated on him with a rival gang member. Kenny is pleasant, organized, has a great memory, and is detail-oriented. He knows everyone's name and is good at reading people. I do a thorough evaluation and leave the room, still looking back at the small creature that has lived a life basically on the streets.

I attend an office party for Evette, the physical therapist who is moving to Seattle. She has been my partner in crime for the last six years. We had a competitive comradery going, but she was always a welcome addition to the team—efficient, thorough, and caring with her clients. The party buffet is filled with a host of different sauces and dips. Their colors are comprised of many shades, and they create that party feel when entering the room. The various aromas that waft through the air further differentiate the office from the sterility of the hospital. I am a chips and dips kind of girl. I delight in a persistent flow of crunchy stuff in my mouth. I take a brief sampling of the dips situated near the entrance of the room. Stephanie joins soon after that. I thank Evette for her professionalism and friendship throughout the last few years, wishing her well. A few members of the medical staff are sampling the dips at the corner of the room and shaking their heads in agreement. I move closer to the red and orange sauces. A few apple cobblers are sitting there, complements of my apple picking. I bump into Stephanie as she whispers, "I have a seven-minute break. What should I taste?" I motion toward the door at the various samplings I have tried and then move toward the corner. Stephanie decides to follow. I dip some pita bread into the dip and immediately turn around, holding my throat. I squint.

Stephanie looks concerned, thinking that I may be choking. Her concern soon turns to a loud laugh as she observes me waving my hands at my mouth to make the heat that's emanating dissipate.

"Wow!" I say. "This gives hot sauce a whole new meaning." I still feel that sting in my eyes, or maybe it is really the burn in my ears that had made its way to my eyes. Stephanie lifts the sauce toward her mouth. A look of surprise crosses her face. I stand there waiting for the full effect of the tasting, but nothing happens.

Stephanie continues to take more pita with a few dips and smiles, "It is not really that hot, Jules."

"What do you mean, it's not that hot? I almost died!" The sensation of heat lingers in my throat, but to prove something to myself, I take another shot at the hot stuff, and with each bite, its effects decrease, but a distinct sting is still present. "Don't ever say I don't give things a second chance!" Evette and Stephanie laugh, and I embrace Evette.

"Oh, Jules, I will miss you," Evette says. "There is no one else who can make a dip that much fun."

The only thing burning worse than my mouth is the skin of my foot. Aside from the general discomfort of designer high heels which I foolishly decided to wear to work today, the insole of my shoe is coming apart. Even the hefty price I paid for these shoes hasn't deterred the shoe from taking this course. Comfort and beauty can't go together, at least not until a worthy voice in the fashion industry will come work for hours on end in a hospital. I can feel every crevice and little bump of the floorboards, and I feel myself walking with inappropriate weight shifts to even out my gait. The small bead that entered my shoe unbeknownst to me this morning is making its rounds under my foot. When I finally take a look and shake out my shoe, I find some respite from the discomfort, and a sigh of relief exits my mouth. When I am wearing a good walking shoe, I don't gauge every step as if it were a life form of its own. I don't sense the unleveled ground or the mild slickness in the flooring of the cafeteria. Thankfully, I have the option of changing this annoyance with a good pair of shoes, but apparently, I am still high on the vanity scale, often opting for the attractiveness of designer shoes.

Some people are hypersensitive to the world around them. Every brush and stroke of the wind against their cheek is magnified. The sensation of a spritz of lemon on their fish is like diving into lemonade. Some people enter their new home to feel encompassed by the scent of fresh wood, while others are oblivious, focusing only on its beauty. Some people chew, grinding their food like a well-milled machine, others barely notice the half-eaten pieces dancing in their mouths. Some people are attuned to every color in their environment, basking in small visual details, while others are oblivious to changes in color at all. My mouth still dances from the hot sauce, but it has significantly dissipated, and now my feet, in the absence of my designer heels which I have briefly taken off, allow me to feel the floor without too much or too little pressure, and for these, I am grateful.

People are all subject to the same environment, yet we all experience it in our very own unique way. I see James in my mind's eye. The child is overstimulated by everything because for so long every touch, sound, and sight created pain. This time I take the elevator to his room, thankful that I don't need to walk the staircase to get there. James is in his room and makes eye contact with me. A subtle differentiation of color in his green eyes is evident. His eyes are more alive and colorful. They have a certain beauty to them, perhaps revealing his soul. He glares at me, looking down at my hobbling feet and my designer shoes now minus the bead. I acknowledge that they make me walk funny and exaggerate my walk even more. A small speckle of happiness crosses his face. The apple must have spurred his appetite because, at least today, he is eating something without it being shoved down his throat. I notice the many dislikes on his plate. "Oh! You poor child," I murmur, imagining that he too has had his fair share of hot sauce today.

He turns his face and eyes toward me, and although no voice is produced, his lips move as if he wants to say something. He takes the sailboat at his side, displaying it before me, as if saying, "I remember you. You came back," and continues, albeit slowly, dipping his spoon into his food in small increments.

Oh, James, I think, *Your poor little body has been distressed by little changes like a pair of high-heeled shoes with a bead rolling in them.* The good thing about me is I try not to make the same mistake twice, at least not the exact same mistake, and I make a mental note to wear my walking shoes tomorrow.

On my way out, there is a commotion, and the staff has convened at the nurses' station. I overhear that the chair of pediatrics has left early. I hear her son's name and the word "overdose." I freeze. My one leftover apple rolls out of the bag onto the floor toward the wall. It is no longer whole and sparkling red but gashed and broken, and I throw it out.

Once at home, I find myself craving a bit of shopping, like it will make something better because if I add something to my wardrobe, it will subtract some pain. Despite the condition of my shoe, I walk slowly to the store, purchase two really expensive sweaters, and then slowly walk home. I have a moment of happiness, noting that the main semblance of my shoes has remained. I watch the cabs go by, thinking that maybe I should hail one even for a short distance, but I don't.

I go home to clean out my closet. I couldn't resist those two beautiful sweaters, knowing that I will likely feel guilty about the purchase tomorrow. For now, I have to find a place to store them. I step inside the closet, rummage through my clothing, and the door starts to close behind me. The closet is quite small, and I can feel my chest rising and falling a bit heavier with anxiety. I can feel the shoebox effect magnified by three. I don't ever recall feeling this in my own closet. It is likely the day's stress getting to me, as I visualize Rigby's face, the boy I believe has overdosed.

I remember another occasion that spurred a similar effect. I recall the day I failed to practice good body mechanics when transferring a nearly completely dependent client, and I felt a wave of heat and pain emanate from my shoulder. I had always had a modified way of transferring my weight, as I had suffered a broken ankle in my childhood. This time I failed to make my usual compensations and felt the force going through my right shoulder as I completed the task. I wasn't certain it had been torn, but felt

185

a deep swelling through my arm. I completed a series of self-administered clinical tests, trying to figure out where the injury occurred, but it's super hard to diagnose one's self.

Well, I needed an MRI, and as they shifted my body under the machine, I felt a sense of panic wash over me. I was surprised that I felt so claustrophobic. It felt like I was being buried underground. I remember not being able to breathe for a few seconds and kept telling myself to pretend I was sleeping, so as not to fear the dark. I kept my eyes closed for most of the full forty-five-minute session. About twenty minutes in, as I lay there, eyes closed, my mind turned to my childhood. My mother often placed me in closets as a child when I "misbehaved". It varied between closets and the boiler room in the basement. I much preferred the boiler room, although the boiler room wasn't a five-minute punishment like the closet. It would generally be half an hour or more, depending on when someone remembered to fetch me. I never really knew what I had done wrong. I was made aware of my vices on only two occasions. "You should have put the cereal box back in the cabinet after you were done with it," is one I recall. "You left your school books on the dining room table overnight" is another.

For the most part, I was a good kid. I tried extra hard to put my possessions and food back in their proper spaces. When I was in the basement, I both feared and enjoyed the punishment. The basement was raw and dark, but I pretended that the boiler was my captive audience. It was there that I would allow myself to sing and dance without judgment. At one point, the washing machine was placed opposite the boiler, albeit briefly, and I recall curtsying to both the boiler and washing machine after singing a song I heard on the radio in my friend's parent's car. I know I dislike spending too much time in the closet. I don't think most people really enjoy time in there. Yet, my strong reaction to being in the enclosed MRI machine was most unexpected. My bursa, the cushioning in my shoulder, was inflamed a bit, but after religiously using an anti-inflammatory, over-the-counter medicine for two weeks, I was able to carry on with my job.

Apparently, I developed this lingering hatred for enclosed spaces, which I initially hadn't realized existed in my psyche. I remember asking a patient with severe obsessive-compulsive disorder what he feels like, and he drew himself locked in a box. For the first time, as I lay under the MRI scan, I had a true understanding of what he meant in both a literal and figurative sense.

As I emerge from the closet, I receive a phone call from Nurse Abbie. "Rigby has passed," she says with a tremble in her voice. She provides me with funeral information. I go back into the closet for just a few minutes, sit on the floor, and allow myself a couple of tears. I remember Rigby. I can visualize the spring in his step and the animation of his face as he made small talk with everyone in the pediatric staff when he visited. He had only met me a few times but remembered that my favorite flower was a peony. He remembered Abbie's favorite drink and recalled each kid's favorite activity. He had a beautiful smile, and his body had still retained some baby fat.

There is a solemn mood the next day as I enter the hospital. Many staff members will be attending the funeral later that day, and the sense of the death of one of our own continues to linger even though the sun is bright and warm today. I walk into Kenny's room. He is in good spirits. He is apparently speaking to his roommate, a twenty-nine-year-old quadriplegic, in an attempt to entertain him. The nurses tell me that Kenny reminds them when his roommate is due for another round on the tilt table, a means of providing him with some necessary movement and circulation. As we work on Kenny's hand strength to better enable him to propel his wheelchair, I notice that he keeps looking at a brown bag near his bed. He admits that he saved some of his lunch to share with his cousin who is coming to visit later on. As usual, he is sure to say, "Thank you," as I make my way out the door. When I turn back for a moment, Kenny is checking in on his roommate, asking if he is okay.

I walk into my next client's room. She has a rotator cuff injury of the shoulder but is also a stage three chronic kidney disease patient. I look over at her almost empty plate from lunch, which consists of protein-dense food, good for the muscles, bad for the kidney, and I wonder why she was provided with this meal given her restrictions. She looks at me in a state of almost euphoria stating, "The food was good." She likely hadn't eaten that much protein in a while, and now felt a sense of satiation that had eluded her. I look at her chart which lists doctors' orders, medications, contraindicated medications, and in large bold letters, I see "no contrast" with her CT scan order. Her file lists a host of doctors, coupled with ailments that have plagued her over the year. Yet, someone with pages of orders and ailments has just consumed quite an elaborate meal. Somewhere a gap has been left open, or miscommunication has taken place.

There is this concept of clinical reasoning that therapists and medical personnel need to employ. In layman's terms, it is the mental processes, and the use of mental resources that guide us in planning, directing, and executing an effective solution. It also incorporates the way we observe our patients and the way we reflect upon our solutions. As a child, I had the same pediatrician for years. When I transitioned into adulthood, I remember the first time I went to an "adults'" doctor. I remember being in awe of this man that really seemed to understand the workings of the human body. He always had a good sense of what was wrong and could be heard thinking aloud about why he was ordering one test or another. He didn't order tests by rote or prescribe medications by frequency of advertisement. I didn't know it at the time, but Dr. Lungy, as I called him, had been a doctor for forty-five years. When you really know and understand subject matter, you can augment information from everything and everywhere simultaneously. I aspired to be someone like him, who knew what, when, and how to provide care, and who could justify why I chose and utilized a specific treatment. Somehow, over time, there developed this discrepancy between medicine based upon protocol and medicine based upon the individualized need. I surmise that protocol was, in fact, created to provide the practitioner with a basis upon which to think and reflect rather than a means to impede our thinking process. The medical practitioners of yesteryear seemed to have achieved medical standards by blending protocol with flexibility naturally. I am generally not consulted for my opinion and don't expect to be, given my low standing on the medical totem pole, but what I think has been lost is practicality, unity in practice, and the basics of listening and observing.

There are those in the medical field that do research and publish hundreds of articles but never deal with real people's problems. There are those that can read many scans and x-rays, MRIs, and CT scans but have no idea where to actually spot an organ in the absence of a device, such as the liver, upon palpation. There are so many co-morbidities in sick people, yet doctors of various disciplines rarely seem to collaborate, and that's why I often see patients whose medications are changed more regularly than their underwear, who, as a result, suffer many side effects. Have you ever noticed a diabetic's lunch plate in a hospital, like blintzes and fruit juice, or the patient that is being prescribed a diuretic, when their skin is already dried out like a prune? Worse yet, patients have been wakened to administer the prescribed medication that his or her doctor had ordered to help them fall asleep. And, my least favorite of all occurrences in a hospital is when medical staff, unwilling to admit that they don't know how to treat something, convince their patients of their need for improved mental health, saying that they need to be more hopeful and keep a positive attitude and might be helped by psychological counseling, while dismissing the patient's concerns. It is not that medical practitioners are bad, it is just that somewhere along the line, they have become part of this alternate universe that just does certain things because that's what they do, without additional thought or reason. Besides, who could have the skill necessary to diagnose and treat effectively based on a few-seconds interview and a one-minute physical. For those physicians that choose to reason further, or take additional time to hear their patient's full story are often deemed inefficient in the eyes of the healthcare world, as they are not treating as many patients in a given time frame with the proven standardized techniques. I hate to admit it, but as time goes on, the vortex is pulling me further into this black hole, from which I am not sure I can emerge. Perhaps this is a new form of claustrophobia, being in your own clinical box.

Stephanie and Slate accompany me to the funeral. We all had interacted with Rigby in some capacity. His funeral, unlike others I have attended, is primarily composed of young faces, faces that will have opportunities that Rigby will not. We return to work with a heaviness in our hearts. A nice, good kid, from a good family, with wealth and a good education, died because of a one-time overdose, at least that's what we have been led to believe. It's mind-boggling, and yet it makes as much sense as most other tragedies—which don't. We sit around during our lunch break discussing the matter, and to lighten the mood, Kevin asks, "What would you want written on your tombstone?" He responds first. "The most-liked person in town. No, scratch that, the most-liked person on the planet."

Stephanie pipes up, "Loving mother, daughter, and wife, tolerable daughter-in-law, and a heck of a physician."

"Good friend!" I add, to which Stephanie blushes and smiles.

Slate doesn't respond at first, but then says, "Jack-of-all-medicine, master of the liver."

Evette: "Never stopped loving to live and went searching for the best restaurants," adding "The ravioli I had last weekend was fantastic!"

I like that one, I think, but I find it hard to articulate what I want. After a slight pause, I say, "Not lazy, sense of right and wrong, truth-seeker."

Kevin interjects, "That sounds like a boring old man's obituary. Jazz it up a bit."

I look out the window and see a cloud. "Led a peaceful and productive existence, and was as free as a sugar-free double-fudge ice cream sundae," I say.

Chase winks, "That's a bit better, Jules."

I have only had a few of my clients succumb to their illnesses, but when they did, their passing struck me very hard as if they had been a member of my own family. In my line of work, there is a close level of intimacy with my clients. I physically transfer them and wrap and bandage them. I learn a lot about their lives, their level of strength, dexterity, cognitive skills, physical ailments, and coordination. I also learn about the layout

192

of their house, their caregivers, their motivations, their goals, and their job requirements. I get to see the childhood enthusiasm in some when they are ready to master a goal, and the fear of failure and sadness at relearning something which they previously deemed simple. I have watched patients struggle to relearn to eat, toilet, and turnabout in bed—the simple tasks comprising our day. I have seen them struggle, wanting so badly to do something when they just can't. I've seen some who are extremely direct and blunt. I've seen others whose body language is in direct contrast with the words they say, and yet others who are seemingly fearful of saying anything at all. I have sometimes become the object upon which they direct their anger and frustration. Some are lonely, while others are overburdened with caring for their families. Some try to hide their pain and anguish, while others accentuate it, attempting to send me the message that they need compassion. Some are happy to have survived, and others wish they hadn't. Some ask me to come closer and assist them. Others ask me to give them more space to try. They often don't know it, but they are never just another "body" to me. I, too, share many of their own insecurities, they are just manifested in a different manner and in a different context.

One of my earliest patients was Jessica Mann. Jessica was a twenty-six-year-old girl. I say girl because she looked so youthful, like a sixteen-year-old. She had undergone a mastectomy following a breast cancer diagnosis. Some lymph nodes were removed as well. Jessica was a petite blonde-haired young woman with big brown eyes. One could barely notice her presence when her small frame was wrapped under a blanket. Her parents had mentioned that she had always been a perpetual smiler, and when she saw me, she tried to fake a smile. At first, she graded her pain level as four, but I could see her grimacing and grinding her teeth. I asked her again what her pain level was. Initially, she hesitated, so I told her that most people have pain with swelling after this surgery, and as a result, she admitted it was a seven. I demonstrated how her pillows should be placed under her affected arm to support it. I also encouraged correct posture, as Jessica tended to favor slouching post-surgery, which was not the best biomechanical position for functional movement and drainage. She was provided with exercises for range of motion and improved flexibility coupled with lymph drainage techniques. In retrospect, Jessica reminded me of Slate. She tried so hard to be an optimist with an underlying fake smile, never groaning or asking for any pain meds, only taking what was given. A part of her was stripped away. I felt naked without my jewelry and accessories in the workplace, yet what she had lost was much more; it was part of her personhood. The scar extended across part of her upper chest, and I was told she loved to play volleyball at the beach. She always tried to look away, refraining from eye contact. I think she didn't want me to see the truth. Her eyes held physical pain compounded by emotional pain that was hidden far deeper than her surgery wounds. "You have really lovely eyes, Jessica," I said.

She turned to me, and her eyes opened really wide, almost glowing from the hospital lighting. She shot me one of those fake smiles and said, "Thank you," in a soft voice. Jessica's journey was far from over; she was anticipated to undergo reconstructive surgery down the road, and it wasn't like I could tell her the source of her pain was in the past, and that she should put it behind her and move forward.

"It's okay to be angry or sad or feel whatever you feel as long as you keep working toward getting better. You don't have to hide it, or you will be carrying an emotional weight on your shoulders, which is far heavier than the extra fluid." Tears streamed down her face, which she tried to wipe away as fast as they came. "It's okay. Leave them. It's cathartic."

I didn't tell anyone, but after that meeting, I went into the bathroom, feeling an overwhelming sensation, like a balloon that was about to burst. I was surprised by the lack of tears, which I thought would have flooded my face. Before long, Jessica left the hospital, ready for the next step in her medical journey. She waved good-bye, and although I did not see her again, I heard through the grapevine that years later, she became a social worker helping battered women. My interaction with Jessica taught me to deflect shame and accept vulnerability.

I don't want to go home today to my empty shoebox apartment. Death can make people's loneliness almost tangible, so I go to Stephanie's house.

I love visiting Stephanie's house. I definitely frequent her house more than anyone else's. She knows better than to expect perfection from

195

herself as a mom, yet, she is the best mom I know. She spends quality time with her kids and always makes it clear that she is there to listen to them. She also makes me feel like part of the family. Tonight, she is serving spaghetti and meatballs, not my favorite meal, but the ambiance is definitely well worth it.

Lee, Stephanie's younger son, isn't that great at catching both a meatball and noodles on his fork. With little warning, while attempting to catch a meatball, his bowl suddenly bounces off the table, half of its contents landing on the table, and the other half falling to the floor. As it flies through the air, some of it, primarily the noodles and sauce, lands on Lee's hands and torso. I freeze in anticipation of what is forthcoming, but Lee just steadies himself, trying to re-fill his bowl with some of the meatball and spaghetti from the table, and then further dirties his hands while brushing off some food from his clothes. Stephanie grabs a dishrag, gives him a sweet smile, and starts to wipe a few noodles that flew over his eyes, sticking to his forehead. She encourages him to come and help her clean up the mess, and as he comes to her side, she grabs his hand, looks at his sauce-filled palm, and draws the shape of a heart. She then places the rag in his hands and says, "Let's clean up." She encourages Sam, her older son, to get a mop and makes clean up into a race. Within no time, the kitchen reverts back to its original form, and Lee gets an additional serving of spaghetti and meatballs, this time with a lesson on improved utensil use.

Stephanie's daughter, Lilly, ties a bedsheet around her neck and steals her mother's pearls, which she further binds and interlaces into a container head, forming a nice crown. Lilly prances around the hallways using a baton as her scepter and curtseys at everyone around her. Her brothers sigh and smile as they had apparently become accustomed to her play. Stephanie grins at her daughter, also giving a mild side-eyed look of disapproval when her eyes meet the pearls bouncing off Lilly's head.

"I really should mete out some kind of punishment for her taking my jewelry without permission, but the truth is I enjoy these little vignettes way more than my jewelry pieces. I loved dressing up as a child. I was usually a bride though, not a princess," Stephanie confesses. "How about you, Jules?"

"How about me, what?"

"What did you enjoy dressing up as?"

I couldn't really recall dressing up as anything, except for two occasions when I dressed up for school plays. Once I was a mountain (which covered my torso and most of my face, so I am not even sure anyone saw me), and the other time, I played a nosy old neighbor that gossips and was not particularly liked by the rest of the community. Everyone else in the play was young and liked.

"So, you never dressed up? Not even for Halloween or costume parties?"

"No, I guess not."

Stephanie continues, "I am sure you took a rag or towel or box and turned it into something else."

"Sorry, still no, not that I recall." In truth, I never even thought about my lack of dressing up in costume or disguise.

It had never been part of my self-reflection, but when Stephanie asked, there was a level of concern in her voice. "You didn't dress up because there weren't opportunities or because it didn't interest you?"

"I am not sure, maybe a bit of both." *It is strange because I am drawn to color, accessories, differentiation of form, imagination, so why hadn't I ever dressed up?* I thought. I could recall my brother dressing up on Halloween, but he seemed to always be wearing black costumes, regardless of what character he portrayed.

I fall asleep quickly in Stephanie's guest room, snuggling into her comfortable bedsheets, only to be woken up at 4:17 a.m. by what I think is some kind of wreckage or bomb. I soon find out it's Lilly jumping on her bed on the floor above.

When she is done jumping on the bed, semi-dressed Lilly is in the kitchen taking out the ingredients to make French toast and is waiting for her mother to do the actual cooking. I offer to do it instead, knowing that Stephanie works really hard and deserves to sleep in a bit. Her daughter guides me throughout the process as if I have never made French toast before. She lists the ingredients and helps me put them together until the end product is on the table. Lilly takes out a heart-shaped cookie cutter. "Here," she says, as she nearly forces my hand onto the French toast,

198

"Make hearts!" Her brother, Lee, joins her at the table, and he smacks his lips as he eats, savoring each bite.

Lilly says, "Yum," as she devours the French toast before her.

"Jules, you should make *your* kids French toasts," she says, "You know, when you have kids. It's good."

Stephanie makes her way downstairs. She goes directly to a cabinet, getting a mixing bowl and utensils. She then finds the soiled utensils soaking in the dishpan, and notices the frying pan on the stove. "Jules, thanks," she says.

Her daughter whispers, "Jules makes good French toast."

"Maybe I should ask you for pointers?" Stephanie responds with a small giggle.

We make our way to work, as Stephanie speaks into her phone, creating a list of chores that still need to be done.

The hospital is having a new data system installed, and the bustle of IT workers on our floor makes my head spin. As I make my way to James's room on the pediatric unit, I pass a group of children sitting in wheelchairs, some with breathing tubes. I hope to make my visit with James memorable, so I bring in the big gun of the pediatric wing, Calvin. Calvin is four years old. He suffers from a rare metabolic disorder. He has been subject to constant monitoring since birth. Calvin dons his cheerful smile accented by roly-poly cheeks. Calvin loves to paint. I think, if given the opportunity, he would happily paint all over himself. Calvin is cheerful and the most outgoing and easygoing child on the wing. He is truly resilient.

Calvin comes in with me, dragging an IV line with Nurse Abbie's assistance. Another nurse carries the paint, as Calvin's grip isn't that great, and some paints have nearly made their way onto Calvin's hospital gown. I know that James's mother was an artist and am not certain how he would react to the paints. Calvin knows how to be enthusiastic and patient at the same time. It is a rare trait.

I was surprised when permission had actually been granted to go ahead with the activity. Even Nurse Abbie was shocked that the wing had granted permission for Calvin to use paints, given their obsession with sterility. Dr. Carter, who has been taking Dr. Kalmar's place as chief of pediatrics, has forewarned that we need to repeatedly wipe down any surfaces should this little get-together with paints be allowed. I willingly agreed. I carry some sheets of paper and place a tray table with some additional paper over the bed.

Calvin approaches James like a big brother would, instinctively protective. Upon their meeting, Calvin exclaims, "Hi cutie!" and then turns to his paper. Calvin starts to paint rapidly using his finger. I push back his tubes to protect them from being in the line of fire, and James watches his friend paint with a new level of interest. I then hand a paintbrush to Calvin which he instinctively knows to share with James. James actually takes it and starts to form lines as Calvin guides him. Calvin enjoys the role of leader and provides intermittent directives to enhance James's painting experience. James can form a line but isn't yet able to draw circles even with imitation, whereas Calvin has mastered shape form and is advanced for his age. James then looks on in horror when Calvin dips his hands in paint, creating a paint print of his hands and looks at me for a reaction. Calvin starts to laugh, making his pudgy cheeks bounce up and down further. Suddenly, Calvin looks a bit unsteady as he attempts to sit up further.

He notices my facial expressions of concern, immediately responding, "I'm okay." He has been sick for so long that he instinctively knows what to say to concerned grown-ups.

I take the opportunity to create a heart in Calvin's palm for which he smiles proudly, takes some of his own paint, and attempts to form a heart in my hand as well. His imitation is quite good, but he hasn't yet mastered a sophisticated heart shape, rendering his like a circle with a dip. I muster some courage and take a deep breath, and then with a smile on my face, take James's hand and draw a heart. It shocks me that he doesn't withdraw his hand.

Then I interlock my finger with James's to form a heart, to which Calvin exclaims, "So cool," and keeps trying to mimic the motion independently. Calvin speaks a mile a minute in a calm and low voice, while James remains silent throughout the whole exchange. Finally, Calvin pipes up and, in a curious tone, with his face in James's personal space, says, "Does your mouth have a boo-boo?"

James's body tenses up, which alerts my concern for the repercussions of this meeting. *Perhaps,* I think, *this wasn't the best idea.* Then Calvin continues, "I have lots of boo-boos too, and I come here to make them better." Calvin is so wise; I could have kissed him if hospital rules were otherwise. Just then, Nurse Abbie walks in with both Calvin's and James's lunches. She takes a look at the paints, raises and draws her eyebrows in a manner I have never seen, then removes the paint from the room. Calvin independently washes his hands while James remains in the same spot he has been since I walked in. Yet this time, he sticks out his hand in my direction, waiting for me to assist in hand-washing without any further prompting. I wipe every surface clean more than once, even chipping my newly manicured nail, and then cover every surface available with towel paper. James watches as Calvin nearly devours his food, for which Nurse Abbie has to slow him down; James picks at his food but eats better than usual.

As the chief of pediatrics hasn't returned yet, the mood is still somber in the hallways. The lightness that Calvin has brought to the room is soon overshadowed by yet another event. Outside, three nurses stand huddled together close to a woman. I can hear the sound of sobbing that ranges from soft to gut-wrenching crying emanating from the group. I cannot make out the figure of the woman that is the focus of the group, but she appears to be leaning against something with her arms firmly pressed against her chest. My feet carry me slowly, as a part of me isn't ready for the bad news that I know is inevitable, given the scene I witness. As I reach the halfway mark toward my target, I can see her face. It is Mrs. Okamoto.

When we first met, she firmly stated, "My name is Aimi." She pointed to her son, "He is Sora." Aimi has been married for fourteen years. She suffered a miscarriage a year after her marriage, which would be followed by three more, and then seven years ago was blessed with a son. Sora was a beautiful child and well behaved. He began having bouts of cold-like symptoms at age four, which were dismissed as being nothing more than a common cold. As the family had moved between states, he had just begun a new school. However, a few months passed, and Sora still appeared weak with cold-like symptoms.

After the doctor's visit, the Okamoto family's life was turned upside down. Sora was diagnosed with an aggressive form of cancer. Neither Aimi nor her husband had ever had any family members diagnosed with cancer. They knew it was a devastating diagnosis but were unprepared for what would come. Sora underwent chemotherapy, then experimental drugs, and constant testing. They moved yet again, closer to a facility that specialized in children's cancers, but their efforts didn't reap any rewards. After close to three years, they returned home to NYC. Aimi had watched her son's beautiful silky and soft hair disintegrate. His nails became discolored. His body color changed often, and his eyes, which had been full of life, dulled more each day.

The first time I met Aimi was seven months ago. Her son had already been in the pediatric wing for a month, but I had never run into either of them. It was only when I went out to pick some fresh fruit from a vendor cart that I encountered this woman, allowing me to pass her in line. She followed me back into the hospital, pushing the elevator button to the pediatric wing. It was the next time we met, and she remembered me, that she pointed out her son, and gave an elaborate picture of the struggles her family had endured those many months.

The pediatric wing did not generally host terminally ill children. They were usually under the care of specialized facilities, but although no one stated it outright, Sora was basically expected to remain here until his death. Aimi spent her days at the hospital, just as she had at all the other facilities. She once confided in me that her son's name meant 'sky'. The day he was born, there was a clear blue sky, and she had hoped his life would be smooth sailing. Her husband had given up a lucrative life in Japan to come to the U.S. and build a life with her. She now felt guilty for having him leave Japan. She felt guilty for not protecting her son. She felt guilty for her previous miscarriages. She felt guilty for not including her parents and in-laws more frequently in her child's illness; perhaps they could have made more successful suggestions for methods of recovery. She had missed so much work during the early stages of her son's illness that she had to give up her job. Here she was, a thirty-six-year-old caregiver, who was jobless and in debt due to her son's medical bills and travel expenses. She had overlooked everything so long as her son lived, and there was a chance he would survive.

But today, her hope was extinguished. The day she dreaded had finally come. Aimi held her son's hand as he passed. There were no marching bands, no full-page newspaper announcements, no alerts on TV that Sora Okamoto had passed. There were three nurses huddled around a woman whose world was shattered, but few people in the world were aware. The sky was mainly clear, with one overstated cloud hanging above. Sora barely had family here; half lived in Japan while the other half resided on the other side of the United States. Aimi was the only relative in her son's room as he passed. What could one say to someone after this kind of loss?

I have been fortunate to have a career that centers around rehabilitation, and a few severely ill patients have crossed my path. I have, however, a lingering thought. There are those that suffer the shock of an unexpected loss, failing to say their goodbyes. Their families often don't have the mental preparation for their imminent death. Others suffer for years, dying ever so slowly. Their every moan and groan acknowledged, but they get to say good-bye, and family members are often prepared for their passing. Who is more unfortunate?

The pediatric wing was now in mourning over two boys' deaths. One family is shocked and unprepared, having just witnessed a vibrant, functional child die in the midst of his beauty and youth. The other family has suffered through watching a loved one slowly lose himself physically and as often happens, spiritually and mentally, as well. Is one more fortunate than the other? When are relatives entitled to grieve more passionately? I once heard someone tell a family member of a man who died from complications from illness at age eighty, "He was really sick; it's a good thing that he won't suffer any longer."

I don't know if that is entirely true. *Was it because he was eighty or because he was ill?* I thought. *Does his family not get a pass to grieve with fervor?* There stood three nurses who had become like family to Aimi and Sora, and their silence and tears spoke volumes. I make eye contact with Aimi, and her eyes seem to give me permission to come closer, so I walk towards her and hug her. Despite my best efforts, I couldn't draw any tears, but I squeezed her hand and slipped her my card saying, "If you need someone to talk to . . ." as I knew she had confided in me before. Yet, another contrast had become evident. Here was a woman who gave up her life for her motherhood, a mother that grieved so passionately for her son, while James's mother inflicted harm on him, denying any ounce of motherhood.

CHAPTER 7: COVERED IN POLKA DOTS AND A SIMPLE SACK

The week has been difficult, and Slate invites me for a trip to Brooklyn tomorrow. I am grateful that the workweek has come to an end. I am hopeful I can find some relaxation during the weekend.

Saturday proves to be sunny, and we take in the sun happily, as the weather forecast predicts the winter will be harsh. Slate and I stroll along the promenade overlooking the Brooklyn Bridge. At one time, Brooklyn was just a borough that was a venue toward glamorous New York City. However, as time progressed, Brooklyn has become a well-known venue in its own right. It boasts various parks, cafés, artistic outlets, and its architecture is variable and unique. As art is one of Slate's passions, he frequents different venues and advises me to take trips to those he deems most worthy. He has been spending more time in Brooklyn lately, almost as an avoidance technique from his current circle of friends and family.

Like the city, Brooklyn is a great place to find a variety of people with different backgrounds and personalities. Their differences often contribute to interesting life stories. On the promenade, we meet up with Carl, who is one such story. Carl is easy to spot; he is wearing a colorful shirt with polka dot pants. He is by far the most cheerful on the promenade today. Pins adorn his backpack We later find out that he has visited all those countries. Carl is in his early forties. His life has taken some interesting turns. He relates that his mother has suffered two bouts of cancer, and his father has undergone six surgeries for various ailments. His mood becomes a bit more somber as he retells his story, but he exudes great energy. His clothing choice makes passersby take that extra glance, but in New York, people have a tendency not to gawk. His build resembles Jonathan's own, but Carl has olive skin with rosy cheeks, and a smile as wide as those of the children around him.

Carl confesses that he had been a drug addict in his early twenties, and his addiction had been so bad that he attempted to burn down his home to collect insurance money that would be allocated toward drugs. He has a loving and forgiving family that put him through rehab and were constantly at his side. Instead of sticking around and helping out when the time came to return the favor, he kept running and running and traveling the world, never staying in one place for more than a few months. He took a few articles of clothing, a little savings, and lived off the bare minimum. While his sisters and mother were at his father's side during surgeries holding his hand, he was usually partying or "living the life." When his mother had chemo and radiation, he was hiking, biking, and even boating around Europe. One day he found himself walking down a desolate road staring up at the hot sun and just started to scream, knowing no one would hear him. He imagined his family before him, those loving faces that had stood by him. He stood there, wishing for their embrace, but the ache of guilt and remorse far outweighed the pleasant image in his mind. He did what he did best, he ran, this time running up the road.

When the road finally ended, Carl found a water source and drank a few sips. Then, taking a polka dot scarf from his backpack, drenching it in water, he draped the now-cold cloth over his back and neck, reveling in its cooling effect. He recalls how he looked at the polka dot scarf which had just provided such comfort and recalled it was his mother's. She once wrapped it around him while he suffered from withdrawal. She was always certain to show her affection, regardless of what her son had done or was going through. Carl never returned that polka dot wrap to his mother. He continued to carry it with him.

He finally admitted to himself that he missed home and that despite having abandoned his family in their time of need, he would face the consequences; he wanted to go home. To his surprise, his family delighted in his return, never spewing a negative word about his sudden and lengthy departure. He has since become an attentive son and sibling. His travels had taught him a lot about different cultures and expanded his understanding of nature. As a way of honoring his travels and trying to evolve further, he offered his services to an organization that helps out kids that have suffered some type of trauma, either via death or abuse. His trademark became his polka dot pants, a nod to his mother's and family's sacrifice on his behalf those years ago. Carl speaks passionately, "People are all different in the way they deal with trauma. The one thing I have consistently found is that everyone wants to be loved, but fear gets in the way." Slate looks at me momentarily then returns his direct eye contact toward the bridge. A young boy, one of the children Carl is mentoring, grabs Carl's hand, leading him toward a sight he has admired at the other end of the bridge, and we part ways. Two passersby take that extra glance at Carl, and he waves at them. They smile. We continue the day admiring the sights and catching a bite to eat.

The weekend serves as a brief reprieve from general life. It passes quickly, and I soon find myself making my way to work Monday morning.

I find a shiny, orange and neon green box sitting on my desk at work. It had Stephanie written all over it. Lo and behold, in it sits a sack, a paper bag, strips of material, sequins, and a few small tubes of glitter. "What is this?" I say as I continue to examine the interior.

"It's a gift from Lilly. You're inventive; make yourself a costume." Then she adds, "You know you have been hanging around the pediatric wing quite a bit. You should be giving something back, some entertainment."

"Are you trying to punish me?"

"No, I am trying to give you a gift. I mean, Lilly is giving you a gift."

"What type of gift is that?" I say, "Shame?"

Stephanie widens her eyes and smiles, "No, a new experience."

The day passes uneventfully, and I continue to greet the large box, or should I say eyesore, sitting on my desk every time I sit down. When it's time to go home, I take a cab because I am no competition for that big box; it will surely win.

That night instead of spending time making myself a healthy salmon and salad dish, I eat a bagel and cream cheese while creating a costume. The sack reminds me of a story a little boy whose dad was a rabbi once told me. There were two young men. One had a beautiful cup made of gold. It was further encrusted with jewels, while the other young man had a simple glass. They were both asked to serve the king. The man with the beautiful cup served the king with his head held high, while the eyes of the man with the simple glass were downcast to the floor. In the end, however, the glass had held the king's desired drink better, making it retain its freshness. By contrast, the gold-encrusted cup left its contents sour. The king was quite pleased with the glass cup and disappointed in the drink bedecked with jewels. The little boy who told me the story was sure to include the moral, speaking as if giving an inspirational speech like his father. His childish words translated, "You don't always derive greater satisfaction, happiness, and functionality from something that is beautiful."

Tonight, I make two sacks, one encrusted with sequins, and the other a plain burlap sack. I create a complementary story to depict this notion. The story is entitled, "Who Wins the Race," where two competing sack racers have opposite sacks. One boy has a tattered but whole sack, the other has a bead and crystal-encrusted sack. In the end, the boy with the bejeweled sack is hindered as he attempts to jump to the finish line, while the boy who wears a tattered sack finds the loose-fitting tatters actually improve the flexibility of his sack to get him to the finish line.

The next day, I take my story and costumes to work. At my first opportunity, I present them to Stephanie.

"What's this?" she asks.

"Well, one is my costume, and one is yours!"

"Why do I get a costume?" she replies in wonder.

"Because this was your idea."

"Okay, I will take the bejeweled one," Stephanie answers.

"That's great. I was hoping you would pick that one." It was only later after reading the story that Stephanie realized she was on the losing team.

"I thought you would make some kind of gown or something," she said.

"You guessed wrong," I chuckled.

We work through the day, a bit tired, but Stephanie and I make our way to the pediatric wing and put on our costumes.

Stephanie eyes me once she is in full gear, "You owe me for this one."

I retort, "Fun, remember this is fun."

James looks at me in surprise as I enter the pediatric wing. His eyes slightly widen, and the skin below his brow mildly stretches. A look of surprise is on his face as he notes the sack I am wearing. Although I am sure he is too young to understand the story and its implications, I can tell he is entertained by the strange costumes Stephanie and I are wearing.

James is seated in a corner, near Nurse Abbie, to diminish his fear of the crowd that surrounds him. As the story comes to a close, we receive much applause, and thus, I assume that everyone was entertained tonight. Mostly, I think the staff thought I must have taken something to be so lighthearted and playful, which was in contrast to my usual self, maybe a little bit of imagination and fun is just as good.

When I get home, I try calling my dad again, but there is no answer. I start to believe that maybe he is avoiding my call.

I walk to work, almost forgetting the significance of the day. Today Slate commemorates his sister's death. I remember the day he told me his secret. It was a Friday night four years ago. Slate had picked me up, and we went to a special exhibit at the museum. The exhibit featured young artists whose works referenced scenes from classic novels. The proceeds were to benefit a charity for young artists that struggled with mental health and substance abuse issues. It only took Slate a few seconds to match pictures to their corresponding novels as he was well versed in both literature and art. We both enjoyed artistry in the gallery and compared notes as to what we perceived the artists' intentions were.

We approached a scene from *Wuthering Heights*, wherein a sickly woman is lying or sprawled out on a bed with a dazed look in her eyes, her body further attested to the fact that she was hanging between life and death. I looked at the picture with some interest and imagined how tortured this artist must have been to create this work. The expression on Slate's face had also changed from that of wonder and amazement to sorrow and worry. It changed so dramatically that it prompted some concern on my part. "Slate, are you okay?" I asked in a gentle voice. He failed to respond and removed his hand from his forehead, now placing his hand over his heart. The concern was exponentially increased after that gesture, and so in a firm and loud voice, I said, "Slate, are you okay? Talk to me."

Finally, Slate came out of his trance and looked at me with a blank expression. "Are you okay?" I said again with a fretful voice, concerned.

His expression returned to normal, and he responded, "Yes, I am fine. Maybe we should get out of here. Let's go get something to eat."

"Do you want to tell me what just happened here?" I responded. "What's going on?"

It was the first time I had seen Slate so tormented, which was further evident in his tone when he responded. "The picture was very intense, that's all. I was captivated by the picture." Slate started walking off until he located a bench near the entrance of the museum. He motioned for me to sit down and left me sitting there without a word and stormed into the men's room. He returned a few minutes later with a freshly washed face. Without a word, he sat down on the bench next to me, and gently, with some hesitation, took out an envelope from his pocket. It was the same en-

214

velope he seemed to carry everywhere, often glancing at it in the hospital. It was never opened, though, at least not in anyone's presence. He handed it over to me. I opened the envelope further to discover a pink paper with a brief message stating, "Thanks for the car, bro!" signed Jenny Slate. On the opposite side of the paper was a date written in a different handwriting.

"I didn't know you have a sister," I said.

"I did have a sister. Jenny was smart and beautiful and kind. She was a ball of energy and vitality. That is, until one day, she borrowed my car to see her boyfriend, and a few days later, she was found in the woods, brutally raped and murdered." As he spoke, he clenched his chest just as he had when viewing the woman in the picture. For a brief moment, my eyes locked with his, but he quickly reverted to downcast eyes.

"I am so sorry," I said in a soft voice. I allowed my cold hands to cover his cold hands and put my head over on his shoulder.

We sat there for a few minutes in silence, until Slate announced, "Let's get something to eat." He refrained from talking about it further for the rest of the evening and never made reference to this story, his story, again.

This explained so much about Slate. How he always requested a change of patient when a woman was hurt as a result of domestic abuse or a victim of violence. Slate was also particularly protective of his car, never allowing anyone else to drive it, let alone to sit in the driver's seat. It also explained why he would never allow himself to be fully joyful. He always avoided his parents even though they seemed genuinely proud of him and appeared to enjoy his company.

The next time we returned to work, there was an awkward silence between us, but then life went back to the way it was before. Slate had several obsessions, reading articles, perpetually going to the gym, and taking in the arts of the city. We never again spoke about that episode, only making brief eye contact with each other when there was news of rape or murder or when a young patient came in seeking help, and Slate hesitated. Part of me wanted to help him, and another part tried to distance myself from him, as I was certain that my own pain would only reinforce his.

Something about little James made my heart feel a bit open, even though it hurt me to look at his wounds, and I thought perhaps Slate would benefit from meeting him, as well. I greet Slate in the hallway today, and he is walking around in a rush coming from a patient's room. He carries another research article in his hands as he makes his way through the hallway. Instead of walking toward his office as he usually does at this hour, he goes outside the hospital and purchases two sandwiches, only returning to his office briefly for his coat. He tells his superior he is leaving and will be back late. I follow him. It is probably wrong of me, and I may regret it in hindsight, but I follow him. I follow him because I am uncertain as to what he will do, and that scares me. He walks in no particular direction, more so on seemingly random blocks, back and forth, quickly. Then he stops abruptly and takes a deep breath. He opens his bag and takes out a sandwich and gives it to the homeless guy on the street. I think I hear him say the name Jenny as he hands over the sandwich. In his crisp shirt and tailored pants, he sits down next to him, and they spend the time eating their respective sandwiches side by side, taking bites almost simultaneously. I see Slate smile. I leave him to his private moments. "Rest in peace, Jenny," I say under my breath.

When I return to the hospital, I notice that I have nine minutes to go. I make my way quickly to visit James on the pediatric wing, but on my way to his room, I see Adam crying. Adam is eleven and a half. He had been on his way to a ballgame with his father when their car was hit by a car driven by a nonobservant driver texting on his phone. Adam's dad had hit his head quite hard, sustaining a head injury and was now a patient in the TBI unit. Adam had sustained a broken rib, pelvis, and elbow. Today Adam's eyes are red, and he is wiping them. He admits that he has been crying about not being able to play baseball. His mother was presently at work, as she had already missed a considerable amount of work following the accident, and his dad was still on the TBI unit. Adam was alone for most of the day and unable to engage in his favorite pastime. Adam's dad was my patient, and during my initial evaluation, I had been informed that his son was recovering on the pediatric wing. Adam's mom had asked if I could be a liaison between Adam and his father should one ask about the other in her absence. Despite some reservations, I agreed.

I motion for Adam to come toward me, and he rolls his wheelchair more fluidly in my direction, as his elbow has significantly healed during the past few weeks. His pelvis is still problematic, but he will likely be discharged before his dad. Recalling that I work on the unit where his dad is recovering, he inquires about his dad's progress. "He is getting better every day and working really hard. Sometimes our bodies have to relearn what they already know." I hear my own voice say, "Sometimes, you need to relearn what you already know."

This gives me an idea. "You know what I think, Adam? I know what can help you. Your body can't yet play the game, but all game strategy starts in your head, so let's use your brain to stimulate and light up all those parts of your body that you use to play baseball. It is like a workout for your body without the workout."

"Okay," he says as he looks at me curiously.

I try my best to recall the motions of baseball, a sport I haven't played since my youth. "You're standing there waiting for the pitcher to throw the ball, your knees are slightly bent, and you feel your weight pulling you a bit back. Your chin is forward, and you don't super squat, feet a bit more than shoulder length apart. You're not shaking the bat. Instead, your hands are securely holding the bat." I eye Adam, "More securely than that, Adam."

Adam smiles, "How did you know?"

"You're eyeing the ball and noticing the movement of the pitcher.

His arm moves forward, and the ball is released. You're standing in the position. Do you feel it in your legs?"

Adam touches his legs as if grading the pressure he feels under his hands.

"Your body tightens up to keep you in position. You hear the rustle of the wind in the background but nothing else, and then, the ball flies through the air. Do you see it flying, Adam?"

"Yes, I can see it."

"So, you rotate your shoulders and hips toward it, slightly increasing bending the knee. You eye the flying ball a bit in anticipation. The ball is closer, and your eyes shift to accommodate the closer distance as it comes toward you. And the force of the ball hitting the bat is felt through your hands and arms and up it goes flying high in the air. You start to run; your legs carry you easily . . . first base . . . and the ball is still flying . . . second base, still up there; your legs, a bit heavier but running . . . third base, and back to home . . . You feel the burn in your legs, but everyone shouts your name, and your body relaxes with happiness."

Adam smiles. I could feel the confidence rushing through him. He opens his eyes. "Yes, I feel it in my legs," he says.

"Keep working at it!" I get up to leave.

"Tell my dad hello," he says.

"I will," and as I approach the elevator, I hear him.

"I am standing at the plate and looking at the ball. . . ." I smile.

It is too late to visit with James now; I will have to come back later, so I walk, or rather run, toward the elevator. The elevator arrives, and I go down to my floor. I exit the elevator walking briskly through the hallways looking for Kevin Chase. There are thirty seconds left to my lunch break, and luckily, he is at the nurses' station. I stand there, and a nurse remarks, "Good afternoon." She sees me waiting for Dr. Chase, but Kevin doesn't turn in my direction, prompting her to ask me, "What's wrong?" Kevin finally turns to acknowledge my existence.

Once I have his attention, I waste no time. "I need you to teach me how to play baseball. You're a good player, right?"

"Well, yes, but why do you need to play baseball?" Before I have a chance to respond, he adds, "Okay, Jules, the master will teach you base-ball." Kevin is not the humblest of men. He chuckles as he leaves.

I call out, "Thank you," and my voice reverberates through the hallway.

Shana, the speech therapist, greets me in the hallway and lets me know that our client has made improvement in his swallowing capabilities, no longer requiring a nectar thickener to enable the food to go down. I have a momentary reprieve from the day; someone is better able to eat, the most basic of human needs. I walk happily toward my next patient, and the remainder of the day goes rather smoothly. Before I leave, I make sure to check on Slate, who is busy writing a commentary on some article that he keeps referencing with his eyes. Turning his head toward the article, he notes my presence, smiles, and wishes me a relaxing night. A good choice of words.

With my day now over, I can go home and relax, perhaps make another attempt at reaching my father. I have tried him a few times now with no response, which makes me a bit apprehensive.

I take off my jacket and place my handbag in its usual spot, making my way toward the house phone. I hear it ring a few times as I am about to hang up. I hear a faint, "Hello." It sounds like my dad. He waits a few seconds before speaking his next words. "Jules, I just want you to know that the doctors found some problems with my heart, and I will need open-heart surgery."

"What? When?"

"In a few days," he says as his voice becomes lower.

"Who's the doctor? Did you get a second opinion? Where is the surgery taking place?" I ask in an almost frantic state.

My father notices my tone and gives me the details, adding, "They tell me I'm going to be fine." He further informs me, "You don't need to come, just giving you an update." I hear the sound of the garage door opening, and he says, "I need to go." I am left standing there in the middle of the kitchen, unable to hang up the phone. When I finally do, I take out all my household cleaners and clean my apartment, for it needs a thorough cleaning. I am a self-admitted neat freak in the way that Slate is an exercise-aholic.

Our activities are a diversion from the preoccupation of the mind, a subconscious break of sorts. I am not big on crying either. It doesn't come naturally. It is usually only after I have tensed myself to the point that I can't take it anymore. I have often put on the vacuum cleaner, not only for proprioception and grounding, but also to drown out the sound of my depressed groans of frustration that come in place of tears. My kitchen floors sparkle; besides for the pride I feel in maintaining a clean house, it is that release of scrubbing down and making something look better that I need. Slate doesn't cry, and James has yet to shed a tear. We are all predominantly flinchers. I want so badly to cry, sitting myself down in the middle of my closet, as I had days ago, but this time no tears flow. I just feel that darkness, the claustrophobia. There is no shame in crying; it's cathartic. It releases neurotransmitters and relaxes the body. I try to convince myself, but it is so unnatural to my existence that on the occasion that tears do fall, it scares me. I finally sense one dangling tear, alone, crossing my cheeks, and I tuck myself into bed, curled up like a child, and fall into a semi-sleep.

As I walk to work this morning, I call in favors from every doctor I know to ensure that my dad gets good care. I find a few articles detailing the surgery my father will undergo and then research the statistics about what and how many things have gone wrong during those surgeries. I avert my eyes, however, as I begin to read the bad stuff that may occur during surgery. Instead, I just stick to knowing what is supposed to happen when everything goes right. I perform my job somewhat robotically today, that is until I note the time. It's lunch, and a small smile appears on my face as I make my way to James's room.

CHAPTER 8: THE HEART OF THE MATTER

Rajad was a former patient. Unbeknownst to me, his grandfather was a well-known businessman in South Asia. He was apparently also known to be a humanitarian and philanthropist. I actually learned how to dance from Rajad. Rajad had acquired an infection, which resulted in neurological sequela that significantly impeded his functioning and daily life. With the assistance of staff, he left three months later in almost original form.

Most patients in the early stages of illness want to learn to move in bed, transfer themselves to another location, complete simple tasks, but not Rajad. All Rajad would talk about was his ability to get fresh air and be able to dance with his girlfriend, and so, I framed all sessions with that as an ultimate goal. Although I was physically fit and fairly rhythmic, I really wasn't the greatest dancer, but Rajad understood the art of dancing to the point that although his body couldn't get it done, his mind could conjure up its steps which he explained clearly. I focused on the simple movements enabling him to do daily tasks all the while, demonstrating how it would affect his dance moves. This was his great motivator. To this day, the only reason I have evidenced sufficient confidence to dance at clubs or weddings is due to Rajad. Rajad's father was extremely pleased with his son's care at the hospital and subsequently made a substantial donation. The money was used to create a rooftop wing in the subacute section of the hospital. With permission from the medical staff, patients from any wing of the hospital could access it. A small sectional with modified windows and other modifications was also introduced. This would shelter those that had restrictions in the amount of time they could stay outdoors. This benefited a variety of patients, such as those suffering from lupus, multiple sclerosis, myositis, skin malignancies, or burns. All modifications were created with the patients in mind, to assist with flexibility, muscle exercises, balance training, transferring, and so forth. The grounds included enlarged cognitive floor games for problem-solving and sequencing. It also included a sandbox with shoveling toys. It was a more pleasant environment when family and friends came together with patients and granted the patients the opportunity to see and feel actual air. Some patients barely made it upstairs, some stayed one to two minutes while others could tolerate longer time frames. Some patients had difficulty tilting their heads upward while sustaining their balance due to either biomechanical issues or physiological conditions that created balance problems. Yet when they finally looked up and saw the sky, I could perceive the fuzzy, warm feeling they were experiencing.

I decided to take James and Calvin upstairs for some fresh air and perhaps to enjoy the sandbox. There were always concerns about germs and sterility, so all equipment needed to be cleaned regularly, and new sand was purchased following two uses (which turned out to be quite an expense). The pediatric wing personnel began to fill it with one-time use items like dry noodles, which were far less expensive. Patients required three exit passes for time to visit the roof, but they all deemed it worthwhile even for the minute or two of fresh air. The hospital staff did understand the importance of nature and outdoors on healing. For this purpose, even ICU patients would often be assigned to a room with a view, either facing greenery or some architectural image. When the first frost fell, the outdoor portion of the rooftop wing would close and could only be viewed via a large picture window.

After a few minutes, I notice two birds sitting at the corner of the gate. They begin exchanging chirping sounds like childhood banter. At first, I smile at them. I so loved birds as a child; they are calming and beautiful. I remember feeding them in a neighborhood park as they gathered together to consume the crumbs I left behind. Calvin watches the birds in wonder, and he begins to move in their direction. Calvin is enthusiastic to see his little animal friends. He alerts James and points, "Birds!" James looks back and forth from the bird to Calvin with anticipation.

At first, I delight in the two boys' enthusiasm and curiosity, and then I recall that birds carry a host of germs, particularly bacteria, which can pose a significant danger for infection in sick people. Suddenly my delight and calm turn to a mild state of panic, as I attempt to shield James and Calvin from this 'terror'. How I wish I could go back to a time when this information was unknown, and a bird was just a bird. Then I remind myself that it is just two kids playing, noting a bird in the distance, which brings them happiness. They are only observing the bird, that's all. The birds aren't wild, and they haven't left their feces. *Is this how it feels to be a new mom?* I ask myself, *like fear of everything all the time.* The birds leave—terror averted. After their play has ended, I order the area to be wiped down, and I return downstairs to the pediatric wing with two seemingly happy kids.

As I walk towards my office, two people enter the hospital chapel. One holds her chest and the other one's hands are wrapped around her friend's shoulders as she says, "Dear God!" repeating it over and over again full of angst and the desperation.

As the hospital chapel doors fling open, and I get a brief view of its interior, I whisper to myself, "Dad, be okay. Please just be okay."

Sandy was fourteen when I met her while volunteering on the pediatric wing. Sandy suffered from reactive arthritis. Her symptoms worsened daily. By the time she was turning twenty, she was lying hopelessly in a hospital bed. There must have been some other diagnosis that eluded the medical profession because her symptoms were so severe. She had tried many different types of medications, including experimental ones. She practiced daily yoga, stretching exercises, rehydrating techniques, and massage; she attempted every alternative diet recommended for autoimmune disease. Sandy also had three binders full of medical testing performed. Her central nervous system had begun to recognize pain as the norm, which is what often happens with chronic pain sufferers. Despite best attempts at splinting and exercise, her fingers were contorted, and during her most recent visit to the hospital, she took off a ring she wore for eleven years that her parents had given her on her ninth birthday and dropped it on the stand beside her bed.

"I can't wear this anymore, my fingers are too swollen, too painful." Then she asked me a question that I try to avoid at all costs. "Do you think that there is a God? Do you think he hears me?"

There is this one subject that I vehemently want to dodge, the subject of religion. I'm not exactly sure what I think about God and religion. I think religion and one's belief system is private and should not be addressed during therapy sessions. Yet, when someone stares at you almost begging you to answer them whether there is a God and whether he is listening, I find myself always answering, "There must be, or you wouldn't be here to have this conversation." People need something to believe in, and I don't want to be the party to deter them from healing, whether it be by the hand of God, or by their belief and hope that a God exists, that will be the impetus to propel them into healing action. There are studies that attempt to corroborate that belief generates healing, but on the other hand, there have been so many that stuck to their faith and died, some even succumbing in very tragic deaths. I am not sure if it is the place of a therapist to discuss this subject matter, but in truth, whose responsibility or right is it to decide if God exists? Scientists? Religious figures? Or the Average Joe?

My grandmother wore a modest cross around her neck; it was set with a green stone. The stone made her green eyes sparkle, and when it caught the light, it gleamed across the room, almost making it appear like a magic charm. When I was ten, my grandmother gave me that cross. Yet, when it hung around my neck, and with my brown eyes, the gleam and magic disappeared. As a child, when I gazed up at the sky, I would tell myself that the clouds block God from hearing me and listening, and when the clouds pass everything will be better, but in truth when the clouds did pass, I would still be in the same rut as before.

Sandy was a wonderful human being despite all her aches, pains, and disfigurement. Still, at this stage of her illness, there was very little anyone else could do. I did something I perhaps should not have done. I bought her a cross, something tangible that she could actually feel, allowing her some peace. To some people, God and faith are just as important as bread and water. I brought Sandy to the window of her room. As we peered out, I said, "There are no clouds out today. God must have a good view of your room."

She smiled her sweet smile and went back to her hospital bed, stating, "I'd better get some rest, so I can get out of here soon." The next day Sandy presented me with a hand-written thank you card while clutching her new cross that she was wearing around her neck. Her condition, however, continued to deteriorate.

The night is still young, I tell myself as the clock shows 1:52 a.m.

I feel my brain wide awake as I attempt to fall asleep. I generally can't remember having had a good night's sleep since very early childhood. I wasn't even sure I knew what that meant. I would sleep five hours during high school, even though it should have been more like ten. I then began taking a series of different supplements to induce sleep and then graduating to higher tier sleep inducers, which generally didn't put me to sleep either. I'm normally not a coffee drinker, as my mother was, but do consume large doses of tea instead to give me that caffeine boost. As a child, I wet my bed once following one of my mother's initial tirades. Subsequently, I would often stay up trying to avoid having another accident. As I got older, it was more daily stressors coupled with nightmares that kept me awake. It had been years since I took something to induce sleep, but I open up my cabinets and still see the bottle which stands there proudly calling my name. I close the door of my bedroom and just allow myself to lie awake for the next few hours until I fall asleep in the early hours of the morning.

This time I arrive to work late, as I had allowed myself to sleep overtime. I work slowly today, unenthusiastic about the fast pace of the hospital, which I usually enjoy.

When I visit James at the end of a long workday, Nurse Abbie advises that he has had three toileting accidents within the last two days. Although he is young, and children his age may still wear diapers, James is different. He actually hates diapers, pulling them off every time someone tries to have him wear one. He is one of a few young children on the wing that wears underwear instead. I wonder who had potty-trained him and when. Perhaps diapers were some sort of punishment from his mother. Abbie had also mentioned that he keeps flinching whenever the a.m. nurse comes to take his vital signs, which had not been the case following his first day in the hospital.

I inquire about any changes that have occurred within the last two days. I come to find out that the a.m. nurse is new. Nurse Eli is carefree and acts lovingly towards her patients. Yet, she has been a change in James's routine, and at this point, any minor change is apt to set something in motion that brings out his 'fight or flight' response. James is extremely observant; his eyes almost poke out of his head with interest when noticing something or someone new. I also note that Eli has a particularly high-pitched voice. Her friendly demeanor coupled with her cheerful voice are appreciated by the remainder of the children of the ward, as I think they deem her playful, but to James, it may be too much of a stressor for his already stressed out and hyper-alert system. Nurse Eli is also a very touchy-feely type of person, the kind that will pretend to tickle you or give you a loving pat on the head. James's small body reacts when someone touches him, even direct visual contact close to his person elicits a jumping response of sorts.

I go into his room, and although he does not smile, something in his eyes seems to appreciate my attendance. James is willing to wash his face on his own and then washes his hands in preparation to eat lunch. He still does not display nearly enough of an appetite expected of someone his age. He even relinquishes his dessert, which has a bear's face on it.

I have brought a book of animals and employ a progressive muscle relaxation script which is intended to help children learn to relax. I model each motion, pretending to be different animals and stressing my muscles to depict tension and then releasing.

James looks on with a great deal of interest, looking at me and then referencing back to the book to see which animal fits with my generated emotion and tension. When I come to the elephant, James puts his hand up to his nose and breathes in attempting to mimic the elephant's trunk. As we approach the end of the book, I invite Nurse Eli to join us as I continue to model the character's emotions and muscle release. Nurse Eli joins in, and James looks up at her with great interest. As she leaves, I say, "Nurse Eli is our friend." I leave the book with James, telling him I will come back another time to read it to him again. This time, before I leave, I give him a small pat on the shoulder, he doesn't flinch. Later, I ask Nurse Eli to speak with a bit less zest to James, and she is very receptive to this suggestion.

I make my way home, my muscles relaxed, and my face is still mimicking some of the animal expressions. I think momentarily that people on the streets are observing my strange behaviors, only to find that the guy that just gave me a second glance was really trying to peek at the store window behind me.

I close my eyes in the comforts of my freshly washed sheets. I see the expression on James's face ranging from curiosity to attempts at mimicking my own facial expressions though not exactly mastering them. I remember his eyes peering at mine as he sat upright in the large chair in his room that almost swallows up his tiny frame but doesn't. I see him relinquish his bed sheet that he generally holds onto for security. I see him kicking his feet ever so slightly with some excitement as I show him a picture of an elephant which he seems to love. For the first time in a few weeks, I sleep a good seven hours, waking up a bit chipper and walking to work with a renewed enthusiasm.

I arrive at the pediatric unit before my workday commences. I am informed that James hasn't had an accident last night and has accepted Nurse Eli's assistance. He has even allowed her to take his vitals without squirming. The staff has informed me that they have observed him touching his nose quite a bit. They didn't know it, but I'm certain it was to signify Mr. Elephant.

I work through the day with the extra spring in my step, even though the hospital is undergoing some construction, creating what appears to be another wing, making me take alternative routes to each division, which is a bit of an annoyance.

I see Slate in the hallway examining a beam that's being installed, which is accompanied by some crown molding. Slate smiles and points out the change in architecture, which I wouldn't have noticed if not for him. We then notice the CEO of the hospital, whom we only encounter about once a year, holding a plaque in hand and pointing to its designated space.

A plaque signifies a donor, which signifies some additional funding for hospital endeavors. We don't know what the new extension is designated for, but everyone's mind plays the game of what if. Although it's a long stretch, I imagine the rehabilitation unit receiving more funding, adding more comprehensive educational materials and enhanced gym equipment and props, wheelchairs that aren't from the 1800s and are better sized for patients, more sophisticated models of equipment, and online technological delivery systems, perhaps even a 3-D printer.

Then Jonathan voices his own thoughts: "More sophisticated imaging technology; the operating room could use a facelift, better yet, establishing a regenerative science wing." We are both reawakened to reality when we hear the annoying sound of drilling, reverberating not only in our ears, but creating mild movement in our entire bodies. For the moment, these dreams are locked away, but not lost.

Early the next morning, I request permission to take James off the pediatric wing briefly, that is, if he is willing to go. This time there would be no Calvin accompanying us. James willingly takes my hand, which was a good first step. We watch the elevator go up and down a few moments before he allows me to lead him inside. In the elevator, we find Brady, another little boy on the unit who has seen James before. He is with his mother on their way out, as Brady has been discharged. James firmly grips the bottom of my skirt as we enter the elevator. I try to take hold of his hand again, but he refuses. Holding my skirt yet tighter, he watches intently as Brady, who

234

was still weak from treatment, curls up in his mother's arms. Brady waves good-bye, and James looks on but fails to return the wave.

Suddenly, the elevator comes to an abrupt halt. James looks as though he is about to panic, but as the door opens, a wave of calm seems to wash over him. He lets go of my skirt and walks at my side as we exit the elevator. James takes my hand. Some doctors come and go as if they haven't seen a child pass them. Others smile and wave as they walk briskly through the doors. Yet others come towards James in an attempt to say a grand, "Hello," and James retreats. He notices Stephanie and pulls me in her direction. He likely recalls her from our little sack performance upstairs. Stephanie is sitting on a rolling stool and demonstrates how it moves up and down. James watches curiously, looking pleased. Stephanie offers him a test run, but he refuses. I sit myself down on an adjustable office chair, motioning to James to sit on my lap for a "ride". To this request, he happily agrees. There is almost a normalness to the routine, a fear of going up and down, followed by a sense of amusement once experienced. It brings to mind the emotion expressed in a child after they master an amusement park ride that they had feared. For a few brief seconds, the floor vibrates as a result of the drilling which could be heard from the floor below, but it thankfully stops rather quickly, as the elevator ride was a sufficient irritant for James for the day.

Mrs. Fletcher, one of my patients, walks past us as she is showing off her ambulatory skills to Gabe, her physical therapist. She waves at James and me. James lifts his arm and hand a bit, waving back. I had hoped we would meet Slate, but Slate was apparently held up in surgery, and it was time for us to leave. Upon returning to the elevator, James holds my skirt, this time loosely. He watches the faces of the people entering and exiting until we reach the pediatric wing. As we approach his room, James clutches my skirt firmly, not letting it go. He looks up at me with a pleading look, as if begging me not to go. "Don't leave me," my ears hear, even though no words are emitted from his mouth. It is the first time in my life I could feel someone needing me, specifically me, and a substitute wouldn't do. It feels good, but I don't want James to become a dependent, needy child. I walk him into his room and come really close to his face. He allows my face to come close to his own, and strands of my long hair dangle next to his, mixing with his own. "I will come to see you tomorrow, James." James semi-waves good-bye and puts his hand up to my face, touching my chin as if in a brief stroke. I refrain from stroking his back, not only for his sake but for my own.

A man I dated briefly seemed to endlessly scrutinize me. I made the mistake early in our relationship of casually remarking that I had had a bad childhood. Though I didn't provide any details, he responded coldly, bluntly stating, "This explains your inability to love." This exchange prompted me to further hide certain details of my life from everyone close to me. The words penetrated not only my mind but my soul. I had always assumed that something in me had been damaged despite having few physical scars, but now this smart aleck had detected what it was. I can't love. I don't know if I love like the rest of the world, but I know that I had great satisfaction and pride when Stephanie received an award from the hospital, and that I gladly wake up early from time to time to get her some coffee, just because she likes it. I know that I feel the need to help Slate whenever he is asked to speak, and I bake modified gluten-free cookies for him to make him happy though I personally dislike them. I know that I have literally felt anguishing pain when my friend and neighbor Sasha was sick. I know that I feel crushing pain when James is scared or in pain, even momentarily. I know that I am happier when they are happy and sadder when they are sad. I can feel anger at those that perpetrate injustices against them. In truth, I don't know if love is a word that people need to say that makes it exist, or if it's a particular type of caress or a look that evidences this emotion.

James looks at my face as I begin to remove myself from his personal space. He watches me walk out the door slowly, as Nurse Abbie returns to change his bandages. He just lies back as she proceeds.

Mrs. Fletcher is a seventy-six-year-old woman who came in for hip arthroplasty, which entailed adhering to certain movement precautions for a few weeks. Mrs. Fletcher's daughter ensures that her mother follows restrictions when moving, making certain that she refrains from bending forward, lifting, or crossing her leg. She lovingly confirms that a pillow is maintained between her mother's legs to ensure proper positioning when Mrs. Fletcher attempts to sleep. Mrs. Fletcher is one of the few individuals that always has a family member around, her daughter Penny. Mrs. Fletcher has been a pleasure to work with. She is always appreciative of any assistance or advice and follows all her precautions to the tee. We have practiced getting dressed using a dressing stick to avoid excessive movements and have implemented stocking aids for putting on her socks, as well as using a long-handled shoehorn to put on her shoes.

Mrs. Fletcher's main priority is being able to return to driving. She prides herself on being an active member of society despite her age. She works for a charitable organization and would often make home visits or pick up equipment or supplies. Her motto was, "My ride is my stride." I have her practice a simulated car transfer by backing up to the "car seat"—otherwise known as one seat of conjoined chairs—with her walker. She practices entering on the driver's side. Mrs. Fletcher will ultimately need her doctor's clearance to resume driving. She is enthusiastically awaiting the day when she can finally go home and start to relive her life.

Mrs. Fletcher likes things in written form. She is a list person. I hand her a pamphlet of precautions, recommendations for work simplification techniques, and safety when engaging in housekeeping, meal prep, and other typical activities. When the pamphlets are all distributed, she opens my hand and places a penny in it. "What's this?" I inquire.

Mrs. Fletcher says, "You have often commented on how wonderful my daughter is. Well she isn't my daughter, not by birth anyway. I married at age nineteen and kept waiting to have a child. By thirty-seven, it still hadn't happened. At the time, I just stopped everything. The crying stopped, but so did the living. I curled up in bed and just didn't go out. Back then, people were less aware of depression. For my thirty-eighth birthday, my husband Ralph took me out to the place where he had proposed to try and cheer me up. It was close to a wishing well. Ralph gave me a penny and said, 'Make a wish.' At first, I hesitated, but then, Ralph kissed me on the cheek. He kissed the penny, took my hand, and we threw it in together. I smiled a little.

"Four days later, there was an article in the newspaper about a couple that had been killed in the vicinity, leaving a slightly wounded infant behind. The only other living relative was a grandparent that was incapacitated and could not take care of her. I couldn't forget the child's face that I saw in the paper and undertook an investigation to ensure that she was okay. This investigation turned into an adoption. My Penny has been the best blessing in my life. It isn't my place, but I am going to say it anyway. I saw you with that little boy, and I think you could use 'a penny' in your life."

I am taken by surprise at Mrs. Fletcher's words. Her daughter returns from re-parking her car, bringing her mother her favorite drink from an outdoor vendor because she is always thoughtful like that. Penny smiles and thanks me when her mother shows off her stack of instructional material that I have provided. "Let's take a walk, Penny," she says as she grabs her walker.

I leave work today, and my nerves are setting in quite fiercely, making me watch three yoga videos in progression to gain some state of calm. Tomorrow is my father's open-heart surgery, the surgery that I pushed out of my mind for the last few days.

As morning arrives, I look at my toast and eggs, which don't appeal to the butterflies that have occupied my stomach, so I just grab the bread and a protein bar, making my way toward his hospital, which is quite a distance from my home. It is still dark outside as I leave my house at 5:39 a.m. My father is scheduled for surgery at seven thirty, but I don't want to risk them taking him in without him noting my presence. For too long, he has failed to note my presence.

Something inside tells me he needs me to be there, or maybe I feel like I need to be there. I have never seen my father cry. I have never really seen him laugh either. He suppresses everything. When he told me that he was undergoing surgery, it was a shock, but it shouldn't have been. His heart has undergone so much, carrying all the weight of all his emotions for many years.

I have resolved to be there for my father, even though it would mean facing the rest of my family, particularly my mother. My father hadn't anticipated my arrival. I think somewhere inside of him, he also couldn't allow himself to believe that someone would be there for him. He seems delighted at my arrival to the room, as he enthusiastically waves me in toward his bed. A nurse comes in, relaying that he is going to be prepped for

240

surgery momentarily, even though it is only 6:51 a.m. I ignore my mother and only nod my head at my sister as she enters. My father thanks me twice for coming, employing a nonchalant tone and look, similar to that of a host that just received a housewarming gift from a guest who came for dinner. Yet, momentarily my father turns to me and his facial expression and tone change drastically, "Thank you for coming," he whispers as he caresses my hand. This time there is a glimmer of care and interest. I haven't felt this much emotion emanating from him since wading in my uncle's pool during summer vacation, wherein my father happily observed me playing. His eyes and tone almost cheering me on. I inform him about what generally takes place during the surgery and what to expect immediately after that, to try and assuage his fears.

As the surgical nurse comes to whisk him away, I whisper, "It will be okay, Dad. Heal well." He smiles. I wait in the vicinity, giving my sister my cell phone number, which she didn't have. "When Dad wakes up, can you call me?"

She willingly agrees but points out, "Sure, for Dad's sake."

I walk around the neighborhood for quite some time, then head to the cafeteria.

After that, I lounge in the lobby like someone waiting for their ride. I check my messages incessantly, but none come. I reference my watch. *It should be over,* I say to myself. I make my way toward the surgical floor, where a nurse notifies us that they are presently transferring Dad to recovery. A doctor makes a brief appearance to say the surgery was a success, and soon, we are informed that only two people can enter the recovery room at a time. My sister pipes up, "You can go, Jules. I will go later," which is great and not so great, leaving me to enter with only my mother.

I look at my mother, as a half-hour has passed, and we are advised that we can make a brief visit with my dad now. Her beauty is still there. She barely aged in twenty years, and her makeup is perfectly applied, with every strand of hair in place. She looks at me no differently than the doctors or nurses that pass her by, only pointing in my father's direction when we enter the recovery unit.

My father looks surprised when he sees me entering together with my mother. He is correct; we make a strange sight. He has some pain but is grateful that he is awake and the surgery is over. I encourage him to plan to go to cardiac rehab, which he initially refuses, but warms up to the idea after the patient in the next bed is forewarned to take better care of himself if he doesn't want to undergo yet a third surgery. Before I leave, my dad looks at me and says, "You are a really good kid, you know that?" I wonder why it took over thirty years for him to tell me that; maybe he didn't know what to say back then. My mother gives me one glance-over as I leave.

I take the long way home, so I can allow myself to have a substantial meal at a restaurant. I sit there alone, eating my perfectly prepared dish, almost devouring it from hunger. As I sit, I compile a list for my father to help him institute a plan for taking meds, relaxation techniques, and daily walks because even from a distance, I have a desperate need to help my father.

I return to work the next day, and the unit seems to have been running just fine without me. I am certain to call the nurses' station to check up on my dad for the eighth time, as I have been doing throughout the night. Shana, the speech therapist, is approaching the gym with Panga Cole, an eighty-one-year-old man with a neurological disorder. He is scheduled for physical therapy in five minutes. She attempts to put the brake on his wheelchair, which is stuck. I go over to help.

"Yes, the wheelchair needs a bit of an update," I say.

The department supervisor stops by. He advises that he has read a batch of session notes, and then looks at Panga, "Oh! Is this the patient with the prolonged lingual elevation, labial leakage, and delayed pharyngeal wall contractions?"

Mr. Cole has a look of confusion. Shana blushes at the lack of discretion by the supervisor, as he relays this information in front of her patient, which not only violates privacy laws but brings concern to the eighty-one-year-old man sitting before her who is neither deaf nor dumb.

Shana turns to him, "Oh, I am so sorry about that. It is just some technical jargon. It means that your swallowing isn't great, and you're leaving some residue behind, and that could pose a risk for choking by blocking your airway. You know that's why we practice those exercises and are modifying your food." The man returns to a more relaxed position, as he waits for his physical therapist, and looks outside. "Bye, Mr. Cole," Shana says and walks away.

Perhaps I am oversensitive today, as my own father is at the mercy of the healthcare system, and I am a bit riled up. I turn to a random nurse, and say, "People are people whether old or young, sick or healthy. They deserve to be spoken to like a human." She agrees but looks at me as if I were a madwoman.

I remember the first client I had. It was a man named Bill. He had a beautifully sculpted mustache. He had suffered a stroke and was unable to move his right side. He was also aphasic, hindering his speaking abilities. Thus, he was unable to communicate well. I remember looking at the asymmetry of his shoulders, noticing that his right side was lower than his left. I placed my fingers between structures on his shoulder, feeling a dip and significant gap between them, inferring that the man's shoulder was partially dislocated. I kept thinking to myself, *I hope I am not causing him pain. He can't voice it.* I kept checking his facial expressions, which appeared expressionless. His mustache is what gave his face more liveliness than other patients in his state. *What if I am hurting some vital structures? Pain is there to forewarn people. It serves a purpose,* I thought. I could feel some level of vulnerability, not sure if it was mine or his. Dan, my supervisor, passed by, and I must have had some self-doubt written on my face.

"Is everything okay?" he said.

"Yes, sure," I responded, thinking I may not be admitting the truth to protect my own pride. As Dan turned to leave, I asked if he could just confirm my suspicion.

Dan palpated Bill's shoulder and detected a partial dislocation as deduced by the extra space between structures, adding, "It's about one finger's width. I believe you are correct, Jules. You can alert the medical team to your findings."

I had watched his hands very carefully, noticing every finger placement and the firmness with which he touched Bill's shoulders, committing it to memory, and asking myself if my technique had been the same. I performed passive range of motion exercises, guiding Bill's shoulders in the correct biomechanical position. It was like cradling a baby, where you are exceptionally careful when you have this precious, vulnerable thing in your arms. Each day, as Bill began to heal, my confidence grew, and my own arms and fingers would move more efficiently.

Chapter 9: Pain Meets Pain

James has been at the hospital for some time now. Slate is about to leave for the local gym; I approach him, almost blocking his path. "Slate, do you have a few minutes? There is someone I want you to meet." It is very rare that I have someone to introduce to Slate. We generally mingle in the same crowd, having mutual friends, and he knows I am not close with family but hasn't been told why. Slate seems a bit apprehensive but quickly consents. He rarely ever says no, particularly to me. He is biting his lip as he follows me.

As we approach the pediatric wing, he starts walking in the opposite direction. "Where are you going, Jules?"

"This way," I point.

"You're going to the pediatric wing? This person you want to introduce me to is someone in the pediatric wing?" He raises his eyebrows, and has a puzzled look on his face.

"Yes."

"Is it a patient or staff?" I detect some impatience in his voice.

"A patient, a sweet little boy named James."

"How do you know him?"

I know that if I provide more details, Slate will never agree to meet the child. He barely can muster enough strength to see the wounds of a child inflicted by illness, wherein intellectualizing allows him to cope. He would become obsessed with the wounds and terms or might speak incessantly about healing the liver, diet, and so forth, but if he knew that this child had been abused, he wouldn't even attempt to approach him.

"Why do you want me to meet this child? Is he a relative or friend's kid?"

"Not exactly either of them, just someone who would probably benefit from meeting you."

Slate freezes as he declares, "I really think this is a bad idea."

I take his hand. "Just follow me." I sense the heaviness of his feet.

We finally reach James's room, and Slate's look of apprehension has turned to disapproval, but he follows me nevertheless. James is sitting up in a chair, with a nurse at his side. His hospital gown is draped over his torso loosely, leaving his collarbone slightly sticking out with his appendages in full view. Slate sees the scars all over James's small frame and comes closer to gain a better view of his injury, but I pull him away.

"You need some distance."

"What's going on? Does he have a vascular disease? Is that why you called me here?"

James glances at the stranger in the room and arches his back toward the back of the chair. I see the fear in his face. I place the sailboat in Slate's hand and tell him to show it to James. Slate rolls his eyes but agrees. I approach James alone, gauging his mood, and say, "Hi, James," noticing him relax. I point across the room. "That is my friend Jonathan. Hi, Jonathan." I wave, adding, "He is Calvin's friend, too. Remember Calvin that you played with?" I point to the painting they created together, the only colorful thing in the room. Slate waves back, and I motion for him to come closer toward James. James's eyes watch as Slate approaches. Slate's eyes start to recognize the marks on the child's body, and James starts to reflect the fear crossing Slate's face.

"Jules, what the heck? Why would you bring me here?"

I pull him out of the room. "You're scaring him."

"What happened to that boy?"

I hesitatingly admit that his mother did this to him.

"Dear God, his mother? His own mother butchered him with artist tools?"

"Is that what those marks are? No one knew what they were."

"Yes, they are artist palette tools used for smearing and mixing," he answers, as he runs his fingers through his hair roughly, almost pulling some out.

"That would make sense; his mother is an artist."

"Listen, I've got to get out of here, okay?" Slate starts moving slowly toward the door.

"No. You can't."

"What do you mean I can't?"

"Listen, you scared him. You need to come in with me to show him you're not a scary guy. He doesn't have anyone. He is alone, and I think you

248

can help him."

"How can I help him? I can only hurt him. For heaven's sake, I am into art like his mother, the butcher."

"He likes to paint. He painted with Calvin. You know Calvin."

Slate looks back at James, noting his small frame and says, "What is he, like two?"

"He will soon turn three," I say, as Slate moves slowly in James's direction.

We try again. This time James looks up at Slate, and they meet eye to eye. Slate attempts to look away from his scars, focusing on his face, and I see Slate's lips turn upwards, his eyes squint, and he smiles for real. "You are a cute little thing," Slate says, as he lifts the sailboat at the side of James's bed and makes the room into a vast sea, with the sails moving everywhere coming closer to James. James seems entertained and leans forward to witness the sight, even standing up at one point for a better view. I never knew Slate could be so playful and lighthearted. As Slate approaches James once again, James continues to lean forward and allows Slate to run the boat toward his nose. James puts his hands together in delight, not coming to a full clap but just from excitement.

"Maybe we should get him some pictures; this room is as sterile as it comes," Slate says as he surveys the room.

"You can draw something for him. Kid-friendly though."

"All right then, a kid-friendly illustration coming right up." Slate's mind mulls over some options as the creases in his forehead intensify. "Can you get me some drawing tools and paper, Jules?"

"Now? You mean you want to stay?"

"Sure. Why not?"

The paper and drawing tools are a bit amateur for Slate, but he makes do, creating all sorts of pictures in a matter of moments. There are balloons coupled with large winding lollipops in whimsical scenes, amusement park rides against a natural backdrop, with a bright sun and clear skies. Slate forms a cloud, and I remove his hand gently from the picture. "Leave it. It's perfect." I provide a storyline for James, and he listens, attempting to examine both Jonathan's and my faces as we go on. The nurses have allowed us to stay past visiting hours. The darkness of the outdoors doesn't deflect the light mood in the room.

Jonathan hangs the three portraits and writes, "For James." He looks at the little boy who is half asleep in the chair, "They are just for you," and waves good-bye as he is dozing. James's arms wrap themselves around Slate's neck for just a few minutes until he is safely tucked in bed.

We both head home, with some color on our fingertips, laughing like giddy kids, and Slate invites me to the bay, which we haven't visited in quite some time.

It's Friday afternoon, and we have both completed an emotionally laden week. Slate and I take a long stroll, finally entering a bay filled with

250

a host of small to medium-sized boats. The area is infrequently explored, and the waters still reflect a bluish hue, not yet a victim of pollution. The air has this indefinable breeze like the one found when you make your way to the beach on a perfect summer's day. The sun casts its light on the water, infusing it with a glow without blinding its onlookers. Slate is certain to comment on the architecture of the boats, noting the subtleties that only its own owner would normally appreciate.

I find a small school of fish making their way towards the periphery of the waters. As they near the edges, they jump up and down in the waters, almost as if creating a dance. The movement creates small circles that widen and spread from the center towards the edges. These visuals delight my eyes. It also provides an inner peace that has long eluded me. *Nature has this magic*, I think, as I smile, watching a fish approach the corner. The natural scents, the consistency of soft rhythmic sound, the mesmerizing visuals that aren't overbearing, I stand there taking in the beautiful scene before me. *Just peace*, I think. I have been so used to coaching people in re-establishing movement, that I have forgotten the beauty of stillness.

I note a full smile on Slate's face, a natural smile, not one forced by circumstances or expectations, just a projection of inner fulfillment. For the next forty-five minutes, we stand there, leaning ourselves against the edge of the gate, feeling as though we are part of the natural setting. For a few minutes, I allow my weight to shift leaning against Slate's, and he allows my weight to fall against him as he moves closer to me to support it.

He smiles again as we leave and whispers, "It was a good day."

"Yes, I agree, a very good day."

As we make our way toward the car, Slate asks if he can come visit James on Monday. I readily agree. He admits that after he left and went home the other day, he had a feeling of longing, as he parted from his new little friend. "Well, it's a date then. See you on Monday," I say as I blush, noting my choice of words.

On Monday, we walk toward the elevator to visit James. Slate tells me that he can only stay for around ten minutes as he is preparing a speech. "For what?" I ask. He blushes like a young boy who has something to hide.

"Well, it seems that I have been chosen to speak at an award ceremony. Apparently, a group of my colleagues feel that I facilitate advancements in medical practice, at least that is the honor bestowed upon its recipients." Slate is humble, but I glow with pride as he casually makes mention of the award.

"You deserve it, Slate," I say as we walk with the same rhythmic pacing toward the elevator door, which is about to open. As we move to enter, I hear Slate's name called from a short distance away. He hears his name as well, only to turn around and find his mother standing there, a bit out of breath, but every hair in place just like her son's. She greets us with a non-English religious reference. The words, though beautiful and poetic, aren't well received in my ears. The last conversation I want to have right now is about religion. She reveals a beautiful satin pouch in her hands, which she informs us was garnered from her recent travels.

Nina, a preacher's daughter, was the meanest girl in the neighborhood. She was able to find a nickname that was undesirable for everyone in the neighborhood. Nina often blocked my path when we were in the playground. She was tall for her age and towered over the younger girls, exhibiting her force on them. I always wondered how someone who came from a household preaching about God could have such a nasty disposition. Worse yet, I never noted her parents rebuking her or chastising her for her behavior. Could it be that they really didn't know?

When I was young, I thought of God as this superhero. I imagined he would suddenly descend, evidencing his powers in an hour of need or distress. However, I never did feel that superpower emerge in my times of distress. This indifference towards religion was further strengthened as I saw people suffer and pray and suffer and pray some more. Some got better, and others didn't. There seemed to be a randomness in it all. I know my father would go to church once a year to commemorate Emily's date of death, but his demeanor wasn't transformed from how it had been before he left. The only way I truly felt a sense of God was from watching the deeds of others. I watched how some close to Him behaved inappropriately, while others were the embodiment of goodness. I envied the people whose compassion was part of their being and felt bad all at once, envying their goodness but feeling bad for them for feeling others' pain, shame, and guilt. I don't know how I feel about God or religion. It is like making a judgment call on a stranger. I can't feel love or hate or anger or any of the other emotions people claim to feel because it is a subject I really don't comprehend.

Slate's mother hands me the silk pouch. It feels great to the touch, and as I open it, it reveals two hands clasped in prayer on a delicately woven bracelet. "It is just a little something I picked up in Southeast Asia," she says. "I thought you would like it."

I look at her face as she presents it. There is warmth and anticipation as she gauges my reaction. Slate has already walked away, as he determined he wasn't the intended party in this exchange. I feel this extreme warmth emanating from my core, spreading out to each of my limbs. She leans forward for a hug, and I graciously return the hug. Slate's mother, Kat, is one of those compassionate people. She is beautiful on the outside, but her inner beauty radiates as well.

She travels around the world, finding ways to better people's lives while hers has been turned upside down. I envision the women who spent their time creating this gift, what type of lives they must live, picturing the small villages that are their homes. Slate paces through the hallways, as I have this exchange with his mother. His body tenses as he approaches her, and he has the onset of annoyance on his face. I quickly put my arm in front of him, "Your mother gave me this gift. Isn't it lovely!"

His body relaxes, and he can't help but appreciate his mother's graciousness. "Yes, that's my mom," he says as he shares a loving momentary glance with his mother. Slate exchanges a few words with her, and they part, both calm and content.

Slate joins me to visit with James and observes me rubbing my new bracelet while in the elevator on our way up. "You know a genie doesn't come out of it," Slate says in a sarcastic tone.

"Really? I thought one would pop up right now," I say with a bit of comedic undertone. "No, I am not waiting for a genie. I am waiting for a superhero, if you must know." We both share a small pure giggle at the notion, and I cover my bracelet with my lab coat.

We walk into James's room, and he smiles at us. I open a book. It's entitled *Danny and His Ball*. James shows an interest. He peeks at the pictures of seven-year-old Danny holding a bright and colorful ball in his hand.

The book tells the story of a boy whose best friend is his ball. He takes it everywhere. He bounces it, catches it, throws it, rolls it up the wall, rolls it down the bed, makes it look like an ice cream cone on his cup, bounces it on the wall, and against a tree. He loves his ball; it always comes back to him. Then one day, Danny can't find his ball. It rolls too far away for Danny to see, but he searches, and as he gets closer and closer, he finds his ball dirty and cracked sitting at the edge of the park. There stands another boy, Jed, holding his own ball, bouncing, throwing, and catching. This time Jed throws Danny his own ball, and they play together.

James says, "Ball," and even HE looks surprised at hearing his own voice. Jonathan stands up, like he witnessed a miracle. James repeats the word "ball" again and adds a few more words. I look back at my bracelet, the hands locked in prayer beam. Perhaps a hero has emerged from these clasped hands. I smile.

When I get home, I hear the crashing of glass and almost a shriek coming from my neighbor, Mr. Dawson's home. *What now?* I think as my life feels like an ever-persistent flow of drama. I bang on his door, asking if everything is okay, but no answer comes out. I bang again and again and take out my cell phone, ready to call the cops. I imagine all kinds of madness taking place in that apartment. I hear Mr. Dawson's voice. I recognize it, even though our conversations have been basically nonexistent. I hear him talking as if he is conversing with someone, but no one else responds. He is talking in some kind of code, and I bang on the door again. Still no response. I start to dial 911, not knowing exactly what is going on, but I hear footsteps come toward the door, and my own heartbeat can literally be heard in my ears.

The door opens, and I see a disheveled Mr. Dawson. He has a mild cut on his wrist, most likely from whatever was broken. I look inside but see no one else. I am afraid of him, not knowing what is going on and not knowing much about him in the first place. However, I find myself asking him if he needs help. He stares at me stone-faced. *Maybe he remembers something,* I think. I tell him that I am going to call an ambulance now, so he can get checked out. Those words are the impetus that changes his facial features, as they have now turned to anger or fear or an expression I have never seen before.

I walk backward, in case he lunges at me, but he now firmly says, "No help," and adds, "Go away."

I do go away; I run into my apartment and get some ice with a first aid kit and return. Mr. Dawson is angry at my return but looks at the kit in my hand. "Is it okay if I just look at your cut?" Surprisingly, he agrees. I walk with him toward his sink at his direction and clean the wound. I put on gloves, which scare him at first, but remind him, "Germs." When he remembers his amputated fingers, he pulls back in shock.

"I work in a hospital. It's okay," I say, and he slowly moves his hand back toward me. "Mr. Dawson, can I call someone for you?" I ask.

"Someone?" he sneers. "I don't have any someones."

"Do you want to go to the hospital for them to check you out? I can hook you up with some great doctors. I think they could better advise you as to what to do."

"No hospitals!" he says with a snarl. I ask again, but he grows angrier. "No hospitals! Go back to your apartment and leave me alone!" he shouts. I do. I tell him if he needs anything, I am right next door.

At night I sleep lightly in anticipation of some rant or sounds coming from next door, but there aren't any, so in the morning, I wake up and knock on the door, saying, "It's Jules, your neighbor."

Mr. Dawson says, "Go away, I am okay!"

So, I gather my belongings and head to work. I anticipate that this man doesn't eat right or sleep, or engage in any meaningful activities given his disposition and physicality.

I call my father as I walk toward the hospital, just as I have done every day since his surgery. He is now home under my mother's care. He says he is okay and has daily nurse visits to tend to his bandages. He sounds like someone homesick, even though he is home. He won't return to work for another few weeks and is catching up on some reading material, which he admits he hasn't done in months. I hear my mother's voice on the other side of the phone, and he reads to me to drown out her voice. Once her voice is no longer heard, he stops reading. My father constantly fixed things around the house. He always had the words 'fix,' 'repair,' and 'assemble' on his tongue, never stating that anything was broken or shattered. It was almost reflexive for him to grab some tools to fix whatever it was, to attest to the fact that things could be salvaged. "It is your turn to fix yourself, Dad," I say. He doesn't hear me because my words are drowned out by the sound of a doorbell ringing, and my father wishes me a good day and hangs up.

With my cell phone still in hand, I walk into the hospital to be greeted with a sound of heavy machinery to further advance the additional wing to the hospital. The sound is less annoying today because it's only the backdrop to a beautiful wall design featuring a dove. I walk upstairs, avoiding the elevator to improve my own cardiac stamina.

I arrive at the same time as a new intern; he comes in bright-eyed with an eagerness to please. He swallows up every word, evidencing a little edge of nervousness that keeps one alert and attentive. Nevin, the new intern, gives the clinical rundown on a traumatic brain injury patient. "She sustained an insult to the arcuate fasciculus." He turns mid-sentence to face me, singling me out for his explanation. "You know, the part of the brain responsible for—"

I pipe up to continue his sentence, "The part of the brain that connects part of the temporal lobe and parietal lobe to the frontal lobe, Broca to Wernicke's area. It plays a role in language—"

Kevin, who is on the team, smiles and says, "He is an intern, be gentle." I feel some remorse at jumping down his throat, but I perceive myself as a perpetual intern, constantly proving my worth at every corner, in every respect, ever since childhood.

Slate was late to work today, which is unusual for him. While responding to Kevin, Slate whisks past the nurses' station and through the corridors that lead to his office. I wasn't sure if it was the right thing to do, but I follow him. I slowly open the door, which is already a crack open. Slate's six-foot-two-inch frame is sliding down the wall until he lands, knees bent, on the ground. He is attempting to keep the tears from flowing from his eyes, but somehow many have escaped. Slate has always been poised and professional. I could not imagine what spurred such behavior but knew it must have been life-changing. I approach him and squat to meet him at eye level. When our eyes meet, he says, "Why don't you ever call me Jonathan? Why can't you call me Jonathan?"

The question catches me off guard. I look at him for a few seconds before formulating a coherent response. "I don't really know why I don't call you Jonathan, but I know that when I say your name, I feel something, an unidentifiable something."

In response, Slate steadies his voice and says, "They have him in custody."

"Whom do they have in custody?" I ask with a level of panic.

"The guy who killed Jenny . . . my *sister*."

"How?" I inquire.

"A friend of his came forward and implicated him in the crime, and shockingly, he confessed. After all these years, he confessed!"

The words are shocking, and I instinctively move toward Slate, even though I am trembling myself. I stroke his cheek. Given the fact that he has disclosed something so personal and allowed himself to be vulnerable in my presence, I take the liberty of saying to him what should have been said years ago. "Jonathan, it's not your fault. All you did was allow your sister to borrow your car. You are one of the best people I know, and I am sure you were a good brother. You are kind and considerate and generous, and unlike myself, you try to pretend you are not miserable for the sake of others' happiness. This is a rare trait." The words keep flowing from my mouth even though a part of me wants to stop them. "Something is

260

wrong with me, Jonathan. I always feel like I need to run away from myself but can't. You know how in vows, one says, 'In sickness and in health, in good times and in bad times?' Well, I guess I only know how to be there for someone in sickness and bad times and have no idea how to engage with them in health and happiness. As strange as it may seem, while others leave their mates when they are disabled and damaged, I only feel comfortable in a damaged environment. I just don't know how to enjoy life in the way other people do."

I can remember my supervisor's voice during my first internship. "You don't know how to express your emotions," she said firmly, looking at me like I was damaged goods. This was the one time I considered quitting my chosen profession. In theory, I know it is important not to keep things to myself, but practically speaking, it just doesn't work for me. This has been proven to me time and time again. *Don't say anything else, Jules,* I tell myself, as I face Jonathan, who seems to want to talk. I am about to make reference to my childhood, but my mouth won't allow the words out. I just can't say them. I can now see my supervisor's eyes glaring at me after she examined my journal. She shook her head "*no*" as she read through each part, which was intended for staff to get in touch with their own emotions, feelings, and concerns to better enable us to understand our clients' struggles.

In a high-pitched voice, she then said each week, "I see you don't know how to do this." After the fourth week, she closed my journal and said, "Well, since you can't do this, I reckon we should stop." Her attitude and demeanor toward me, which she must have thought was constructive criticism was, in fact, destructive. She had convinced me that I am incapable of sharing my emotions effectively. I felt another blow when I further recalled her saying in a harsh tone that I don't know how to ask for help, like asking for help is part of the job requirement. In truth, I have been alone for a long time and had to make do with me, myself, and I.

For the most part, I wasn't provided with "help" in childhood. I had to figure things out on my own and fend for myself. The next time the opportunity presented itself, I asked another coworker for advice on how to write up an assessment. Apparently, my coworker told my supervisor that I asked for help, and now I was being penalized for it. My supervisor's words lingered in my mind with every one of our meetings. I volleyed with the idea of leaving school and the profession for the next several days, but it was actually a client that changed my mind.

Gale was severely depressed, remaining within the confines of her room and sleeping most of the days. She had quit her job, and her bed was her only friend and family member. As time went on, she began to attend workshops, and soon, interacted with staff. This woman, who initially deemed her existence unworthy, was the impetus for my not abandoning my aspirations and giving me some hope for the future. Aside from learning that I had been emotionally uncommunicative and that I wasn't able to trust others for help, the one valuable lesson I did learn was never to dismiss anyone else's emotions, regardless of what I may feel at the time.

Emotions belong to others; like their personality, it's part of them. I don't get to dictate how they should feel, only to ensure that their manifestations of a given emotion are neither detrimental to themselves nor to others.

After I finish my tirade. I look Jonathan in the face, and it's a face I have never seen; I find it to be uninterpretable. Then as I look eye to eye at Jonathan, I realize that I had put my foot royally in my mouth when I blurted out, "I only know how to interact with the damaged." The words now echo in my ears. Jonathan may have interpreted it as though I consider him to be damaged, but he remains silent. I feel not only guilt, but I know I am wrong at having made this whole episode about me when it should have been about him and his sister. It was his turn to vent and let his emotions out freely. It wasn't about me. I have stolen his moment.

I give him my hand, and he takes it. I help him up toward the chair in his office. He readjusts his perfectly ironed shirt that became untucked as he sat on the floor and smooths down a few raised hairs. He looks at me for a moment before responding. His eyes are like a small child's looking for a hug from his mother when he has injured himself. He then takes out a paper from the envelope that he has carried with him for years, tears it up, and throws it in his trash bin. His face returns to its old self, and I remember all those times this man came to get me out of a bind.

"Maybe we both start again?" he says. Then his eyes brighten, and he adds, "Jules, its Jonathan, okay? Call me Jonathan." He looks at me once more, reinforcing, "Jonathan."

I turn to leave, but before I do, I reach over and squeeze his hand, and I can feel the full pressure of his hand squeeze back. *He doesn't know my secret,* I think at first, but then I remember he has known me for a really long time. Jonathan is unsure how to respond but nods and says nothing.

The day goes on with a strange silence between us like he is trying to figure out what to do with his life now that there is some level of closure, and now that we have opened another Pandora's box.

Stephanie notices my solemn mood and invites me over to her home. As we leave, I see a small flower growing on the fence that surrounds the hospital. It hasn't yet succumbed to the changing autumn weather. It sits there alone, but its beauty is astounding. Its color is bright, and its leaves open, not yet ready to die. I vow to appreciate its presence and beauty, so long as time will allow it to live. It brings a smile to my face.

Stephanie meets me outside and remarks about the smile on my face. "Oh, so you don't need cheering up. That's great because my kids like the fun Jules better."

Jules and fun don't seem like they go together in a sentence, but it is still nice to hear.

Chapter 10: Combat or Tickled Pink

Stephanie's home is considerably larger than mine, but it's much smaller than my childhood home. Her home has a country-like charm, but with modern undertones. One can see small items in need of repair, like a spindle on the banister and a few little nicks in cabinets, a stained floorboard, a broken tile in the bathroom. Stephanie is very detail-oriented; she has far surpassed me in that respect. That's why she is a great doctor, but she chooses to look away from these minute failings in her overall beautiful apartment because she knows what is important. She is very sentimental, still keeping her sticker album from childhood, her paddleball from grade school at which she was a pro, and has every picture ever taken with friends and family neatly bound in binders by date. Her daughter, Lilly, grabs my hand enthusiastically, while almost jumping up and down in anticipation. She drags me by the hand up the stairs toward her room. My hand feels a bit out of whack, but I graciously accept her little pudgy hands. The look of joy on her face is priceless. She points, jumping up yet higher with a little squeal, and there stands her wardrobe, no longer a pristine white but a pink color, her favorite color.

"Oh, wow! Pink!"

"No," she says with her eyebrows dancing in delight. "It's ballet-slipper pink!"

"It is a beautiful fit for a princess like you." She blushes. She then holds up two matching pink pillows to accent her bed. Her delight in small things reminds me of her mother. It's an important characteristic for a child to have, particularly in this day and age.

We return to the kitchen to meet up with Stephanie.

"It was the grandest room ever," I say in earshot of Lilly, who is still giddy. In a hushed tone, I tell Stephanie, "She is a great kid. Like mother, like daughter. How did that piece of furniture come to be a ballerina pink?" I inquire.

"It is ballet-slipper pink," Stephanie retorts with the same smile as her daughter's. "We worked on it together last weekend."

Now I understand why those nicks and scratches in her tiles and her cabinets aren't yet fixed and why she missed a great theatrical performance last week when she had waited months to see it because she prioritizes. She emotionally prioritizes. Giving children *things* only serves momentary pleasures, it's the *experiences* they share that create lifetime memories and brings true joy. In my own home, I had toys, but siblings wouldn't play with me. There were few shared experiences with our parents, yet my home was pristine and beautiful.

I share one trait with Stephanie. I seek happiness in simplicity, despite being a self-proclaimed pessimist. Those small things give us a few moments or even seconds of delight like when you snuggle up to your newly washed sheets; when a person smiles at you on a bad day; when rain dissipates as you exit a building; when someone holds the door for you at just the right moment when you're carrying a box bigger than yourself; when you find an unbroken seashell along the polluted beach trail; when your figure fits perfectly back into your old skirt or jeans after losing an inch; when you get that last slice of pizza that has your favorite topping on it; when you take that first sip of water after you haven't had a drink all day; when your pen doesn't fail you at a time you're signing important documents; when you stand back and admire that you were able to independently repair your toilet without the wait and expense of the plumber; when the paint color you chose actually works on the walls in your home; when the workplace ID lets you in on the first try; when the amount due on your bill is twenty-seven dollars instead of the thirty dollars you had calculated. The list is endless, but it is only a detailed eye that can see these small things and smile with gratitude, but like muscles in our body, developing a detailed eye comes from awareness, training, and from repetition.

My father phones me, letting me know that he has arranged for cardiac rehab training to be initiated in a few weeks. He thanks me for the names and numbers I provided. This time his voice is muffled, and I think him incapable of raising his voice.

"Are you feeling okay, Dad?" I ask.

"I am fine."

And then I hear it, the sound of a tool which he has forgotten to turn off. "Dad, you are supposed to be resting," I say in a firm voice.

"Calm down, Jules. I just wanted to hear that sound. It will help me sleep better."

"Goodnight, Dad," I say, thinking we have exchanged more words in the last few weeks than practically ever.

When I get home, Mr. Dawson is standing at my door, no smile, but he says, "Hello," which is so unusual that it scares me. He apologizes for the day before and looks at me again and says, "You look like my daughter."

"Oh, you have a daughter? Why don't we call her?"

"I told you yesterday, I DON'T HAVE A SOMEONE!" he says angrily. I think that maybe his daughter died, and that haunts him in the way that my aunt's death haunted my father's family. I hear him mumbling like I have in the past, something to do with politics. " . . . human life without politics . . . politics without human life . . ."

I put my hand on his arm. I feel him jump back like someone startled in combat, and then I glance at his hands and his demeanor. *Like combat,* I say to myself. "Mr. Dawson, I don't want to pry. Are you . . . were you a soldier?" The words seem to strike a chord, as his eyes now evidence a similar vulnerability to the type my patients' eyes express when they are told they need to have a catheter or have to wear adult diapers.

He answers, "My daughter doesn't know me." He looks down at his hands, "The war took her away from me." I don't fully understand. At first, he fails to elaborate, but he then adds, "The war took everything away from me." He turns toward his apartment, ready to go back in.

"Mr. Dawson," I say, this time in a quiet manner. "I had a really hard day, and I am sure you have had many really hard days. When I am stressed, I create notecards from recycled paper, and I have some paper prepared in my apartment. If you want, you can join me." He refuses, so I add, "I will leave the door open. You can come if you like."

I am still a bit in fear of him, not knowing his mental state. But I remember my dad pointing out a group of soldiers as we walked near a pier one day. "These people defend your right to play in the playground, walk the streets, go to public school." It was only one of a handful of times that my father spoke with such fervor. I recall those words and think that regardless of whatever happened, this man is still some kind of hero. In the midst of my putting together my notecards, Mr. Dawson arrives. I wonder what my friends would say about my inviting a stranger into my home, especially Mr. Dawson, who Sasha, my old friend and neighbor, would reference as, "that scary old man next door." Sasha provided me with a good dose of fear, and I know that drama has its way of following me around. I, therefore, leave my phone on, ready to dial.

As Mr. Dawson walks in, at first, he yells about the mess. I allow him to say it without retorting because I don't feel belittled by his words; I recognize that it is just a man who wants to command something in his life. He touches the different textures and eyes the varied colors of my notecards, asking who they are for. "I don't have lots of someones either, at least not family," I say, "These are not for my family, but they are for a few someones that are my friends. They enjoy it."

He pushes a chair over to the table and joins in. His eyes have softened.

"Maybe we can send one to your daughter?"

"I don't think my daughter would want one even if she knew it was my last written word ever. Even if I died tomorrow, she wouldn't care."

"Well then, let us send one to someone who helps you out."

"Margaret."

"Oh, Margaret? Who's Margaret?"

"The lady at the bank. She always helps me fill out my slips." As he answers, he looks down at his imperfect hands.

"We can make one for her, Mr. Dawson. Do you know how to use the computer?"

Mr. Dawson looks at me, "You mean that technology stuff? I don't like that stuff." He returns his focus to the note-making, which I modified to enable him to grasp the shreds before him. He starts to talk. He talks a lot. I imagine he talks more than he has in a long time, almost failing to swallow. He shares how he lost his friends in combat; that his wife divorced him after he came home; that he distanced himself from his daughter for her to have a better life; the feeling of dread when he realized many of his fingers were gone; and his inability to get a good job. He also spoke about the war, the changes in temperature he endured, the small daily annoyances of having limited food choices, his inability to sleep, the time a kidney

270

stone formed when he was in intense heat. He lost every role in his life, husband, father, friend, soldier, and he lost his fingers that were requisite for most daily tasks.

He relies upon people to do tasks that he might be able to do by himself with the proper tools, and I open the computer to show him how much easier it would be for him to write the letter, but he refuses to try. I create a small ball-like structure from the material in my home, place it in his palm, and put a band around it that secures it to his remaining fingers, and he glides along the page, attempting to write.

Instead of the thank you note to Margaret, he writes, "Dear Emma." I feel like I am intruding on a personal moment. "I am so sorry, Emma, that I wasn't a good father to you . . ." He writes a bit more about his feelings for her and explains why he left. It takes time for him to get used to not only the writing implement but to expressing thoughts that haven't been expressed in written form in a while. He must have imagined the likes of such a communication many days and nights throughout the years but hadn't fathomed that he'd ever actually be capable, either emotionally or physically, to write it. He ends the letter, "Politics breeds war, people make peace, humanity makes progress." He looks at it in disbelief that his own hands composed this letter. I provide him with an envelope.

"What's your name?" he asks.

"Jules," I say, while reflecting on the fact that this man has divulged many years of secrets without knowing my name.

"What's your full name?"

"Julianne Lovell Westcott."

"I am Sergeant Henry Radford Dawson. Nice to have met you."

"Nice to have met you, too," I say, feeling my cheeks form a full smile.

Before he leaves, he adds, "I'll bet your dad is really proud of you," and I nod, wishing for its truth. And he walks out, this time closing the door gently behind him. I look at the beautiful notecards. They are quite feminine looking, and yet a strong sergeant looked like he had a few moments of tranquility while making them. Mr. Dawson was a great diversion to the affairs of the day. I think I will ask Stephanie for her advice about Mr. Dawson, given that her father is a veteran.

The next morning, I look at my notecards, stacking them neatly at the side, ensuring that they remain crisp. I leave my apartment, at first ready to knock on Mr. Dawson's door, but refrain. *He needs his own time*, I think. I leave and walk a block, noting the sight at the other end of the corner across the street. It is Mr. Dawson standing at the mailbox. He takes a deep breath and throws an envelope in. He stands there for a few seconds and keeps checking that it has gone down to join the other letters in the box. Mr. Dawson doesn't see me, but I whisper, "Have a good day, Mr. Dawson," hoping the same for myself.

I return to work and am informed that Dr. Kalmar, chief of pediatrics, has returned. Mr. Dawson is trying to reconnect with his daughter,

272

and Dr. Kalmar is learning to disconnect from the memory of her son. I make my way upstairs to the pediatric wing but have no idea what to say. What do you say to someone who has lost a child so senselessly? Her loss is surely compounded by her professional role being a doctor and caregiver of children. I fear that she will feel judged by me, or that I will cause her more grief, so at first, I only nod as she passes me by. She nods back, but as she nears the end of the hallway, I run after her. "Dr. Kalmar, I'm sure I am the hundredth person to accost you in the hallway. There aren't any words that probably are right, but I remember your son. He was a good kid. He was a good kid on a bad day. I hope you can find peace and your heart heals." She nods and makes a quick getaway, looking back at me momentarily.

Nurse Abbie approaches me in the hallway and happily reports that James was really good today. He asked for his toothbrush and allowed the nurse to brush his teeth, even attempting it on his own. I am glad to have some positive news, and I return to my caseload downstairs.

The next day, Jonathan arrives to work, walking slow-paced in the hallways. I notice the bags under his eyes, as I see him in the office. He looks exhausted, but acknowledges my existence with a friendly, "Hel-lo." He has his laptop with him and is taking small bites from a perfectly semi-unwrapped protein bar. Within seconds, he is staring into the screen almost in a trance-like state. When he is agitated, he writes everything down, like a machine that just had its battery changed. I reason that the source of his agitation is me, but I soon realize that he repeats, "mast cell activation," as he vigorously devours the research articles before him. "It is not just allergies," he whispers. "It's mast cells . . . mast cell activation," he says. He turns to me with a look I have seen before. It is a look of defeat.

"Jonathan, you can't always help everyone. You can only try your best, and you always try your best!" My words must have calmed him a bit because he keeps writing, albeit at a slower pace. This time, he allows himself a brief reprieve to shake out the arm cramp he previously ignored. Before I leave, I turn back, "Slate, I mean Jonathan, I know you're really busy today. Can we meet up tomorrow?"

"Yes, we should meet tomorrow," he says in a decisive voice. He looks at me briefly as I exit, only to immediately return to his work.

Kevin passes me in the hallway, asking me to wait, as he runs into his office and grabs a stack of papers and books. He carries it, making him slouch a bit from the weight. "Jules, these are my baseball gems. Everything you want to know. You can look through it. I will leave it in my office for your perusing, and maybe you want to meet up next Saturday for a run-through with the master?" Kevin points at himself a big smile across his face.

"Sure. Thank you!" I take the first available book from the pile, which has lots of pictures, as I definitely need visual referencing for base-ball. I walk away, surprised that Kevin took all this time for me. I also imagine Adam's face lighting up as he flips through the book, which thus far seems quite interesting.

274

The next day, after I have completed my day's paperwork, I bump into Jonathan standing near my office as I exit. He asks if we can go for a drink. I agree, and we make our way to the nearest café.

While taking our seats, Jonathan says, "Listen, I am really sorry about the other day." He then starts apologizing for his tears, adding, "I was in a really bad place."

I find it surprising that he apologizes for his tears. It was actually refreshing to see him cry. Just knowing that he could cry was some sort of reassuring factor. "Don't apologize for crying or for your emotions. I actually think it was good that you got a release of some sort, similar to a workout in the gym." He nods a bit. His latte arrives, making him take a sip, which allows me to take deep breaths and relax before I make my next statement. When he is done, I cut him off—although he is in the middle of expressing his opinion about the latte, which was served with some sort of fancy cream and is new on the menu—because if I don't say it now, I may never.

"Jonathan, I need to tell you something." He perks up his ears like he usually does, being the good listener that he is. "You know that I moved out of my house in my teens and have lived alone for a long time?" He nods in the affirmative. "You know how I never really visit my family, and usually just go somewhere else for the holidays." He nods again, this time crinkling his forehead with anticipation. "The truth is, I don't really have a great relationship with my family, particularly with my mother. Well . . .

Well . . . Well . . ." I hesitate—"It's because when I was younger, my mother hurt me a lot. She would hit me, tug at me, throw things at me, and it was compounded further by her negative words. It was only directed at me, not my siblings, and somehow they, too, learned to treat me differently."

I could see Jonathan's eyes flaring. I add, "Not nearly as bad as James," to decrease the severity of the visual that his brain may be conjuring. "When my grandmother moved in, it stopped. After that, I was generally just ignored by my mother. My grandmother was kind to me; she made things semi-normal."

Jonathan takes my hand. "I'm so sorry, Jules." I see him deflecting a tear as my own have started rolling down my cheek.

"I never tell anyone about it because it was a long time ago, and I should be over it. I lived in a house, had food, clothes, went to school, played in a yard, and it wasn't like the abuse some other kids suffer. I treat people all the time who can barely manage simple tasks, and whose lives are upside down." My brain recalls Jonathan's words yesterday, 'Mast cell activation' Someone's immune system is failing, and I am burdening him with baggage that happened years ago. "I feel like my brain knows I should forget about it, but my heart can't. I know that when I am around you and James, I feel a little more alive."

Jonathan looks at me with a surprised expression, "Do you actually feel guilty about not forgetting, Jules, because you weren't as badly hurt as some other people are and because you had a home?" He takes a deep

276

breath, "It is never okay for someone to hurt you, especially not a parent."

I feel him clenching his hands in anger at the thought. I wipe my tears, which I hadn't initially sensed streaming from my eyes. "I guess you're right." I take the opportunity to add, "And you shouldn't feel any responsibility or guilt for your sister's death. You were just her brother, a good one, and shouldn't reflect on yourself any other way."

Jonathan adds, "You are not damaged. You never were damaged. We are both not damaged, just in pain."

We continue to sip our drinks, remaining quiet for a few minutes. I remember the book on baseball in my handbag and take it out to show Jonathan. Despite not being as big a baseball enthusiast as Kevin, he, nevertheless, enjoys the various photographs and facts.

I walk home, feeling a lightness to my step and relief at Jonathan's reaction. When I reach my apartment, I create a bit more floor space by placing objects over the highest shelf, so that I can practice my pitching skills. I find it more difficult than depicted in the illustrations, and get a bit sore after my twenty-second attempt, but sense the endorphins that the activity generates, which feels quite good.

Chapter 11: Just Shuffling Along or Purposeful

It's Saturday, and the phone rings. I chose not to go out today due to rough weather and am happy I stayed at home. It's a voice from the past, the recent past. A voice that I welcome to hear, "Hi Jules, its Sasha." She hardly has the opportunity to finish her sentence when I speak, barely catching my breath for five minutes, updating her on life at the hospital, and the craziness that has become my existence. I also tell her of my good fortune to have stumbled upon this little boy named James. Sasha is my surrogate mother, former neighbor, and has also been one of my closest friends. I never told her about my being abused as a child, but she sensed something was wrong early on in our relationship and became my shoulder to lean on. Sasha and I share a love of nature, and she often accompanied me on strolls. She was able to demonstrate tough love, yet her caring nature always came through.

Sasha was now fifty-four, but I had met her in her early forties. She lent a listening ear, as I confided in her about the bumpy road I call life. She smiled, offered words of encouragement, never holding me back from venting. She was also a great cook and helped me sharpen my culinary skills. "Stop following recipes," she would say, as her hands whipped up a meal without much thought. "Just feel it. Look at the consistency and texture. Touch it, and smell it, and you will know." However, I was never able to achieve the level of skill that Sasha had. I could discuss almost anything with her, and she was a never-ending source of advice. She suggested the best laundry detergent to buy, the best way to get stains out, how to grout and tile, and she provided good dating advice. She had worked on Wall Street for many years and had raised a son as a single mother. Her son, now a computer engineer, had subsequently moved to California's Silicon Valley.

At age forty-seven, Sasha began to feel somewhat fatigued and attributed it to the general aging process. She began to sleep in longer, but her fatigue persisted. In addition, she began to have gastric pain that was somewhat unusual, coupled with constipation. She never mentioned any of those symptoms to me, but I initially noticed how slowly she was climbing the stairs. One day, she admitted she had been tired, actually, very tired.

"Are you tired every day?" I asked, and she gave me a brief nod of the head. "Does anything else bother you?"

She shrugged her shoulders at first but then pointed to her stomach area. When she did this, I observed that her clothing was hugging her a bit tighter than usual, and the area was quite swollen. As I moved my hand toward her stomach, she pushed it vehemently away. I asked if she had any itching or muscle aches, and she replied, "No." I hadn't observed any change in her coloring, but when she admitted that her pains had persisted for a few months, I strongly urged her to see her doctor. Sasha was not the type to go running to doctors for every ache and pain. She was from

Eastern Europe and had mostly been exposed to alternative medicine and natural remedies in her youth, particularly as she was from a remote area. As a child, she had received bee-bite therapy for muscle aches, which got better within three months. Her father had undergone a cooling procedure for heart problems. She was the type of woman that laughed at me when I said that two miles was a distance to walk.

Sasha continued with her daily routines, only scheduling an appointment with the doctor for six weeks later. She was becoming progressively weaker but was also cutting back on extracurricular activities to try and even the score. She went to the doctor who took a basic panel of blood work, which was when the unfortunate news arose. Sasha's liver enzymes were way off the charts. After further investigation, it was discovered that she suffered from primary biliary cholangitis. A biopsy revealed her liver damage was extensive. The damage had been accumulating over some time. It came as quite a shock as Sasha generally ate well, wasn't a smoker or drinker, and hadn't shown signs of any autoimmune disease or inflammatory condition.

Sasha was in such a state of shock that she failed to process what was happening to her. She tried to avoid the topic, always asking me to share my own news. She became weaker but kept going to work, making different excuses for why she wasn't up to par. She was constantly flinching from pain but denied her great discomfort when asked. Her skin became drier, and she avoided walking in the sun to prevent further dryness. She was fighting for her life, not necessarily fighting for her liver. She was trying to hold on to the strong Sasha and was ignoring what she needed to do. The strange thing is that Sasha had very little outward appearance that indicated she was a sickly woman. She looked beautiful, particularly as she was a well-dressed and put-together woman. External scars and facial discoloration are what people think of when they think of illness. Yet, surprisingly, at this point, she had none of that. Although she was placed on an organ transplant list, she filed any medical records away in a drawer, making them almost inaccessible. She didn't even confide in her son about her disease until three months after she found out. Her workload was becoming impossible, her eyes eventually bearing a yellow tinge, and her skin becoming a bit itchy and discolored. Social outings became nonexistent, fatigue coupled with dietary restrictions precluded monthly restaurant visits, and even daily chores were a hassle.

I didn't tell her, but the news of Sasha's illness hit me hard. She had been a constant in my life for a few years now, and conceptualizing that she may no longer exist in the near future was heart-rending. It was as if my grandmother was dying all over again.

The liver, I think of it as Slate's obsession, is an organ that can regenerate, but only until it's significantly destroyed. It removes toxins, and when it fails, toxins accumulate in the body. It is known as an organ that represents anger in some philosophical ideations.

My mother was an angry person, but Sasha was the opposite. She knew how to provide tough love with gentleness. Why was she being punished like this? Perhaps I was the toxicity that brought on her condition. I contemplated the thought only to dismiss it; I realized we have had a mutually beneficial relationship. Sasha taught me the difference between constructive criticism and being put down. She was a strong, independent woman. I confided in Slate to garner more medical information, and he provided several suggestions. I sat in my apartment for a full day recording and searching the different options.

My mind and body needed a break, so I went to the local park, where I often go to clear my mind. I noticed a bird perched on the branch of a tree and then caught sight of a nest with a few baby chicks. The nest had previously been obscured from my vision. They were chirping to each other in harmony like a coherent group. I believed that they were sparrows, given their small frame and color. It was unusual to see so many birds in autumn. They would soon likely disappear, along with their banter. Their presence, though fleeting, would be missed during the cold winter months, and when they return in the spring, their voices would be welcome. On this occasion, a woman sitting at the other end of the park had drawn a number of pigeons to congregate around her. Upon a second look, I noted her feeding them crumbs from a plastic bag. Her bag rested on her walker as she sat on a park bench. She watched them fly up and down, and then when they finally departed, she got up and began to move toward another area. Actually, it was someone else that she moved toward, and the other person took a photo of them together. *How sweet,* I thought, perhaps this man was her son.

The man then took off, moving in my direction. He held his cell phone and texted enthusiastically like something great just happened, and as he passed me, he nearly knocked me over, failing to look directly in his path.

"So sorry," he said, even though we had not collided. "Do you know whom I just met?" he shrieks and names a famous singer from a formerly well-known rock group. "Can you believe it!"

I looked back to see the old woman, but she was gone. *Wow,* I thought, *I'm sorry I didn't have the opportunity to meet with her.* I then scolded myself for my thoughts; no one is "just" an old woman sitting on a bench; everyone has their unique story to tell. An old woman still has a rocker soul, and an ill woman can still be the strongest and most independent woman I have ever met. Every person has value, I remind myself. *That's it,* I think, as a lightbulb goes on in my head, *Sasha forgot she has value.*

I returned to the apartment complex. I banged really hard on Sasha's door, but there was no answer. I knew she was in there; I could hear her TV on, and so, I barged into the apartment. She stood there with a displeased look on her face, holding her side.

"Listen, you can hate me if you want, but you are really important to me, and you're not doing what is in the best interests of someone I really care about, so I am going to put my foot down right now." Sasha smiled, looking at me as if I was incapable of forcing anyone to do anything. She was well-aware of my usual mindset, and my present behavior was inconsistent with that. I stormed through her dining room door, gaining access to the kitchen. Her apartment was more disorganized than usual, and her cabinets and fridge were understocked.

I turned to Sasha, who now appeared upset at my intrusion. "I really care about you, and I need you to let me help you. Please, Sasha, let me help you." I began to cry, which she knew was unusual for me. Sasha pushed her hair back, which had become disheveled from too much time spent in bed. She drew a tissue from the tissue box, and as she handed it to me, she hugged me and began crying herself. I had never seen her cry, not even at her mother's funeral, which I attended. She was crying for herself and for me, for her roles of listening ear, employee, housekeeper, mother figure, all of which she realized she had been losing.

Sasha and I sat down at her dining room table and together compiled a list of things that could be done to lighten her burden.

- Place bed closer to bathroom. Sasha was taking a laxative-like medication that prevents toxic backup and thus reduces the likelihood of stomach swelling and swelling of extremities. Since it precipitated more frequent bowel movements, being closer to a bathroom would be beneficial.

- Create a calendar of doctors' appointments and have a friend or relative accompany her. I offered my own services for some of them and then helped her list other close neighbors that would likely accompany her as well.

- Create weekly grocery lists. She could order items via the internet or call in to a local grocery for delivery.

- Coordinate her laundering with others in her building, only necessitating her going every so often.

- Have all medical staff, neighbors, friends, and any other support-unit numbers programmed into her phone for easy access.

- Provide me with a list of library books that pique her interest. I will pick them up for her on my way home from work.

- Practice energy conservation techniques to prevent fatigue, yet allowing her to be as independent as possible.

- Maintain range of motion with brief exercise activity.

- Watch a movie with Jules every Sunday night, listen to her ramble, and offer good advice.

Sasha smiled when she read the last item on the list.

Sasha was also particularly good at understanding the stock markets. I gave her a notebook to document any news or information regarding stocks and financial markets, so she can be well prepared, as she desired to return to work.

When accompanying Sasha to doctors, I observed that she just sat and agreed with everything the doctors said, never asking any questions or posing any concerns. She became this passive figure, disempowered, and unlike her former self. I wasn't sure if it was fear or fatigue that prevented further conversations.

"Sasha, I know you are reading up on your condition. I have brought you some library books myself covering those topics. So why don't you ever ask the doctors anything? I know you have questions and concerns." She just looked at me. I continued, "You know you are really smart, articulate, and you are entitled to have answers, particularly as they relate to your own body."

Sasha gave a mild nod. I went home thinking she won't change, but to my surprise, she asked some really good questions the next time I accompanied her to the doctor.

Sasha constantly needed to be close to the hospital. She stayed in, continually waiting for the call to come that she would finally be a liver recipient. She barely went out, fearful that her cell phone may lose service. Her home became almost a prison cell; she was chained to the phone.

The time came when she was unable to return to work. The physicality was just too burdensome. After a few weeks, she obtained a commissioned job writing for a small financial firm. The pay was minuscule, but it gave Sasha something to do and lightened her mood.

Also, although she didn't show it, she had concerns not only about her health and her ability to obtain a transplant, but also about finances as she was living off her savings.

Another year passed, and one day, an ordinary day like all the others, I received a call that Sasha had been taken to the hospital for her transplant. A liver had finally arrived.

I ran to the hospital, barely explaining anything to anyone, but Slate was able to fill them in on the details as he had met Sasha on many occasions. I knew Slate was fascinated by the liver, the organ that he called one's second heart and brain.

When Sasha awoke, I think they assumed I was her daughter and let me in without question. Later in the day, her son arrived from California. She was still swollen and provided with pain medications after the surgery. Her eyes barely opened, but she nodded to me with a half-smile. "I am so happy to see you," I whispered, and she squeezed my hand in return. I told her I would be back later as the visits post-surgery were limited to a few minutes.

While in the hospital, Sasha was provided with lists of medications she was to take. In addition to organ transplant rejection meds, antivirals, antibacterials, and antifungals were prescribed to avoid infection. Sasha was to avoid crowded areas, particularly for the first few months as interaction with people would increase the likelihood that she would be exposed to infection. She was also to avoid activities like gardening that posed a higher risk for infection. Precautions were to be taken when eating foods, and fruit and vegetables were to be soaked in a solution before eating. After about a week, Sasha went home. Her son had hired a cleaning crew to scrub down the house to further minimize her risk of infection.

This time Sasha had a very visible mark, a surgical scar indicating sickness. But the irony was that the scar was the beginning of her transformation. Although, to the naked eye only, she appeared far more sickly than she had previous to the surgery, this was not the reality of her bloodwork analyses and her organ function.

When Sasha finally came home, at first, it was as if nothing had changed. The pain from the surgery site was severe. The fatigue still there; moreover, she now had a long list of medications to take during specified times in the day. She was tired, as sleep in the hospital was limited, and interrupted by constant blood draws and other tests.

When I came to visit Sasha in her home, I sat quite a distance from her and refrained from hugging her. It was early in her recovery, and I didn't want to pose any threat to her with infection, particularly given that I worked in a hospital, increasing my exposure. Sasha recalled the former list we had made, and she requested that we make another one now. I was really proud of her for asking. She was trying to empower herself.

We now composed another list of what would be necessary for success.

- Place pills in pillbox noting time of day, and set a timer as a reminder.
- List important phone numbers of transplant team members should

questions or concerns arise and of nurses for biweekly home visitation and inspection of incision site.

- Continue with grocery list call-ins or internet orders.
- Arrange for help with showers and assistance with bandage changes on days when a nurse is not present.
- Take short walks to build endurance.
- Daily log of blood pressure, glucose levels, and assessed pain levels.
- A separate log for daily food intake.
- Ensure fruit and vegetables are soaked in solution before cooking/eating.
- Replace gardening with floral design.
- Have ample access to soap and other supplies to minimize possibility of infection.
- Arrange rotating caregivers to accompany to doctors' appointments and blood draws.

This time Sasha added, "Make sure to watch movies with Jules Sunday night, and she will listen to me complain!" This time I smiled.

A few months into Sasha's recovery, she compiled her own list:

- Compile list of employment opportunities for the interim.
- Take a language course on internet.
- Attempt own grocery shopping.
- Gain clearance from doctor for driving again.

- Ensure use of sunscreen, order a supply of surgical masks accessible for daily wear.
- Rearrange bed to original location and walk to bathroom.
- Take daily fifteen-to-twenty-minute walks to build endurance.
- Thank God and send formal thanks to the family that lost a loved one—the liver donor.

This would take a long time. Although her independence was slowly returning, and Sasha felt grateful, it was mixed with a sense of guilt at living on account of someone else's death.

Some of the fatigue still endured, and Sasha never fully recovered to her former self but made significant improvement. After six months, she returned to working part-time in an inferior position but admitted to herself this was in her best interest. She also took on more activities for herself and was a listening ear again. After a year, she flew to California for a week's visit with grandchildren. This vacation turned into a permanent move. For over a year and a half, I was once again devoid of a mother. The only consolation was our monthly conversations.

After Sasha's transplant, I basically stalked her, ensuring she was okay. She hated it and liked it all at once. I told her, "If the shoe were on the other foot, you, too, would be standing over me making certain that I was adequately caring for myself." She agreed it was true.

It was hard for Sasha to reacquaint herself with social activities.

She had become accustomed to avoiding these tasks due to fatigue, generalized pain, gastric distress, and overall limitations. She had been devoid of normal social interactions outside her intimate family setting and my presence. She also feared crowded places, as it posed an opportunity for infection. Getting back into this part of her former life took the longest.

Sasha advises that she is doing well and then point-blank asks, or tells me, "So, you're going to adopt this boy; is that the plan?" Sasha is abrupt and generally understands me.

"What?" I say, surprised. "Me? Adopt James?"

"Jules, you are going to adopt James," she states almost matter-of-factly. The thought lingers in my mind like she was nurturing a seed that perhaps was already there.

She adds that Jonathan is a good guy; she knew it the first time she met him when he picked up litter in the street, remarking, "Someone could fall."

Then she asks, "Well, are you adopting James?" The thought of keeping James forever makes me happy, but I know it is an impossibility. I must have said the words impossible out loud because Sasha retorts, "Jules, I thought it was an impossibility for me to get a liver, yet I got one so . . ." I hear her grandson in the background calling her.

I say, "Speak to you soon," saving her the pain of hanging up on me during a possible life-altering dialogue.

Before she leaves, she tells me, "Call me any time, day or night," and hangs up with her usual melodic, "Good-bye friend."

Of all the patients I have ever treated, one of the most memorable to date was Anna, a beautiful, well-spoken, nineteen-year-old. She suffered from a progressive illness that affected every system of her body. One wouldn't know it though; her beauty was so overpowering that it overshadowed her pain. Perhaps it wasn't a blessing, but rather a curse. Her mother had died in a car crash before her first birthday. She was raised by a stepmother and had two older sisters and a half-brother. Her family was very loving and were continuously at her bedside whenever she was admitted. They always brought DVDs, music CDs, and "how-to" books and magazines to keep Anna busy and entertained.

As her twentieth birthday approached, I asked her what she wanted for her birthday. To this day, her response haunts me. "I want to be given permission to die." Three days before her twentieth birthday, Anna wrote a poem about a caterpillar. When it finally morphed into a butterfly, it was unable to fly away, as there were too many other butterflies crowding around and blocking its path. Although beautiful and caring, they were hindering it from taking flight. Anna placed the poem over her chest, took a mixture of pills from a bottle, lay down, and died. By the lip prints on the photographs near her bed, we could see that she had kissed pictures of every member of her family. I knew she was riddled with pain twenty-four hours a day and that she wasn't really living a full life. I knew she wanted to die. We tend to make assumptions that when someone has a loving family and doesn't appear outwardly ill, that somehow their illness is an illusion or is a transient part of life.

I went to her funeral and saw how pained her family was as they laid her to rest. A part of me was jealous of how much love her family held for her, but another side of me never wanted to experience such love that would bring equal or perhaps greater pain than the pain I witnessed that day. Maybe that's why I stayed away from both love and from the resulting pain and continued to be numb. I know I miss Sasha, her absence is painful, and suddenly, I am engulfed with a sense of intense loss at the thought of never seeing little James again.

The weekend passes quickly. As I scan through patients' medical files, I note that I have a large caseload to fill today, predominantly with patients recovering from a fractured hyoid bone, an unusual body structure to break, making me believe that the universe is sending some kind of message, although I have yet to discover what it is. Evette meets me at work today, reminding me to join her at six thirty p.m. for a Broadway show. I look forward to it, having that extra pep to my step as I work.

It is six thirty p.m. I make my way to the Broadway show; it will be Evette's last opportunity to attend a performance in the city before her big move. As I stand at a two-block distance from the theatre, I see a woman walking slowly, her walk unsteady, as she shuffles along. Her shoulders droop forward, her arm swing is diminished. Her arm freezes midstride, she has difficulty navigating a soda can in her path. Her initiation is labored, and I walk toward her. An asymmetry of the shoulder is also forming. Her eyes meet mine, and I know those eyes; they have aged, but I know them. She looks at me, then away, then back at me. It's Mrs. Devons, my biology professor. She was an exuberant and proficient teacher. She always had a real-life case study or a model to support every lesson, which further made life interesting. I can still see the vignette she produced on the parts of the cell, wherein each cell part had a video demonstrating its use; it was both informative and entertaining. She waited until you knew the answer, believing that you did and would always say, "Correct!" when someone answered a question. It was as if she was a game show host, and you had won a prize. As she spoke, her eyes twinkled. She had profound respect for the body and personhood.

The next semester, she was also my anatomy professor. She treated the bodies that others called specimens with the utmost respect. She apologized to them as she moved a body part over for a demonstration. She was always certain to reference them with a name. "Thanks, Sandra, for squeezing my hand." "Here are the levator scapulae; this is where Sandra's dress would lie." Ms. Devons was very gentle. If she needed to grab your hand, arm, or shoulder for demonstration purposes, you could barely feel her touch. It was graceful, coupled with tenderness. We weren't allowed to see the patients' faces; they were covered, but the jaw would peek out.

"Isn't David's jaw structure interesting?" she would say. "It is superb. He had the structure of a true model." Mrs. Devons had a look of fascination when presenting the attachment of muscles and how they twist and turn at given junctures.

I remember the dissection of a cat; I remember the sterile instruments and the fur peeking out. "Every creature is beautiful; treat your furry friends with respect. Remember that." And when she demonstrated dissection, it wasn't butchery, it was like the brushstroke of an artist just making a small imprint. My lab partner took the scalpel enthusiastically and, with a heavy hand, plunged it into the cat. I covered my eyes. I think she expected blood to gush out or something, but it didn't. It had been placed in formaldehyde. She found boredom in the absence of gushing blood while I found solitude, and we both looked at each organ, tendon, and ligament.

Mrs. Devons made me feel a certain compassion for humanity and for all beings, living or deceased. I learned from her that patients are people and to show respect. It is because of her that I have learned to forewarn my patients what will transpire during our sessions and tell them how and why they are being touched. It is a basic tenet of human respect.

I watch her now, how her own body fails to move appropriately. The mild pill-rolling tremor of her hand she displays is accompanied by the mild tremor of the upper body. Her vibrant red hair no longer matches the vibrant facial expressions she displayed. As she speaks, a mild decline in the intensity of her voice is present. I hope in my heart of hearts I am seeing incorrectly. *She is just tired,* I tell myself. I tell her how I enjoyed her classes, get her up to date on my job, and thank her again for being an excellent instructor. She looks down and smiles. I am glad the muscles of her mouth can still form a smile. I look at her and know the signs; I have seen them before. She has Parkinson's disease, but I pretend I know nothing, that I am just a former student meeting her former teacher. "Mrs. Devons," I say before I leave, "here is my number." I push it deep into her hands and squeeze. "It would be great to catch up with you again soon."

I watch the theatrical performance. It is great, but my mind plays a different scene. It visualizes wonderful Mrs. Devons and her future. I imagine her in the later stages of Parkinson's, the taut mouth, the drooling as saliva piles up in her mouth, the difficulty with gastric emptying and the constipation, the inability to swallow her food or her meds, the reduced facial expression, urinary infrequency, decreased smell and taste, the diminished quickness of wit coupled with a delay to responding to questions, and perhaps changes in sweating. I think about all the essential therapy she will need: the range of motion exercises for her neck, shoulders, and torso; expiratory muscle training and the small gadgets that facilitate tongue exercises; the food-thickening agents to support her poor swallow; the requirement for smaller meal consumption; the extra dental visits; the herbs and minerals that potentially help with symptoms; the exercises for strengthening her voice and improving her breath support; the prompting for successfully carrying out activity; the necessary support systems to be in place. I recollect her son, then a small boy of ten who came to visit one afternoon when his class was dismissed early, and I imagine his fear looking at his mother's significant frailty in contrast with her former vivacious self. I imagine his worry that she shouldn't fall and hurt herself, or worse yet, that she doesn't choke when eating. I imagine him assisting in her medication regimen and looking out for side effects. I attempt to reassure myself that things aren't as bad as they appear. That there are things to be done like exercises, use of cueing, and implementation of adaptive equipment.

Diagnosis is only one aspect of treatment. It doesn't tell you about someone's personality, their wishes, their thoughts, and it doesn't let you know exactly how much someone has suffered as a consequence of a particular malady. It also doesn't let you know the level of support someone has, and by support, I don't only mean the number of relatives or friends that one has; it's the people that will help you change your bandages, lovingly take you to appointments while providing reassurance, the ones who help you with your routines and look out for you when you are vulnerable. The ones who give you a smile even when you're grumpy. The ones who see you at your best and still accept you at your worst. Several dynamics truly comprise "the sick person."

I imagine Mrs. Devons's medical chart, the medical jargon, and treatment protocols she will likely undergo. I want to write a few extras in her chart. I want to at least tell staff that they are treating Mrs. Devons, the best professor ever, but it is not a criterion for reimbursement or an insurance code. It will likely only be diagnostic referencing, procedures, and medication that they will look at when Mrs. Devons is treated.

I watch the show almost in a trance-like state, not because its beauty has transferred me to another dimension, but more so, because my mind is on other matters. The show has song, dance, and color. I get fragments of its delight, and the young patron on my right is mesmerized, admitting that he is from Kansas, and it is his first. I return my eyes to the beauty of the show just as it is ending. "Mrs. Devons, you will always be that feisty redhead who made me love science and who fostered my curiosity."

My thoughts are interrupted by the round of applause, and the young kid from Kansas has just knocked my Playbill to the floor as he got up to provide his own enthusiastic standing ovation. Evette turns to me as it ends, her eyes sparkling, and I get up to applaud and look at the actors that attempted to delight me and whose efforts were quite evident in the show.

I turn to Evette, "Enjoy your life. Really enjoy it!"

"I'm not dying, Jules, just moving," she says. She looks back one more time before the curtain closes. "Weren't those costumes superb? We should get a wardrobe like that."

She lightens my mood.

It's been a long day, but I need some groceries, so before I make my way home, I stop at a local grocery store. I feel emotionally drained, perhaps morphing into an existential crisis. Since my apartment is a shoebox, a trip to the grocery store consists of picking up a maximum of nine essential products. Yet, selecting them doesn't go quickly. As it is unwise to shop when you are hungry, it is truly ill-advised to shop when you're volleying with someone else's health crisis, which somehow seems to be becoming your own. I find chickpea noodles, a breakfast cereal made of peas, the ninety-nine percent chocolate as well as lychee nuts. I quickly add the new multicolored quinoa to my cart. I locate the extra virgin olive oil and buy the greenest one that's gold standard imported. I purchase a bar of soap with only two ingredients and buy the environmentally friendly laundry detergent. I feel guilty but can't give up my whitening toothpaste, so I leave the organic toothpaste behind. I admit I am curious about them all, imagining their taste, which is generally not like the traditional food product anticipated, but I am up for trying. I overspend by about thirty dollars on organic and health food products, convincing myself it is the right way to go; health is way more important than seeing another movie or finding another entertainment source.

I get home and start on my meal immediately. I make a chickpea noodle, leek, and apricot soup, which kind of tastes weird but flavorful at the same time. My plantain pancake is complimented by the lychee nuts. I always have extra virgin olive oil sitting on my counter. I admit that the olive oil has softened my chapped lips. Even with all the treats, I don't sleep like a baby. I am a stressed-out adult. The next morning, my stomach fails to thank me for the organic and high-end extras I consumed, and I crave a piece of bread. Instead of taking whole grain, I stick to a standard piece of rye.

CHAPTER 12: FISHING FOR PURPOSE

Before I leave for work today, I notice a postcard in my mail. I slip it out from amid the pile of envelopes sitting on my small desk, so small one may mistake it for a child's desk. I see a beautiful picture of five people standing proudly with big grins. It is my dad's brother, Uncle Tray, and his family. My uncle Tray took my siblings and me for outings as a child. Most memorable was one when I was eight years old, right before my grandmother moved in. Tray was an avid fisherman. His truck was filled with fishing gear, wading boots, and a camouflage hat adding to the intrigue of the outing. Tray is my father's youngest brother. He is a bit livelier and has this sarcasm that mimics my own. Tray was the only one of my father's brothers to work a white-collar job. He was an investment banker, yet all his free time was spent in the outdoors. Whenever time afforded him the chance to travel, he sought out great adventures in the jungles or wilderness, sometimes scaling mountains. Despite working at a desk for most of the day, his hands were still rough, and his skin chapped from the elements. For every word that my father refrained from speaking, Tray spoke twice as much. He enjoyed chatter and had an eclectic group of terms he employed frequently when speaking. Tray had a vivacity to him, perhaps because he was too young to recall Emily's death.

Tray was one of a few of my relatives that I felt liked me. He called me Curlicue as a child, as I had the only curly hair in the family, and he'd wink in my direction when we left his house. Tray gave me pony rides and took me to the zoo. Tray delicately fed the animals like they were his own children, giving them all a nickname despite their already having a zoo-given name. Sometimes he would let me name them. Tray was one of those lost people who perpetually traveled to find themselves, only to continue to travel when they are still unfound. Still, I would definitely deem him the kindest of my extended family members.

Tray invited my siblings and me on a fishing trip. As we approached the waters during our first fishing expedition, Tray pointed to the fishing gear and explained how to make use of it. We each had our turn. My brother thought he caught a fish, but it turned out to be a pollutant, a plastic bottle. Next, it was my turn. I had this intense determination to catch a fish on that hook. I felt a sudden pull and a tug. Tray came to help me when he noticed the force pulling me in. I wiped my eyes in disbelief. There it was, a beautiful fish attached to my hook. It wasn't a really big fish, though it appeared grand in my eyes. I beamed with pride at having been the family member to achieve the goal, and then I looked down at the fish as it thrashed around over and over again, its eye wide open and seemingly peering at me. I could almost hear it beckoning for me to throw it back in. It was the only time that I can recall my siblings cheering at my victory, but as every second passed, I felt the pit in my stomach growing. I was watching a living being struggle, brought on by my own hand. Tray must have sensed my tension.

"Jules, this fish was made just for you. When God created it, He made it so that one day it will serve to make a perfect dish for you." In this strange sense, Tray made me feel important and made the fish purposeful. Life is about having a purpose. Tray had a weird sense of compassion, and although he tried to hide it, he was a religious man at heart. That night I assisted in preparing the fish, making certain that nothing tainted it and that it was cooked just right. Before I took my first bite, I whispered, "Thanks for being made for me."

When I was fourteen, Tray moved to Australia and would soon marry and establish a family there. He would send postcards and continues to do so to this day, even forwarding them to my Manhattan apartment. I haven't seen Tray in many years, but I still feel his presence. I am pleased to see the photo of Tray and his loved ones looking so happy. I never went fishing again. It isn't an experience I enjoy, but to this day, when I consume a piece of fish, I say my blessings; it is kind of a knee-jerk reaction.

We all want to be purposeful. We want to know that our existence isn't for naught. Disability often overshadows people's sense of purpose, making them feel only the burden of human existence without that internal benefit of meaning. I look at all my clients today; some will heal, becoming better versions of themselves, others will continue to be victims of chronic disease, and others may not be here much longer, but I view them all as purposeful.

My clients are the best teachers. They have not only made me enhance my techniques, but I have also come to learn about the nuances of life, anger, frustration, fear, love, hate, trust, confidence, reliability, freedom, appreciation, diligence, resilience, hope, compassion, friendship, forgiveness, letting go, and self-expression. They have given me a purposeful existence, and I hope I have contributed to theirs. I understand that purposefulness is why my father is fiddling with his tools even though he shouldn't be using them, and why Mr. Dawson feels dead even while still alive. I understand why Jonathan seeks out a homeless stranger to give his sister's sandwich to because even in death, this minute act gives her life more meaning.

I walk through the hallways at the hospital and see one of my clients whom I haven't seen in a few months. I wave.

"Hi, Tara!"

She returns the wave, but as she approaches me, she says, "I'm not Tara. I'm—" and my mouth moves to say it, though I am in shock.

"Evian, is that you?"

"Yes," she says.

My mouth gapes open, standing for a few seconds utterly surprised. I remember our meeting four years ago when Evian's face evidenced fatigue, and her body carried lots of extra fluid, making her appear much older and less beautiful than her identical twin sister, Tara. Here she is standing firmly on her two feet with a bit of coloring to accent her face, in a slender and form-fitting outfit.

304

There are those who aren't the subjects of medical care, but nevertheless, suffer vicariously through the illness of a loved one. They are the children, parents, siblings, other relatives, and friends who stand there, watching the horror unfold. Yet, they don't leave. I remember standing at the nurses' station when a five-foot-eleven-inch, beautiful woman traversed the path. Her golden skin tone accented her almost purple-gray eyes, a color I had never seen before. She was dressed in the finest material and had a walk not unlike those on the runway. She dashed through the doors quickly, and I found myself entering the same room as she did. At her side lay a patient, a woman resembling her own distinct features, with the same long hair and bone structure, but dressed in lounge day-wear as patients are. Her eyes, though similar, were swollen, and one could almost feel her fatigue.

I learned that Evian was the name of the patient and that Tara, the other woman whose beauty I had just admired in the hallway, was her identical twin. These women were genetically identical, but an environmental affront affected them differently. Both women had seen a doctor for a cough, which the doctor deemed viral and stated, "Leave it alone." One of them, Evian, would not improve but would suffer from a severe heart infection. This, resulted in heart failure, and she was on the brink of death. While awaiting a transplant, Evian had been placed on a LVAD machine, a Left Ventricular Assist Device. The device would facilitate blood flow from the chambers of her heart to the aorta, ultimately reaching the rest of the body. The cables from the device exited her abdomen. The cables required charging using an external battery pack and controller. Evian was required to keep this abdominal port area clean and was cautioned about getting it wet.

I was well acquainted with the two sisters as Evian had been in and out of the cardiac unit and the intensive care unit on more than one occasion, and despite not being Evian's therapist, I could often hear her small "ouches" or "oohs," stating how tired she was while I worked with other patients around her. Tara always ran toward her like a slave ready to do her master's will. Her eyes were the eyes of a sister filled with care and worry. She constantly asked Evian if she needed anything or wanted anything, often several times in a row. I learned that when Evian wasn't in the hospital, Tara helped her shower and helped her clean the wound. She stood over her, ensuring that her battery power wasn't low and that the connections were secure and functioning. She helped her with daily chores and tasks. Tara took Evian's vitals often and ensured that she followed dietary and fluid restrictions. She also provided entertainment, like books and movies. Tara often scoured activity books, finding just the right entertainment source for her sister. Evian anticipated that she would soon die, but fortunately, after being ill for quite a while, she was able to secure a heart transplant.

Once the transplant was completed, and she began healing, I would meet her exercising in the cardiac gym. Tara waited outside, placing sticky pads on every page in the book or magazine that Evian might enjoy. Tara now helped her sister with her medication regimen and with performing activities and exercises to keep her new working heart functioning. Although this had been a tough medical journey for Evian, both women had a hard time reintegrating socially and functionally to the world they once knew, neither felt like their former selves. Evian had physically suffered for a long time and had death hanging over her, unhinging her emotions. Tara watched her sister become a battery-operated individual, afraid that the port or batteries that provided her with life would fail. She put her own life on hold, awaiting her sister's return to life. All this distress resulting from a mild infection that ballooned out of control had been unrecognized by medical personnel. I once asked Evian why she was named so, her name being quite unusual. She said her parents had gone on vacation and lingered, reluctant to leave the French Riviera. The sight was beautiful, but after hiking for many miles that day, her father's lips were parched, and he began to feel weak. His wife ran into the store and brought him Evian water. He recalls his thirst being quenched and how he had regained his strength to truly enjoy the beauty of the French Riviera. Upon news of the pregnancy, he asked his wife to name the child Evian. However, they were unaware that there was a second child. When she made her appearance, they decided on the name Tara, which means 'Hillside.' What better complements the beauty of water if not the hills?

Tara was the one making certain that Evian was alive. The physicality of it and the emotional burden took a toll on her. She suffered from a form of survivor's guilt wondering why her sister's cough and illness had evolved to a near-death experience while hers did not. At one point, Tara became my patient. She was in an ever-constant state of doing on behalf of her sister that she developed de Quervain's tenosynovitis, which resulted in pain and swelling near her thumb due to all the repeated lifting and grasping she had been doing.

During sessions, she was riddled with stress, not from the injury, but from worrying about who will take care of her sister now. When you meet individuals with a simple illness that morphs into something unexpected, there isn't only a greater challenge in physical rehabilitation, there is a distrust for the medical profession that failed them. As her sister had initially been misdiagnosed, Tara had a general distrust of all medical personnel, which likewise extended to me, and it was as if she was constantly watching her back, even more so, her sister's. She documented every word I said and had a special notebook for the cause. When I told her it is important to relax, she responded, "Relaxing is what got us here." It was hard to gain Tara's trust to let me help her. We shared a learning curve in how to interact with each other. Establishing rapport and trust is a true challenge for achieving therapeutic gains when it's compounded by fear. I constantly monitored her comfort level.

I head to James's room. I can't wait to see him. As I make my way into the elevator, I am greeted by the same face I had just seen moments ago in the hallway. This time it's Tara, my former patient. She appears glad to see me and wraps me in a sudden embrace.

"You look good, Tara," I say. I let her know that I just met up with her sister, who seems to have made great strides, admitting that I had mistaken her sister for her.

She tells me that time does heal wounds, as does communication. "When I finally admitted how I felt and asked for help, it magically arrived. I am no longer alone caring for my sister. I thought I had to bear it alone because my sister had been my primary source of encouragement throughout my life, even while enduring my own rough patches." She explains that as Evian began to heal, she sensed herself healing, as well. Seeing these two women makes me momentarily believe in fairy tales and happy endings.

Evette is still humming a tune from last night's show. She has hummed it so steadily today that Kevin Chase is now humming it too. As they pass me in the hallways, they make a point of humming it in my ears. It is annoying but drowns out any remaining negative thoughts.

I walk toward James's room, feeling light and airy, waiting to be greeted by his cuteness. He has begun to smile a bit, allowing one dimple to emerge.

On my way, I come in contact with Garret. He is a six and three-quarter-year-old freckle-faced, gapped-tooth boy. Garret is a tickler; his mother finds his behavior frightful when he approaches and tickles strangers, yet is delighted that despite illness, her son still finds enjoyment in a good tickle. Garret speaks his mind and interacts well with adults. He often hums or sings to himself. He is great at arts and crafts and is constantly on the lookout for a good project. Garret enjoys bold colors and larger-than-life personalities. Garret is a fun kid, the type most kids want to be around to forget about their troubles, but for a boy like James, Garret is too much, too soon.

James's facial expression changes as Garret approaches him in the hallway. I see fear emerging, as James quickly retreats. I intercede and ask Garret what his last project was. James watches Garret's interaction with me. He is still cautious, but he has stopped retreating and has moved away from the wall, moving in Garret's direction. Garret waves good-bye, as he is taken for testing. I take a good look at James. His eyes show a distinct interest when I take his hand, and we re-enter the room. He moves toward me, rather than waiting for me to initiate. He speaks few words, but they are always directed toward me. He has some light back in his eyes and makes eye contact with others. On occasion, a shy smile emerges, but he quickly covers it up. He eats small portions of food and no longer recoils when his "boo-boos" are treated. He enjoys the three characters on his toothbrush and will use it willingly even though he doesn't accurately brush his teeth. He has a select group of three children he interacts with on the ward, albeit in a passive capacity. He engages in some imaginative play.

Love has a sound. It's the reverberating sound of a kiss, a pat on the shoulder or a stroke on the head, the tune sung especially for someone, the sound of the differentiating steps taken to run to someone loved. Love has a feel; it's the feel of muscles in your face that move easily to create a smile, and the calmness in your organs and body when in a loved one's presence. It is the airiness and lightness in your step; the warmth and coziness; the squeeze of the hand to show your compassion or comradery; the delivery of water when lips are parched. Love has a distinct visual; the way you look at others even when they don't feel their best, the intertwining of hands, a streaked teary-eyed face when you laugh so hard with them you cry. On the other hand, it's sometimes the visceral pain you feel when you share in their pain.

I look at James. He is winding down from the day, as he begins to doze. His soft end curls hit the pillow and are standing up, likely from static. "Goodnight, Curlicue," I say. I sit there looking at him. I finally whisper in his ear, "I love you, James." I know he can't hear me, nor would he fully comprehend what my words mean. As his eyes close, I stand before him and say, "You didn't deserve this, James. You didn't deserve any of this pain." I look at this little boy, this vulnerable little creature, and feel so happy watching him sleep. His existence has made my heart feel things that it had never allowed itself to feel; it's more open. I feel love.

My mind cannot believe that my mouth uttered those three words. I leave feeling calm, missing that little face until morning, but I feel a lightness, and I sleep well.

The next day, I visit with James again. He welcomes my presence, even seeming to look forward to it. Abbie comes to advise me of the foster parents James will be staying with following his discharge, which will likely be in a day or so. I think I mishear and ask her to repeat that. "Yes, he will be leaving in a day or so."

"In a day or so?" and with those words, the euphoria and lightness turn to a profound sense of pain. I know my heart has grown, as I could feel its own weight. Somewhere inside me, I knew it was inevitable that a child I had come to know in such a brief time frame would leave. Still I couldn't imagine he would have such a profound effect on my heart. I look to leave the room, to avoid looking at him because that little face of his is now a source of distress, a symbol of what is to be lost. Yet, I can't leave. My body doesn't let itself move out of the room, and the images that Jonathan created hanging on the wall are almost serving as guards, reinforcing my need to stay. I continue to sit and read books and mimic characters for the duration of my break, and when the time is up, I drag myself out of the room, blowing him a kiss that he won't see from his vantage point, as I feel pressure rising in my chest.

When I return to my shift, I bump into Kevin Chase; he is in his usual state of cheerfulness, but he asks if I'm okay. "Sure, I'm okay. I am great," but he doesn't let me pass. He blocks my way. Kevin knows that I visit with James often. Kevin almost forces me to explain what happened, so I just say, "James is going to foster care within the week," and walk away. I feel anxiety rising within me and deep-breathe my way to my next patient. I feel my diaphragm almost spasming as it moves up and down, and I try to make it stop, so I take small deep breaths, my abdominal pressure increases, and my breaths now move in a synchronized pattern in and out. I feel a little bit calmer, but the overarching doom still remains.

I enter Karen's room, Karen is twenty-nine. Her mother who appears to be about seventy is in the room. Karen is a professional young lady. She has suffered a tear of the ulnar collateral ligament of the thumb when she stretched out her hand to catch her ski pole in an attempt to break her fall while skiing downhill. It is already a few weeks past her surgical repair, and she has initiated flexion/extension of the injury. Her mother has come along, even though Karen protests that she doesn't need her "mommy". Her mother kisses her head like one kisses a four-year-old. Karen smiles and accepts it; she is used to her mother's presence and concern as she is the "baby" of the family. Despite moving out in her early twenties, she visits her childhood home often. Her mother is optimistic, feeling thankful that her daughter's injury wasn't worse. The older woman wants to be involved in Karen's therapy, so she asks if she can help at home with any exercises or anything else. Instead of talking to her like I normally do, I pull out a pamphlet and hand it to her. She thanks me, as she stands at the wall, and I observe her body swaying forward and backward more than it should. She rubs her back a bit, prompting me to ask, "Wasn't your hotel stay comfortable?"

"Yes, it is just age. I am getting old. My back has been acting up lately." She is talkative and also admits that she has been eating lots of prunes lately, "Like old people do." I notice her breath, which comes from her upper thoracic region, her chest, instead of her abdominal area. She now evidences a more pronounced back and forth sway. She mentions that her blood pressure has been increasing despite trying to walk more frequently, and mentions that she has persistent GERD. She makes some GERD jokes; her daughter looks on, a bit worried.

This isn't just old age, I think. She breathes out quickly, uncontrolled and steady. I can feel my own breath being in a more hyperventilative state due to my stress. *Her diaphragm should lower itself to increase abdominal pressure, and then appropriate trunk movement and pressure can take place. She isn't breathing correctly,* I think in between my own unsynchronized breaths, but my usual intrusive self can't intrude today, and I don't offer my advice. I pretend to be a regular onlooker. I'm quiet, only nonchalantly adding, "Maybe get a routine checkup. It can't hurt." I just want to get home, as fast as I can. The two women leave, and I wish them well.

All I crave is getting into my bed and allowing the blankets to swallow me. I have this feeling of loss that keeps penetrating my soul deeper and deeper. But the day isn't over yet, there is still one more patient I need to see. I feel overwhelmed, and amid the undercurrents of hyperventilation, I feel a tap of the shoulder. I jump back, and it's only Shana, the speech therapist, "Sorry to have startled you," she says, followed by her informing me that our mutual client is being discharged tomorrow. After I take a few minutes to refresh myself, my breathing is back to normal, I'm hydrated, and my hair is now as perfect as it was this morning, which is perfectly imperfect.

I move on to Eduardo, my last patient of the day. Eduardo is a forty-four-year-old male. He had suffered a rotator cuff and back injury as a result of a boating accident. I have always found him to be a very patient man. He has a good sense of humor and is always sure to thank those around him. He continually observes everything. Unlike many of his inpatient counterparts, Eduardo's facial expressions and body language change often. Sometimes I feel as though he is picking up on some energy wavelength I am emitting as he seems to mimic my emotional states. After a tough day at work, and given the James situation, I enter Eduardo's room slowly. Upon his first sight of me, he cringes, his tone and voice change. As I approach him, he retreats as if someone is about to pounce on him. I think he is experiencing some kind of medical emergency, so I rush over to him, asking if he is okay.

"Am I okay? It is you, Jules. It's you who is the source of my distress."

I find myself thinking that perhaps I am emitting an unpleasant odor. I smell my shirt quickly imagining that some droplets of sweat may have made their way onto my person as a result of running down the hospital steps in haste. I discover that my shirt smells as fresh as it did this morning. Although I rinsed my mouth after lunch, I quickly check my breath

315

for the lingering scent of onions from my lunch sandwich. It doesn't appear to be the source of his distress either, so I inquire further, "Eduardo, I haven't touched you yet. What is it? Did you have some pain after I left last session?"

"No, it's your mood; it's killing me."

"My mood?" I have been trying my best to hide it, and thus far, only Kevin has commented.

"I'm feeling your pain literally, and you're making me feel weighed down like sandbags during a storm."

"What?" I said.

"Yes, I can literally feel your pain, Jules, and you're giving me way too much sensation today. I can mirror people's moods," he says nonchalantly like he is telling me the weather. "I can kind of feel your pain, and trust me, you are giving me lots of sensation today. It is hard enough to share a room with a guy whom they constantly prick and has tons of bandages. I feel every prick and every rip of bandage, but having a therapist . . . honestly, you're adding to my suffering."

Eduardo is blunt, and I am not sure what exactly I have done, but obviously, I can't hide anything from him. He is right. I am a Debbie Downer and am constantly trying to nurse my own wounds, and this poor man is unfortunate enough to feel it. I am not sure what to do with this information. I offer Eduardo the option of having another therapist come in my place for therapy today. Instead of responding, Eduardo passes me a card composed by his six-year-old son. It is colored with bright colors. It states, "Dear Papa, I can't wait to arm wrestle with you. Feel better, Love, Matias." The card is beautiful, and the letters are crafted with different sizes in bubble-letter form. At first, it makes me think of James, and I must be evidencing a look of distress because Eduardo is cringing like someone who just cut himself, but I reread the card, and a smile forms. I could see Eduardo's face and body relax.

"Thank you," he says, "I feel much better. You have calmed down now. We can get started."

We work through the session just as we have on previous days, as I continuously eye Matias's card on the nightstand, giving me the impetus to continue. I leave the room, a bit less depressed than I came; however, the situation continues to weigh me down. I write my progress notes for the day and leave, forgetting my jacket. The bluster of the wind outdoors reminds me when it hits my face, and I return to my office to retrieve it.

I pass Kevin again, but he must have noticed some improvement in my mood, as he waves good-bye cheerfully, no longer an inquisitor. "Have a good night. Don't forget about our baseball meeting." I nod, then hurriedly make my way out the door.

I walk home. Each foot follows the next toward my apartment. When I finally reach home, I feel some comfort at being in my own quarters, even though it's a shoebox, because suppressing my emotions all day was grueling. The anger, frustration, and sadness all rolled into one. I finally allow myself the freedom to shriek. I don't stifle it like I normally do. The sound bounces off the walls back to my own ears, and I could literally feel the vibration.

I am glad Mr. Dawson, my neighbor, is away and that he cannot hear me. He hasn't yet received a call or communication from his daughter, but his ex-wife has contacted him, and he traveled to go meet with her.

I put on my most comfortable pajamas and cook comfort food, downing it quickly, and then have a piece of cake to wash it down. At night, the euphoria and lightness are long gone, and I struggle to find comfort in my own bed. I drown the sound of my thinking with blasting music to the point where my ears hurt, and then drift off to sleep.

The sun's strong rays and warming touch in the morning bring no comfort. I sit curled up on the couch, holding the phone to call in a personal day. Today is the day James is leaving, and I don't want to watch that scene unfold. I don't want to watch his reaction to being taken to a new home, learning to cope with new people, and I don't want to feel my own distress, knowing that I can't visit with him each day.

I hear Sasha's melodic voice in my ears, "Aren't you going to adopt him, Jules?" and I laugh at the absurdity of the idea. I am a single woman living in an NYC shoebox, with no family to count on and limited resources. I redirect my thoughts toward the phone, pushing each button as I call in to my superior, letting him know I won't be coming in today. After I end the call, I instinctively dial Jonathan, but quickly hang up.

I have often observed greater vulnerability than shame in my patients. In addition to allowing me to see their physical struggles, they often tell me intimate details of their lives. Yet, despite realizing that I should voice my own struggles, I just can't. I still can't discuss them with anyone else. I can't face my own vulnerabilities. For a brief moment, I examine what seems to be my reality. Just as in my youth, I felt I was basically an appendage, present but not vital for the functioning of my family unit. Now I am once again awakened to the fact that I am no longer necessary anymore. James has a home. Jonathan finally has some closure and a level of contentment in his life. Sasha is at home in California with her real family. Evette is leaving, and Stephanie and Kevin were fine before I appeared. To top it all off, my favorite professor is fighting a battle that would soon turn to a war, and I likely can't help her. I haven't even seen my siblings in quite some time. They surely know more about strangers than of me. The last time I saw one of my siblings, other than my sister at my dad's bedside, was when I accidentally met my brother Dean at a local Chinese restaurant, his favorite.

Dean is only one year younger than me. I remember him sitting beside me on my bed when he was five, staring at the scratches on my wrists after one of my mother's rants, not knowing what to say. Instead, he just sat there. He almost patted me on the back, in an attempt to comfort me, but retracted his hand. Other than Dean, I hadn't seen my siblings in many years. My siblings and I had engaged in only a few brief phone conversations in recent years. I wasn't part of their lives, nor were they part of mine.

I look at myself in the mirror with my oversized pajamas and unkempt hair. I can't be of use to my clients in this state, or perhaps I never was. I don't feel purposeful. I feel sad, empty, and angry, all at once. I feel my limbic system in overdrive and don't know how to stop it. Emotions shape the way we think and the way we think, in turn, shapes our emotions. This is the dance our limbic system does as it interacts with other thought processes. Somehow, I just got lost in this dance, crashing at every turn.

Chapter 13: Rebirth

I decide to get dressed, this time wearing a jogging suit. I don't go running, I go to the liquor store, not even knowing what I am supposed to buy. Everyone else seems to use alcohol to suppress some type of emotion, so why shouldn't I? I ask the clerk what strong stuff he has, and after looking me over and volleying whether he should supply me with something, he brings out some vodka. I come home and fuddle through the cabinets for a large glass, pouring the vodka in slowly, and stare for a few moments at the glass before me. I feel a headache coming on, and I haven't even taken a sip yet.

I lie down in my bed, all the while thinking how I got here. Just as I place the glass to my lips, my phone rings. I debate for a few seconds about answering it, but the ring persists, and I pick up. The voice on the other end is surprising. It's Kevin Chase. He asks me if he can come over, which catches me off guard. I look down at the vodka bottle. I really lack skill in closing the top. I fumble, and the cap flies across the room. I could smell the liquor wafting through the air, which makes my stomach a bit queasy. Despite my state of shock at both Kevin's call and the strength of the vodka's smell, I agree to Kevin's request to come over.

"I will be there in about fifteen," he says as he hangs up.

I hear a loud knock on the door, bordering on a bang. I drag myself toward the door opening it. He lets himself in.

"Well, you look bad," he says matter-of-factly as he looks me over, his eyes going up and down swiftly. In addition to my casual wear, my ponytail holder is coming out, making my curly hair look like it has just been electrified. I pull at it to find my own hair too intertwined with it.

"Why are you here?" I say in an annoyed tone.

Kevin catches a glimpse of my glass filled with vodka. He looks at me peculiarly and is surprised by the mess of unopened mail on the table. Kevin sits down, and I hesitantly sit down, allowing a throw to cover my shoulders and trail behind me. He doesn't appear fazed by the smell of the liquor, which by now has fully entered my nose and is creating a bad headache.

He places a box on the table and opens it. In a musical but off-key loud voice, he says, "Happy birthday!"

My headache is now throbbing, and I ask, "What . . . What are you talking about? It's not my birthday."

I look at the bottle, thinking that maybe that was the source of the confusion, but then Kevin says, "You know what your problem is, Jules? You are a quitter. You're a quitter, and worse than that, you never trust yourself to make wise decisions on your own behalf."

Now my apathy or sadness turns into anger. "You are really stupid, Kevin, you know." I retract my harsh tone and words. I say, "Sorry," but I am still visibly angry.

Kevin responds, "You seem to have an abundance of tolerance for others but not for yourself. That's the difference between you and me, I execute my plan without a million caveats." I never knew Kevin to talk this much, and apparently, he isn't done. He continues, "You just don't fight for things that are important to you. James is important to you, and you won't trust yourself to be his mother, even though you would make a really good one, at least, in my opinion. The two of you are like a meant-to-be kind of thing. Let it be your birthday. Allow yourself to be reborn and make the changes you really want." For the first time, I perceive his depth. I also sense his sincerity. I look down at the cake with my name, "Happy Birthday Jules." It's the first one I have ever received.

While I have Kevin's attention, I finally ask, "Why did you choose me, out of everyone else, to go to your reunion a few years ago? And why did you ask me to pretend to be your wife?"

Kevin blushes. "Well, it is because you get people. Even when you think you haven't fully understood them, you keep trying to get them. I guess I wanted my classmates to think that I married someone with that quality. I was quite popular in school. I knew the best hangout places, had designer clothes, frequented the best clubs, but I just don't really get people like you do, the deep stuff. I thought if my classmates were to see you and realize how great you are, it would reflect on me."

Kevin puts down another box as he talks. I open it, unable to imagine what's inside. There is a list of names and a bunch of paperwork. "What is this?"

"This is what is going to help you get James." I look at the list of names, each followed by Esq. "The first three are my good buddies from law school," Kevin says, not realizing what he said.

"Oh, so you did go to law school," I state in surprise.

"Yes, for close to two years, but it wasn't as interesting as medicine. Don't tell my father I said that."

"There are no words to thank you, Kevin."

"You can thank me by getting the kid."

Kevin lets himself out, and I rummage through the papers. I spend the rest of the day calling and searching and searching and calling to find the best lawyer in Kevin's pile.

I find out there is lots of administrative stuff, paperwork, and medical forms, but it's the only way I can get to James, so I work diligently and with enthusiasm.

I think about what it takes to be a parent, the provider of food, clothing, and shelter. I grew up in a nice home, my laundry was washed, there was sufficient food for breakfast, lunch, and dinner. I had toys. It was the main things that only a parent can give that my parents didn't provide.

My grandmother was the one who acknowledged my pain when I scraped up my finger. She gave me some solution to wash it off and a Band-Aid. She comforted me all the while. She helped my body and mind calm down. In my earlier years, she tucked me in at night and took me for outings in local parks or just for walks to spend time with me in the area. She

324

wished me good luck when I had a test. She seemed to empathize with me when I grimaced after tasting my first sourball. She allowed me to believe there was a Santa Claus and unicorns. She bought me McIntosh apples because they were my favorite. For a while, I started to feel trust toward humanity, a respect for the nuances of my personality, a sense of safety, a sense of curiosity and learning, and I came to appreciate the sound of my own voice, as I felt I had someone who appreciated that I was born.

Unfortunately, my time with Grandma was short-lived, but I realize that that is what good parents do, at least that's what I think. When she died, that small bit of sense of self that had developed died with her, as it had still been flourishing in its early stages. It would only be through my interactions with strangers, some of whom later became good friends, that my sense of self slowly returned.

Three days have passed, and my table is now submersed in paperwork that will need to be completed for James's adoption. I don't mind eating my chicken and broccoli in the corner where I scrounge for space. I look out the window as it's night, but it appears to be rather light. There is a full moon, and instead of assuming that trouble is on the horizon, I admire the moon as a reflection of the sun's light, a promise that morning will eventually come, bringing yet an even brighter light.

I change the linen, taking in the scent of the newly washed sheets, and am ready for a good night's sleep, only to remember that in the morning, I am scheduled to meet with my father. I prepare my clothing, taking a brief glance at myself in my full-length mirror, admiring my image, which looks significantly better than it did three days ago. This time, I perceive my full face, not just a profile, and find myself saying, "You didn't deserve all the hurt, Jules. You didn't deserve any of it." I snuggle up in bed and fall asleep as the moon stands outside my bedroom window.

In the morning, I visit my father. The drive is long, and I am a bit weary upon arrival. As I enter, my mother is standing there. Unlike our last meeting, this time she is in close proximity, close enough for me to make some comment that she can't so easily ignore. When my sweater's edge accidentally knocks against her skirt, I say, "So sorry," but then my words turn to rebuke. "I have always done the right thing, the good thing, even as a child. My room was tidy. I didn't complain. I worked on my homework silently. I didn't deserve being hurt; I didn't deserve any of it. Oh! And I wasn't clumsy. Just for the record, my wounds were not inflicted on my own. It was you, and even if I had been a bad kid, no one deserves to be treated like you treated me. Despite your mistreatment, I turned out to be a good person, have good work ethics, I'm loyal to my friends, and they are loyal to me."

I stand there in shock at the words that spewed from my mouth as if someone else was saying them. My mother barely flinches. I wait for her retort, for a change in the look on her face, some evidence of regret, remorse, something, but she doesn't say or do anything. She just goes about

326

her way, as if I have said nothing.

My father has overheard my rant, and I see the distress in his face. The conversation was unintended and unwise given his present state, but he looks at me, pain in his eyes. "Jules, go home. Don't take care of me. Take care of yourself." He repeats the same words, "Take care of yourself," until I start to exit the room, and when I look back, he recoils from pain but still waves good-bye.

On my way home, my cell phone rings. It's Mrs. Jones confirming our meeting for tonight. She is Stephanie's mother-in-law's friend. I arranged to come by weeks ago, and it seems that I have forgotten about our meeting given the events of the week. This is something I never would have done in the past. I try not to allow her to hear the surprise in my voice nor my hesitation when she mentions the visit today, but I make my way over because reliability is step number one when you want to form a therapeutic relationship, or any relationship, for that matter.

Mrs. Jones suffers from rheumatoid arthritis. She lives in a really small house with minimal preparation space for daily chores, including cooking. She wants to be able to do everything herself without adaptations as she wants to continue to achieve gold standard mom status for her two children, who are teenagers. She is fifty-one and not looking forward to being an empty nester, as her seventeen-year-old son is already looking toward college next fall. She wants to be able to cook food, do laundry, and get her own clothes. She has been taking a biologic for joint pain, which has helped somewhat, but she still has a way to go. The co-payments for her meds are a large financial burden, and the money she saved for her sons to attend college are now put aside towards this cause. She had been enlisting her husband's help until he suffered an onsite work injury leaving him with intense back pain. Mrs. Jones is a religious woman, referencing her faith during the session. She tells me she has trouble bending, reaching, walking, lifting, grasping. She describes her joint pain like a jarring impact that she relives over and over. Her hands throb during every activity, but she is learning strategies to protect her joints and limit their burden. In addition, she has a mild inflammation of her eye.

To my surprise, she tells me how lucky she is. She lets me know all of her strengths, barely taking a breath as she speaks. "I know how to find things on my own, and recognize them. I know what they are used for, and how to use them. I can remember details and can enjoy games and family discussions. I know where to go and when to go. I can manage my money, and more importantly, my emotions. Even though I have little, I can laugh and cry at will. I know whom to call and how to contact my family and friends if need be. I know how to have patience and how to attend to things. I know how to command my body to work, even if it sometimes fails to listen. It is just discomfort, not pain. Pain is something much worse."

It surprises me when she fails to describe her jarring impact and burning sensations as pain, but when she divulges the next part of her story, I begin to understand.

She relates that her sister has been suffering from Pick's disease, a frontotemporal dementia. Her sister was only forty years old when she was diagnosed, and she will be forty-eight in a few weeks. She paces and wanders. She becomes hostile at times and anxious at others. She has deficits in language and has overall difficulty with thinking. Mrs. Jones feels like she is the fortunate one. Her son introduces himself as he enters the room. She lifts her hand to wave, saying, "Ouch," and blows him a kiss good-bye.

Mrs. Jones has me show her how to position herself and heighten her chair so that she can mend her son's favorite pants. She is already completing some non-resistive exercises to keep her as limber as possible.

I provide her with energy-saving techniques to enable her to accomplish her tasks wisely and avoid further injury and pain. She provides me with her weekly schedule, and I create short rest breaks where applicable. I place her microwave, which she uses religiously to prepare basically every type of fruit and vegetable imaginable, at an appropriate elevation to reduce further strain on her back. She is well known for her smoothies. I organize her food by size and frequency of usage to avoid the extra stress of taking down food items when it's unnecessary. Lids are removed to avoid additional finger and hand stress when opening. I provide her with simple gadgets for decreased joint stress when opening the dreaded doorknobs, to avoid leaving every door in her home uncomfortably open. We order more efficient and less strenuous jar and can openers, and peeling devices. She has modified bottles that are easy spritz and spray. She distributes large bulky loads into segments to avoid carrying weighty loads from room to room.

As I prepare to leave, she dials her sister's home, awaiting a home attendant to update her on how her sister is doing. She briefly lowers the phone from her ear, which appears to be difficult for her to hold. She says, "Hold please" and quickly turns on speakerphone. She smiles as she no longer holds what has likely been perceived as a significant weight in her hands and continues the conversation.

I sense her concern about being a great mother to her kids and a good wife, so before I leave, I tell her, "Mrs. Jones, it's easy to see you're a really great mother." She thanks me for coming. This time, she grasps the doorknob as practiced and closes the door behind me. The juxtaposition of today's two meetings is ironic, the mother who is overly concerned, and the mother whose concern is nonexistent.

She tells me to send regards to Qiao, Stephanie's mother-in-law. I readily agree.

Everyone has a store of energy that needs refueling on occasion. I can feel a bit of a release of my limbic system. My emotional state is less chaotic. *It is just discomfort,* I tell myself, *not pain.* My cognition now follows suit, and I am in a much better frame of mind. I have a woman with rheumatoid arthritis and her sister with Pick's disease to thank for that.

Day after day, I wait for my mother's call, but the call never comes. I come to realize it likely never will. I look at my calendar with a red marking, indicating that I will return to work, after my brief hiatus, the following Monday. In the interim, I initiate contact with the lawyers from Kevin's list, and I choose the one most willing to be of service.

CHAPTER 14: ANOTHER GRANDMA

A few days have passed, and I return to work, with some changes in attitude and perspective. When meeting up with Kevin, I let him know how good the cake was, and that the sparkling letters bearing my name were a beautiful touch. I add, "It could have used a bit more icing but otherwise perfection."

"Okay," Kevin says with a wink.

I add, "I made good use of the box too, Kevin. Thanks again."

Although the workload is heavy today, I feel light and carefree as never before. I notice Dr. Sarim, trying to decipher a puzzle. He squints and cranes his neck for better viewing, and I remind him to sit upright, particularly as his neck pain is finally subsiding. "Yes, how quickly we forget," he says, as he sits up and moves the puzzle onto a book cover for better viewing. He munches on some sweet potato fries, whose crunch is both annoying and entertaining at once. He says it helps him think. The puzzle is made of a series of symbols that, when rotated appropriately, create some sort of phrase.

I mosey my way into his space to view the puzzle and provide a bit of advice for some of the clues. I solve some of it and find myself munching on a few of his fries. Once solved, the words appear. "When you hide behind others, your view is partially obstructed; when you hide behind yourself, you're still in plain sight."

Jonathan returns from his visit with an old colleague who is establishing an institute for organ regeneration. He is a bit weary but in an exceptionally good mood.

The months pass by, and a thorough search is undertaken to determine if any relatives may come forward to challenge the adoption. In this case, only one living relative can possibly oppose it; however, it is an important one, James's grandmother, Jacqueline Rodclif.

I was told she lived on the Upper West Side and requested a meeting with me. A meeting was, thus, set up by my lawyer. I had been hoping to hear her voice by phone before our meeting. This would perhaps have provided me with some glimmer of her personality. I approach with apprehension, my legs shaking a bit, but I keep walking until they come to an abrupt halt halfway down her block. I move in small increments to get myself to the brownstone. The meeting is scheduled for 4:45 p.m., and my watch reads 4:41. Two minutes go by as I pace near the house, trying to make my brain stop racing, and as the time on my cell phone turns 4:44 p.m., the front door opens. I look up. There stands a woman in her sixties with dark hair accentuated by a few strands of gray. Her hair is in an updo with not a hair out of place, looking like she has just come from the beauty shop. Her makeup accentuates her cheekbone structure, which is quite beautiful. She looks at me and asks, "Are you Ms. Wescott, Ms. Jules Wescott?"

"Yessss, I amm," I answer, my voice a bit strained. She invites me in, pointing in the direction of her living room and leads me toward an exquisite sofa, motioning for me to sit down. She smiles with one dimple, like James. My tension decreases a bit, but I am still wary.

"Would you like something to drink?"

I feel a little quiver on the inside and goosebumps on the outside like when you are out in the cold for a while. "Just a cup of hot water please," knowing that the cold chill came from within, but hope that perhaps it will calm my nerves. Mrs. Rodclif brings the hot water and sits down opposite the coffee table on the matching love seat, her legs crossed like she was nobility. She refrains from speaking, but her eyes are on me, and I imagine her coming to a conclusion based on my casual wear, and the walking shoes that I wore to perform my duties at work.

"Ms. Wescott, thank you for coming. I'd like to get to the point. My husband died from pancreatic cancer last year, and Karen was my only child." It was the first time I had heard the name Karen without James associated with it or a last name. It almost made James's mother human-like, less of the monster she was depicted as when he was in the hospital. "I am sixty-nine years old, and old age continues to creep up on me. I truly love James, but can't take care of him the way I think he should be cared for. I had you investigated."

I am shocked that I was unaware of the fact that I had been under investigation. I feel a bit intruded upon and wonder what this woman had discovered. She looks at me, and her mouth turns into a proper smile.

"You seem suitable to be James's parent. A Dr. McConnel, who is acquainted with you from the hospital, had particularly nice things to say about you. He said he was certain you would care for James just as if you bore him yourself. You care for strangers like they are family."

"Dr. McConnel?" I ask, thinking I misheard.

"Yes, Dr. McConnel." I nearly spill my hot water as I hear McConnel's name mentioned, but then recompose myself as Mrs. Rodclif continues.

"Karen was a rebellious child. She was never satisfied with anything and would have tantrums and shout uncontrollably about minor issues. I admit that she was quite spoiled, having everything and anything at her fingertips. I assumed that having so much made her less appreciative and just thought of her as an ungrateful child. I could never have imagined that she was capable of such evil. I couldn't imagine that she would inflict such pain on her own child. I saw the pictures. I saw the wounds and the indentations. She made her own child, her own flesh and blood, into an art project. I hope she never gets to lay eyes on beautiful, sweet James again."

Mrs. Rodclif redirects her focus, looking up at the photos on the mantel. There stands a picture of a prominent looking man who commands my attention. I assume it is Mr. Rodclif. His portrait is next to three other pictures that Mrs. Rodclif takes from the mantel. She sits down next to me as she shows me the first photo. It is James at two months old. He looks content in his grandmother's arms. "He was a sweet little boy and didn't cry." Mrs. Rodclif hands over the next photos saying, "This is James at six months, and here he is at nine months."

There are no photos of Karen. Perhaps they were discarded or never there at all. "He was a good boy. I haven't seen him in close to a year as I was busy mourning my husband. Had I known what Karen was doing, I would have gone to any means to stop her." She looks at me, eye to eye. "I will do whatever is in my power to ensure that you get James and that Karen will never see him. She will never be able to hurt him again. I will stay out of your way. This way, he won't have to see anyone from this family, and he can have a fresh beginning."

By now, Mrs. Rodclif's voice is choking up. I recollect my own grandmother and imagine how much greater the damage would have been in her absence. "Mrs. Rodclif, I didn't have an easy childhood, and I am not sure that your absence from his life is a good thing. More people loving him and caring about him wouldn't be detrimental."

She looks up at me with a smile penetrating through her tears. "You know, James was named for my father, James Marson II. He was a good man, philanthropic, inventive. I was surprised Karen was willing to name her child after him. She had already changed her name from Karen to Kendra years ago, always wanting something different than what she had. I don't know who James's father is, nor do I believe Karen does. She gravitated to art, to anything unusual, not specifically dark or morbid, just unusual. Never in my wildest dreams . . ." Her perfectly applied mascara drips at the corners of her eyes. "Just please tell James one day that I loved him."

"Perhaps you should tell him yourself." With those words, I stand up, gathering my belongings, ready to escort myself to the door. Mrs. Rodclif, who now appears less threatening, gets up from the couch, and I give her a semi-hug. The shock of the embrace initially makes her retract, but her tenseness dissipates, and she returns the embrace. "I'm not a child psychologist, Mrs. Rodclif, but sometimes what we think someone needs isn't what they need in the long run, so I can't promise that he will never see his mother again, nor do I think it wise that you are not a part of his life. I can only tell you that I will try my best to make him a happy child and help him become a trusting person who feels protected and loved." I approach the door. "Thank you for entrusting James to me, Mrs. Rodclif. He is very dear to me."

"It is Jacqueline. Call me Jacqueline." Her loneliness is almost tangible. Her home is beautiful, but I would guess she feels somewhat confined in its emptiness, not void of things but of people. She has no family members to accentuate her virtues nor tend to her raw wounds.

CHAPTER 15: MOVING ON

It was a bright and sunny Saturday morning, and Jonathan gets me on my cell as I am preparing a load of laundry. He sounds cheerful on the phone, with expressive intonation as he talks. "Let's go to Coney Island," he says, almost with childlike enthusiasm. I haven't been there in quite a while and have heard that its popularity has once again been on the rise. It's autumn, but Jonathan advises that the boardwalk and part of the amusement park are still open. We will take the train, as parking is almost nonexistent.

The train ride is uneventful. A group of teenagers shows off their vocal skills. They get no applause other than a quiet tap of the hands from me. I watch the changing station signs as we enter Brooklyn, and I count the stops to Coney Island like an impatient young child. Jonathan is fiddling with his pen then wringing his hands apprehensively with a bit of a tapping action, compliments of his right leg, but he has a genuine smile on his face as we make eye contact. "Are you okay?" I ask as I watch his right leg tap further.

"Yeah, I'm great. Why do you ask?" Jonathan replies.

"No reason." When we finally reach the station, I stare up at the sign. I haven't been to Coney Island in years, and it's one of a few times that I don't mind reminiscing about something. We walk the boardwalk, all the while commenting on the beauty of the landscape. The sun warms my back and neck, making my shoulders loosen. Jonathan recommends that we walk through the amusement park. I walk slowly, basking in my childhood nostalgia of the place. Jonathan walks with a quick stride, and a bit of mischievous curiosity is plastered on his face. We look at the various rides that line the park and imagine our visceral response and respective scream time on each of them as we pass.

Jonathan stops at an arcade. He rummages through his wallet, and with his eyebrows elevated, he says, "Let's play."

I am glad to see his excitement, and I readily agree. We engage in a few games of skeeball, followed by a hit-the-target activity then play one of those games where you just keep feeding quarters to something in anticipation. I have amassed quite a number of tickets, and I look Jonathan straight in the eyes. "Stop letting me win!"

"Jules, I can assure you that I am not letting you win. You're just better at this."

As we are all played out, we approach the counter to claim our trinket prizes. I have amassed 627 tickets, which makes me eligible for many small gifts. I look at the prize selection, sticky hands, stickers, mini-magnifiers, fancy pencils, scented erasers, and for some reason, this selection brings me such joy. Jonathan and I look at each other, "Sticky hands!" we say in unison, and I am ready to provide my tickets.

Jonathan seems on edge, but he has this childlike giddiness that calms me and brings yet more inner joy to the surface. Soft rock music is playing, and Jonathan points out the boom box that is its source. As I return my gaze toward the prize selection, a small white box sits on the counter. Jonathan points, "Jules, you should definitely choose this." Seven people surround me waiting their turn to select a prize. I look back at Jonathan, puzzled. He passes the box closer to my hand, and I unwrap it piece by piece, angle by angle like a small child waiting to find buried treasure. When the box cover is fully opened, there on a black cushion sits a circular diamond ring; its sparkle is enhanced by the colored lighting that surrounds us. I gasp as I hold my chest in surprise. Jonathan takes the ring out and faces me with a soulful look in his eyes. "Will you marry me, Jules?"

I feel overwhelmed, forgetting about the people waiting around me. "Why? Why would you want to marry me, Jonathan?"

He doesn't look surprised by the question and readily answers. He takes my hand. "Let's see now . . . You're kind and compassionate, loyal, intelligent, and really great to look at . . . I like the way you water your plants twice a day, notice every flower on your path as if they were unmined diamonds, the faces you make when you eat hot sauce, the way you guzzle down a cup of water like its vodka, the elegant way you throw a skeeball, the way you listen to your patients, the way you listen to me. But mostly, I love you because you're you."

The words, "I love you," tickle my ears that are so sensitized that I could hear my heart beating, and then the tears start to stream so fluidly as if they had been bottled up waiting to fall precisely at this moment. I waited thirty-four years for someone to tell me they loved me, and when it comes from the mouth of a man that has more emotional baggage than I do, I know it's authentic. I had already whispered the words, "I love you," to James, but now, I summon my vocal cords and, in a really loud voice, say, "I love you, too." The strangers around me all hear it. Some smile, a few applaud, and offer congratulations. Jonathan beams, and with shaky hands, he places the ring on my finger, and I admire it for just a couple of seconds until I ask, "Can we pick a prize now?" We pick a variety of different trinkets and lots of sticky hands. The air is now crisp, the sun less present, but I feel my lungs have greater capacity.

When I return to the city, I provide Stephanie and Kevin with sticky hands from our adventure. Stephanie takes my hand, "Well, Well! The man finally did it!"

After my engagement, I take a long-overdue trip to the cemetery in upstate New York where my grandmother is interred. There are large tangled vines growing into the gate at the perimeter of the cemetery. A lone rose stands there in its glory, like the one that had long ago perished at the hospital. Roses were my grandmother's favorite. I smell it but refrain from picking it and placing it on my grandmother's grave. "You need to keep living," I say. I bend down, peering at her name and admiring the upkeep of her headstone. I tell her about my engagement and tell her about James, but my primary goal is to thank her, to thank her expressly for those years that she gave me a childhood, expressing my gratitude for how she gave me a springboard from which some level of goodness could flow from me. I tell her how beautiful and smart and kind she was, how her stories delighted me, and how her voice was angelic. The words flow easily from my mouth as if she were still standing in front of me. Before I leave, I bend down to her grave, touching her name that is inscribed in stone. *Thank you, Grandma, thank you for helping me make good memories. I love you, Grandma. I love you a lot!* And I leave, still recalling her face before me, sharing in my long-awaited happiness.

A week has passed since my visit with my grandmother. My mood is rather pleasant, and I am particularly agreeable because I am going on a shopping venture. Though shopping has never healed my wounds, it has been quite the Band-Aid. I go to the store and purchase a rather costly dress because now I will be accompanying Jonathan to his award ceremony not only as his coworker and friend but as his fiancée.

Jonathan has a profound fear of public speaking; this is the one place where his sense of panic is evident in his full body language. He is being honored today and should feel very fortunate and upbeat, but he has basically locked himself in one of the adjacent rooms and keeps saying, "I will be out soon." Jonathan is one of the most articulate people I have ever met. He employs the English language most skillfully. He has the physical presence and the words, but his enemy is his own mind. I allow him to practice his speech over and over again in my presence so that it becomes

342

less of a novel experience.

His name is called, and as he walks up to the stage, I see him loosen the top button of his shirt, as if he were choking. On most every other occasion, he has managed to "man up." Perhaps it is this internal struggle that has facilitated the growth of a small number of wandering gray hairs. Speaking in a crowd of people he knows is way more frightful than speaking with individual strangers. "Strangers," he says, "will only judge you once, but being judged by the people you know, will linger indefinitely." Jonathan looks quite handsome. The blue of his eyes compliments his shirt, and the dim lighting creates a glow that reflects the light of his eyes, softening them further.

Jonathan looks at his fellow professional audience members, predominantly hospital staff that he has greeted numerous times. He gulps, then gazes directly at me until the crackle in his throat subsides. He makes a speech referencing evidence from just about every source known to man about blood and vascular disease, and then says:

"I am not certain how it came to pass that my voice was the one chosen to grace this stage tonight, as there are so many others more befitting to have been on the receiving end of this award; however, since I am here, I will let you in on a secret.

"As I accept this award, I accept it on behalf of hundreds, if not thousands of people. You see, the relationship between medical staff and patients is an ever-evolving one. Doctors facilitate healing, while patients are the catalyst guiding doctors to evolve further by causing them to reflect and revise their attitudes and methods and sharpening their skills to further facilitate healing. This cyclical relationship continuously broadens the advancement of treatment and restoring patient health. Once the circle is broken, there is a decrease in efficiency and effectiveness. Thus, all members of medical and supporting staff must be active listeners and efficient observers, both to patients and to each other, to allow this evolution to take place.

"So today, I thank my patients for teaching me determination, and pushing me forth despite their pain and hardship; they have sharpened my discernment of illness and helped my skills evolve. I thank my medical staff and colleagues, as all of us harmonize to help forge ahead with this evolution. I am also grateful for their teaching me dedication and pushing me forward to maximize my potential both in intellect and proficiency. I cannot omit thanking my fiancée, Jules, for listening to me ramble on about one medical advancement or another, and for helping both my heart and my brain merge in concert, by always encouraging a feeling of compassion and consideration which is highly contagious. Thank you, Jules." And there is loud applause.

My heart feels itself growing with deep gratitude at having such a wonderful human being like Jonathan in my life. Jonathan has mastered the art of science because he understands the way this journey works. We are an ever-flowing cycle. We affect other people's lives, and they affect ours. Even a lone patient curled up in bed feeling purposeless improves our understanding of ourselves, our own weaknesses and strengths. They make us confront our fears as we make them confront theirs. We may fear our own inadequacies at failing to help them, or we fear that one day our destiny is to be as vulnerable as they are, probably a bit of both. We have learned so much from them, and we hope we have benefited them and trained them, as well.

As I learned to release my tears and let them flow, the heaviness of the dark cloud which had followed me all my life began to disperse, as if washed away by rain, allowing rays of sunshine to penetrate through.

CHAPTER 16: HOME

During the process of adopting James, I look at a myriad of apartments as we will need more room. This would require a significant loan from the bank, which also means more paperwork. After much back and forth, the final piece of paper to secure my loan stares back at me. I look at my signature, which is in perfect cursive. It reads Julianne Lovell Westcott. A nice complicated name for a complicated girl. Names intrigue me, as they tell a story. My name also tells a story. It has historical significance. This information would have eluded me if not for my great aunt Kay.

My parents never referenced me by my second name, nor did they ever call me by my full name; it was always just "Jules" for as long as I can remember. My great aunt let me in on a bit of information when I turned thirteen. Lovell was the place where my parents met. I was their only child that had not been named for a relative. My father was up in Maine, helping a friend repair his cabin. It was quite worn down, and my dad loved fixing things. He was creating some sort of concrete mixture when he had his first encounter with my mother. My mother was traveling with a friend during spring break. Apparently, they craved some fresh, crisp air and made their way to Maine. They opted to visit the unfamiliar corners of Maine as part of their travels. This is a bit different from the mother I grew up with, the one that runs from the picnic table when she notices an ant and prefers to remain indoors in her air-conditioned home. Her designer shawl was blown off by the wind, landing in my father's mixture. My father wasn't well versed in designer logos, probably thinking it was just a plain old scarf and wondering why my mother felt it necessary to don a scarf in this weather and area. My father sensed her distress, apologized, and tried to assure her that the world wouldn't come to an end even given that the dirt on her scarf may be hard to remove. I guess my mother was visibly upset as he tried to comfort her. This was in Lovell, Maine. My mother's friend opted to stay at the hotel, while my parents spent the next two weeks exploring Maine together then returning to New York together. My father isn't the biggest conversationalist, but he spent early mornings building a rocking chair for my mother to show he cared. He carved his own name on one handle and hers on the other.

Once they married, the rocking chair stood on the porch of our house. My mother asked my father to repaint it. Dabs of paint marred my father's first name, but it stood on our porch for many years, tarnished by the elements, but still there. I don't think my mother ever truly appreciated its full worth and meaning. I only caught sight of her sitting on it twice. She had no smile when she passed it. I feared sitting on it, being unworthy and all, and feared it would break even though I was the leanest in my family. But, at age ten, when my parents were away, I sat there for an hour rocking back and forth and singing, not yet knowing the story behind it.

The wind was fierce, and it was cold, but it felt tranquil and cozy. Perhaps my mother's blown scarf was proof that this marriage wasn't one made in heaven, but then again, my father bought her a new scarf beyond his means for their sixth-month anniversary. I do love nature and rocking chairs, and I do love my scarves, so somewhere in my genes, my parents continue to exist.

Fortunately, the bank approves the loan, and I seek out a two-bedroom apartment, nothing like the house I lived in as a child.

My childhood home was quite large in comparison to city living. The entryway led to a massive living area and a large white kitchen. We had lots of crown molding thanks to my dad, and every entranceway had a beautiful wooden door with carveouts. My grandmother ultimately changed the décor, adding bits of color and wallpaper here and there. There were four large bedrooms. My sister and I shared a room.

New York State afforded us the experience of four seasons. The backyard boasted a large oak tree with a wide trunk and gnarled roots indicating it was aged. I imagined it to be from the era of George Washington, but doubt it was. The tree branches were stretched out like massive arms and gave us sufficient shade when the sun beat down on us. In summer, rose bushes and lilies grew around the backyard that were woven through a trellis, contributing to the elegance of the yard. I loved the flowers. I put my nose up against them until I felt that tickle from the fragrant scent.

When I was six, I tried to bottle the fragrance by using an olive oil jar and standing near the rose bush for ten minutes, but surprisingly, only a faint smell of roses could be detected and it came from the petal on my sleeve, while the bottle smelled of remnants of olive oil that had been rancid. The squirrels walked upon the white wooden fence that differentiated our property from our neighbor's, and we created a little picture or doodle on every fourth board to denote our presence.

In the winter, Dean borrowed a neighbor's sled and perched it against the outdoor staircase of six steps pretending we were descending a mountain. Once or twice, Dean even pushed me down. My turn would always be last, guaranteeing that I received the least number of trials, but the experience was still pleasant, and I never complained. Dean loved bike riding so much that when the snow fell, he would shovel a few feet, leaving two mounds behind. He perched his bike wheels on the mounds and would just pedal, creating the effect of a stationary bike. I enjoyed the snowball fights. It was the one activity where I did most of the throwing, as my aim was best. I hated that the flowering plants had died and sat there with their dried-up petals facing the ground. The environment was too white, and I would take some watercolors or fruit juice to spray-paint some of the snow before it melted. The color was like random dots that sometimes melded together, and although it didn't last, in the moment, I enjoyed the change.

In the spring, we brought out the lawnmower, not that we had

acres of land, just some. It had been in our garage from the previous owners, so we kept it and took pleasure in mowing a few feet of grass.

During autumn, the large tree shed its leaves, and it looked sickly.
Its strong bark even faded, but it allowed the sun's rays to shine through
and create warmth. My grandmother had brought a swinging loveseat with
her, and we would just swing and enjoy the caterpillars, ants, and ladybugs
crawling around, watching their desired progression. On occasion, my father would have a barbecue, busying himself with food preparations. His
eyes focused on his task at hand and not the people around him, and as a
result, he never ended up eating at the same time as we did.

My criteria are now simple. I only require a home that is clean and
neat, with nearby access to a park. Some outdoor area in which I can place
a swinging chair. A large window to watch the changing of the seasons and
welcoming ample light. I don't seek out the frills and whistles of my former
house because it wasn't a real home anyway.

After a long search and a bit of bargaining, I finally find a fitting
space. This time, it's "our space," not just mine.

I no longer live in a shoebox. I live in a two-bedroom apartment
with shelves that don't need to constantly be reorganized to make room
for my belongings. Although larger, it still has that New York City coziness. My things have been transferred over, with the addition of toys and
clothing for James. He has a little child's bed with a railing that matches

his cuteness.

I don't want the circumstances or individuals involved in James's first three years of life to dictate his future. I want his future to be far better.

When Jonathan and I go to pick up James from his present foster home, he stretches out his hands, and his face literally lights up. He has a new wardrobe with new shoes, and his physical wounds have significantly healed. There is little physical remnant of the boy we knew from the hospital. As I pack his things, there are a few folded papers among them. They are covered with artwork, compliments of James and Calvin. I sought the art with fervor, opening every drawer, even searching the trash bin in the hospital, wanting a little piece of James before he was taken to foster care. I now have the good fortune of picking up the real thing, James in the flesh, almost pinching myself to ensure that I am not dreaming.

We walk outside, and I hold his little hand that has grown just a bit, enabling him to clasp my own hand a bit more firmly. We enter Jonathan's new minivan, making our way to our new home. James looks on in wonder as we pass the many neighborhoods in New York City. When a large dump truck is parallel-parking while we wait at a traffic light, James's eyes widen in fear only momentarily, and he holds his ears. As we pass, he refocuses his attention on the sights and smiles as he notices me peek at him from the front seat.

We finally reach our new apartment. The weather is changing, and a glistening light flashes outside my apartment. that comes and goes outside my apartment. The sun is setting, and I look down at James's face that reflects the sun's departure. I watch his expressions and gestures as he carefully takes in the sights that surround his new home. As I approach the entrance of my apartment, I see a firefly dancing back and forth. It isn't the season for fireflies, yet there is one flying before me. I watch the firefly dance, and I am momentarily transfixed. I smile and look back at James; he, too, has made the same discovery. At first, he waves his hand, making me think he is swatting the small creature, but as I examine the scene closer, I note his hand trying to grab hold of the bright element. He looks on in wonder, and a shy smile begins to cover his face. I take out a plastic cup from my bag and attempt to catch the firefly, but I am glad this time that I have no jar to trap a part of nature that yearns to be free. "Let's go home," I say.

CHAPTER 17: BEYOND THE CLOUD

I make myself comfortable in my new home. I am no longer shifting items around, constantly changing the environment to accommodate my apartment size.

I briefly rummage through my relatively spacious closet in search of one of James's toys that seems to have disappeared. As I search, I come across my puffy wedding gown. Its layers and grand appearance resemble a cumulous cloud. As I run my hands over its intricate exterior, I recall every joyous detail of my wedding. The gown is in great contrast to my general sleek, designer taste, but it finally afforded me the opportunity to dress up like a princess.

The mail arrives as I finish my first round of laundry in my new washing machine, which is actually in my own apartment now. I look through the mail to find a beautiful vanilla and lace envelope. It's from the hospital. I wonder what it could be. I open it to find an even more beautiful card. It turns out to be an announcement. It is announcing the opening of a new wing to the hospital. "Mental Health Advocacy and Care," it reads. It lists a donor's name, perhaps the one that was on the plaque that the CEO of the hospital held months ago. I don't recognize it, but then I look toward the end of the invitation. It is "in memory of a young boy who died before his time, Rigby Kalmar," the chief of pediatrics' son. I see the image of doves atop the invitation like the doves that graced the walls at the new wing's entrance. There will be no sophisticated databases or 3-D printers, no new equipment, nor updates to the gym. Jonathan will not have a new study forum for his liver research nor an updated operating facility. Perhaps though, there will be people who will finally get the peace they seek, and that is okay in my book.

I open my computer. There before me stands the promise of the unlimited storage of the cloud. In informational technology, cloud computing is an invisible vehicle for the sharing of data and accessibility. It isn't part of the general computer infrastructure but has become a vital medium for enhanced services and resources. It increases and magnifies the individual's or organization's ability to network or communicate many-fold. It serves to empower its users. In some stages in life, we become this cloud, whether intended or not. We manifest as a vehicle for change or growth. Our interactions with others become a venue for further fostering communication and networking and for the distribution of information. This cycle is inevitable. Sometimes we recognize our role in this cycle, and at other times, we don't.

Every client comes with their own memories, life situations, experience, habits, personalities, as do I. I try to understand their attitudes, relationships, strengths, and weaknesses to create a picture of who they are and what they need. There is an interplay between my own circumstances and theirs, and we work in tandem for their greatest outcomes. Some are easier to understand and empathize with than others; some attitudes and life events have been in direct contrast to my own. Yet, they have all taught me life lessons. It is through them that I have come to reflect upon and examine my own being with all its intricacies, to understand myself better, and appreciate the uniqueness of my character. It is all these people, with our similarities and differences, that have greatly enhanced my journey, as I hope I have enhanced theirs. In their vulnerable states, at a point in their lives when they were humbled and felt less than human; they have so enriched mine. We are an ever-evolving society, influencing and changing each other, even when we don't know we are. I remember telling my client, "Every person we meet becomes a memory." Somehow when I wasn't looking, these memories, and lessons, effects of my environment, changed me.

I look over at James as he plays happily with the new toys in his new room. I realize that despite having a far from perfect childhood, I can think of all the people who have had a constructive hand in my evolution. My grandmothers, my patients and coworkers, and my friends. Perhaps though, the greatest source of my learning and healing came from a child, a wounded child. I have learned that although I have received many of my life lessons in bits and pieces and in fragmented patterns, while others have learned them in a more unified whole, my lessons are no less valuable, nor is my personhood. I understand more clearly now what I hadn't before.

Almost a year has passed since James's adoption. I stand in my kitchen, making French toast with hearts, his favorite. He is a little over four, and when we celebrated his birthday, there was a birthday cake with his name on it, accompanied by a few guests singing songs. I hear the pitter-patter of his feet as he makes his way from his room, which he calls "his place." His room lacks molding and a skylight but is graced by many pictures; some are Jonathan's artwork, and others were created by James's own hand. He enjoys color, and his pictures are cheerful. His artwork displays a small half heart, which he has copied from Jonathan, who always hides a half heart amongst his work. James is unable to form the curves of the heart, making it appear more like half a lemon.

Jonathan graciously bestows piggy- and pony-back rides to James, despite the backaches that follow as he relishes every moment with James.

James is adamant about sleeping with a nightlight and always asks for the window shade to be down even during daylight hours. He likes for all doors to be open, so he can get a good vantage point from every part of his room. I never force him or prod him to speak about his past but give him the opportunity to speak freely. I often wonder what other tortures he endured beyond what I have already discovered. James has learned to apologize when he makes a mistake, like when something spills on clothes or the floor but is no longer in terror about its consequences. He attempts to help out with daily chores, even attempting to fold laundry, which he just mashes together and puts in his drawer. His favorite chore is wiping the counter clean, and I think he has learned the art of scrubbing from me.

"Clean," he says with an emphasized tone as he stands back, admiring his handiwork.

He is still quite shy around other people, always looking to me for approval, but he willingly greets the neighbors with a hello, no longer lunging at my skirt for protection. Surprisingly, he will approach animals of all kinds, even when they appear to be threatening, like the big black guard dog that lives across the street. He must understand their special language because, as he approaches, they are gentle.

When we first brought him home, trying to convince him to go to preschool was a struggle in itself. He required lots of forewarning, and a few practice-runs before actually walking into the classroom. It was a miracle, or so I thought, when he first walked into the official classroom. I waited for the wailing or fleeing to begin; it didn't. I stuffed his briefcase full of toys from home to remind him that we were still with him. Although the wailing or fleeing never happened, as I turned to leave the room, a sad expression was visible on his face depicting a feeling of abandonment. My heart sank. I should have known it was his style to be silent yet give me lots of guilt. I told myself it was normal for a child to have fear on his first day of school, but this wasn't the first day for the other children. They had already been in school for about a month. And this was James, my James, and I wasn't sure what his normal was, so in a moment of concern, I gave him the key to my apartment. He loves dangling keys. It's one of the few noisy surprises he tolerates. He likes opening boxes with keys to see what is inside. Perhaps somewhere unconsciously, he likes the thought of unlocking something, letting it be free.

As I dangled the key before him, he recognized it instantly as the one that opens our front door, as indicated by the bright multicolored tag he once drew. He finally let me leave, no longer sporting the abandonment expression. When I came to retrieve him at the end of the day, I took the opportunity to peek inside and noted his face. It wasn't a carefree ambivalence or an inner happiness that the other children displayed, but it wasn't sadness or terror either. It was more of a curiosity, like the curiosity James displayed during our interactions in the hospital. The teacher said he refused to participate but sat tailor-style on the floor and seemed to observe all the events and people in his environment. He appeared to be listening intently as she spoke and read books. When James spotted me, he greeted me with a cheerful smile.

When we got home, he passed me the key. As I opened the door, he rattled off a few things he learned in school. It was as if another child just entered his body. James never takes naps; he won't close his eyes in an environment other than the home. He was exhausted and quickly made his way to the floor in his room, where he fell asleep. He often enjoys sleeping on the floor even with a quite expensive, comfortable mattress. Perhaps it is there that he feels grounded.

In the days that followed, James exhibited a greater calmness about going to school. Each day I continued presenting him with our house key.

A few weeks after school started, I forgot to hand him that key, and he managed well anyway.

James has befriended two classmates and remembers the names of several others. He willingly does pre-academic tasks, but it's the extra stuff that is more difficult. He will march during circle time but performs no other exercise routine. He smiles when the teacher gets into character while reading books. He participates in some crafts. In school he still will not sit in the center of a circle, always veering towards a corner spot. He watches and waits when interacting with others, but evidences greater facial expression during his observations. He sings all the songs he learned at school, just not at school. He sings them at home, but he quiets down when he catches me peeking at him.

At present, he has only initiated limited conversation, saying, "Hello," and "Can I play with your ball?" with one boy in our neighborhood that he has seen several times in the vicinity. However, he often waves to everyone, particularly good-bye. He will not ever fall asleep in the car. He needs to be awake to see where and with whom he ends up. He went into the blow-up pool at the neighbor's house for three minutes, but when he realized his legs were fully submerged, he quickly got out. But he tried again the next visit, for the same three minutes.

On this day, the first day of autumn, Jonathan and I plan a trip to the playground, last licks in tolerable weather before the winter. James walks down the hallway carrying one of his favorite toys, which was a gift from Kevin, a child's umbrella, which James assumes was intentioned to be a tent of some sort. He makes his way toward the breakfast nook as he awaits his French toast. He always eats his French toast with one spoonful of jam. As always, his fingers have gotten dirty, and he goes to wash them, leaving just a drip on his face.

"Maybe I should eat you up," I say, "You look delicious!"

He replies, "No, Mommy. I am not tasty."

I still hear the word "Mommy" echo in my ears; it is beyond pleasant.

James looks all around him as we travel in our minivan towards our designated destination; he is one of those kids that notices the yield sign before the adults. As we arrive at the playground and make our way to the slide, a soda can flies through the air. He flinches a bit as the can hits the garbage can near him. James will now slide down without starting and stopping and without even holding on to the slide's side rails because he knows I am down there and trusts that I will catch him. He still fears walking along the winding path and stays many feet away from bikes or people. He ducks when he sees a ball even in the distance, assuming he is the target. He jumps back when the water fountain is barely on because it once began spritzing overtime. He watches the other children swinging with anticipation and excitement, moving back and forth, being pushed or self-propelling on the swing; he still needs those initial prompts to get him to sit on the swing, but once he is on, he pumps back and forth happily allowing me to be a safe distance away. He attempts to place two feet on a spider wall climb, but shyly turns around and goes back off, this time dangling one foot on it, and one foot on the ground. He runs near every sprinkler in the park, which strangely is still on in autumn, but only allows his fingertips to get wet while other children emerge drenched. He smiles as it tickles his hands. He asks for his sailboat toys when we sit down on the park bench. He snuggles himself up toward me as he imagines himself the captain of the ship. He likes imaginary play, sometimes dressing himself up in Jonathan's good clothing, pretending to go to 'his' office, which is the den. He makes the tugboat noise. He allows me to peck his cheek, which now has an evident dimple, and I pat his head as my grandmother patted mine. I receive a phone call from James's grandmother, Jacqueline, confirming her expected visit with him tomorrow, and I put James on the phone to hear her voice. A bit of excitement conjures up in him, as he really likes Grandma Jacqueline.

I still talk to my father. Mostly I do the talking; he is more of a listener. He is the only member of my family that came to support me when I adopted James. When he first met James, James looked fearfully at the tall statue-like man that faced him, but my dad was gentle and quiet, and it was his stillness that allowed James to accept him.

We look up at the sky. There are many clouds out today. The three of us peer upward. I point out their various shapes. I unfold James's imagination as to what images the clouds have formed, and we discuss what they could possibly be. As I glance up at them, I think, *We are like clouds. We have presence and power, we can shape ourselves into many forms and identities, and sometimes we just need to let our emotions flood without restraint.*

Epilogue:

James holds his three-year-old little sister's hand tightly, as he always does. Her hair is blonde and her eyes a sky blue. She resembles my mother, but when I look at her, I don't feel hate or anger, rather my heart melts with happiness. She is warm and loving and likes to cuddle. She hugs her brother every time he comes through the door, and he willingly accepts and reciprocates. I see pain in her eyes when I stub my toe and love when she brushes my curls through with her fingers. She pats my face as I read through the pages of her favorite book, *Cinderella*, for yet the second time before bedtime.

James is the best big brother. He wraps his hands around her shoulders when she cries, and he waves his spoon like an airplane to encourage her to eat the vegetables which she dislikes. He sits with her and plays with dolls and carriages, making up imaginative scenarios in his mind even though he says he "hates girls' toys" like many boys of age eight do. As they exit the house, James helps the old man next door up the stairs because his cane has something stuck to it, rendering it useless for the moment.

Jonathan gets into the car, already a bit late to his meeting at a new facility studying liver regeneration. However, he doesn't start the engine as he notices the yellow bus waiting and his two children walking hand in hand as they approach the school bus. It is our daughter's first day of school, and James is comforting her and encouraging her to mount the

363

school bus steps. I watch them go hand in hand, and they both wave good-bye through the glass windows. Jonathan's broad smile and sideways look at me tells me more than his words ever could.

I have learned what true contentment is, and now when I laugh, I let it flow freely from my mouth with the accompanying jiggle of the stomach. When I see nature, it is not a means of calming my nerves from the past, but a hope for what the future holds. I look down at my tattoo or "mark" of freedom created at age eighteen, and although the memories will never fully fade, I can truly say, "I am free!"

End.

ACKNOWLEDGEMENTS

First and foremost, I thank the first person I have ever met, my mother. Thank you especially for listening to the seven-year-old girl who said, "I can't write this composition," and for showing me that organizing my writing doesn't have to be a big deal. Thank you for encouraging me to find an alternative phrase or a different way of making my point clearer. I probably would not have grown to love words without you. I appreciate your most recent contribution, reading through my manuscript and providing constructive criticism and encouragement. Most importantly thank you for your patience.

I am also very grateful to my father who has always made himself available to assist me, and whose supportiveness has never failed me. With his vast array of knowledge and intelligence, he has provided me with scientific curiosity and has always filled my head with philosophical thoughts. Thus, showing me that various disciplines can meld into a beautiful creative endeavor.

I also thank all those people who have contributed to my professional knowledge over the course of years including, but not limited to, instructors, supervisors, and co-workers. They have advanced my ability to examine the actions of my characters and elements in the story. They have also helped me to think critically of small details and factors, and to differentiate between those factors and elements that were fabricated for creative purposes as opposed to those that reflect authentic therapeutic intervention.

CPSIA information can be obtained
at www.ICGtesting.com
Printed in the USA
JSHW041610221020
8962JS00006B/134

9 781735 691077